Passionate protector by day...
sinful seduction by night!

——— THE ———
BODYGUARD

Julie Miller attributes her passion for writing romance to all those fairy tales she read growing up, and to shyness. Encouragement from her family to write down all those feelings she couldn't express became a love for the written word. She gets continued support from her fellow members of the Prairieland Romance Writers, where she serves as the resident "grammar goddess". This award-winning author and teacher has published several paranormal romances. Inspired by the likes of Agatha Christie and Encyclopedia Brown, Ms Miller believes the only thing better than a good mystery is a good romance. Born and raised in Missouri, she now lives in Nebraska with her husband, son and smiling guard dog, Maxie. Write to Julie at PO Box 5162, Grand Island, NE 68802-5162, USA.

Donna Young, an incurable romantic, lives in beautiful Northern California with her husband and two children.

Debra Cowan, like many writers, made up stories in her head as a child. Her BA in English was obtained with the intention of following family tradition and becoming a schoolteacher, but after she wrote her first novel, there was no looking back. After years of working another job in addition to writing, she now devotes herself full-time to penning both historical and contemporary romances. An avid history buff, Debra enjoys traveling. She has visited places as diverse as Europe and Honduras, where she and her husband served as part of a medical mission team. Born in the foothills of the Kiamichi Mountains, Debra still lives in her native Oklahoma with her husband and their two beagles, Maggie and Domino. Debra invites her readers to contact her at PO Box 30123, Coffee Creek Station, Edmond, OK 73003-0003, USA, or via e-mail at her website, www.debracowan.net.

THE —— BODYGUARD

JULIE
MILLER

DONNA
YOUNG

DEBRA
COWAN

MILLS BOON

Mills & Boon, an imprint of Harlequin (UK) Limited, Eton House, 18-24 Paradise Road, Richmond, Surrey TW9 1SR

THE BODYGUARD © Harlequin Books S.A. 2012

Protecting Plain Jane © Julie Miller 2011
Engaging Bodyguard © Donna Young 2006
The Private Bodyguard © Debra Cowan 2010

ISBN: 978 0 263 90195 5

024-0812

Harlequin (UK) policy is to use papers that are natural, renewable and recyclable products and made from wood grown in sustainable forests. The logging and manufacturing processes conform to the legal environmental regulations of the country of origin.

Printed and bound in Spain
by Blackprint CPI, Barcelona

Protecting Plain Jane

JULIE MILLER

For all my friends on the www.eHarlequin.com boards and Intrigue Authors Group blog.

2010 was an especially tough year for me, but I truly appreciated all your kind messages and cyber hugs and prayers. Pretty cool. Classy, too. Thank you.

Prologue

The laughter rang in Charlotte's ears and cut through her innocent soul. The muffled music echoing through the school that had filled her with anticipation only moments ago now pounded through her head like a death knell.

"Right. Like I'd go out with some nearsighted brain-iac like you when I could have this." Landon, the Prince Charming who'd saved her from coming to the prom with her quiz bowl partner, Donny, leaned over and kissed the raven-haired beauty from the school he'd transferred from earlier in the year. Tears of shock and anger were already blurring Charlotte's vision, but Landon's victorious taunt came through crystal clear. He waved his copy of the prom photo they'd taken a few minutes earlier as proof of their date. "Goal and game for me, sweetheart. I just passed my varsity initiation and earned a hundred bucks, to boot."

Charlotte was shaking beneath the fancy updo of hair that had been straightened and lacquered within an inch of its life and was supposed to make her look pretty. "Asking me out was a bet?"

He stuffed the photo into his pocket. "A man's gotta do what a man's gotta do to fit in around here."

And making Charlotte Mayweather, the dateless wonder, think someone special had seen through her plain Jane facade was his way of fitting in? She should have been *smarter. None of the other boys she'd had a crush on ever saw her as more than a kid sister or one of the gang. Being smart was the one thing she was really good at. Why hadn't she seen the sham of this boy asking her out? Why couldn't she read people the way she could read a book?*

Landon blew her a kiss and grabbed his real date's bottom through her clingy satin dress, letting Charlotte know that while he'd picked her up and brought her to the Sterling Academy's big spring blowout, he had no intention of walking her through those doors into the auditorium and sharing even one dance with her. "All the new guys on the soccer team had a task to complete. You were mine."

Charlotte sniffled and wiped away some of the mascara that was streaking her glasses. "Aren't you the only new guy?"

He shifted back and forth in his black tuxedo, possibly feeling one teeny, tiny iota of remorse. "Hey, look, Char— nothing's stopping you from going to the dance."

"By myself?"

"Isn't that how you spend all your nights?"

She took that one like a sucker punch to the gut. She was Charlotte Mayweather, damn it. She had friends. She had scholarships. She had a stellar future traveling the globe in search of historic artifacts and running her father's museum as soon as she finished Yale and earned her doctorate.

But all she felt was hurt. All she could think of was the betrayal. "You're slime, Landon."

"Yeah, but I just earned my place in your high-falutin' school, I'm starting goalie and I'm gettin' some tonight." He held out his arm for his real date and pushed open the double doors leading to the auditorium. "Let's go, babe."

Charlotte jerked at the instant assault of loud music

on her eardrums and got a heartbreaking mental snap-shot of the couples and colorful decor inside as the doors drifted shut behind him. She spotted her friend Gretchen floating through the crowd in her tiara, celebrating her win as prom queen. Her best friend Audrey was dancing with Harper Pierce, the tall blond boy she'd had a useless crush on since they'd been lab partners in chem class. Her homeroom gossip buddy, Valeska Gordeeva, had one guy cutting in on another as they danced.

But when the doors closed and the music muted, Char-lotte didn't open them again. As much as she treasured those friendships, she was not going to be a third wheel on anyone's night or humiliate herself any further.

Charlotte tossed in bed, moaning a warning in her sleep as she watched her teenaged self turn and walk toward the school's front door. "Don't go," she murmured, feeling the terror creeping into her nightmare. "Don't."

But after ten years of reliving the same inevitable horror, she still couldn't make it stop.

Charlotte ripped the corsage off her wrist and took one last look at the beautiful red rose and silver ribbons before flinging it to the asphalt and stomping it beneath her foot. "Take that, Landon Turner."

The petty satisfaction of destroying his gift lasted long enough for Charlotte to come up with an even better idea.

"No." She knocked her pillow to the floor, helplessly reaching out in her sleep. "Stay in the moment. Stop."

Pausing long enough to get her bearings in the rows of parked cars, Charlotte pulled off her glasses and furiously wiped away the tears on her cheeks. Ignoring the streaks of makeup left behind, she put them back on and brought her vision and her impromptu scheme into focus. She changed

*course from her aimless escape and cut through the cars,
heading for the opposite end of the parking lot.*

*The limousine drivers hired for the night—who wanted
a family employee ratting to parents about what went on in
the back of the car?—were all parked on the far side of the
lot, beyond the student cars. She'd find the driver Landon
had paid for and have him take her home. Then she'd ask
her father to double whatever Landon had paid, maybe
send the driver to Vegas for a weekend on the Mayweathers, and Landon and Miss Boobalicious back there could
find their own way home.*

*Charlotte saw the car a couple of rows away, hiked up
her gown and hurried her pace. That'd piss him off. Using
her first official date with a handsome guy as a joke? He'd
be out more than the hundred dollars he'd just—*

"Miss Mayweather?"

*"Aggh." She pulled up short when the man in the tan
coveralls stepped out from behind a car. She clasped her
hand over her racing heart. "Yes?"*

*He swiveled his head back and forth. Was he lost? Look-
ing for someone? "Charlotte Mayweather?"*

Tears squeezed between her lashes, steaming against
her feverish cheek.

*The man faced her again and his fist followed right
after.*

*The blow knocked her to the ground, and her glasses
flew beneath the car beside her. Her head was still spinning, her stomach nauseous when she heard the squeal
of tires on the pavement and felt the rough hands on her,
lifting, dragging. A white van screeched to a halt in front
of her. The men who threw her onto the rusty, dirty floor
inside were little more than blurs of movement and hurtful
hands.*

She was scarcely aware of scratching at those hands,

kicking, twisting. The blood on her nose was the last thing she saw as a dark hood came down over her head. The slam of a sliding door was the last thing she heard.

The prick of a needle in her arm was the last thing she felt before blessed oblivion claimed her.

"Wake up," she cried into the sleeve of her pajamas, fighting to make the nightmare disappear. "Wake up."

Charlotte woke up to the jarring, concussive sounds of the men beating on pots and pans again. She'd drifted off again. She was losing track of the hour, losing track of the days. Oh, God, they were coming into her room again. "Charlotte! Charlotte!"

They yelled like that to keep her off balance, to keep her from thinking or getting any real sleep, to mess with her head.

"Don't come in." *She tried to sit up, but she was too weak to do more than push herself up onto one elbow. She hated when they came in. It was safer when they left her isolated, alone. She was starving, but she could drink her water and pee without anyone watching.*

The door was opening. They were coming in. She always got hurt when they came in.

"Come on, girlfriend." *The one with the big fists from the parking lot threw aside his pan and held up the scissors he'd been banging it with.*

"No," *she begged when the other two held her down on the bed.* "Please, no."

He splayed his hand over her bruised face and turned it into the stale bedding. "I'm tired of waiting for my millions. It's time to show Daddy just how serious we are about the money."

He brushed aside her hair with his long fingers. When she felt the cold metal against her neck, Charlotte screamed.

Charlotte screamed herself awake. She sat up in bed, a cold sweat trickling down the small of her back as she kicked away the covers that had twisted around her legs. She tapped the lamp beside her bed three times, flooding her room with the brightest light possible.

"Max? Stay in the moment," she chanted aloud, repeating one of the mantras her therapist had taught her over the years. Her heart was racing, she couldn't catch her breath. She needed to think. "Max!"

A black-and-tan terrier mix that looked like a miniature German shepherd hopped onto the bed and into her lap. He licked the tears from Charlotte's face as she ran her hands over his short, soft fur, seeking out the grounding realism of the dog's body heat and thumping heart.

Once she was certain she was awake, once her panicked brain truly understood that this was now, not ten years ago—that she was home, not in that smelly beige room—that she was safe—she hugged the dog until he squeaked.

"Sorry, boy." She scratched at his scarred-up ears, kissed the top of his head and pushed him off her lap so she could climb out of bed. "Sorry."

Moving with practiced efficiency, Charlotte picked up the pillow trimmed with Battenburg lace off the floor and tossed it onto her rumpled bed. She pulled her red, narrow-framed glasses from the bedside table and put them on, already heading into the connecting sitting room. She waved her hand in front of the switch there and lit up the crowded oak tables and desk stacked with papers, the bookshelves and antique Americana rugs, the overstuffed sofa and chairs, and went straight to the locks on the door.

While she could visually verify they were all secure, she needed to touch each one—the dead bolt, the doorknob, the chain and the computerized keypad that glowed green to show the high-tech Gallagher Security Company lock was engaged. Once she was certain she was safely locked inside her private rooms at her father's mansion, she spared a rueful thought for her father, stepmother and stepsiblings. Had she wakened anyone on the estate? But just as quickly, she breathed out a sigh of relief. One advantage of living behind soundproof walls was that the same loud noises she wanted to keep out also prevented the rest of the household from hearing her on nights like this one.

After stopping in the bathroom to check the barred window and splash some cool water on her face, Charlotte padded back into her bedroom, pulling aside the thick drapes to check that the locks and laser alarms were still all engaged. Only then did she really stop to breathe. And think.

She hadn't completely wigged out the way she once might have, but she hadn't been able to stop the nightmare, either—a sure sign she was overly fatigued, or more worried than usual about something. Maybe she'd been keeping too many late hours, working at the museum long after closing. Maybe she was feeling like a twenty-seven-year-old imposition to her father and his new wife. Maybe it was agreeing to install the telephone in her quarters after all those years of even refusing to answer one.

The press and police and friends had called around-the-clock. Landon had called her so many times after her release. "I'm sorry. I didn't know. Forgive me," he'd begged. Sometimes, he'd be drunk and would simply say her name, over and over again. The restraining order had finally stopped him.

Maybe it was all those things that had triggered the nightmare again.

Maybe it was nothing.

Max lay over her bare feet as Charlotte looked through

the glass and bars up into the night sky. Frothy, finger-
ling clouds sailed past the full moon and disappeared
into a bank of darker clouds, sure signs that a storm was
gathering.

She had a sense that something else was coming, too.
Something very, very bad.

But in the ten years since she'd been kidnapped and
ransomed for five million dollars, she almost always felt
that way.

Resigning herself to that reality, Charlotte wiggled her
toes to stir Max to his feet and closed the drapes. But
the memory of the nightmare—of the real events she'd
survived—still sparked through her blood. The notion of
sleep, of facing the uncertainty of even the next few hours,
took her past her bed and back into the sitting room where
she pulled on a pair of white cotton gloves and curled up
on the sofa with a box of pottery shards she'd brought
home from the museum. She picked up the first piece and
a magnifying glass, resuming the painstaking process of
identifying and dating the fragments from a dig near Ha-
drian's Wall in England.

When she got up to retrieve a reference book, she saw
the dusty high-school yearbooks on the shelf and briefly
wondered why she thought she needed to keep any remem-
brance from that time in her life. She nodded and headed
back to the sofa.

It was because she treasured the past. The now was a
frightening thing, the future uncertain. But the past was
complete. Done. Finished. Nothing could be changed.
There were no more surprises.

She was safe with the past.

It was the present and future she couldn't handle.

Chapter One

Three days later

Charlotte Mayweather eyed the canopy of gray clouds that darkened the Kansas City sky beyond her front door and shivered. She pretended the goose bumps skittering across her skin were in answer to the electricity of the storm simmering in the morning air rather than any trepidation about stepping across that threshold into the world outside.

But with a resolve that was as certain as the promise of the thunder rumbling overhead, she adjusted her glasses at her temples and stretched up on tiptoe to kiss her father. "Bye, Dad. Love you."

Jackson Mayweather's gaze darted to the flashes of lightning that flickered through the thick glass framing each side of the mansion's double front doors. "Are you sure you want to go out in this? Looks like it's going to be another gullywasher."

"You know storms don't bother me." Charlotte cinched her tan raincoat a little more snugly around her waist, leaving the list of things that *did* bother her unspoken. "You can't talk me out of going to the museum. I want to get my hands on those new artifacts from the Cotswolds dirt fort before anyone else does. I have to determine if they're of Roman origin or if they date back to the Celts."

Her trips to the Mayweather Museum's back rooms and storage vaults—where the walls were thick, the entrances limited and locked up tight, and she knew every inch of the layout—were the closest she'd ever come to experiencing an actual archaeological dig. Unpacking crates wasn't as intriguing as sifting real dirt through her fingers and discovering some ancient carved totem or hand-forged metalwork for herself. But it brought more life to her studies in art history and archaeology than the textbooks and computer simulations by which she'd earned her PhD ever could.

It was normal for an archaeologist to be excited by the opportunity to sort and catalogue the twelfth-century artifacts. And it had been ten long years since she'd felt *normal* about anything.

Her father scrunched his craggy features into an indulgent smile. "Those treasures will still be there tomorrow if you want to wait for the storm to pass. Better yet, I can arrange to have them brought here. I do own the museum, remember?"

Thunder smacked the air in answer to the lightning and rattled the glass. Charlotte flinched and her father tightened his grip, no doubt ready to lock her in her rooms if she showed even one glimmer of hesitation about venturing out into a world they both knew held far greater terrors than a simple spring thunderstorm.

Wrapping her arms around his neck, she stole a quick hug before pushing herself away and picking up her leather backpack. *Go, Charlotte. Walk out that door. Do it now.* Or she never would.

She plucked a handful of short curls from beneath the collar of her coat and let them spring back to tickle her mother's daisy clip-on earrings. "I'll be okay." She pulled the check she'd written from her trust fund out of her pocket and waved it in the air. "I'm paying to have those artifacts shipped from England, so I intend to spend as much time as I want studying them."

"I don't like the idea of you being alone."

She zipped the check into the pocket of her backpack. *Alone* was when she felt the safest. There was no one around to surprise her or betray her or torment her. There was no second-guessing about what to say or how she looked. There were no questions to answer, no way to get hurt. *Alone* was her sanctuary.

But he was a dad and she was his daughter, and she figured he'd never stop worrying about her. Still, when he'd fallen in love with and married his second wife just over a year ago, Charlotte had vowed to venture out of her lonely refuge and live her life somewhere closer to normal. Giving her father less reason to worry was the greatest gift she could give him. What years of therapy couldn't accomplish, sheer determination and a loyal friend who'd survived his own traumatic youth would.

"I won't be alone." She put two fingers to her lips and whistled. "Max! Here, boy."

The scrabbling of paws vying for traction on the tile in the kitchen at the back of the house confirmed that there was one someone besides her father in this world she could trust without hesitation.

A furry black-and-tan torpedo shot across the foyer's parquet tiles, circled twice around Charlotte's legs and then, with a snap and point of her fingers, plopped down on his tail beside her foot and leaned against her. She reached down and scratched the wiry fur around his one and a half ears. The missing part that had been surgically docked after a cruel prank had triggered an instant affinity the moment she'd spotted his picture online. "Good boy, Maximus. Have you been mooching scrambled eggs from the cook again?"

The nudge of his head up into her palm seemed to give an affirmative answer.

"Figures," her father added with a grin. "When we rescued him from the shelter, I had no idea I'd be spending more on eggs than dog food." He bent down and petted the dog as well. "But you're worth every penny as long as you keep an eye on our girl, okay?"

Her father's cell phone rang in his pocket and Charlotte instinctively tensed. Unexpected calls were one of those phobias she was working to overcome, but until her father pulled the phone from his suit jacket, checked the number and put it back into his pocket with a shake of his head, Charlotte held her breath. When he offered her a wry smile, she quietly released it. "It's your stepbrother, Kyle."

"You could have taken it. Maybe there's a crisis at the office."

"With Kyle, everything's a crisis. That boy is full of innovative ideas, but sometimes I wonder if he has a head for business."

"Come on, Dad." It was easier to defend the family member who wasn't here than it was to stand up for her own shortcomings. "How long did it take you to learn all the ins and outs of the real estate business? Kyle's only been on the job at JM for a year."

He understood the diversionary tactic as well as she did. "No one is going to think less of you if you decide not to go in to the museum today. I don't want to rush your recovery."

A sudden staccato of raindrops drummed against the porch roof and concrete walkway outside. Clutching both hands around the strap of the pack on her shoulder, Charlotte nodded toward the door.

"I'm fine." Well, fine for her. After ten years of living as a virtual recluse, she was hardly *rushing* anything by going to the museum today. She caught his left hand in hers and raised it between them, touching her thumb to the sleek gold band that commemorated his marriage to Charlotte's stepmother. "You're moving on with your life. I am, too."

"I don't want anything Laura and I or her children do to make you feel guilty, or push you into something you're not ready for. I know you feel more comfortable at the house—"

"Dad." Charlotte pulled his fingers to her lips and kissed them. "I'm happy for you and Laura. I know Kyle will turn out to be a big help to you at the office and Bailey is, well…" She flicked her fingers through the golden highlights that her stepsister had put in to turn her hair from blah to blond. "We're becoming friends. I've seen you smile more in the past few months than in the ten years since the kidnapping. Think of your marriage as inspiration, not something to apologize for." She released him and retreated a step toward the front door. "My hours may be a little funny, but I'm going to work—just like millions of other people do every day of their lives."

The silver eyebrow arched again. "You're not like other people."

No. She'd seen more, suffered more. She had a right to be wary of the world outside her home. But therapy and a loving parent could take her only so far. At some point, she was going to have to start living her life again.

And stop being a burden to her father.

"There's no miracle happening here, Dad. It's not like I'm going to a party. I'm taking advantage of the museum being closed for the weekend, and this endless weather keeping crowds off the street. I know my driver and don't intend to go anywhere but the car and the back rooms of the Mayweather. I'll be fine once I get to work."

"I can see you've thought it through, then. Are you sure

you don't want me to call the security guards in to watch over you?"

Her no was emphatic. "If I don't know them on sight, then—"

"—you don't want them around." His smile looked a little sad that that was one phobia she'd yet to overcome, but she had plenty of reasons to justify her fear of strangers. "Make sure all the doors and windows are locked while you're working—even the doors into the public area of the museum. Double-check everything."

She jingled the ring of keys hooked onto her backpack. "I will."

The front door opened behind her, the wind whooshed in and Charlotte instinctively ducked closer to her father. Just as quickly, she eased the death grip on his jacket and smiled at the retirement-aged chauffeur closing the door. Richard Eames collapsed his umbrella and brushed the moisture off the sleeves of his uniform. "The car is ready, Miss Charlotte. Just a few steps from here to the driveway."

Her father nudged Charlotte toward the man who'd been with the family for more than twenty-five years. "Richard, you take good care of her."

"Yes, sir." Richard took the backpack off her shoulder to carry it for her, then opened the door and umbrella.

For a moment, Charlotte's toes danced inside her high-topped tennis shoes, urging her to run outside the way she once did as a child. It had been years since she'd felt the rain on her face. She lifted her gaze to the dramatic shades of flint and shale in the clouds overhead and breathed in deeply, tempting her senses with the ozone-scented air.

But her father's cell rang again, shutting down the urge.

She clung to Richard's arm while her father took out his phone and sighed. He held up his hand, asking her to wait while he answered. "Yes, Kyle. Uh-huh. Your assistant didn't inform you of the conflict? I see. Of course, the meeting with the accountants is more important. No. I'll handle your mother. You'll report this evening? Good man."

"Is everything okay?" Charlotte asked as he put away the phone.

"Richard." Instead of giving an answer that might worry her, Jackson turned his attention to the chauffeur. "Clarice Darnell and her assistant Jeffrey Beecher are coming to the house this afternoon to go over the estate layout and setup requirements for Laura's spring garden party and some other events for the company. Kyle was going to handle the meeting, but I'll be taking it now. Be sure to return Charlotte to the private entrance at the back of the house. That way she can go straight to her rooms and avoid our guests."

"I will."

While Richard and her father discussed her trip to and from the museum, Charlotte dropped her gaze from the sky and scanned the grounds outside the white colonial mansion. The trees she'd climbed as a child had been cut down to allow a clear view from the house to the wrought iron fence and gate near the road. She searched the intricate maze of flowers and landscaping her stepmother had put in for any sign of people or movement.

"I saw on the news this morning that some of the creeks south of downtown are closed due to the flooding. Do you have alternate routes planned?"

Richard nodded. "I've been driving in Kansas City going on fifty years now, sir—I think I know my way around. I'll find a dry street to get Miss Charlotte to the museum."

"Good man." Jackson turned to his daughter. "You have

your list of numbers to call if you sense any kind of threat or discomfort?"

"Programmed into my phone and burned into my memory."

Jackson reached down and wrestled the dog for a second before scooting him toward Charlotte. "Keep Max with you at all times, understand?"

"Always do."

"And Richard, I'll double your wage today if you stay with her."

The older gentleman grinned and held out his arm. "I don't charge extra for keeping an eye on our girl, Mr. Mayweather."

Jackson reached out and brushed his fingers against her cheek, as though reluctant to let her out of his sight. It was up to Charlotte to summon a smile and face her fears for both of them. "Bye, Dad."

She set her shoulders, linked her arm through Richard's and took that first step out the door.

The second step wasn't much easier. Nor the third.

With a nervous click of her tongue, she called for Max. The dog bolted ahead and jumped inside the backseat of the BMW as soon as Richard opened the door. She paused, clinging to the roof of the car, fighting the urge to dive in after the dog. "Is he still watching?"

She didn't need to say her father's name. Richard knew what this brave show was costing her. "He's standing on the porch."

A drop of cool water splashed across her knuckles, momentarily snapping her thoughts from her father and her fears. Almost of their own volition, her fingertips inched toward the drops of rain pooling on the Beamer's roof. How she missed being outside in the—

"Miss Charlotte?" Richard prompted, as the rapid patter

on top of the umbrella indicated the real deluge was about to hit.

The impulse to reach out vanished and the paranoia returned. Curling her fingers into her palm, Charlotte climbed in and slid to the middle of the leather seat. Richard set her backpack beside her and closed the door, saluting a promise to her father before shaking off the umbrella and slipping behind the wheel.

Charlotte pushed the manual lock as soon as he was in, even though the automatic locks engaged when he shifted the car into gear. Hugging Max to her side, she turned her nose into his neck. The moisture that clung to his wiry coat was as close as she'd come to feeling the rain on her cheek once more.

Richard found her gaze in the rearview mirror. He smiled like the caring Dutch uncle he was. "Breathe, Miss Charlotte. I know you're leaving the estate for your father's sake, but try to enjoy your day out. The car is secure, my gun is in the glove compartment and I'm driving straight from here to the museum. I'll walk in with you to make sure everything is secure, and I'll wait outside the door until you're ready to come home. I promise you, it's *perfectly safe* to leave the house today."

Perfectly safe. Since that fateful night in high school, perfectly safe had become a foreign concept to her.

The three men who'd abducted her were now in prison, would be for the rest of their lives. But not one of them, not Landon, not the kidnappers, had paid the way she had. Disfigurement. Phobias. Self-imposed isolation.

That night, and the long days that followed, had ended any hope of living a normal life.

Stay in the moment.

This wasn't high school. This wasn't a date. She was

older, smarter. She had Max and Richard with her. She'd
be all right.

"I'm okay," she insisted, tunneling her fingers into Max's
fur. "Drive away so that Dad will get out of the rain."

Richard nodded and pulled away. "Why don't you get
out some of those photos and shipping manifests from the
museum to distract you while I'm driving?" he suggested.
"You'll get lost in your work soon enough."

Giving Max one more pet, inhaling one more steadying
breath, she nodded and reached for her bag. "Good idea,
Richard. Thanks. As always, you're a calm voice of reason
in my life."

But she crunched the papers in a white-knuckled grip
as they drove away from the one place where she *knew* she
was safe.

EVEN INSIDE THE PRISTINE atmosphere of the museum's
warehouse offices, enough humidity from the rain-soaked
air outside had worked its way into Charlotte's hair, taking
it from naturally curly to out of control.

She pushed the expanding kinks off her forehead as she
straightened from the worktable where she was document-
ing the artisan's crest burned into the iron hilt of the sword
she'd been cleaning. Her back ached, her empty stomach
grumbled and Max sat in the workroom doorway staring
at her—all certain signs that she'd lost track of the time.

If she'd been at home, more certain of the coded locks
protecting her, she might have been grateful that she'd so
fully engaged her brain with the task of cataloguing artifacts that she'd actually gone for several hours without
her obsessive insecurities dogging every thought. But she
wasn't at home. And as she adjusted her glasses at her
temple to check her watch, she nearly flew into a panic.

"Why didn't you say something?" She slammed the book she'd been using, startling Max to his feet.

She'd told her father they'd be home by nine, that it was okay for him to go out to dinner with Laura. It was a rare treat for him to enjoy a night out with his wife. The museum was deserted, locked up tight. Charlotte had been in heaven to have the place and all its treasures to herself, *so yes, Dad, enjoy your evening out.*

She slid the sword back into its crate. "It's eight-thirty."

Half an hour past the time Richard was supposed to pick her up. True, he'd been parked in the staff parking lot behind the warehouse all day long, working his puzzles, watching the sports channel on his mini satellite TV, napping. And he'd promptly come to the door each time she'd called him. To walk Max. To bring her lunch. Just to check in and assure herself he was there. If she didn't call him, he knocked on the door. Every hour on the hour.

They hadn't spoken since 7:00 p.m.

Richard was never late.

In a flurry of scattered activity, Charlotte shut down her computer, plucked her raincoat off the back of a chair and shoved her arm into one sleeve. In a miracle of klutzy coordination, she grabbed her bag, pulled out her phone, tutted to the dog and raced him to the steel door that marked the museum's rear exit.

And stopped.

A nervous breath skittered from her lungs. She couldn't go out there. There was no way to know if it was safe. Evil hid in the shadows at night. Men with fists and needles and greed in their hearts lurked in the dark. They'd lie in wait until it was late and she was alone, and then they'd hurt her. And hurt her. And…

Charlotte squeezed her eyes shut. *Stay in the moment. Stay in the freaking moment!*

"Richard!" She opened her eyes and shouted at the brick walls, even as she pulled out her phone and punched in his number. She tried to focus on getting the other sleeve of her blouse into her coat instead of counting how many times the cell phone rang.

Richard knew how changes in her routine upset her.

That was the third ring. Maybe he'd fallen asleep.

She shifted anxiously on her feet. Four rings.

Charlotte tugged the belt of her coat around her waist and held on as a flash of lightning flickered through the darkness shrouding the unreachable windows above her. Even though she knew it was coming, she winced at the boom of thunder that followed.

Charlotte blinked when she realized her eyes were drying out from staring so hard at the door. Max danced around her feet. "We need to get a peephole installed."

She worked her lower lip between her teeth and reached out to touch the door. The steel was cool from the temperature outside, its texture rough beneath her fingertips. Did she dare open it? Did she risk going outside on her own? She leaned closer and tuned her ears to any sounds of movement in the alley way beyond the door. But a blanket of rain continued to fall outside, drumming against the awning over the door, muffling all but the quickened gasps of her own breathing.

And Max's singsongy growl.

Charlotte's paranoia wasn't fair to the dog's bladder. "I'm sorry, sweetie. Richard?" she called out again, doubting her voice would carry through the steel and bricks and storm to the car parked outside.

The sixth ring.

Max left her side to scratch at the bricks. He whimpered.

What was wrong? Why didn't Richard answer? Her fears multiplied with every single…

The ringing stopped.

"Charlotte."

"Richard? Where are—"

Click.

What the…? He hung on up her? A burst of anger surged through her. He knew what that did to her—how she'd received all those calls and hang-ups in the weeks following the kidnapping. It had taken months of therapy afterward before she'd even allow a phone in her rooms, longer than that to carry one with her.

Richard knew that. He knew… "Oh, my God."

Embarrassment washed away her unkind thoughts, leaving Charlotte's knees weak and her heart racing with concern. What if Richard was hurt? What if he was having a heart attack and needed her help? What if he hadn't called her because he couldn't?

She pocketed the phone and grasped the dead bolt above the doorknob. But her fingers danced over the steel pin, hesitating to grab hold. Could she turn it? Did she dare? Richard had been with her family from the time she was a child. He *was* family. He'd stayed on when he could have retired because she could almost function like a normal person when surrounded by familiar faces, by the handful of staff she trusted. If he'd been driving her the night of her high-school prom, he'd have gotten her safely home. He would never, ever intentionally frighten her.

What if Richard needed her?

Listening to her worries instead of the fear, shutting down her brain and following her heart, Charlotte curled her fingers through Max's collar and turned the bolt.

She nudged the door open, barely wide enough for the dog to stick his muzzle out. Charlotte leaned into the crack until the moisture in the air splashed against her cheek. Max strained against her grip to squeeze through to the gap. "Hold on."

She wasn't ready to do this. She *had* to do this. *Face your fear.*

"Okay." Taking a deep breath and holding it, Charlotte put her left eye to the narrow opening and peeked outside. Her glasses fogged up almost instantly, blinding her. But she pulled the frames away from her face and let the lenses clear. Once she'd readjusted them on her nose, she huffed out a curse at her temerity. She could see the light from the streetlamp at the edge of the parking lot reflected in every rivulet of rain that streaked the polished black fender of Richard's BMW. The car was right there, parked a couple of feet beyond the edge of the green-and-white awning.

Charlotte pushed the door open a few inches more and let Max run out to sniff the rear tire. "Richard?" she shouted through the downpour.

She hurried out to the car. Rain spotted her glasses, distorting her vision before she got the back door open. But Charlotte never climbed inside.

"Are you okay?"

Reprimand gave way to relief. Then her mind seized up with a whole different kind of fear.

She darted around her door and pulled open the driver's door. "Richard!" Her beloved friend was slumped over the steering wheel. "Richard?" Charlotte pulled out her phone, punched in a 9. She swiped the rain from her glasses and glanced around, making sure the narrow lot was still empty, before lightly shaking his shoulder. She punched in a 1. When there was no response, she slid her arm across Richard's chest, her fingers clinging to something warm and sticky at the side of his neck as she pulled him back against the seat. "Oh, my God."

Richard's eyes were open, sightless. Blood oozed from the neat round bullet hole at his temple. She couldn't bear to look at the pulpy mess she'd felt on the other side of his head.

Charlotte.

She jerked her hand away.

Richard never called her anything but "*Miss* Charlotte."

Charlotte whirled around. "Face your fear," she chanted. "Face your fear."

He had her number.

Whoever had done this had taken Richard's cell phone. She'd called him, and now he could call her back.

She shut off the traitorous phone and stuffed it deep into her pocket. She checked every corner and shadow, marked every movement—a car speeding past on the curiously empty street, a wadded-up fast-food sack skipping across the pavement and Max giving chase. "Max…?"

She put her lips together and tried to whistle.

But any fleeting sense of security sputtered out along with the sound. Was there something moving beyond the Dumpster at the end of the alley?

The rain had finally pummeled its way through her thick hair and crept like chilled fingers over her scalp. There were brick walls on three sides of her—three stories high with shuttered windows and iron bars.

And the Dumpster.

"Face…" How could she face what she couldn't see? Her heart raced. Her thoughts scattered. The nightmare surged inside her.

Besides the dog and the dead man, she was alone, right?

She saw no one, heard nothing but the wind and rain and her own pulse hammering inside her ears.

But she could feel him. A chill ran straight down her spine.

She caught sight of the blood washing from her stained fingers, dripping down into the puddle at her feet. She snatched her fist back to her chest, her feet already moving, retreating from death and horror and *him*.

Whether the eyes watching her were real or imagined didn't matter. Charlotte's reaction was intense and immediate. Run. Hide. She clicked her tongue. "Max! Come on, boy. Come on."

But the scent of trashy cheeseburger wrappers was too enticing.

"Max!" Operating in a panicked haze, she put her fingers to her lips and blew. The shrill sound pierced the heavy air and diverted the dog's attention. "Get over here!"

Max bounded to her and she scooped him up, yanking open the museum's back door and dumping him inside. Charlotte slammed the door behind her and twisted the dead bolt into place. Oh, God. She hadn't imagined a damn thing. Softer than the pounding of her heart, more menacing than the bloody handprints she'd left on her coat—footsteps crunched on the pavement outside. Running footsteps. Coming closer.

Charlotte grabbed Max by the collar, backed away.

"Charlotte!" A man pounded on the door.

She screamed, stumbled over the dog and went down hard on her rump on the concrete floor.

"Charlotte!"

She didn't know that voice. Didn't know that man.

How did he know her name?

Flashing between nightmares and reality, between Richard's murder and her own terror, the pounding fists seemed to beat against her.

"Charlotte! Come on, girlfriend. I know you're in there!"

They couldn't take her. She'd die before she'd ever let them take her again.

Scrambling to her feet, she scanned her surroundings.

"Shut up," she muttered, trying to drown out the pounding on the door as much as she wanted to drown out the hideous memories.

She wiped her glasses clear. Yes. Safety. Survival.

"Max, come!"

She ran back to the workroom, shoved the top off a wooden crate and pulled out the long, ungainly sword from the packing material inside. The weighty blade clanged against the concrete floor and, for a moment, the pounding stopped.

She pulled out her keys and unlocked one of the storage vaults. "Max!" The dog followed her into the long, narrow room, lined with shelves from floor to ceiling.

"Charlotte! I'm coming for you!"

The banging started up again as she turned on the light and locked the door behind her. He was so angry, so menacing, so cruel. Charlotte crouched against the back shelf, holding the sword in front of her. Max trotted back and propped his paws up against her thigh. The smell of wet dog and her own terror intensified in the close confines of the room. "Stay in the moment," she whispered out loud. She petted her companion, to calm herself, to take control of her scattered thoughts, but stopped when she saw the blood she'd transferred onto the dog's tan fur.

"It's okay," she lied. "It's okay."

But she'd chosen the smart, well-trained dog for a reason beyond his scarred ear. Max scratched at Charlotte's coat, nuzzled her pocket. Call someone. The words were in her head, hiding in some rational corner of her brain.

"I can't. If I turn on the phone, he'll call me."

We need help.

The deep brown eyes reached out to her, calmed her.

Charlotte nodded and pulled out her phone. She couldn't face the police on her own. Couldn't handle crowds. She turned it on and immediately dialed the first number her terrified brain could come up with.

The pounding outside continued, beating deep into her head. After three rings, a familiar woman's voice picked up. "Hello? This is Audrey...Kline," she whispered in a breathless tone.

"Audrey?"

Pound. Pound.

"Charlotte?" Her friend's tone sharpened, grew concerned. "Is that you?" A second voice, a man's, murmured in the background. "Alex, stop. Charlotte, is something wrong?"

Alex Taylor. Audrey's fiancé. "I'm sorry. I forget other people have lives. I'll call Dad at the restaurant—"

"Don't you dare hang up!"

"What is it?" She could hear a difference in Alex's voice. He, too, sounded efficient, rational, concerned.

"Talk to me, Char."

"I'm at the Mayweather Museum. There's a man at the door. Richard's dead. I can't—"

"Richard's dead?"

The scratch of a dog's paw reminded her to breathe. "Someone shot him and I'm here by myself. There's a man..."

"Alex is calling the police now."

"No."

"But Charlotte—"

"What if it's like…?" Before. Swallow that damn irrational fear. Breathe. "I won't come out unless it's someone I know. Have Alex come."

"We're on our way," Audrey promised, relaying the information to Alex. "Are you safe?"

Alex must be on his phone, now, too. She could hear his clipped, professional tones in the background. "He's not calling 9-1-1, is he? I won't come out for a stranger."

"Shh." Audrey was hushing her, talking to her as if she was the paranoid idiot she fought so hard not to be. "He knows."

"I locked myself inside. Max is with me." Charlotte needed to hear her voice, needed the lifeline to sanity to keep herself from flinching at every pound on that door. "Audrey?"

"Alex is calling a friend of his. Trip's apartment is close to the museum. We're twenty minutes away, but he can be there in two."

"No. I want you to come."

"Trip's a friend. He's a SWAT cop, like Alex. He helped save my life during the Demetrius Smith trial. He won't let anyone hurt you."

"I haven't met—"

"We're leaving the house now. I don't want you alone any longer than you have to be."

"Wait. How will I know him?"

"Trust me, Char. You can't miss him. He'll be the biggest thing in the room."

The biggest thing in the room? Audrey meant the description to be concise, comforting. But Richard was dead and she was alone, and whoever was banging on the outside door was no small potatoes, either.

The pounding stopped, filling the air with an abrupt silence even more ominous than the deafening noise.

Charlotte's breath locked up in her chest. Was he looking for another way to get in?

"Char?"

She jumped at Audrey's voice. "Biggest thing in the room. Right."

"Trip will be right there. The whole SWAT team is on their way."

The instant Charlotte disconnected the call, it rang again. The name and number lit up with terrifying clarity.

Richard's number.

"Oh, God."

It rang. And rang.

"Stop it!"

She pulled her hand back in a fist, intent on hurling the tormenting object against the door. But a paw on her thigh and a glimmer of sanity had her shoving it onto the shelf beside her instead. She'd need it on to know when Audrey got here.

Then she huddled in the darkness with the sword and the ringing and her dog and waited, praying that her friends got to her before whoever had murdered Richard did.

"AUDREY CAN'T RAISE HER on her phone, big guy. You have to go in."

"Got it." Trip Jones stuffed his phone into the pocket of his jeans and peered over the Dumpster into the parking lot behind the Mayweather Museum of Natural History. He pulled his black KCPD ball cap farther down across his forehead to keep the rain out of his eyes, but it didn't make what he was seeing any less unsettling. *What have you gotten me into this time, Taylor?*

Trip retreated a step after his initial recon, wrinkling his nose at the Dumpster's foul smell and running through a mental debate on how he should proceed without the rest of his team on the scene yet to back him up. The rain beating down on the brim of his hat and the metallic bang of an unseen door, swinging open and shut in rhythm with the wind, were the only sounds he could make out, indicating that whatever trouble had happened here had most likely moved on.

Alex and Audrey had lost contact with their friend, and that wasn't good. But he wasn't taking any unnecessary chances. He had to leave the cover of his hiding place and go into that alley. Alone. But he'd go in smart. Flattening himself against the brick wall, he cinched his Kevlar vest more securely around his damp khaki work shirt and pulled his Glock 9 mil from the holster at his waist. He rolled his neck, taking a deep breath and fine-tuning his senses before edging his way around the Dumpster.

Alex had told him three things when he'd called about the off-duty emergency. Find a woman named Charlotte. Keep her safe. And...don't go by your first impression of her. Odd though that last admonition had been, the concern had been real enough to pull Trip away from the book he'd been reading and haul ass over to the museum in the block next to his apartment.

You owe me for this one, shrimp. Trip towered over Alex by more than a foot, and while he might not be quite the tallest man on the force, he was damn well the biggest wall of don't-mess-with-this muscle and specialized training KCPD's premiere SWAT team had to offer. But even he didn't like the looks of what he was walking into. A woman alone at night, in these conditions—something about a murder... Trip frowned. This was all kinds of wrong.

The place was desolate, deserted—solid walls on three sides with bricked-up windows. Rain poured down hard enough to muffle all but the loudest cry for help. A skilled hunter wouldn't have to work hard to isolate and corner his prey here.

And apparently one had.

Trip approached the car at the museum's rear entrance.

Don't be her. Don't be Charlotte. He didn't want to have to explain showing up a couple of minutes too late to Alex and his fiancée. Or his own conscience.

Gripping his gun between both hands, Trip crept alongside the black BMW. He breathed a sigh of relief and cursed all in the same breath. The driver's side doors stood open, the interior lights were on, but no one was home. He put two fingers to the side of the slumping chauffeur's neck. Hard to tell for sure with the cooling temps, but he'd been gone for a couple of hours.

At least the pool of blood was localized. No one else had been hurt at this location. No signs of a struggle in the backseat. But Trip said a quick prayer as he reached in beside the dead man to pop the trunk of the car. After closing the door to preserve what he could of the crime scene, he edged around the back to peek inside. His breath steamed out through his nose.

No body. No Charlotte.

That left the museum's steel door, caught by the wind and thumping against the bricks beneath the awning. After pulling a flashlight from the pocket of his jeans, Trip caught the door and quickly inspected the lock. Scratch marks around the keyhole for the dead bolt indicated forced entry.

He hadn't completed his task yet.

Gritting his teeth and his nerve against whatever he might find on the other side of those bricks, Trip swung the beam of light inside. The museum's warehouse section was dark, with tall, blocklike shapes forming patterns of opaque blackness amongst the shadows. A second sweep led him to the switch box just inside the door.

The electricity had been switched to the off position. The need to move, to act, to fix something, danced across his skin. Dead man aside, someone had broken in and cut the power.

Alex's friend was in serious trouble.

To hell with stealth. "Charlotte Mayweather!"

A rustle of sound answered his echoing voice.

That itch kicked into hyperdrive, pricking up the hairs on his arms and at the back of his neck. "Charlotte!"

Thump.

Perp? Or victim?

He wasn't waiting to find out. "KCPD. Come out with your hands on your head."

He squinted his eyes and flipped on the power switch, creating a shorter recovery time for his vision to adjust as the cavernous interior flooded with light. The shadows became shelves stacked with crates from floor to ceiling, and tables in aisles where more boxes were stored. He swung the light around toward a shuffle of sound and discovered a row of three closed doors marked…

"Not now." He focused the light at the sign on the first door—Z3CVP3 ZTOPVÇ3—and let the letters swirl inside his head until they read SECURE STORAGE.

He didn't have to read the sign on the door to detect the movement behind it. He lowered the beam of light. Another lock. But no signs of entry.

No key, either.

"Charlotte?" He slipped the flashlight into his pocket, tucked his gun into his belt. He jiggled the knob. Sealed tight. He slapped the door with the flat of his hand. "Charlotte!"

Either she couldn't answer or someone was keeping her from answering him.

Trip looked to the right and left, spotted what he wanted and went for it. "Charlotte?" he called out in a booming voice that was sure to carry through the brick walls themselves. He lifted a crate and set it on the floor. "My name's Trip Jones. I'm with KCPD. I'm a friend of Alex Taylor and his fiancée, Audrey. Are you able to answer me?"

His answer was a soft gasp, the crash of a whole lot of little somethings tumbling down inside that room, a woof and an unladylike curse.

"Charlotte?" The work space around him held a treasure trove of useful gadgets—box cutters, twine, screwdrivers, a drill. He could pop the lock or cut his way in in a matter of minutes.

But the woman might not have that long.

His arm muscles tensed as he set the second crate on top of the first. "I'm comin' in, Charlotte."

Trip tilted the table onto one end, jammed it up beneath the door's hinges and shoved. With one mighty heave, he separated the door from its frame.

The table fell to one side as he pried the busted door open. It shielded him until he could angle around and see into the deep recesses of the closet behind it. "Charl—"

He caught a glimpse of short curly hair and glasses before the woman inside hollered a piercing rebel yell and charged him.

The first blow knocked the door back into him, slamming into his nose and making his head throb.

"Ow!" He tossed the door after the table, held up his hand and reached for his badge so she could see he meant her no harm. "Relax. I'm here to help."

Seriously? Was that a sword? She screamed a deep, guttural sound that was all instinct and fear. The long metal blade arced through the air.

The blow caught him on the forearm and Trip swore. He felt the sting of the blunt blade splitting the skin beneath his sleeve and knew he had only one option when she raised the archaic weapon again.

Forget reassurances. With a move that was as swift and sure as breathing to him, Trip ducked, catching her wrists and twisting her around. He hugged her back against his chest, lifted her off her feet and shook the sword from her grip. "Damn it, woman, I'm one of the good g—"

He tripped over something small and furry that darted between his legs, and down they went.

Chapter Two

Trip clipped a crate with his elbow on the way down, landing on the unforgiving concrete floor with the panicked woman sprawled on top of him. Thank God he'd broken her fall instead of crashing down on top of her. "Are you okay—?"

"You can't take me!" A swat of thunder echoed her protest and a heel clocked him in the shin, jarring the few bones that hadn't already taken a beating. A dog barked in his ear, lunged at him. Trip swatted it away, but it barked again. The woman he'd come to rescue twisted on top of him, fighting as if *she* was the one who'd just been attacked.

"Sheesh, lady. You're all ri— Scram!" As he pushed the dog out of his face, her fist connected with the gash in his forearm, making the wound throb, and she slipped from his grip. When he felt her knee sliding up his thigh and saw her fingernails flying toward his face, Trip was done playing hero for the night. He caught her wrist, blocked her knee and rolled, pinning both her hands to the concrete above her head and crushing her flailing legs and twisting hips beneath his. "That's enough!"

"Get off me!"

"Miss Mayweather…" Despite the weight of his body, and the unforgiving wall of Kevlar that shielded him from further injury—he hoped—she fought on with futile persistence beneath him. Her funky red glasses flopped across her lips instead of her nose and her exposed eyes were open wide, terrified, like a spooked horse. And hell, it was his fault. "I'm sorr—" But she was still too much of a danger to him to release her outright and let her bang away like the storm outside. "I'm sorry." What he wouldn't give to be armed and built a little less like a tank right now. She was scared and he was probably scarier than whatever had sent her to hide in that room in the first place. "Look, ma'am—"

"No!"

"Hey!" He tried to pierce her terror with his voice. But he was breathing hard, too, and the dog was barking, and he couldn't find the calm tone he needed. "Hey."

"Let me go," she gasped.

"Are you gonna hurt me again?"

Bang. The wind caught the outside door. It slammed into the bricks and every muscle in her body jerked with the sound.

"Richard's dead. He'll kill me this time."

"Lady—"

"Don't kill me." She squeezed her eyes shut, straining against him, tiring.

Trip's blood ran cold. Those were tears on her lashes.

"I'm not gonna… Ah, hell." Shoot him. Make him run ten miles in full gear. Give him paperwork. But do not… do *not* let a woman cry on his watch. "Stop that. I'm not the bad guy here."

"Don't hurt me," she gasped.

He needed to end this. Now.

"Shh. Nobody's gonna hurt you. You're safe. Come on now. There's no need to be cryin' like that." Trip eased himself down, covering her like a blanket with his body, erasing the distance between their chests, controlling her tenacious struggles with his superior size and strength. She'd pass out from exhaustion before he even worked up a sweat at this rate.

"No," she moaned, pushing against his shoulder as soon as he freed her hands. "Please."

"Charlotte, you need to breathe." He brushed a kinky tendril of golden toffee off her cheek and dropped his voice to a husky tone. "Look at me." She shook her head and tears spilled over her cheek, flowing as steadily as the rain outside. "Look at my badge…" Nope, not on his belt. It had gone flying in the initial tumble. She squirmed valiantly, her tired fingers curling into the shoulders she'd pummeled moments earlier. He was desperate to calm her down, to stop those tears, but he wasn't about to go retrieve it with the way she was still writhing so unpredictably beneath him. Ignoring the twinge in his forearm, Trip propped himself up on his elbow and reached for the brim of his cap. She grunted with renewed energy, shoved hard against his chest. "It says KCPD…"

He felt the dog's hot breath in his ear a split second before he felt the pinch on his fingertip. "Ow! Back off, pooch."

"No!"

The mutt was after his hat. "Get out of here!" He wanted to play tug-of-war? Trip closed his fingers around the dog's muzzle and shoved him away. "Give it—"

"Don't hurt my dog!" Charlotte Mayweather pulled her hands away and went suddenly and utterly still beneath him. The mutt pulled the cap from Trip's startled grip and trotted off to a corner. A plea wheezed from the woman's throat. "I'll do whatever you want. Just don't hurt my dog."

She'd refused to give up the fight or listen to reason for her own safety? But she'd surrender for the dog's sake?

Although her golden lashes still glistened with tears, her eyes were suddenly clear, focused and looking right up into Trip's. For several seconds, his vision was filled with deep dove gray. The scents of dampness and dust and heat filled the air between them, filtering into his head with every quick, ragged breath.

For a woman who had as much feisty terrier in her as the dog gnawing on his cap, she'd suddenly gone all quiet, all submissive, all ready to listen to civilized reason now that she mistakenly thought her furry sidekick was going to get hurt. Trip was the one who was bleeding here. Charlotte Mayweather was one seriously twisted-thinking, incomprehensible, crazy...

Woman.

The realization short-circuited the adrenaline still sparking through Trip's body, leaving one sense after another off-kilter with awareness. Curvy hips cradling his thighs. The most basic of scents—soap and rain and musky woman.

And those big, soulful eyes.

"Don't go by your first impression of her," Alex had warned.

Made sense now.

Charlotte Mayweather was a menace to herself and anyone trying to help her. And, while he wouldn't call her beautiful, she was definitely...distracting.

As soon as his conscious brain registered what his banged-up body had already noticed, Trip pushed himself up onto his hands and knees, putting some professional, respectful, much-needed distance between them.

"I didn't hurt the dog," he assured her, swallowing the growly husk in his deep voice. Yeah, he had a right to defend himself, but his badge didn't give him the right to be making goo-goo eyes at a possible victim or witness. Besides, she wasn't his type. While Trip had never really considered exactly what his type of woman might be, he was pretty sure that pink high-top tennis shoes, flying fists and flaky eccentricities weren't on the list.

He shifted to one side, easing the bulk of his weight off her while keeping a careful eye out for any sign of further attack. "You, I'm not so sure about. Sorry about the takedown, but you forced me to protect myself. Anything bruised up?"

She shoved her glasses back into place, masking her eyes as she scooted just as fast and far across the floor as she could, until the brick wall at her back stopped her. She whistled and the dog jumped up as she pulled her knees to her chest and hugged them tight with one arm. The dog, with Trip's cap locked firmly in his teeth, settled beside her and her free hand drifted down to clench a fistful of fur at the dog's nape. "Did Max bite you? It was an accident, I promise."

"You didn't answer…" Trip crouched where he was a few feet away, keeping close to her level on the floor instead of towering over her and sending her into a freak-out again. Her eyes darted to the black-and-tan dog and back across the warehouse aisle to look at him.

Okay, so she wasn't going to speak rationally about anything besides the fur ball. Fixing a more sympathetic expression onto his features, Trip held up his hand and waved his fingers in the air. "Max, is it? He got a nip in, but I'll survive."

"He didn't mean it. He's not a vicious dog. His job is to keep me from losing it." Um, maybe the pooch needed a little more training? Or was the armed charge and barely controlled panic that moved her body in those rigid, jerky motions her idea of keeping it all together? "He's never been with me when I've been attacked before."

"Hey, I wasn't the one attacking—"

"I don't know if he was defending me, or maybe just wanted to play—but he didn't mean to hurt you."

Trip breathed in through his nose and out through his mouth, forcing himself to relax—wishing she'd do the same. He was guessing she hadn't meant to hurt him, either.

"No harm done." There was barely a blister on the tip of his index finger, but the gash in his forearm was oozing blood through the tear in his sleeve. "On the other hand, I think your sword wound is gonna need a few stitches." He fingered open the rent in his shirt and examined the cut. "You know, I've been stabbed, tasered, shot at—even dislocated my shoulder once on a call. But I've never had to report being brought down by a twenty-pound dog and a broadsword before." Maybe if he kept his voice somewhere short of its natural volume and kept smiling, she'd quit inching up against the wall like that, putting every millimeter of distance between them she could. "Makes you kind of unique."

She didn't so much as blink at the offhand compliment, and offered not even one flicker of a smile at his teasing. "Max weighs twenty-five pounds."

"My apologies." Okay. So he wasn't making any points with Alex's eccentric friend. Better swallow his guilt and stick to police work. Her eyes followed every movement as he plucked his badge from beneath the broken crate, dusted it off and clipped it onto his belt. Trip sank back onto his haunches on his side of the aisle. "Could you at least tell me if any of that blood on your coat is yours?"

Finally giving him a break from that accusatory glare, she glanced down at the stains on her sleeves. With a stiff, almost frantic effort, she rubbed at the reddish-brown spots, turned her hand over to grimace at the slickness that clung to her fingers. With both arms, she pulled the dog up into a hug and choked back a sob. But when her eyes nailed Trip again, there were no tears—only sorrow and distrust. "It's Richard's blood. Maybe yours. I'm not hurt."

"Good." So the woman had been scared spitless, but she hadn't been physically harmed. He was so not the negotiator on his team. Give him something to blow up, break into, fix, and he could handle it just fine. But talking a woman off a mental ledge like the one Charlotte Mayweather was apparently teetering on? Ignoring the tweak at his conscience that *he* had as much to do with putting her on that ledge as her dead friend and an unknown assailant did, Trip focused on the things he *could* handle. He straightened enough to sit on the edge of a table and reached up to his shoulder to tear off his right sleeve. "Did you see the killer? Is that why you were hiding?" He paused midrip. "Ah, hell. You thought I was him, didn't you. Is that why you attacked?"

Her eyes were tracking his movements again. "I know that assaulting a police officer is a really bad thing, but—"

"You have a knack for not answering my questions."

"—to be honest, I didn't know who you were, and after seeing Richard and all the blood, and the noise, and he knew my name—"

"Who knew your name?"

"The man on the phone. The man who called me on Richard's phone. The killer knew my name. He was taunting me." She hugged the dog tighter, and the pooch turned his head to lick her jaw. "He pounded on the door. The calls and the pounding reminded me of…he knows things about me."

"Charlotte…I mean, Miss Mayweather." He'd never seen a person pull herself into such a tight little ball of terror and uncertainty. He didn't understand *pounding* and *calls* and what exactly those meant to her, but he wanted nothing more than to brush those dark gold curls off her cheek, wrap her up in a hug and prove that he was nothing like the man who'd frightened her into such a state. "He won't hurt you," Trip vowed, wisely busying his hands by going back to work on a makeshift bandage by breaking the last threads and peeling the sleeve down his arm. He had a feeling that touching her, or even moving closer, would send her into another panic. "As long as I'm here, nobody is getting to you. And I'm not leaving until Alex Taylor and the people you know and trust get here. Okay?"

After watching her eyes lock on to his without any real relief registering there, Trip looked away to check his watch. Surprisingly, only a few minutes had passed since he'd answered Alex's call—and, he suspected, only a few minutes longer would pass before Alex and the rest of his SWAT team arrived to deal with this off-the-clock rescue. But Miss Hug-the-Dog over there was looking at him as if she'd been sentenced to a night of terror with the beast from some gruesome fairy tale—and he'd been cast in the starring role.

It was hard on a cop's ego, and humbling to any man, to be perceived as the villain—especially when he was used to doing his job and saving the day. He needed the diversion of the pain that made him wince when he pressed the wadded-up fabric against the cut on his forearm to stanch the bleeding there.

The wind outside caught the door again. Trip didn't know if it was the startling noise or him standing that made her eyes widen like saucers. But he figured an apology was useless and strode over to pull it shut.

After wedging a shim of wood between the door and frame to keep it closed, he faced her again. Yep, those suspicious eyes had followed every move he'd made. "Did you know this outside door had been jimmied open?"

"No."

"Then the perp was in here." He perched on the edge of the table again. "You were right to hide. And attack."

"It's not right to hurt somebody else like that." She tucked the swath of curls behind her ear, exposing a flash of a big white-daisy earring. "I'm sorry. I swear I didn't know you were a police officer. I get a little…stuck in my head sometimes."

Trip dabbed at his wound again. "I'm not pressing charges."

"You're not?" She sat up a little straighter, confusion mellowing the distrust on her face for a few moments. But then he could see her gathering her thoughts as she swiped the crystalizing tear streaks off her cheeks. "You're not pressing charges against Max, either, are you?"

"Nope."

"Thank you." A long silence, muffled by the cocoon of rain falling outside, followed as Trip tore off a strip from his sleeve and continued to doctor his wound. Maybe as long as he stayed calm, she would, too. He even thought he saw her hands reach out to help him as he used his teeth to help tie off the pack on his forearm. But as soon as he spotted the gesture, she pulled away and curled her fingers into the dog's fur. "You're Alex Taylor's friend?" she asked instead.

"I work with him at KCPD. We're on SWAT Team One together. Special Weapons and Tactics."

"Alex is…a sweet guy."

"If you say so. I call him *shrimp* when he annoys me. But I can count on him to have my back."

Half a smile curved her full lips. She was testing the option, as if unfamiliar with the idea of relaxing and sharing friendly conversation. "He counts on you, too, I think. He speaks highly of Captain Cutler and your team. I'm friends with Audrey Kline, Alex's fiancée. Audrey is with the district attorney's office. We went to high school together."

"I know the counselor." Trip had a feeling there was no problem with Charlotte Mayweather's mental faculties, but he could see her waging a battle to keep the panic she'd shown earlier from swamping her again. He hoped he didn't say anything that would screw up the tenuous peace between them. "My name's Trip. Don't know if you caught that while you were bustin' up my face and arm."

"Joseph Jones, Jr., Triple J or Trip." If she'd relax just a fraction more, that'd be a real smile. *Please let her smile.* "Audrey told me. And please, it's Charlotte. 'Miss Mayweather' sounds so spinsterish." She touched her slim red glasses on her face. "And I'm already battling that stereotype."

"Thanks…Charlotte. Audrey mentioned you, too. Look, I'm sorry I scared you. If you'd have just answered me…I had no way of knowing if you were stuck inside that closet with the perp—or if you'd been injured. I had to get to you."

She stroked the dog and nodded. "My brain knows that. But sometimes I—"

A cell phone rang in the closet behind Trip, and Charlotte pushed herself straight up that wall. She hugged her arms tight around her waist. It rang again, and he could see any hope of coaxing a real smile or a little trust out of her had passed.

When it rang a third time, Trip was on his feet, digging through the mess in the closet to put a stop to the ringing.

Cripes. She'd said the killer had her number. That he'd called to torment her somehow.

He snatched the phone off the floor and answered. "Trip Jones, KCPD. Who is this?"

"Trip? It's Audrey." He could hear the siren on Alex's truck in the background, heard him on the radio to the other members of their team. "We're a minute away. Did you find Charlotte?"

Trip immediately regretted snapping into the phone. No wonder Charlotte was afraid of him. "I found her. She's…" Unpredictable. Frightened out of her mind. Unexpectedly charming. "…she's safe."

He glanced over to see a woman whose jaw was clenched so tight it trembled. That wasn't right. No one should have to cope with that kind of fear churning inside her.

Trip looked her straight in the eye to reassure her. "It's your friend Audrey."

Although Charlotte nodded her understanding, she didn't say anything until the dog dropped Trip's hat and stretched up on its hind legs, resting a paw against her thigh. Looking down into the dog's tilted face, Charlotte's fingers immediately moved to scratch behind a tattered, scarred-up ear. "Good boy. Mama's fine. Good boy."

What was it about this woman that kept getting under his skin? Guilt that he hadn't gotten the job done he'd been asked to do tonight? Frustration that *he* couldn't make her feel any better, but the dog who'd stolen his hat could?

Or was it something about those haunted gray eyes that triggered all the protective instincts he possessed?

As if she was even interested in being protected by him.

"You can't get here soon enough," Trip admitted, turning back to the phone. "I don't know what to say to her."

"I warned you that she's a little eccentric."

"Yeah, well she's scared enough of me that I don't know if I'm being much help."

The strident sound of a siren, made faint by the building's thick walls, pierced Trip's thoughts. The rhythm of the pulsing sound was different from the siren he could hear over the phone. Or was he hearing both sounds over the connection to Audrey's phone? Wait. He could make out three, five, at least six different siren signals approaching—a lot more than the other members of SWAT Team One could account for.

Audrey was hearing them, too. "Did you call an ambulance? Oh, my God. It's like a parade. Alex?"

Trip tensed, then forced his muscles to relax as he jogged toward the door and pulled it open. "Audrey, put your boyfriend on the phone," he commanded. "Taylor. What's going on? What are you seeing?"

Trip stepped out beneath the awning and spotted the swirls of red and blue lights bouncing off the wall of the building across the alley. Rain pelted his face and streamed down beneath his collar. So much for a low-key response to an *eccentric* friend's call for help.

He recognized Alex's truck turning into the end of the drive and parking at an angle to block the other vehicles. "Looks like we've got more backup than we asked for."

Trip hung up as soon as Alex hopped out of his truck. With his gun drawn, he hurried to the museum's back door, slowing just long enough to catch Audrey by the arm and hurry her on past the limo with the dead driver inside.

"Talk to me, Taylor."

Alex Taylor, wearing the same KCPD SWAT flak vest over jeans and a sweater, shook his head, pushing his auburn-haired fiancée beneath the relative dryness of the awning. "I don't know, big guy. I called Sergeant Delgado and Captain Cutler and that new gal on the team, Murdock.

I didn't call the army for backup. Word must have gotten out that it was Jackson Mayweather's daughter who was in trouble. That means the press will be here any minute, too."

"How is she?" Audrey asked, her face wreathed with concern.

Trip felt the heat at his back a split second before he heard the soft husky voice whisper behind him. "What's wrong?"

"Charlotte!"

Trip's impulse to shield the woman taking shelter behind him was thwarted when Audrey scooted past him and caught Charlotte up in a tight hug. "Oh, honey. I'm so sorry about Richard. Are you okay?"

Charlotte's denial was a quick shake of her head. "It's happening again. It's like before."

"Before what?" But Trip's question went unanswered. Again. Vehicles screeched to a halt out on the street's wet pavement. Car doors opened and closed. There were shouts and a few choice curses.

"What's going on?" Charlotte tipped her chin and blinked against the rain, throwing the question to Trip as if the approaching chaos was all his fault. "Why are all these people here?"

"I'm guessing it's the response to your 9-1-1 call."

"I didn't call anyone but Audrey." Charlotte was hunched over, holding tight to the dog's collar. "I don't want to see anyone. I want to go home." She hid behind Trip as the first uniformed patrol officers dashed around the corner into the alley lot. "I don't like people."

He spun around to keep her in sight. "You don't like people?"

"I don't like strangers. I can't handle people I don't know, especially all at once."

"They're here to help."

"Like you did?"

Ouch. The big gray eyes nailed him with the accusation.

Give it up, Jonesy. You're not going to win this gal over tonight.

"I'm sorry." Apology colored her voice, and she reached out as if she was going to touch him. But she quickly snatched her hand back to her chest. "I shouldn't have said that. All the rumors you've heard about the crazy woman at Mayweather Mansion are true."

"I don't listen to rumors—"

"It's not your fault." The woman was going into panic mode again. "Audrey? What am I going to do?"

"C'mon." Audrey wrapped her arm around Charlotte's shoulders and turned her toward the door. "Let's get you back inside. Alex, keep them away if you can."

"I'll do my best, sweetheart. I'm gonna need you, big guy."

After stowing his Glock back in its holster, Alex squeegeed the rain from his sleek black hair and put up a hand to hold back the officers hurrying toward them. "I'm Alex Taylor, SWAT Team One. The scene is secure, guys."

One of the uniforms kept coming. "Is that your truck? You're gonna have to move it. I've got two ambulances on the scene, with orders to get them in here."

Trip stepped forward, making a bigger blockade. "You need a coroner's wagon, not an ambulance." He nodded toward the BMW. "The vic is an elderly gentleman. Richard…?"

"Eames," Alex supplied the missing info. "Gunshot wound to the head."

The officer glanced inside the car, clearly questioning Trip's authority. "I'll have to check with my superior."

"Do that."

That took care of the first two officers, but the second wave was pulling up at the end of the alley, grouping up to assess and discuss the scene. The response to one frightened woman's call for help was bordering on overkill.

"Just how rich are the Mayweathers?" Trip asked.

"Jackson Mayweather is worth more than you and I both will make in a lifetime—and then some. Once word gets out that his daughter has been harmed again…"

"Again?"

Alex grinned ruefully. "You read all those books and yet you don't know front-page news? Charlotte was kidnapped when she was seventeen. Tortured. Ransomed for millions of dollars. Testifying at her kidnappers' trial was the last time she made an official public appearance. According to Audrey, a situation like this could send Charlotte back into seclusion for…forever, I guess."

Kidnapped? Tortured? Trip felt the blood draining from his head at the memory of him wrestling the terrified woman to the ground. "You didn't think I needed to know that before you sent me over here? I could have done some real harm."

Alex's dark eyes narrowed, surveying Trip from head to toe and back up to his bare arm and the makeshift bandage there. "Maybe we need that bus, after all. What happened?"

"Don't ask."

More people arrived on the scene, this time ranking detectives wearing suits and ties. A pair of EMTs, carrying their boxes of gear, followed close behind. The crew of a news van was already unloading equipment and setting up shots.

Alex's deep breath matched Trip's own. Any chance of secluding Charlotte from the cops and the media was quickly spiraling out of control. "If Charlotte didn't call 9-1-1, who did?"

Trip looked at the phone still clutched in his hand. He remembered Charlotte's instant terror at the idea of the killer calling her again.

"I think I know." Trip lifted his gaze, sweeping the rooftops and bricked-up windows before he advanced to meet the red-haired detective striding toward them. The bastard was still here. The man who'd killed the driver and forced Charlotte to arm herself with an ancient sword was someplace close by—maybe even a part of the frenzy—watching, feeding off her terror. "Get the team on the radio. We need to set up a perimeter."

Chapter Three

He was walking away.

The biggest man in the room, in the whole parking lot, was walking away.

Charlotte pulled away from the hand tugging at her wrist, pushed away the stethoscope sliding beneath her blouse and scooted forward on the gurney to peer through the lingering drizzle of rain to watch Trip Jones rise from the bumper of the second ambulance where he'd been sitting. He smoothed his big palm over the pristine white bandage where he'd been given sutures and a shot. He said something to the paramedic working on him and then turned to follow his commanding officer—a salt-and-pepper-haired man who'd introduced himself as Captain Cutler earlier—over to a meeting of bowed heads and nods with the rest of his SWAT team. Captain Cutler. Trip. Her friend Alex. Another dark-haired man wearing a perpetual scowl. A blonde woman with a ponytail.

Surrounded by a busy anthill of uniformed officers, detectives, CSIs, reporters, EMTs and family members moving around the museum, alley lot and blocked-off street, her eyes were drawn to the controlled stillness of Trip's SWAT team. Yes, they occasionally glanced around, or turned an ear to their shoulders when a message came over the radios clipped to their flak vests. But they were focused on their own discussion, gesturing occasionally, nodding agreement to one suggestion or another.

Charlotte couldn't explain her fascination with Trip Jones. Although she'd heard Audrey and Alex talk of him, she hadn't met him before tonight. It had been years since she'd met any man who wasn't family or didn't come to the house.

There was something to fear about all that size and strength and specialized training. For one irrational second inside that warehouse, she'd thought he meant to snap Max in two with one hand. Heck, he could have snapped her in two if he'd wanted, and she wasn't any skinny twig of a woman. She hadn't been pressed against that much man and muscle since, well…ever. He'd had every right to get physical with her, but he hadn't hurt her. Although built like a mountain, he was perhaps more like a volcano—a quiet, intimidating presence on the landscape, friendly enough unless all that inherent power in him erupted. Then she could imagine he'd be a far scarier opponent than the man who'd wrestled her to the ground tonight.

Fascinating indeed. She hadn't dated or acknowledged a hormone since the kidnapping. Yet here she was processing an almost intellectual curiosity about a man. One she would most likely never see again.

And who most certainly wouldn't want anything further to do with a screwy piece of work like her.

Charlotte could feel herself disconnecting from the confusion going on inside her head and closing in around her. It was a long-ingrained coping skill—but not the healthiest way of dealing with stress, so she turned away from Trip Jones and struggled to stay engaged with the three men sitting on each side of the gurney and standing with a notepad at the ambulance's open rear door.

Still she longed for her father and Audrey to leave the

press interviews they were conducting, to keep the reporters away from her, and take her home.

"Miss Mayweather, I asked if the attacker left you any kind of message." She didn't think it was any accident that the red-haired detective in the suit, tie and raincoat had waved his pen into her line of vision to force her attention back to him. "You were friends with Valeska Gallagher and Gretchen Cosgrove, weren't you?"

He wanted to know about two murdered friends?

Stay in the moment, Charlotte. Engage.

But she couldn't do it alone. She clicked her tongue. "Max. Up here."

Her companion leaped from the damp pavement into the back of the ambulance and crawled up onto the low bed where she sat.

"I went to school with Val and Gretchen." And Audrey Kline and a host of other overachievers at the Sterling Academy. She knew what the detective was asking. "The Rich Girl Killer doesn't murder sweet old men. And no, I haven't received any threatening letters. Richard's killer called me on my phone." She nodded at the plastic evidence bag with her cell sealed inside that Detective Montgomery held. "I think he was trying to find out where I was. He wanted to scare me into revealing myself. He must have read about my kidnapping. He knew…"

She dipped her face down to Max's and welcomed the comforting lick on her jaw.

"Miss Mayweather," one of the EMTs protested the muddy paw prints on the crisp white sheet, "that's hardly sanitary."

The other poked the stethoscope at her again. "If you work with us, this will only take a few minutes longer. Since you refuse to go to the hospital, your father asked us to give you a thorough once-over."

He pulled at Max's collar. She pulled back. "I have a doctor who comes to the house when I need one. I'm fine."

"Miss Mayweather?" The EMT shooed Max outside when she turned her attention back to the detective.

"I've answered enough, Detective Montgomery. I need to go home."

With a nod, he acknowledged the blatant hint to leave her alone, even though his faintly accented voice never wavered from its cool, calm and collected tone. "How can you be certain it was Mr. Eames's killer who called you?"

"I know."

"Would you care to elaborate on how you know that?"

Charlotte smoothed a damp kink of hair off her cheek and tucked it behind her ear. "Would I care…?"

Her ear.

Oh, God.

Charlotte's heart stopped for a split second then raced into overdrive. "Where's my earring?" She tugged at the exposed lobe, scarred and rebuilt from a graft of skin taken from her scalp. Hiding the disfiguring reminder with her hand, she whirled from one EMT to the next. "Did you take my earring? It's a white-enamel daisy. Did you take it?"

She recognized that knowing look exchanged between the two men. "Ma'am, we don't have your earring."

Right. She'd probably lost the keepsake from her mother in the struggle with Officer Jones. She swung her legs off the bed, but strong hands caught her and pulled her back onto the gurney.

"Max? I need Max." The EMT gently took her shoulder and slipped the chilled stethoscope against her skin. Charlotte twisted away.

"We can back-trace the number off your phone."

"To Richard's." She swung her gaze back to Spencer Montgomery. "But you didn't find his cell, did you? I'm telling you the killer took it." She brushed her curls back over her ear to hide the scar. "I want to look for my earring."

"You think the killer took your earring? The Rich Girl Killer takes souvenirs. Did you see him?"

"No. I just…" The panic was taking hold again. She had no keepsake to hide behind, no companion to focus on and keep her thoughts clear.

"Miss Mayweather?" The EMT who'd checked her pupils and pulse dabbed something cold and wet against her arm. When she saw the syringe on the bench beside him, she knocked the alcohol wipe away.

"I don't want any drugs." She put her fingers to her teeth and whistled loudly enough for all three men to pull back for a moment. "Come here, boy."

But the respite was brief.

"Ma'am, clearly you're upset by tonight's events. I need to give you something to calm you. Your heart's racing. We're worried about shock." Max had jumped back inside the ambulance, but the EMT was blocking him from climbing onto the gurney with her. Oh, great. The whistle had caught her dad's attention, too. He was watching her from his press interview, clearly concerned. "Just let me go home. Please."

"We need to remove the dog."

"One more question," Detective Montgomery prodded. "Can you be certain it wasn't your chauffeur calling for help? Perhaps a dying utterance?"

"No!"

"Move it, Fido."

"Max—"

"I need you to lie down."

"Could you identify the voice?"

"No. Please don't." Her mind was spinning, her heart racing. She wanted Max.

"Lie down."

"…hear a gunshot?"

What happened to one more question?

"Give her the sedative."

"I don't want…"

"…identify the killer?"

"Max?"

"The dog stays." The deep-pitched voice silenced the madness, and everything inside Charlotte went suddenly, blessedly still.

The only thing Charlotte could hear was the rain dribbling on the asphalt. The only thing she could see were the broad shoulders of Trip Jones filling the opening at the back of the ambulance.

He looked down at the detective beside him. "This interview is over."

Charlotte's attention danced down to the bandage on his arm, up to the tanned angles of his exposed biceps and triceps. She read the white SWAT emblazoned across his vest, took quick note of the gun and badge on his belt. But in a matter of seconds, before the protests of the three men around her started in, her gaze went back to Trip's grizzled jaw and the green-gold eyes looking down at her with a glimmer of something like intimate knowledge and understanding shining there.

"You're a crazy woman, all right. And I'm not sure I fully understand why. But…" He picked up Max in his arms and set him squarely in her lap. "The dog stays with her."

"Officer, we can't—"

"He's a service animal. With him here you don't need any sedatives. The dog stays."

"We have a job to do."

"You're out of line, Jones."

"With all due respect, Detective, she's been through enough." Trip's eyes cooled and his expression hardened as he looked at Detective Montgomery and the two EMTs, ensuring their cooperation. Charlotte hugged her arms around Max's chest and lowered her chin to the top of his warm, damp head as Trip pulled something from the back of his belt and turned to shout to his friends. "Taylor, let me borrow your cuffs. Sarge? Murdock? Yours, too."

Charlotte watched in fascination as his big hands deftly linked the handcuffs into a long chain. He hooked the last one to Max's collar and placed the jerry-rigged leash into her hand.

"There. Now you can control him and he won't be in anybody's way." As confidently as if they were long-lost friends, he reached out and mussed up Max's fur. "He won't bite." When he pulled away, he winked at Charlotte, startling her, drawing her focus back to his teasing eyes. "As long as you're nice to the lady."

For a moment, her eyes locked on to his. The teasing faded and something warmer, regretful almost, filled the air between them. Unused to her body's curious response to a man who was practically a stranger to her, she hugged her arms tighter around the dog. But she couldn't look away.

Caught up in those eyes, in the kindness he'd unexpectedly shown her, in the confident strength of his presence, she breathed deeply, freely—once, twice. Maybe he was more serene mountain than volatile volcano, after all.

He nodded, breaking the spell. "Charlotte."

And then Trip Jones walked away. Again.

Taking Charlotte's gratitude, and something less familiar and curiously unsettling, with him.

THE MAN SITTING IN THE dark vehicle adjusted the focus on his zoom lens and snapped one more photo, congratulating himself on capturing the image of a bloodied, harried woman, curled into a ball and hugging her dog in the back of an ambulance.

Pleased with his work, he powered down the camera and zipped it neatly into its carrying bag beside the cell phone he'd already crushed beneath his shoe. He tucked the bag into its spot on the floor behind his seat. Then he pulled his computerized notebook into his lap and clicked out of his file of old newspaper files and photos, which had provided all the information he needed to recreate the most vivid, frightening moments in Charlotte Mayweather's life. With two more clicks he was online. He smiled. Yes. People were already chatting and blogging about Charlotte Mayweather coming out of hiding and being involved in another unfortunate incident.

His anonymous post of tonight's events had generated the response he wanted. Just as his helpful phone call had created the crowd of chaos he was enjoying tonight.

Success flowed through his veins as he closed the computer and packed it in its pocket as well. Risking someone spotting the distant glow of his cigarette, he inhaled one last, long drag before pulling it from his lips and putting it out in the ashtray. He crushed the butt down—once, twice, three times before laying it neatly atop the ashes and shutting the tray.

He picked up the gaudy daisy earring from the dashboard and cradled it in his open palm, smiling at the perfect order of things tonight.

A good smoke.

Tidy surroundings.

An unexpected souvenir plucked from the floor of the Mayweather Museum's warehouse.

Yes. She'd just realized it was gone. His old friend was so terrified by his actions that he could see her practically crawling out of her skin as cops and medics and family alike tried to keep her on the gurney in that ambulance. Getting to the reclusive Charlotte Mayweather had been a cakewalk for a man like him.

She'd always thought she had all the answers—that she was smarter, better than him—that her father's money gave her the right to dismiss his talents. She'd made that mistake once—couldn't be bothered with what he had to offer, refused to listen to reason. But he'd proved her wrong tonight. Not only was he intelligent enough to get to Charlotte, he was clever enough to get inside her head.

He breathed in deeply, savoring the lingering smoke in the air, enjoying the satisfaction of a job well done.

Nailing the old man had been simple. All he had to do was walk up and knock on the car window. The chauffeur had actually smiled, perhaps recognizing him, then rolled down the window as if he wanted to offer help. He reached over and stroked the gun and silencer on the seat beside him. The old man *had* helped, had served the necessary purpose. It wasn't the first man's death he'd agreed to in order to make his vengeful plan come to fruition.

He was halfway through his list of wealthy women who'd slighted him over the years. Women he'd once trusted. Women who had used, betrayed and laughed at him. There'd be one more name checked off that list if Audrey Kline's zealous boyfriend hadn't gone into 24/7 bodyguard mode last November. Or maybe it had been his own mistake, thinking he could trust a gang of thugs to follow the rules of his plan.

He bristled where he sat, the sweet aroma of his rare cigarette souring into a foul memory in his nose and lungs. He didn't make mistakes.

His fingers curved around the earring and squeezed, its sharp edges cutting into his skin.

Normally, he preferred to put his hands on his victims, to feel them writhing with fear, to hear them begging for mercy. He opened his hand and forced himself to breathe deeply, recalling Charlotte's screams of terror when he'd beat on the door. The erratic rhythm of his pulse evened out as he replayed her helpless gasp over the phone in his head. He turned from his hidden vantage point and watched her manic movements and pale expression as she dodged reporters and battled with cops and medical personnel amidst the glare of headlights and spotlights and television cameras. Seeing her weakness paraded on display in front of her family and the press strengthened his resolve, calmed him.

This was all going to plan. Charlotte Mayweather craved security, predictability—she needed to know and trust everything and everyone around her in order to function like a normal human being.

He'd take all that and more from her.

Feeling tonight's victory coursing through his veins again, he tucked the earring into his pocket and started the engine. Power over those who had wronged him, control of his own destiny—those were heady things that restored the equilibrium inside his own head.

He pulled onto the street, driving two blocks before turning on his lights and heading across the city.

His thorough research into her kidnapping ordeal, and into the hellish trial that followed, had paid off. He was in her head now, exactly where he wanted to be.

Charlotte Mayweather didn't stand a chance.

Chapter Four

Trip downed the last of his beer in one long swallow and plunked the empty glass on the table. Of all the nights he'd been to the Shamrock Bar, celebrating successful missions with his team, commiserating over the rare loss of a hostage or saluting a fallen friend, he'd always been able to tune out the noise of too many conversations and television sets and concentrate on his friends. Or on a pretty face who didn't mind a little flirtation. Or on one of the classic novels he'd been too frustrated to get through when the rest of his classmates had been reading them back in school.

Thank God for Classic Comics—or he might not have the high-school diploma he'd needed to get into the police academy eleven years ago.

He rolled an imaginary crick from his neck and turned his attention back to the paperback he was reading at the corner table. It might take him all year long, but he was determined to get through the entire *Lord of the Rings* trilogy.

Only, Ents and elves and the scramble of letters he called Mordor kept getting sidetracked by sword-wielding women with pesky dogs and curvy hips and expressive eyes that shouldn't be hidden away behind a pair of glasses.

He turned his page toward the light hanging on the wall

beside him and tried to focus. *The qeaçous…no, beacons of Gondor are alight, calling for aid.*

But Trip's thoughts weren't in Middle Earth.

The swirling lights and sirens meant backup had arrived. They meant somebody else was here to convince her that he was one of the good guys. "They're here to help."

"Like you did?"

Trip's gaze drifted to the blank margin at the bottom of the page. Where did Charlotte Mayweather get off, all but accusing him of making a horrible night even worse for her? He'd volunteered on his own time to check on the friend of a friend in need. The dead body and forced lock he'd found had put him on full-alert-combat mode. The woman was safe with him there. She didn't need to be afraid or cry or go psycho on him.

She just needed to believe that he'd protect her—at any cost—because that was his job. It was who he was. It was what six feet, five inches of brawn, resourceful instincts and a talented set of hands was best suited for. He'd told her as much—had shown her—but she still didn't believe he was one of the good guys.

And then she'd cried on him? The stitches in his arm and threat of a killer on the loose he could handle. But those tears trickling over her cheeks had twisted his stomach into a knot and made him useless to her.

And why was that stunned feeling of incompetence the memory that niggled his conscience two nights after the fact? Why wasn't he analyzing the syrupy heat that had stirred in his veins when she'd halfway smiled at him for answering her tomboy whistle and plopping the dog in her lap?

Why was anything at all about Charlotte Mayweather still stuck in his head?

Trip closed his book and reached for his empty glass, tuning in to the other people in the bar. Captain Cutler sat at the end of the table, reading over the report from their performance-evaluation drill this afternoon. Alex Taylor sat directly across from him, on the phone with Audrey. Rafe Delgado was up at the bar, leaning in to stand nose-to-nose with their favorite bartender and adopted little sister, Josie Nichols.

Whatever that hushed argument was about, Josie was standing her ground, flipping her long dark ponytail behind her back and tilting her chin, despite the fatigue that was evident in her posture. For half a moment, Trip considered poking his nose in and warning Sergeant Delgado to back it up a step. Couldn't he see how she braced her hands at the small of her back? The woman was dead on her feet, attending nursing school by day and working long hours at her uncle's bar at night. She didn't need whatever grief Rafe was giving her right now. But then Trip's rescuing skills seemed to be a little on the fritz right now.

Still, Rafe seemed to be taking his overprotective-big-brother thing with Josie a little too far. Since she was the daughter of his first partner, who'd been killed in the line of duty, there was probably a stronger connection there. But it turned out there was no need to intervene. Josie flattened her hand in the middle of the sergeant's chest and pushed him out of her space before spinning around and returning to her duties behind the bar.

Seemed like Charlotte Mayweather wasn't the only woman who didn't want SWAT Team One looking out for her.

"Here we go." Randy Murdock, the newest member of the team, was driven and talented and female. *Miranda,* a feminine name that didn't seem to fit either her personality or her deadly aim with a Remington sniper rifle, set a tray of beers on the table. The unwritten law was that the new guy bought the second round of drinks, since Josie Nichols seemed to always find an excuse to serve their first drinks on the house. "Everyone wanted a draft, right?"

"Works for me." Trip reached across the table and picked up his second beer. He wouldn't resort to getting drunk to get his frustration with a certain toffee-haired heiress out of his system, but getting his hands busy with something else might. "Thanks, newbie."

Randy slid into the chair beside Trip's, pulling a beer in front of her, too. "I don't want you guys to think that just because I'm the only woman on the team that I'm going to be serving the drinks all the time. And don't expect me to bake brownies or darn your socks."

"Don't expect me to darn yours, either," Trip teased, appreciating the normal interaction with a woman.

"You can sew?" she countered.

"You can cook?"

The blonde's cheeks blossomed with a blush that she quickly hid behind a swig of her beer.

"Down, you two." Captain Cutler chided them like a stern father, setting the report down on the table and picking up a glass. His dark blue eyes zeroed in on Randy. "As long as you keep making a perfect score on the target range, you don't have to bring me another beer."

"I don't mind doing that for you, sir."

Michael Cutler grinned. "Relax, Murdock—I'm paying you a compliment. Team One's score today was the highest ever recorded on the course. Captain Sanchez on Team Two owes me twenty bucks. And I intend to collect."

"Congratulations, sir."

"Congratulations to my team." Cutler raised his glass and signaled to Sergeant Delgado to come over to the table and join their toast. "Now, you all perform that well on the street, and I can rest easy when I go home to my wife at night."

Trip raised his glass and took a drink to honor his team's performance on the mock-terrorist-attack drill this afternoon. Even during those lucky stretches of time when there was no real bomb threat or fugitive alert or hostage crisis that needed SWAT on the scene, they trained in weapons and strategy to keep their skills and instincts sharp. Today's drill had gone by the book—full cooperation, each playing to his or her strength, no mistakes.

So why couldn't he be savoring that victory instead of stewing over some eccentric kook…?

Trip's gaze skidded to the neat shock of red hair on the man walking through the Shamrock's front door. One thing about hanging out at a cop bar was that eventually, almost every cop in KCPD, active or retired, would stop by. Even the ones he didn't particularly like. Trip barely knew Spencer Montgomery, but something about a detective relentlessly badgering a witness in an ambulance when it was plain to anybody who looked that she was about to lose it, put him on Trip's don't-turn-your-back-on-him-yet list.

Detective Montgomery must have felt Trip's eyes on him because he paused before sitting and turned, trading nods of acknowledgment, if no smile of kinship, with him. Montgomery and his dark-haired partner had been assigned to the Rich Girl Killer investigation. A serial killer had already tortured and strangled two of Kansas City's wealthiest beauties and was believed to be responsible for one or two more unsolved deaths. Just last year the killer had targeted Alex's fiancée, but the perp had eluded identification and gone underground. Did Montgomery think there was some kind of connection between the dead chauffeur and the murderer he was after?

Trip sat up straight in his chair.

Was *that* the killer Charlotte Mayweather feared?

The man she'd thought *he* was?

Maybe the prickly heiress's paranoia wasn't all about the trauma of being kidnapped ten years ago.

"All right, sweetheart, I'll see what I can do. You will *not*. You will not." Alex's voice interrupted Trip's silent speculation. "If that's the case, it's not up for negotiation. As soon as I'm done here, I'll swing by to pick you up."

"Problems with the soon-to-be missus?" Trip felt he'd better make a comment before anyone noticed his unusual preoccupation with his thoughts tonight.

"Just a little discussion about taking unnecessary risks." Alex closed his phone and slipped it into the pocket of his jeans. "We reached a compromise."

"She'll go ahead and do what she wants and you won't complain about it?"

"Ha-ha, big guy. I wouldn't be giving me too much grief. You've been all kinds of quiet since that night at the May-weather Museum." So his brooding hadn't gone unnoticed. "On the other hand, whatever you said or did, Charlotte's still talking about it. Audrey's at her house right now."

"Is she filing a harassment claim with the D.A.'s office?"

"Not exactly."

"What *exactly* is she saying about me?"

Captain Cutler put an end to the conversation. "What is this, junior high? You two settle your love lives on your own time. I just won a bet."

"Congratulations, captain," Alex took a drink and then pushed his glass away. "Sorry to cut the celebration short, but, since we have the next couple of days off, I've got a favor to ask." The others stopped their joking and drinking long enough to listen in. "Well, Audrey's the one making the request, but—"

"What does the counselor need?" Sergeant Delgado asked. As moody as he'd been lately, he had a soft spot for Audrey Kline, the assistant district attorney who'd put away the murderer of a little boy who'd died in Delgado's arms back in November. They all owed Audrey a favor for that conviction.

"She's looking for some extra security to keep an eye on the guests at Richard Eames's funeral tomorrow. I guess he'd been with the Mayweather family so long that they're all attending the service and hosting a reception afterward at the estate."

"They're *all* attending?" Trip was still pondering what accusations, or unlikely compliments, Charlotte had to say about him. She'd made it clear that she had a phobia about people, about strangers—about big, scary men like him, especially. He couldn't see her standing with a crowd of mourners around a grave site, or welcoming them into her home.

"Charlotte said Richard Eames was like an uncle to her. They're going to find a way to sneak her in to the graveside service," Alex explained. "But they're worried about paparazzi and curious fans. Anything about the Mayweathers is usually newsworthy, but if word gets out that Charlotte is finally making a public appearance after all these years, it might bring the crazies out. They'd like to keep their mourning as private as possible, of course."

"They're about the wealthiest family in Kansas City," Randy pointed out. "Don't they have their own security?"

Alex nodded. "Gallagher Security Systems—the same private outfit that protects the estate where Audrey's father lives. They'll provide extra guards at the house, in addition to all the electronics Gallagher designed. But they're more gadgets than manpower—they don't have the resources to secure a cemetery the size of Mt. Washington as well."

Rafe Delgado leaned back in his seat, a frown settling back on his expression. "Didn't Gallagher provide the security at the estate where Gretchen Cosgrove was murdered, too?"

Randy picked up on his suspicion. "That's not a very good recommendation for Gallagher's company."

"Gallagher's wife was the Rich Girl Killer's first victim," Captain Cutler reminded them.

"If his company had access to all the crime scenes, maybe the second murder and other attempts are a cover for his wife's death." Randy wasn't getting the hint stamped on Cutler's unsmiling face. "Has anyone investigated him?"

The captain cleared his throat and simply looked at her.

Randy wilted in her chair. "Too soon in our relationship to speculate about something like that, hmm?"

"Quinn Gallagher is a friend of mine," Cutler explained. "Any connection between his company and the murders is a cruel coincidence. Or a plot to discredit him."

Trip's gaze instinctively shifted across the room to the table where Spencer Montgomery and his partner were sipping drinks. Son of a gun. The red-haired detective was looking over the rim of his glass, meeting Trip's gaze—as if he knew the conversation around SWAT Team One's table centered on his investigation.

The detective didn't so much as blink before turning back to his partner. A guy that unflappable would have no qualms about exploiting Charlotte Mayweather's grief if it meant solving his case.

Uh-uh. He had the stitches in his arm to prove *he* was the man Charlotte could count on if there was any other threat to her person or sanity—from killer or cop alike. Whether she believed it or not.

Trip pulled back to answer Alex. "I'll volunteer."

The mood around the table grew sober. They were all shifting back into wary-protector mode.

"Jackson Mayweather is looking for some off-duty officers to help with crowd control, in exchange for a generous donation to KCPD's widows and orphans fund."

"Whatever the Mayweathers need. I'm there."

"Thanks, Trip."

Captain Cutler was nodding, pushing away from the table and standing. "Call or text us with the times and setup. We can coordinate our efforts once we're on-site. And remember, protecting the Mayweathers is strictly voluntary."

"I'll be there," Trip repeated, rising.

Alex stood, too. "Audrey will be there all day, so that means I will, too."

Randy shrugged and joined in. "It's not like I've got a hot date tomorrow."

Rafe was looking over his shoulder, watching Josie serve a beer and a smile up to one customer before hurrying behind the counter to greet someone new and fetch the next drink. Whatever was troubling him didn't appear to be a concern for her.

"Sarge?" the captain prompted.

Rafe stood as well. "I'm in."

Trip grabbed his jacket off the back of his chair and shrugged into it. With thoughts of Charlotte distracting him from his normal routine, he hadn't really been in the mood to celebrate, anyway. As the others headed for the door, he picked up his book and fell into step behind them. Any mental thumbing of the nose as they filed past Spencer Montgomery's table was a silent bonus.

This was a team he could trust. Just like that drill this afternoon—they'd get the job done. Together.

Sure, maybe he was looking to redeem himself in Charlotte's eyes. Maybe he couldn't make her feel safe, or put the woman at ease, but he damn sure could handle a little routine security and crowd control. He could ensure that she found the privacy she needed to deal with her grief.

And maybe that knowledge, at last, would put his guilty conscience to rest.

Chapter Five

Charlotte's palm was sweaty around the wrapped bouquet of white roses she'd been clinging to for the past twenty minutes.

While Max chewed on his new leash at her feet, she sat at the tinted back window of her father's limo, secretly watching the mourners huddled around a green tent some fifty yards from where the driver had parked near the beginning of the procession line. Her head ached with a terrible mix of guilt and grief. The sweeping hillside, studded with tall trees and marble markers, was curtained by rain and shadows, giving a twilight cast to the afternoon service.

The event-planning team her father had hired to put together a reception at the house later was to be commended for stepping in to help with the ceremony here, as well. Not only had they taken over the task of coordinating transportation from Mt. Washington Cemetery to the estate, they'd issued umbrellas to any guest who'd shown up for the wet proceedings without one.

Like a sea of black mushrooms sprouting across the hillside, the faceless mourners only added to Charlotte's unsettled nerves. Logically, she understood there were people here she knew and could trust. But she couldn't see any of them. Her father and stepmother would be standing beneath the awning with the family and minister. Audrey and Alex were there, too. She'd seen him drive up in his black SWAT uniform earlier, no doubt taking a break from work to attend the service with his fiancée. But without the anchor of a trusted friend or family member to cling to, an illogical sense of isolation was creeping in, making Charlotte question the impulse to pay her personal respects to an old friend.

A flicker of movement at the edge of the crowd caught her attention and she shifted in her seat. Her stepbrother, Kyle Austin, turned away from the ceremony to check his watch. The shoulders of his tailored gray suit lifted with a deep breath and another check of the time before he disappeared beneath his umbrella again. While she'd grown up with Richard Eames, the Austins had been part of the family for less than two years, and Kyle was such a workaholic at her father's real estate development company that he barely knew the staff's name. He was here strictly as a courtesy to her father.

Drawn to another ripple of movement, she spotted her stepsister Bailey's strawberry blond hair. She was standing with her arm linked to a tall blond man. Charlotte squinted. If he bent down from beneath that umbrella and whispered to Bailey just one more time...Harper Pierce? Charlotte smiled as he kissed her stepsister's cheek, recognizing the society prince she'd once gone to school with.

In the very next breath, she frowned. Harper had proposed to their classmate Gretchen Cosgrove last year. According to her best friend Audrey, within a month after Gretch was murdered, he'd made a play for her. Audrey, of course, an eloquent woman who rarely minced words, told him in no uncertain terms that Alex Taylor was the man she loved and Harper needed to move on.

Now he was spending time with Bailey? They knew each

other well enough to hold hands and exchange a kiss? When had that happened? Gretchen had been dead for only four months. A man that desperate for constant female companionship seemed a far cry from the high-school soccer hero she'd once had a major crush on. When she was sixteen, even though he'd never looked at her as anything other than his study buddy, she'd willingly typed Harper's papers and tutored him in whatever subject he struggled with in order to maintain the academic standards needed to play sports at Sterling Academy.

The notion of high school and longing for a boy of her own turned her memories to the stupid choice she'd made with one of Harper's teammates the night of the prom. It was a plain girl's foolish mistake to turn down attending with a friend and accept Landon Turner's invitation. Finding out he'd issued the invitation on a lousy hundred-dollar dare, and had another girl waiting for him at the dance, had led to a humiliating exit. And to the man waiting in the parking lot. And the speeding van and the…

"Nope." Charlotte turned away from the window, thinking she could turn away from the memories, as well. "I'm not reliving that nightmare again."

And yet she was. Right now. Hiding away in a car because she was so damn afraid of some other stranger out there. How was she any less free of her kidnappers now than when they'd held her down and cut off part of her ear as proof of life for her father?

Landon had paid for his unwitting collusion with the kidnappers by being kicked out of Sterling Academy and losing his most prestigious scholarship offers. Once he'd outgrown the need to play pranks on the school's resident bookworm, he probably had gone on to lead a normal, successful life.

But she was still paying for that night. She was still

afraid, still obeying the threat that her kidnappers would find her and hurt her even worse, in any number of ways, if she tried to escape and trust her own decisions and be free again.

With a weighty, sorrowful sigh, she pulled her black trench coat more tightly around the skirt and sweater she wore. She let her fingers slide into her pocket to touch the brand-new phone with the unlisted number that her father had given her. She could call for help anytime she needed to. Too bad there wasn't a number she could call to make her feel truly warm and confident and normal again.

When the low tones of "Amazing Grace" filtered in through the walls of the limo, Charlotte turned her attention toward the green tent again. The service was winding down and people were moving, probably to lay a flower on the casket or express condolences to Mrs. Eames, her children and grandchildren. Charlotte's heart rate picked up a notch in anticipation. She wanted to be one of those people trading hugs, holding someone close to share her grief.

But she couldn't. Even if she could see some faces now, they were all strangers to her. How could she face them, wondering if the man who'd killed Richard and terrorized her was one of them? Was there someone else in that crowd waiting to knock her senseless and take her away from everything she knew and loved in exchange for her father's money? Was there someone out there who wanted to kill her, too?

Besides, the mourners weren't the only crowd at Mt. Washington today. Down at the bottom of the hill, at a restricted distance beyond the line of cars, was a gathering of reporters, complete with microphones and television cameras. They might be waiting for a glimpse of Jackson Mayweather or a sound bite from one of his stepchildren or second wife, but there'd be a crazy dash if they knew that, after ten years of hiding from Kansas City society, the Mad Miss Mayweather had ventured out of her ivory tower. And no matter how badly she wanted to pay her respects, she wouldn't risk the potential media circus of her appearance detracting from the Eames family and the sadness of the day.

So she'd sit right where she was until the crowd cleared and her father came to get her to walk her up to the grave site.

When she realized she was watching the clock as closely as her time-obsessed stepbrother, Charlotte flipped her watch around on her wrist and reached down to scratch Max's head. "We just need to be patient. After ten years of solitude, you'd think I'd know how to do that, right?"

Max answered with a sniff of her hand and a bored look in his round brown eyes. Leaving him to polish off his chew toy, she returned to the task of spying from her anonymous vantage point. The mourners were spread out across the hillside now, trickling down to their cars—walking in small groups, stopping to chat with old friends. As the crowd thinned, she spotted Alex and Audrey with one of the uniformed guards from Gallagher Security. Two motorcycle cops from KCPD cruised by, pulling into position at the front of the procession.

A tall man climbed out of a police SUV parked up ahead, hunching his shoulders against the rain as he crossed the road to speak to the traffic cops. Charlotte pulled one knee beneath her and sat up taller. She recognized that man in the black SWAT uniform. Salt-and-pepper hair. Air of authority. He was Alex's captain, one of the men she'd seen him talking to the night of Richard's murder.

A second man from Alex's team, lanky, with dark brown hair beneath his black SWAT cap, climbed out from the passenger side of the SUV. He lowered the walkie-talkie he'd been speaking into and pointed up the hill.

Spinning in her seat, Charlotte followed the direction of his arm. She searched higher up the hill, beyond the green tent, and saw the policewoman with the blond ponytail looking through a pair of binoculars.

Charlotte searched the entire crowd, from one tree line to the next. If the rest of Alex's team was here, did that mean…?

Trip Jones.

Her pulse skipped a beat then drummed into overtime. How had she missed seeing the oversize mountain of a man in the black uniform and boots standing near the media cars and trucks, squinting into the drizzling rain because he had no hat?

The water added nutmeg-colored streaks to his light brown hair. The rain had to be running down the back of his neck, making his crisp uniform damp and sticky. One hand rested on the butt of the gun strapped to his thigh, the other tapped at the tiny microphone clipped to his ear as his lips moved in some sort of terse reply. But she detected no hint of discomfort in his implacable stance, no trace of complaint in the methodical back-and-forth scan of his eyes.

"Maximus, I think we owe the guy a new hat." And an apology. And maybe an explanation for her odd behavior.

And maybe while she was doing that, she could study those hazel eyes again, to see if she'd only imagined the gentle humor and unflinching support there when he'd handed her Max and told the others at that ambulance to bug off.

Of course, to do that, she'd have to meet him again. She'd have to be close enough to make that eye contact.

She'd have to speak. Rationally. But she hadn't seen any pigs flying around—

A sharp knock on the window beside her made her jump halfway across the seat. Max's woof matched her startled gasp. Clutching her hand over her thumping heart, Charlotte reminded herself to breathe and called herself twenty kinds of fool once she identified the man with the wire-rimmed glasses waiting patiently outside the car.

Jeffrey Beecher was the executive assistant for the event company handling the memorial reception today. The earbud he wore and corkscrew cord that curled down beneath his suit jacket confirmed that he was the hired help. Her stepmother often employed Jeffrey and his crew to coordinate parties and fundraisers. Charlotte didn't attend those functions, but her father ran thorough background checks and made sure that she was introduced to any staff who came onto the estate. Just in case she would need to leave her rooms during an event, she would be able to identify the employee and not go into a panic.

She briefly considered staying where she was and not responding to the knock. But Max had barked and she had yelped, and the man with the business suit and umbrella really was standing ever so patiently in the rain, so he had to know she was in here.

Just do it, Charlotte. She had no place to withdraw to right now. *Engage.*

Crawling back across the leather seat, Charlotte pushed the button and lowered the window a few inches—just enough to peek through and smell the green, woodsy dampness in the cool outside air. "Yes?"

Jeffrey's umbrella blocked the rain as he bent over far enough to line his eyes up with hers. He adjusted his glasses on his nose and smiled. "Miss Mayweather. Sorry to intrude on your privacy. But I need to tell you there's been a slight change in plans."

"Oh?" She didn't like change. She didn't like surprises.

Something of her confusion must have read on her face, because he put up a hand and patted the air in a placating gesture. "Don't worry. We'll still get you up to lay a flower on the grave and say your goodbyes. But I'll have to ask you to wait in the car a little bit longer."

She reached down to stroke Max's ears. "Is something wrong?"

He quickly shook his head to reassure her. "We weren't anticipating the numbers of reporters here at the cemetery, so we're having to improvise. Clarice," his boss, "actually invited them to attend the reception. As long as they stay outside of the gates, of course."

Charlotte climbed up onto her knees again, her gaze flitting over to the news vans and photographers and the mountain of a man keeping watch over them. Would they really try to intrude on the family's privacy with Trip standing guard?

Her father apparently thought so. "Mr. Mayweather is going to send your stepmother and stepsister on to the house so that the press corps will follow them. Then he'll come back for you to lay the flowers on the grave."

"What about Kyle?"

"Oh, yes." His gaze darted over to Kyle Austin, jogging down the hill. Charlotte saw her blond-haired stepbrother collapse his umbrella, climb into his white Jaguar and speed away from the service. She had no time to speculate where he was going in such a hurry because Jeffrey was pulling an envelope from inside his jacket and sliding it through the crack in the window. "Kyle said a man handed this to him, but he needed to get back to the office, so he asked me to deliver it to you."

Charlotte plucked the envelope from his fingers. "What man?"

"He didn't know him, but he said he had on a uniform of some kind. Your name is on the envelope." Jeffrey shrugged. "I'm assuming it's a condolence?"

She turned it over to see her name neatly typed on the front. But there was no return address, no glimpse of handwriting to give her any clue as to who it might be from. Maybe this was Trip Jones's idea of sending her an apology?

Only, *he* wasn't the one who needed to apologize.

She pulled the envelope into her lap and tried to be civil. "Thank you, Jeffrey."

"No problem." Something buzzed into the earbud he wore and he answered with a "yes, ma'am" before pulling away. "Sorry to intrude on your privacy, Miss Mayweather, but I'd better get to the estate and make sure everyone's ready when the guests arrive. See you there."

Probably not. Charlotte rolled the window up and sat back to open the envelope and pull out the neatly folded letter inside, alternately checking out one window and then the other for any sign of her mysterious pen pal. So a man in uniform had given it to Kyle. One of the security guards? Someone on the florists' staff? A courier? Police officer? Trip?

Or someone very different.

It's your turn, Charlotte.
All those brains, yet you never saw me coming.
I'm here now. Watching. Waiting.
The old man couldn't stop me from getting to you.

*No one can. I'll take what you owe me and enjoy
watching you squirm.
Scared yet?*

"Oh, God." The silent assault pushed the blood to her
feet, making her feel dizzy, light-headed. Her vision blurred
the vile words as she crumpled the letter in her fist. "Max?"
She instinctively reached for the dog. "Max?"

He hopped onto the seat beside her and she hugged him
tight. But she still felt cold, isolated, afraid.

"Why is this happening to me?" she whispered into the
dog's fur, rocking back and forth. "Why does he want to
hurt—?"

The phone in her coat pocket rang and she screamed
out loud. Max barked but licked her hand as her shaking
fingers dug into the pocket of her coat.

It rang again, the chirping sound creeping along her skin
and raising goose bumps. It was him. She knew it was him
and she answered anyway. "What?"

A single, satisfied breath. And then, "Did you get my
message?"

"Stop this." Anger and confusion colored her plea. "I'm
not like other people. I can't handle this."

Another soft breath ended in a low-pitched laugh. "Don't
you think I know that?"

Charlotte slapped the phone shut and hurled it across
the limo.

It started ringing again as soon as it settled into a carpeted corner of the floor. "Stop it!"

She snatched Max's leash and shoved the car door open.
Her feet slipped on the red bricks that lined the road, and
she grabbed onto the door handle to keep from falling.
One shoe came off and tumbled into the ditch. She didn't
care that her stockings were soaking up the oily residue on

the asphalt. She had only one thought in mind as she spun around to search the hillside. "Dad?"

Her gaze darted from umbrella to umbrella, from marker to marker. She needed the cool rain splashing her face to clear her senses enough to realize that she'd just captured the attention of half the people milling through Mt. Washington.

For an instant, Charlotte froze. Her skin heated with embarrassment, her thoughts raced with panic. The man who'd called her was here. Watching. Taking delight in her phobic reaction to his threats.

Stay in the moment, Charlotte. Don't let him make you crazy.

What a fool she was. *Just go home. Don't give him the satisfaction of seeing you like this.*

Using her hand more than her vision to guide her, she tugged Max's leash and sidled around the front of the car. She knocked on the driver's window, peered inside behind the wheel. Empty. Where had he gone? This wasn't part of the plan.

"Did you need me, Miss?"

The smell of smoke filled her nose as she twirled around. "My father gave you specific instructions to wait…"

Uniform.

"I was just taking a cigarette break, ma'am. Union allows it. I was right over there."

She read the name on his chest beneath the event company's logo. *Bud.*

She didn't know any Bud.

"Did you…?" She raised the crumpled note in her hand. "Did you give this to my brother?"

"Ma'am?" Bud tucked a toothpick into the corner of his mouth and frowned. "Is something wrong?"

"Charlotte Mayweather!"

She turned to the sound of the voice. Snap. A bright light flashed in her eyes and she jerked her face away.

"Hey, pal." Bud in the uniform stepped between her and the photographer who was trying to snap another picture. "You leave her alone."

Move.

The photographer with the receding hairline wasn't the only reporter calling her name. While he traded curses with Bud, Charlotte blinked her eyes clear and looked over the hood of the limo, seeking out a familiar face. Any familiar face.

Red hair. "Audrey?"

The moment she spotted her friend hurrying down the hill with Alex Taylor at her side, Charlotte limped around the car on one shoe. With a click of her tongue to command him, Max leaped over the ditch with her and scrambled up the hill.

Another light flashed in her peripheral vision and she turned up the collar of her trench coat, pulling her head in like a turtle and skirting past a black-marble marker to reach her friends.

"Charlotte, what's happened?" Audrey wrapped her up in a hug and Alex's strong arms folded around them both.

"He called me on my new phone. He's here."

Alex urged them both down the hill toward the cars, his chin tipped toward the microphone on his collar. "Come to my location now," she heard, as he guided them across the ditch. "And get those photographers back. Lassen, you son of a…" Alex pulled back and pressed a kiss to Audrey's temple. "Get her in the car while I take care of this rat."

With Audrey's arm around her shoulders, they turned toward the limo. "Steve Lassen is that tabloid opportunist who gave me such grief during my gang-leader trial last November. He and Alex have history."

Charlotte saw Bud circling around the limo, opening the back door for them. She planted her feet, tripping out of her second shoe before they stopped. "I don't want to go with him."

"Char, the press…" She pulled the letter from Charlotte's hand. Audrey's pale cheeks flooded with color. "Where did you get this?"

Men in black uniforms were closing in on their position near the hood of the limousine. Orders were shouted, protests made. But the press was retreating to the opposite side of the road.

"Oh, my God." Charlotte willingly turned her back to the cameras and squeezed Audrey's hand, worried by her friend's reaction to the threat. "This is just like the one I got last November. Alex!"

"Jeffrey—the guy organizing all this—said it was from Kyle, that a man in some kind of uniform had given it to him."

Alex was back. He wound his arm around Audrey and read the note.

"Where's Jeffrey now?" Audrey asked, futilely trying to look beyond Alex's protective grasp.

"Leave that to the detectives. He's back," Alex announced grimly.

"Who's back?" Charlotte whispered, more alarmed by the way Audrey's cheeks blanched than by anything that had happened in the past few minutes.

"The Rich Girl Killer."

It was a bleak, terrifying pronouncement.

"The man who killed Gretchen and Val?" The man who'd worked with a gang to terrorize Audrey? He was after *her?*

"Here," Alex ordered, thrusting out the letter. Charlotte shivered from head to toe at the wall of black looming up behind her. She recognized the hand that reached around her to take the paper from Alex and shrank away from the fading bruise of a dog nip there. "Get that letter out of the rain—it could be evidence. I need to get Aud someplace safe."

"We'll get the family home." Captain Cutler was there, too, snapping orders. "Jones, get this one back to the limo and tell that guy to drive."

"Sorry, I've got to do this." Trip's deep voice seemed to hold a real apology as he stuffed the letter inside his vest and pulled Max's leash from her fingers. But there was nothing forgiving about his big hand clamping around her arm, pulling her into step beside him. "But the closer you are to me, the safer you'll be."

"Let me go." Charlotte struggled every step of the way. But her wet feet found no traction and Trip's grasp on her arm showed no signs of freeing her.

"Get in the car," Trip ordered.

Her eyes zeroed in on Bud, rolling his toothpick from one side of his mouth to the other as he waited for her.

"No." She didn't know Bud, couldn't ride with him. "No!" When she realized she couldn't stop the freight train of Trip's long strides, she reached up and grabbed a handful of his sleeve. Her fingers curled into the damp material, wrinkling it in her fist. "I don't trust him. He's wearing a uniform."

Trip planted his feet and faced her, his hand on her arm the only thing keeping her from pitching forward at the sudden stop. "*I'm* wearing a uniform."

There was no humor in the green-gold gaze bearing down on her now.

Her fingertips brushed against the muscle flexing beneath his sleeve, their pleading grasp stuttering at the unfamiliar sensations of hardness and heat. She snatched her fingers away, fighting the unexpected urge to hold on tighter, wiping the moisture from her glasses instead. "A man in uniform handed the letter to Kyle, who gave it to Jeffrey, who gave it to me. But I was watching you when I received it, so I'm guessing you didn't—"

"You make no sense. Back up!" She flinched as he pointed over her head toward a reporter inching across the road. She flinched again when his hand settled on her shoulder. With a sotto-voce curse, he moved it away. He bent his knees, hunching down to bring his gaze more even with hers. "Why did you get out of the car in the first place? The plan was to take you up to the site after the procession had left."

"But he said the plans had changed—"

"Who said? The driver?" He swung his gaze toward Bud, patting his chest where the letter was hidden. "You think *he* sent this?"

"He's wearing a uniform."

"Miss Mayweather?" a voice shouted from the other side of the road. "Does today's visit mean you're coming out of seclusion?"

"That's Jackson's daughter?"

"How does she look?"

Charlotte's world shrank to the wall of black Kevlar in front of her face as Trip straightened and shouted a second warning to the reporters clamoring for the scoop of the day. She couldn't tell if he was moving or if she was the one drifting closer when the cameras started flashing.

"Is your driver's murder part of another threat against your family?" one reporter asked.

"Oh, my God." It was definitely her who had taken that

step away from the limelight. "I don't want the Eames family to hear any of this today. It was a mistake to come."

"Miss Mayweather—hurry." Bud was waving her toward the limo's open door.

"This is crazy." Trip grumbled his frustration and released her to pick up Max and drop all twenty-five pounds of him into her arms. Instead of pushing her toward the car, he tucked her to his side and hustled her in the opposite direction, half lifting her so that her toes touched the bricks and asphalt only every third step or so. "I guess you two are stuck with me."

"Stop. Where are you taking me? Put me down."

"I'm obeying an order."

Too close. Too fast. She couldn't breathe. She needed to think. Charlotte squiggled her hips and pushed with her elbow. If she let Max go, maybe she could free herself. But if she let go, there'd be nothing between her and Trip Jones. "You're not listening to me."

"You can have Bud or those reporters or me."

Somewhere between the sensations of chilled toes and warm man, she'd missed seeing just how far he'd taken her. Her feet scraped the ground as he wedged her back against the side of a heavy-duty black pickup truck. Max was squirming, woofing under his breath at the flashes of light that warned the reporters were pursuing them, but Trip put an arm beneath hers to keep the dog in place as he pulled out a set of keys. The lock beeped and he had the door open before she pulled away from his helping hand and her fear found its voice. "I feel like I'm being kidnapped again."

"What?" He retreated half a step, his eyes narrowing, perhaps judging her sincerity, perhaps deeming her a lunatic. "If you want to be safe, get in. Hell, I'll give you the damn keys and you can drive if you'll just move."

"I don't have a license anymore. I can't drive. I'm afraid we're at a standoff." Instead of voicing the argument that rounded his lips, he put his hands on her waist and lifted her and Max into the truck. "Hey!"

After tossing aside a paperback novel that had been sitting on the seat, he reached across her and fastened the seat belt around her. "Now get down before those cameras or someone else gets a clean shot at you."

He gave her a split second to pull Max out of the way before he closed the door and jogged around the truck to climb in behind the wheel. Charlotte's fingers toyed with the handle then hesitantly reached down to pull the paperback from the floorboard. She ran her fingers over one of her favorite titles as she folded it shut. "You bent your book cover."

Trip reached across the center console and snatched the book from her hands, tossing it onto the folding seat behind him. "It's been a long time since anyone made me think I was some kind of stupid bully."

Feeling trapped but a fraction more secure in here than she did on the other side of the door, she huddled against it, slinking down behind Max while Trip started the engine. "I never said you were stupid."

"Nice distinction." Trip scrubbed his hand over his face, taking the rain and his frustration with it, before turning to look at her across the seat. His deep voice rumbled inside the cab of the truck. "You're my only concern, Charlotte. What I say to you will always be the truth. I've got your back. I won't hurt you. And I won't let you get hurt."

"You can't promise something like that." She pulled off her fogged-up glasses and squinted to keep him in focus. "I know I'm a bit of…" an odd duck? a crazy lady? "a para-noid freak—"

"You're not."

"—but I have reason to be. It's hard for me to trust anyone besides Dad…or Richard." Her eyes lost focus as the grief and injustice of the day took hold again.

Trip put the truck into gear, honked to clear the road and pulled out. "Honey, I don't need you to walk and talk like every other woman on the planet. I just need you to believe that I'm one of the good guys. Have a little faith."

Hearing a grown man call her *honey* diverted Charlotte's thoughts long enough to lose her grip on Max. The traitorous dog had no confusion whatsoever about Trip Jones. He walked right over to Trip's lap and sniffed his face.

With a muttered reprimand and a tussle around the ears, Trip pushed him away. "Your dog likes me. Why can't you?" He braked the truck before taking a hairpin turn toward the cemetery's main gate. "Now hold on."

As they picked up speed, Trip called his captain on his ear mike, giving something called a "twenty" and promising an ETA as soon as he confirmed a destination.

Like him? So she was a little fascinated with his taste in reading and the way he handled her dog and why on earth he'd call her *honey*. And she was more curious than she should be at the self-deprecation she'd heard in his "stupid bully" line.

But trust him?

Charlotte kept her eye on Trip's stiff expression, held tight to Max and prayed.

Chapter Six

The craziness they'd left behind at the cemetery was waiting for her at home, too.

A team of Gallagher Security guards was sorting out
the traffic jam at the front entrance to the Mayweather
estate, asking for IDs and punching in security codes to
allow expected guests through the gates, while filtering out
any paparazzi or curiosity seekers posing as mourners and
trying to sneak in. Jeffrey Beecher, wearing a clear plastic
raincoat over his suit and tie, carried a clipboard and his
cell phone. He greeted each vehicle, checked his guest list
and either signaled to the guards to let the people inside
pass, or got on the phone to verify whether someone should
be allowed to enter.

Charlotte was still hunkered down in the passenger seat
of Trip's truck, absently stroking Max's fur, barely peeping
through the bottom of the window. They were seven vehicles back, with more cars and limousines pulling into the
queue behind them. A television news crew had a camera
and antenna set up on top of its van across the street, and
another was filming a live feed with its reporter on the
street. Trip was on his phone, calling in a situation report,
telling his captain that she was fine but that he was going to
need backup on the scene if they had any hopes of securing
it. Not an encouraging thought.

There were whistles and bright lights, shouts and honking horns. The strident echo of sirens pierced the thick air, probably in answer to neighborhood complaints about the streets being blocked. The windshield wipers beat at a steady cadence and her heart thumped in the same quick rhythm. Her feet hurt. And every time she tried to inhale a calming breath, her nose filled with the pungent scent of wet dog fur and something even more unsettling that had taken her ten miles of riding in the truck to identify—the earthy scent of wet, warm, male skin.

"This is my own home," Charlotte murmured, wilting at the assault on her senses. "My sanctuary."

She needed quiet, alone and safe right now. But there was nothing outside the truck or inside her own head that could generate any sense of calm.

"Yeah, it's a real zoo here." Even as he continued to speak on the phone, Trip's right hand moved across the center console.

Was he reaching for her? Offering comfort? For one disjointed moment, Charlotte pulled her fingers from Max and let them drift across the seat toward the long, bruised fingers.

"You okay?" he mouthed the words and Charlotte looked into those unflinching eyes and almost nodded.

But just as she imagined she could feel the heat emanating from Trip's big hand, the screech of tires on the wet pavement drew her attention back outside. The crunch of metal on metal grated against her ears as she sat up in time to see one of the cars ahead of them plow into the rear bumper of another.

"Son of a gun." Trip sat up straighter, too, his taut posture instantly putting her on guard. "Gotta go, sir. Fender bender. Could be the tension of the day, could be a diversion. I'll keep you posted." The captain said something else and Trip glanced over at Charlotte. "Like glue. Jones out."

Trip's promise to Captain Cutler as he disconnected the call should have reassured her. But now people were out of their cars, inspecting the damage. One of the guards hurried over to assess the situation.

"You think the wreck was deliberate?" Charlotte asked, hating the possibilities.

Trip checked his rear- and side-view mirrors, his suspicions fueling Charlotte's own. "Half of Gallagher's men are leaving their posts, and there's no way a traffic cop could get in here fast. We're stuck."

"So what do we do?"

"Stay put." But Trip ignored his own edict and unfastened his seat belt. "Ah, hell."

Charlotte curled her fingers around Max's collar when Trip leaned forward. "What is it?"

"Are you sure that guy's working *for* you?"

She followed his gaze to see Jeffrey Beecher pointing to her in the truck and saying something to the guards. He might as well have shot up a flare because a pair of guards was now heading toward the truck. Even though Jeffrey's gestures indicated that he wanted to get Charlotte inside the gate as quickly as possible, car doors were opening, windows were going down and the line of cameras parked across the street swiveled their way.

"It's happening again," Charlotte despaired, feeling the unwanted attention crawling across her skin. "Why do they care so much about me being here?"

"They don't care about you. They want to sell papers."

"My father has friends at the *Kansas City Journal* and local TV stations. Ever since the kidnapping, they've agreed not to publish pictures and stories about me. Why would they risk their relationship with Dad to get a couple of pictures?"

"Steve Lassen's a tabloid photographer. He's independent, like a lot of these bozos. I'm guessing your daddy's influence hasn't reached the rags he works for yet." Trip scanned from side to side, and she could almost see him checking off one observation after another. A wary energy pulsed around him, filling the truck, stirring Max to his feet and adding an edgy blend of excitement and trepidation to Charlotte's fragile nerves. "You're a national story. After ten years of being a mystery woman, you made a public appearance at your chauffeur's funeral. Sounds like a headline to me. I'm guessing, in their minds, Daddy's influence only covers the privacy of your own home."

"That's not very comforting."

"If you want a guy to say it'll be all right when things are this crazy, I'm not your man." A muscle tensed along his jaw as he tempered the snap of his voice. "I'm more inclined to do something about the problem."

"I don't need any false platitudes."

"Fine." He shifted in his seat to pull his badge from his belt and loop it onto a chain around his neck. "You want to lie low in here until the guards can get us in? Or do you want me to clear a path now and take you straight to the house?"

"You can clear a path?"

He grinned, as if whatever permission she'd just given pleased him. "Like I said, I've got your back. Watch me work." He hopped out and faced her in the opening between the door and the frame. "Lock the doors and stay in the truck."

A spray of rain blew in, splashing her face like a wake-up call before he shut the door. He didn't budge until Charlotte scooted Max aside and scrambled across the seat to lock the door. Then, after laying a hand against the window he was gone, holding up his badge, identifying himself as KCPD and shouting orders that made the guards jump and people hurry back inside their cars. With each long stride that carried him into the fray, Charlotte felt more and more isolated—a pariah on display in the middle of all the chaos.

Steadfastly ignoring all the curious eyes turned her way, she wrapped her fingers around the steering wheel and held on, keeping Trip in sight. People straightened when he approached, jumped when he spoke. The gates swung open and he ushered the first two cars through to the driveway. Then he climbed onto the hood of one of the wrecked cars, rocking it up and down to unlock the bumpers.

Trip really was clearing a path to the house. One man versus a hundred, and he was winning. Her lips trembled with the unfamiliar urge to smile, but they settled into a straight line instead. What was it like to have that kind of confidence about the world? Would she ever be able to reclaim the adventurous spirit she'd had as a child? Before the kidnapping? Before the phobias and therapy and seclusion transformed her into this shadow of the woman she'd once hoped to be? Would she ever reclaim even half the strength that Joseph Jones, Jr., commanded?

As her thoughts took her to a darker place, Charlotte tightened her fingers on the wheel, willing the vibrations of the engine to flow through her and keep her anchored in the here and now. To trust Trip's word. To believe he could accomplish what he promised and get her safely home.

The dented cars separated and Trip, along with three other men, pushed both up onto the curb. He waved the fifth car in the queue into the narrow opening they'd created and pointed to the car just in front of her.

And then she caught the flicker of movement in the rearview mirror.

A man carrying a backpack darted from one car to the next, ducking down and hiding as he moved between them. Charlotte's knuckles popped out as she tightened her grip on the steering wheel and shifted her attention to the side-view mirror. There he was again, poking up behind another car. Oh, no. Even the rain couldn't mask the distinct points of his receding hairline or the camera slung around his neck.

"Steve Lassen." Charlotte breathed the vile paparazzo's name, hunching down and peering over the dashboard at the same time. True, he was staying across the street, but he was creeping closer and closer. "Hurry, Trip."

Then, boom. A loud smack hit the back of the truck and Charlotte sat bolt upright. Max propped his front paws on the back of the seat and barked at the bed of the truck. Had *she* been rear-ended, too? Charlotte checked the mirror. Nothing but the line of vehicles and endless rain behind her.

"Hush, Max. Hush, boy." She petted his flank and pulled him back down to the passenger seat.

A second mini-jolt hit and Charlotte spun around at the pinging sound. Was someone throwing rocks?

A bright flash from the trees across the sidewalk momentarily blinded her. That creep Lassen had maneuvered himself into position and finally had his picture of her—sitting behind the wheel of Trip's truck, wild-eyed, confused, afraid. Trip was running toward her, shouting something—drawing his gun and waving at her to get down.

A third projectile struck the glass beside her and Charlotte jumped. Max barked and barked and barked as she watched the window splinter into a fist-sized web of cracks right before her eyes.

"Shots fired!" She heard Trip's deep voice shouting in the distance. "Get down! Everyone, get down!"

Run. Fight. Move.

A surge of adrenaline, tamped down by caution and futility for too many years, screamed through Charlotte's veins, demanding she take action. She'd fought the night she'd been kidnapped, fought until too many blows and the mind-numbing drugs had taken away her ability to scream or struggle or even think.

"Charlotte!"

When she saw another, smaller flash near Steve Lassen's hiding place, Charlotte's instinct to survive grabbed hold of that adrenaline. *Gun!* She stepped on the brake and shifted the truck into Drive. The shot hit the window, shattering the glass as she stomped on the accelerator.

Trip slapped the side of the truck and jumped out of the path as it lurched forward. Max tumbled to the floorboards as Charlotte scraped past the car in front of her. "Sorry," and clipped the next one. "Sorry!"

"Charlotte, stop! Let me in!"

She heard Trip's curse, loud and clear, but couldn't seem to lift her foot off the accelerator or turn her focus from the haven of her home waiting at the end of that driveway.

Perched on the edge of the seat to reach the pedals, she held on tight as she bounced over the curb and spun for endless seconds, churning grass into mud. Finally, she remembered at least one thing from driver's ed in high school, hit the brake and twisted the wheel. With Trip charging up in her rearview mirror, she found the traction she needed and roared through the gate.

Her skills were rusty, but her speed was certain. Bypassing the parking attendants and cars and guests at the front of the house, she drove around to the service entrance in back and skidded to a stop.

"Sorry, Max. Sorry, sweetie." Dragging the excited dog from the floorboards, Charlotte climbed out of the truck and ran to the back door.

The world outside was too frightening for her, too dangerous. She needed to be home. She needed to be safe.

She punched in the lock's security code, swung the door open and ran straight through the mudroom and kitchen and carpeted foyer. Concerned shouts and worried glances fell on deaf ears and tunnel vision. Max loped beside her as she turned down the first-floor hallway to her private suite of rooms. Blinded by the panic attack, she had to pause for a moment to catch her breath and steady her fingers to type in the unlock code to her room.

M-A-X-I-M-U-S.

Click.

She was in. "Go, boy." She released Max's leash and forced herself to breathe.

No more bullets. No more strangers. No more spotlight.

Push the door shut. You're safe—

A black boot wedged itself in the opening, stopping the door with a jerk. A big, bruised hand snatched hold of the door and pushed it back open.

Charlotte was forced to retreat as Trip Jones filled her doorway and marched into her sitting room. "What the hell were you thinking?"

She spun around, snatching up the first object she came to—a small bronze shield from the museum. She held it up in front of her as her hips butted against the back of the sofa. "What are you doing here? I'll call security. This is my home. Get out."

"Uh-uh, honey. You stay right with me this time." He easily pried the shield from her hands and tossed it onto the cushions behind her. "I don't care what kind of crazy you are—you look me in the eye and talk to me."

"Hey, that's Etruscan."

"I don't care if it's the Mona Lisa." In the time it took her to glance down and ensure the security of the artifact she was responsible for, Trip had her pinned against the back of the couch, with one fist on the fabric at each side of her. His thighs were like tree trunks pressing into hers, his hair was dark with rain, his uniform splattered with mud, and his chest rose and fell in a quick, deep rhythm while he dripped on her. He was too big, too furious, too much man to be in here. "I just tracked mud all through that nice reception in the front rooms to get to you. Now, I said I had your back. I told you to stay put."

"It's not your job to protect me." She shoved at the big white letters on the front of his uniform, but neither the Kevlar nor the man moved.

If anything, he was coming closer, leaning in, forcing her to tilt her head back, way back. "It's my job to protect everyone in this city, especially when my captain gives me an order. Get you home safely." His hazel eyes searched her face, looking for an understanding that wasn't easy to give. And then they crinkled with concern. "Cripes, Charlotte—some unknown perp was shooting at you, and your response is to run from help?"

"I couldn't stay out there any longer. I had to get inside."

"I had to let that shooter go so I could run after you. You want me to cite you for driving without a license, inflicting property damage or scaring the crap out of me?"

He was scared? Huh? Her fingers drifted beneath the hard edges of his vest, needing something to hold on to to stop their trembling. She felt the abundant warmth and rapid beat of his heart beneath her fingertips and realized she wasn't the only one shaking here. "I'll pay for any damages. I'll buy you a whole new truck. Where's my backpack? I can write you a check from my trust fund right now."

"Missing the point." With cooler air rushing in between them, he turned away, raking his fingers through his short hair, leaving a mess of shiny wet spikes in their wake. When he faced her again, he propped his hands on his hips, assuming a posture that she guessed was supposed to make him look less threatening. He failed. "Normally I'm an easygoing man. But you are pushing my buttons right and left, lady. How was I supposed to know whether you'd been hit or not?"

With Trip standing between her and her bedroom door now, Charlotte had nowhere to go unless she made a mad dash to the bathroom. He deserved better than another door slamming in his face. Besides, after sharing that much forced contact with his thickly muscled body, she wasn't sure her legs would carry her that far.

She hugged her arms around her middle, mentally trying to hold her ground. "I couldn't think. I saw the man in the woods with the gun. I mean, I didn't see his face, but I saw the flash and then the window shattered. I had to do something."

She held her breath as he closed the distance between them again, then released it on a shaky sigh when he reached out with a single finger to unwind a lock of hair that had twirled around the temple of her glasses. The gentleness of the gesture, the husky softness of his tone, were completely at odds with the drenched warrior who'd been pushing *her* buttons a moment earlier. "*Are* you hurt?" He reached into his pocket and held up a tiny metal ball in his palm. "Thank God he was just shooting BBs."

"BBs?"

"I picked this one up off the street. I'll call in my team to sweep the area as soon as they're done at Mt. Washington—see if we can find any trace of the shooter." He looped the curl around his finger and rubbed it with his thumb. "He didn't get to you, did he? No cuts or bruises?"

Charlotte slowly shook her head, savoring his touch on her hair almost as if it was a caress against her skin. "If he wanted to kill me, why not use real bullets?"

"You tell me."

Her voice hushed to match his. "Someone wanted my attention."

"Someone wanted to scare you."

"He succeeded." But neither of them laughed at the joke. Instead, she leaned toward the warmth of his hand near her temple. But when his fingers tunneled a little deeper and brushed against her damaged earlobe, she jerked away. "Please don't."

"Sorry, I thought I was reading the okay signal."

"You were. I mean, what does that mean?"

His eyes narrowed a moment in confusion, but then he reached for that single tendril of hair again. "It means you're interested in seeing what up close and personal is like between us. But not too close."

She nodded. "Just don't touch my ear."

"Sensitive, hmm?"

More than he knew.

"Your hair's wild."

"It's out of control."

"It's so soft." He was inspecting the curl with an almost scientific fascination. "Yet it's strong enough to hold on to me."

Was this…banter? Why wasn't he moving away? Why wasn't she pushing him away? She thought all the rain

would leave her chilled, but with him so close, she felt…
feverish.

"I really am sorry about the truck. And your hat. And
the stitches in your arm." Wow. She was a freak. But he
still had her hair curled around his finger, stroking it. It
was a sensual, soothing gesture, an intimate one between
a man and a woman. They'd argued and now they were
making up. It felt so…

Normal.

Her whole body began to shake now. She so couldn't do
this.

"Trip," she wanted to confess, "I'm not like any other
woman you're likely to meet."

"I noticed." His hard face turned boyish with a sly half
grin. "You sure know how to keep a man on his toes."

"That's not what I'm trying to do." She reached up to
straighten her glasses and to tuck the curl, still warm from
his touch, behind her ear and beyond his reach. "I wasn't
always this way—with the phobias and panic attacks. But
I guess it's who I am now. I appreciate you doing the favor
for Audrey and Alex, and checking in on me. But we have
security here. It's probably better if you go now, before I
find some other way to ruin your—"

"Miss Mayweather?"

Charlotte clenched her toes into the carpet at the sharp
rap at the open door behind Trip. She hadn't locked up. She
hadn't barricaded herself in the way she needed to. And
now she had a man in her room. Two men.

"Ma'am. Just wanted to return this."

Bud held his cap in one hand as he rolled a toothpick
with his tongue from one side of his mouth to the other
and held out a cell phone. Her new cell phone. How had
she forgotten, for even one moment, that the outside world
wanted to hurt her? *"Did you get my message?"* A strange

man's laughter echoed in her memory and chilled her to the bone.

"That's not my phone," she lied.

"I found it in the back of the limo. Who else's would it be?"

"I don't want it. These are my private quarters. Please leave."

"You need to step back into the hall, my friend." Trip swept past her—in one stride, two.

Charlotte reached for his hand. He stopped.

She'd just dismissed him, just denied wanting to feel anything like a normal man-woman relationship with him. And now she was clinging to his hand.

For a split second, he seemed just as stunned by the impulsive contact as she was. But then, before she could tell herself to let go, he folded his strong fingers around hers and pulled her close behind him, shielding her from an unwanted visitor more effectively than the carved Etruscan bronze had.

Trip's deep voice took command of the room. "You've been dismissed," he paused to read the name on the gray uniform, "Bud."

"I'm just trying to do a nice thing here."

She buried her face between Trip's shoulder blades, clutching both hands around his. "He called me on that phone."

"Whoa, I didn't call anybody. I didn't use any of your minutes." Trip was pushing Bud out the door. "I'm just returning what I found."

"I don't want it. Take it away."

"You heard the lady. Wait." Trip pulled one of the black gloves off his belt. He understood the *he* Charlotte was talking about. "I'll take the phone. Now go."

As Trip wrapped up the cell and closed the door, she

could hear Bud whining all the way down the hall. "Thanks for going out of your way, Bud. Just trying to do my job, ma'am. Lousy thanks."

Trip turned before the voice faded. "When did you get another call from the killer?"

"How did he get that number? It was a brand-new phone."

He squeezed her fingers. "Charlotte, when?"

"At the cemetery. Just after I got that note. He was laughing at me, at…rattling me. That's why I panicked."

Trip swore. "That means he was close enough to watch you. He's getting off on your distress. Who has that kind of access to you?"

"No one does." With a jerky shrug, Charlotte pulled her fingers away from the warmth and strength of Trip's hand. Trying to hug away the chill that shook her from inside and out, she stepped around him and turned the doorknob. "At least, no one does when I'm locked in here. You'd better go, too."

Every muscle inside Charlotte reached out to the comforting, abundant heat of Trip's body when he walked up behind her. But her mind wouldn't give in and move the way her body wanted her to.

"There's safety in numbers, Charlotte—not isolation. Whatever's happening isn't going to stop just because you lock that door."

"What's happening is that someone's trying to drive me crazy. The phone calls, the notes, the loud noises—they're all things that happened to me when I was kidnapped. I know what they all mean now—the taunting and the terror. If this guy knows everything that happened—if that's what is waiting for me…"

"Why would someone want to do that to you?"

"I don't know." Her shoulders sagged. "But I can't go

through that again. I'm not strong like I used to be. I just can't do it. Security and predictability in my routine mean everything to me now. Trip?"

Damn, couldn't the man take a hint? Now he was wandering through her sitting room, peeking into her bedroom and bath. He looked at the artifacts set on nearly every table and desk, checked the books on her floor-to-ceiling shelves, studied pictures on the walls. Charlotte huddled at the door and watched him circle.

"You know, when I was growing up, a lot of people misjudged me because I was already about this big when I started high school. Plus, I wasn't…the best student on the planet. I didn't like it when people pointed it out to me." He stopped in front of her wall of books, stroking the spine of one leather volume and then pointing to one of her degrees she had hanging on the wall. "You must be pretty smart."

"You're not a stupid bully, Trip."

"I said that out loud, huh?" His self-deprecating smile tickled something deep inside her, waking a compassion she wouldn't have thought a man of Trip's skills and strength would need or want. His eyes sought hers, and dared to look beneath the surface, from clear across the room. "My point is, people can change. If we're not who we want to be, we have the power to do something about it. I have dyslexia. Don't get me wrong, I've outgrown some of it as I've matured, and retrained my brain on how to read things. But it takes me time, you know, to read books and take tests and fill out forms. I've got so much to catch up on that I'm never gonna know everything I want to."

Charlotte took a step into the room. "How is that like surviving a kidnapping and having every decision you make, every person you meet, colored by that nightmare?"

"I'm guessing you've never been called stupid."

Her heart ached for the young man he'd once been. She couldn't imagine absorbing such an insult, especially as an adolescent. But surely that was all behind him. He was a grown man now, exuding enough confidence to fill the room. "I imagine it's a struggle—something you should take pride in for overcoming. Clearly, you're an intelligent man or you wouldn't have the job you do. You wouldn't be able to break down doors with tables or rig up leashes from handcuffs."

"Thanks. But I didn't always see myself that way." Trip strolled back toward the door. "You want to change. You cared about your friend who died and wanted to be there to honor him. You love that mutt of yours to pieces. Your eyes—" he shook his head, as if in wonder "—say everything you think and feel." He waved his fingers in front of her face. "You're the one who took *my* hand."

He was standing right in front of her now. She answered to the letters emblazoned at the middle of his chest. "I was more afraid of Bud than I was of you. It doesn't mean I'm ready to be normal again, that I'm ready to make myself a target for some sadistic stalker who seems to know exactly what scares me the most. How am I supposed to fight when I don't know who or why I'm fighting?"

"All I'm saying is, you can change if you want to. You can be stronger. I'll protect you all the way until you get there if you say the word. But it won't be easy. I discovered I didn't have all my demons licked when I met you in that museum the other night."

Charlotte tilted her head to find a curiously indulgent smile waiting for her. "What does that mean?"

"In some ways, every time I run into you, it's like high school all over again. You make me feel like I have to prove something, and I haven't had to prove anything to anyone for a long time."

"You don't have to prove anything."

"Yeah, I do. You still don't trust me."

Well, he'd certainly kept his word about one thing. He didn't lie. So they both had things they wanted to change. *Good luck with that.* "If we were in high school, I'd be the four-eyed brainiac in college-prep classes and you'd be the resident bad boy in shop or auto mechanics. Our paths would never cross."

Her smile faded along with his. But then something warm and mischievous colored his eyes. Before she could speculate on the change, he slid his finger and thumb beneath her chin and tipped it up another notch. He caught her startled gasp beneath his lips and pressed his mouth against hers. The kiss was tender, warm, brief.

He paused for a moment, his breath whispering against her skin. Then he tunneled his fingers into the curls at her nape, dipped his head and kissed her again. More firmly this time—a little less gentle, a little more possessive. He caught her bottom lip between both of his and drew his tongue along the curve, triggering a moist arrow of heat that made her fingers latch on to his biceps and her insides go liquid. Her lips pouted out, chasing his, foolishly wanting more, when he pulled away. Trip grinned. "Then I'm glad we're not in high school."

She didn't deserve that grin, wasn't sure she could even remember the last time a man had kissed her—didn't think a grown man as sexy and strong as Trip ever had. Charlotte's brain was spinning with questions, and she felt a little too flustered to speak coherently at the moment.

Fortunately, Trip Jones had no trouble with words or kisses or flaky plain Janes with a quirk for every day of the week. He scooted her to one side and opened the door. "Lock this behind me. And remember, you haven't seen the last of me yet. I've got your back."

She pushed the door shut after he stepped into the hall-way, then scrambled the code on the keypad to lock it securely. She turned and leaned back against the door, drawing in a weary, thoughtful breath. Could she really conquer her phobias the way Trip had apparently conquered his reading disorder? Could she stand up to a killer who seemed to want to literally scare her to death? Could she ever be normal enough to act on this unexpected bond she was building with Trip?

I've got your back.

Charlotte knew that Trip believed that promise.

But could she?

THE MAN RAN HIS FINGERS around the tiny circular dent on the tailgate of the black pickup truck, relying on the steady fall of rain to wash away any prints he might leave behind.

The shot wasn't terribly accurate if the prankster had been aiming for Charlotte. The scattershot approach was definitely too messy for his tastes. The randomness of firing into a crowd left entirely too much to chance.

He flipped up his collar and walked around the truck that was still steaming from the heat of the engine and counted one, two, at least three or four shots, judging by the shattered glass sitting in a puddle on the driver's seat. He'd wager the press had gotten some interesting pictures for the evening news, although he doubted if Charlotte would ever see them or the headlines surrounding the day's events. Jackson Mayweather and all his money would see to that.

So what was the advantage to his unknown and un-wanted accomplice's attempt when his call and missive at the cemetery had already produced the desired results of tearing away at Charlotte Mayweather's fragile sense of security?

Straightening, he slowly turned 360 degrees, squinting into the rain as if the other man was still out there. Who the hell would shoot at her?

He had his plan carefully mapped out. One step at a time. Take away her safety net of familiar faces and staid routines. Make the phone calls, send the notes. Make her face everything she feared—loud noises, strangers, crowds, drugs, violence, isolation—everything that had been in the papers about her kidnapping. And then he'd add death to her story.

On his terms. In his own good time.

He buried his hands in his pockets and chuckled, the sound swallowed up by the storm. There *was* something extraordinarily delightful in watching Charlotte screaming like a crazy woman behind the wheel of a truck as she barreled through the gates of her own home.

Crazy was good. Crazy was justice.

But he wanted the satisfaction of showing Miss Brainiac that she was no better than him. Telling him no. Treating him like the hired help. Ignoring the gallantry she didn't deserve.

She was *his* to destroy.

No one else's.

Now to get out of the damn rain and get back to work.

Chapter Seven

Trip cradled the china cup that was far too delicate for his
fingers in his open palm, and settled for smelling the coffee
he'd been served this morning. A good ten years had passed
since he'd been summoned like a rookie being called on the
carpet for blowing an arrest. And his morning briefings had
never taken place at a swanky, old-money estate where this
dining room alone was as big as his entire apartment.

But Captain Cutler had okayed it—had encouraged Trip
to answer Jackson Mayweather's invitation to breakfast,
especially if the serial killer who'd targeted Alex Taylor's
fiancée last year was now back in the picture and had set
his sights on Charlotte. SWAT Team One had a personal
connection to this case. The captain had told Trip that
as long as there was a threat to someone the team cared
about, then the team itself was at risk. If he had an in to
keep tabs on the investigation, then use it. Let Alex hole up
with Audrey on twenty-four-hour protection detail while
Sergeant Delgado, Randy Murdock and Captain Cutler
held down the fort at KCPD headquarters. Trip was here
amongst the businessmen and lawyers and Fourth Precinct
detectives to represent the interests of the team.

Besides, the scenery here was more interesting than any
morning roll call meeting or team briefing. And he wasn't

talking about the suits and ties seated around one end of the long dining room table.

Trip leaned against the oak frame beside a bank of windows and peeked through the sheers into a tiny square of lawn surrounded by a tall fence covered in ivy. It had no gate he could see and was only accessible from an entrance in the back of the house itself. It was separate from the rest of the detailed landscaping on the grounds, nothing but grass and a small patio. And he guessed it served one purpose.

Max, an energetic, one-eared mix of shepherd and terrier, jumped into Charlotte's arms. The two went down on the slick wet grass and rolled, and she came up laughing.

For one surreal moment, he thought the rare glimpse of sunshine between storm fronts was playing tricks on his eyes. Charlotte Mayweather laughing, unguarded—her mouth open and her toffee-colored curls bouncing around her head—stirred something warm and appreciative in his blood. Made him think of that unexpected urge he'd had to kiss her yesterday—and the even stranger sense of territorial rightness that had flowed through his veins when she'd kissed him back.

Maybe some ancient magic had gotten inside him when she'd cut him with that old sword. Because there was something about all the crazy that was Charlotte Mayweather that kept getting under his skin.

Maybe it was the glimpses of the woman she was meant to be, like the one he saw now, surrounded by fresh air and her precious pooch, that intrigued him. She was wearing bright red rain boots and didn't seem to care a lick that she had mud and grass stains splashed on her bottom and the elbows of her red-and-gold-striped rugby shirt. Her jeans skimmed over her healthy curves nicely, and other than the funky earrings that glistened like gold Aztec sunbursts, she looked more like an outdoorsy kind of woman than a locked-up recluse—a woman better suited to running with Max in a dog park, traipsing through archaeological ruins or camping out in a tent with him, a campfire and one sleeping bag.

Time out, big guy. One sleeping bag? So when exactly did that idea pop into his head? The woman had forced him to get a tetanus shot, put his truck in the shop and wounded his pride. So why was his body humming with the idea of discovering what other hidden treasures Charlotte possessed?

He had to be honest with himself and admit that the team wasn't the only reason he'd agreed to come this morning. He still had something to prove to Charlotte, and he wasn't giving up on getting her to believe that he was one of the good guys until she stopped looking at him with those big gray eyes as though he was part of the nightmares that made her so afraid of the world beyond that fence.

Detective Montgomery set his cup in his saucer and expressed his frustration with Jackson Mayweather's version of cooperation. "I would have preferred to interview your daughter yesterday at the cemetery, or here after the shooting. Eighteen hours after the event, memories get sketchy, clues disappear and so do my suspects."

Jackson leaned back in his chair at the head of the table. "If you want to question Charlotte, you'll do it here, with my lawyer and me present, or not at all."

Trip tuned back in to the conversation, guessing for a moment that no one had bothered to tell Charlotte about this meeting of the minds that seemed fixated on using her to solve the Rich Girl Killer case. And then he decided that Charlotte was too observant a woman to miss the vehicles lined up in front of her home, and suspected she was out there throwing a tennis ball for Max and muddying up her clothes in an effort to hide from any possible contact with the men in this room.

Including him?

Now there was an irritating thought.

Jackson Mayweather's svelte blonde wife, Laura, signaled to the attendant waiting by the breakfast buffet to circle the table with the coffeepot again. "You keep talking about Charlotte. What are you doing about protecting my Bailey? She's a rich girl, too."

Jackson reached across the corner of the table and squeezed her hand. "Don't worry, darling, I've stepped up security here. I'm paying Quinn Gallagher's security company for a round-the-clock physical presence on the estate."

"That protects Charlotte—she's a homebody."

Trip shook off the attendant's offer to heat up his full cup of coffee. "She goes to work at the museum, doesn't she?"

"When it's closed." Laura Austin-Mayweather dismissed Trip's question as easily as she dismissed the servant. Her focus was on whatever her husband had to say. "What about when Bailey has a party to attend? Or is out on a date?"

Jackson patted her hand as he pulled away. "I'll assign one of the guards to follow her 24/7."

Trip crossed to the table and set his cup and saucer down. "Are you making the same arrangements for Charlotte?"

With a gesture to an empty chair, Jackson asked him to sit. "That's why I invited you to this meeting, son. You and I need to have a discussion."

"I'm listening." Trip rested one hand on the back of a chair and the other near his badge on his utility belt, opting to stand. He didn't fault Mrs. Mayweather for worrying about her daughter's safety, but he had a feeling the psychological and physical attacks on Charlotte were specifically *for* Charlotte, and that no one else in this family was in any real danger. He had a feeling Jackson Mayweather sensed that as well, but was humoring his wife.

But Spencer Montgomery wasn't in the mood to humor anybody. He reached inside the pocket of his suit coat. "My job isn't security. It's solving these murders. I would think getting a serial killer off the streets would make everyone feel safer. Now if you and your lawyer will allow me to resume my interview? Even secondhand observations might be helpful." He set a clear plastic evidence bag holding the cell phone Trip had taken off Bud Preston on the table. "Can anyone here tell me how this phone got into Miss Mayweather's hands? From what I understand, *she* doesn't go shopping for such things."

Trip scanned the men and woman at the table right along with Detective Montgomery. Mrs. Mayweather looked to her husband, who looked to his stepson, Kyle, whose gaze fixed on the man with the glasses sitting across the table from him.

Jackson seemed displeased with the silence. "As soon as Charlotte told me she wanted to attend Richard's funeral service, I realized she'd need a new phone to keep in contact with me."

The brown-haired man with the wire-framed glasses dabbed his napkin against his lips and cleared his throat. Jeffrey Beecher was here representing the event staff that had worked on the estate and at the cemetery. "You hired our company to make sure everything ran smoothly yesterday. Maintaining communication between your family and our staff at Mt. Washington and here was key to a successful day. So I took the liberty of providing phones for each family member."

Detective Montgomery made the notation in his notebook. "Who had access to the numbers besides you?"

"The clerk at the phone company. Anyone with access to their database."

"I'm talking about anyone here at the house—before the funeral."

Jeffrey returned Kyle's pointed glare, apparently willing to share information, but not to take blame. "Mr. Austin told me to get five phones that he could hand out before everyone left for the cemetery. I set them on the credenza in the foyer, like you asked."

Jackson tossed his napkin on the table and faced his stepson. "Kyle, I asked you to get that new number for Charlotte—to help your sister. She trusts the family."

"I had things to do yesterday, Jackson. Meetings. The hired help was right there, willing to do whatever we needed. I delegated."

Trip cared less about the family dynamics and more about the obvious lapse in security. "So the phones were sitting there all morning. Anyone in this house could have gotten the number and called her with the threat—family, regular staff, event staff, guests."

Jackson drummed his fist on the table. "You will not accuse my family of any wrongdoing. We're the victims here."

No, Charlotte and Richard Eames were the only victims in this house. "Sir, with all due respect, you asked me here this morning to report everything that happened while I was with your daughter. You wanted someone from the outside with no connection to your family to share his observations. You must have some suspicions."

"I asked you here because you're a SWAT cop, as finely trained as any elite military officer."

Kyle snickered into his coffee cup. "He called you because you're the only man with a gun and a badge that she's let close enough to do her any good these past ten years."

"Kyle," Laura chided her son.

He swallowed the last drop and set down his cup. "The last man she trusted enough to protect her outside this house was murdered. I can see why he'd rather have this Robocop than an old man around to look after her."

Trip's hand fisted around the top rung of the chair. Thank goodness Charlotte wasn't here to hear that cold bit of compassion. "Well, then—speaking as a representative of Charlotte's best interests—her stalker is someone who's been in this house, right under your nose. Now I don't know if it's the same guy as the Rich Girl Killer, but I do know she's not safe here. It's an illusion you can't keep letting her live with."

"My daughter is very fragile."

"Thank you." Kyle threw up his hands as if he'd just scored a point. "I've been trying to tell you that Char's eccentricities border on mental instability."

"You're not helping, Kyle."

"I'm the one watching your money, Jackson. She's the one who's giving it away like candy."

"Her charities give her a connection to the outside world. Writing a check isn't the same as being strong enough to face that world."

The woman Trip had seen wrestling with the dog, the woman who'd come at him with a sword and a rebel yell, wasn't fragile. And the woman he'd kissed certainly wasn't mentally unstable. "Give your daughter some credit, Mayweather. It's not the way I would have done it, but she was resourceful enough to save herself yesterday, and that night your chauffeur was killed."

Spencer Montgomery smoothed his tie and stood. "The Rich Girl Killer doesn't shoot his victims in the middle of traffic jams."

"Somebody was shooting yesterday." Trip reminded

him, "He worked with gang members last year when he was going after Audrey Kline. Maybe he has another ally this time."

"The RGK is hands-on." The detective continued to quote his by-the-book profile of the man he was hunting. "His failure with Miss Kline is fueling his pursuit of Charlotte. He likes to terrorize, torture and strangle. He's methodical and precise—very much an in-your-face kind of killer. I believe he suffers from an obsessive-compulsive disorder and perceives that these wealthy young women have wronged him somehow. He's exacting punishment. He's coming. He can't help himself."

Laura Austin-Mayweather's shocked gasp pretty much summed up the growing tension in the room. These people were talking about ongoing cases and estate security, placing blame and deflecting accusations. He was talking about one woman. "He's already here. If you're so smart, Montgomery, tell me—how do you plan to identify your killer and catch him before he succeeds in his quest?"

The detective's light-colored eyes barely blinked. He'd be a tough one to go up against in a poker game. "We were misled by the gang involvement when he went after Miss Kline. But we know how he works now. We set up twenty-four-hour surveillance on Miss Mayweather, tap her phones and the security cameras here. Any time he calls we need to keep him talking as long as possible to help us pinpoint a location, or get some clue to his identity. The next time he delivers a message or tries to approach her, in any disguise, we'll be ready."

"That's your plan? First, she's too fragile, and now you're using Charlotte as bait?"

"I hope that we can assemble evidence from enough of these stalking incidents to piece together their source—

where he's getting his inside information on these women. We find the common link and we can zero in on him."

Trip scrubbed his hand over his jaw, not believing what he was hearing. "So you're hoping this bastard terrorizes Charlotte long enough before killing her so that you can find your answers?"

"It's a difficult choice, but I'll be saving lives in the long run."

"You're not saving hers." Trip turned to Jackson. "And you support this idiotic idea?"

"If we don't find a way to catch him, my daughter will die—if not by his hand, then by driving her mad. I nearly lost her once—when she came back from those kidnappers, she was broken. I won't let that happen again."

Just a few long strides took Trip around the table and put him in Montgomery's face. "How do you protect Charlotte when your unsub is living or working or regularly visiting in the same house where she lives? She has a fear of strangers. But how does she identify the enemy when all of your suspects are people she knows? How do *you*? She'll be dead in her locked-up room before you figure it out."

The huffing noise of a panting dog made Trip's heart sink.

He spotted the red glasses and muddy jeans as soon as Charlotte appeared in the archway to the dining room. Max sat beside her, his leash held in a white-knuckled grip. She'd heard every word out of his big, stupid mouth. "Interesting plan. Maybe someone should ask me first."

"AND YOU WONDER WHY I have trust issues. Now I can't even mourn in peace."

Trip stood at the bathroom door watching Charlotte, leaning over the edge of the tub, rinsing the last of the mud and suds from Max's fur. Her bottom bobbed up and down as she moved, and he rolled his eyes away so he could concentrate on the discussion and not the distraction of all those curves emphasized by her clingy wet clothes. The woman really did have a seriously sweet figure, and a surprisingly sharp tongue for someone the rest of the world considered an introvert.

"I can't believe it, all of you eating breakfast, plotting ways to intensify my nightmare or even get me killed."

"I was the one defending you in there."

She shut off the water and warned Max to stay put. "Because I'm too incompetent to defend myself?"

"Because you weren't there." Trip picked up one of the towels stacked on the toilet lid and handed it to her. She wrapped the towel around Max and rocked back on her heels as the dog climbed out of the tub. "Personally, I think Montgomery's plan sucks. There has to be more investigating he can do, more suspects he can bring in, more clues he can uncover before resorting to surveilling you and hoping something new breaks on the case."

Max licked her face while she toweled him dry—the perfect excuse for not making eye contact with him, the perfect barrier for keeping Trip at a distance. "Detective Montgomery told me he's been investigating the RGK murders for two years now. I suppose he's getting desperate. He must be if he thinks I can help him."

"You don't have to do this, Charlotte. Your father thinks catching the killer is the only way to save your life. But I don't think he fully realizes the risk he's taking."

"And you do?"

"You do, too." She was the only person in this house who'd been the victim of a violent crime. She knew better than any one of her well-meaning family the emotional and potentially deadly price they were asking of her. "Tell them no."

Charlotte's cheeks paled at the grim reminder. But her only response was to let the dog loose. The dog took two steps and shook himself from nose to tail, spraying water all over the bathroom—and Trip's uniform. Point made. Discussion over. Shut up, already.

Or not. After letting out the stopper in the tub, Charlotte picked up a second towel and crawled around the bathroom, wiping splatters of water off the cabinets, walls and fixtures. "You said I could change things. That I didn't have to be afraid the rest of my life."

"I didn't mean this." Trip stepped aside to let the dog trot into the sitting room to find a warm spot on the rug to take a nap.

"How then?" Charlotte shifted her attention to the floor, mopping up the trail Max had made across the tiles. "One thing I agree with Detective Montgomery on is that this sicko will come after me again. He'll leave a note or make a call—I haven't revisited everything that happened during my kidnapping yet, and he's enjoying the game too much. It's like he was there. But those men are all in prison. How can he know so much about those weeks I was a hostage? Why is he doing this to me?"

"Charlotte." Trip knelt down and pulled the towel from her hand.

She snatched the towel right back and kept working. "If I'm the one he'll make contact with, then maybe I should help capture him. That's being strong, isn't it? I'd be taking control of my life, instead of the life outside these doors controlling me. Right?"

"It's a crapshoot. I wasn't talking about risking your life yesterday."

Her hands stilled for a moment and she looked straight at him. "But catching him would make him stop, right?"

Oh, God. Those had better not be tears glinting in her

eyes. Now Trip was the one rocking back on his heels as her pain, her bravery, her desperation twisted something deep inside him. But this was a woman he couldn't lie to. "I think the threats will only escalate until we arrest him or—"

"—he kills me."

"I don't like that option."

Trip's husky whisper held her attention for one hushed, intimate moment in time.

And then she reached beneath her glasses to wipe the moisture from her eyes and resumed her work on the floor. "That's why Dad is paying you to be my bodyguard, isn't it?"

"I work for KCPD, not your father."

After a brief hesitation, she ran the towel over the toes of his boots, drying the water droplets off them as well. "So I'm just a plain ol' citizen of K.C. that you've sworn to protect and serve. Just like anyone else."

He finally realized that all her cleaning was busywork, avoidance of him. And he very much wanted her attention. He needed to touch her and have her be okay with it. He took the towel away and tossed it on top of the hamper. Then, with a hand beneath each elbow, he rose, pulling her to her feet in front of him. "Honey, there's nothing plain or old or like anyone else about you. I'm here because you're in danger. I wouldn't be doing my job if I let you get hurt."

"There are plenty of guards around here. Dad hires the best."

Her hands hovered in the space between them before finally, cautiously, coming to rest at the placket of his black uniform shirt. He liked that, feeling the gentle heat of her fingers seeping through the crisp material to warm his skin.

He dared to pull her closer, to turn her cheek into the pillow of his chest and wrap his arms around her. He rested his chin at the crown of her wild silky curls and savored the small victory of feeling her lean against him. The smells of wet dog and shampoo didn't matter. Damp clothes soaking into his didn't matter. Holding Charlotte mattered. Feeling her softness—under his chin, against his body, in his arms—mattered.

Trip felt stronger, yet oddly more vulnerable when Charlotte snuggled against him like this. Purely masculine instincts were stirring behind his zipper at the decadent sensations of heavy breasts and generous hips fitting up against his harder frame. Yet something scarier and completely unexpected was waking deeper inside him at the fragile trust she was showing by simply letting him hold her.

At least, he hoped it was trust. He prayed it was the beginnings of trust—and not some fear of what he might do if she resisted that allowed him to hold and inhale and feel and touch. That notion alone kept him from tightening his arms around her the way every sensitized cell in his skin yearned to. The idea that Charlotte wasn't completely sure that his attraction to her was genuine kept his hands securely in the middle of her back instead of sliding up to test the weight of a luscious breast or dipping down to that sweet bottom to pull her more firmly into his masculine heat.

Instead, he rubbed his cheek against the caress of her hair and whispered into her ear. "You need someone from the outside looking after you. Because the threat is right here, in this house. We just can't see it. I want to look after you."

He didn't mind when she curled her fingers more tightly into his shirt, pinching a bit of skin underneath. She was holding on, moving closer. "Don't take away the one place I feel secure, Trip. I need my things, my work, my routine."

"That doesn't have to change. I won't ask you to go to a safe house." It would be a hell of a lot safer and easier to defend than leaving her to serve as the bait in her gilded mousetrap. But he hadn't had any luck convincing Detective Montgomery or Jackson Mayweather. He doubted he'd have any more success making Charlotte see reason. So that left plan B. "But I will ask you to let me be a part of that routine."

"You've already barged your way in to my rooms and my life. It's not like I can stop you."

He reluctantly leaned back, leaving his hands at the curve of her waist. She tipped her head up, tilting her gaze at him over the top of her glasses. Her eyes were storm-cloud gray, turbulent with questions and wary suspicion.

Yeah, *that* was the look he needed to get off his conscience and out of his head.

"Oh yes, you can." A little frown appeared between her golden brows, telling him that his response confused her. But he wasn't going to explain what he barely understood himself. Trip pushed her glasses up onto the bridge of her nose, masking her eyes before releasing her. "I'm asking you to let me stay. Let me be a part of your life until we get this guy. I promise I'll keep you safe. Or I'll die trying."

She crossed her arms and drifted back a step. "I thought the whole idea behind a SWAT cop was to keep people from dying."

He didn't laugh. "Let me stay. Trust me, Charlotte. Please."

"Why does it have to be your personal mission to protect me if Dad isn't paying you?"

Guilty conscience? A very real fear that no one else fully

perceived the danger she was in? Those big gray eyes that haunted his waking thoughts and dreams? "Let's just say, you'd be doing me a favor."

"I don't understand."

"I'm not sure I do, either. But I don't think I could stand it if you got hurt and I could have done something to stop it."

"I said you didn't have to prove anything—"

Screw patience. Trip caught her face between his hands and pulled her up onto her toes, covering her mouth with his—silencing the excuses she used to push him away, silencing the frustrated need simmering inside him, silencing his own fears that he was growing way too attached to a woman he was completely wrong for.

He pressed his thumb to the swell of her bottom lip, coaxing her to part her lips for him, taking advantage of her warmth and sweetness when she did. Charlotte's fingers crept up around his wrists, holding on as he plunged his tongue inside her mouth to introduce himself to hers. She answered back, her tongue chasing his as he learned each taste and curve. A husky moan, deep in her throat, quickened his pulse as surely as the graze of her curious lips across the jut of his chin. His blood hammered in his veins and pooled in all sorts of achy places when her fingers moved up higher, settling against his jaw and guiding his mouth back to hers as she sampled one lip, then two, then pushed them apart to touch her tongue to the softer skin inside.

Trip wound his arms around her, temptation taking his fingers down to the delicious curve of her bottom and lifting her into the full tutelage of his kiss. She opened for him, welcomed him, taught him a thing or two about the benefits of curiosity and enthusiasm when it came to assuaging and fueling needs like this. He slid a supporting arm around her waist and dropped one hand lower, cupping a buttock that perfectly fit the size of his hand.

It was only when he felt two pert nipples brushing against his chest and the need to take her down to the floor right here in the john surged through him that Trip remembered that business and safety had to come before pleasure. Scaring her off with his baser needs was one risk he could avoid, so with a reluctantly determined gasp for saner air, he summoned the strength to pull her fingers from his neck and lift his mouth from her full, pinkened lips. "Whoa. Whoa, honey. We need to slow down."

Her eyes were dark and hooded and sexy with an innocent desire as she peeked over the top of her glasses at him. He pushed her glasses back into place, making sure to keep his eyes glued to hers and not to the tempting rise and fall of breasts as she crossed her arms beneath them and retreated. "Why do you keep doing that?"

Trip's next several breaths came as deeply and erratically as hers. "Seriously? I didn't think our second makeout session in your father's home with everything else going on around us was the best time or place to go all the way."

"All the way?" Her cheeks blanched a shocked shade of pale. "I meant, why do you keep kissing *me?*"

Ah, hell. Another encounter with Charlotte Mayweather had just taken a sharp turn into crazy land, and suddenly he was the bad guy again. "I don't know. Why do you kiss me back?"

"Because you're an overwhelming presence and apparently it's hard to get rid of you when you put your mind to something."

He scrubbed his hand over his mouth and jaw, and squared off against what sounded a lot like an accusation. "Like wanting to kiss you? Like feeling something and acting on it? I'm a healthy male and a human being, and you are gettin' into my head in ways that make me want to…" *Pull out my hair? Protect you? Bed you?* Maybe he was the one riding on the crazy train. "What do you want me to say? How do I get you to believe in me?"

"Trip, you can probably guess that I don't have a lot of experience with men. The truth is, I have no experience. At all. I don't know how to kiss."

"Then you're a natural talent."

That made her blush.

"I've never had sex. I don't know how to make a relationship work. I don't know if I even can." She shook her head, scattering toffee curls around her face as she retreated another step. "I'm not used to feeling or kissing or needing or whatever it is you want from me."

Frustration gave way to something infinitely more tender, and Trip found his patience again. "I want all those things from you. But only if you're willing to give them."

"I am feeling something for you, Trip. But do you have any idea how much that scares me?" She tucked a curl behind her ear, but it sprang back out to fall on her cheek. "I need to feel safe. In all things."

"I said I've got your back." He caught the independent curl with the tip of his finger and smoothed it back into place, then leaned down to press a kiss to her temple. "In this, too. Just give me a chance to show you I'm not the bad guy here. If I say or do anything you don't like, you tell me."

His body could scream away in protest if denying any physical or emotional need for this woman is what it took to see trust shining in her eyes.

Maybe it was time to go back to proving that. He pulled his hand away and turned into the sitting room. "You don't have to worry about any *us* right now. Finish drying the dog and get his collar and leash. You said you wanted to go to the cemetery? Let me call the rest of my team. We'll get you away from this house for a little while.

"You're under KCPD's watch now."

Chapter Eight

Charlotte knelt down to lay the bouquet of roses on the turned-up mound of earth beside the flowers that had once been draped over Richard's coffin. Max came over to sniff her handiwork and she scratched his head before shooing him on his way to follow the path of some squirrel or rabbit that'd come through earlier. She kissed her fingers and touched them to the plastic marker that held Richard's name and dates until a permanent stone monument could be fixed into place, knowing it was as close to trading a hug with him as she could ever get again.

"Thank you, my friend. For everything. I'm sorry. So sorry." Tears burned in her sinuses and squeezed out through the rapid blink of her lashes to warm her cheeks in the cooling air.

In the middle of the spring afternoon it felt like twilight. A storm was brewing overhead again, filling the sky with fast-moving clouds. Tall oaks and pine trees dotted each side of the road that twisted up through the hills of Mt. Washington Cemetery, their thick trunks and budding branches casting long shadows over her. But no shadow seemed as tall and foreboding as the sturdy bulk of Trip Jones standing beside her, with a handgun strapped to his thigh, a military-looking rifle draped in the crook of his elbow and a stone-cold expression of wary alertness stamped onto his rugged features.

"You okay?" Trip's voice rumbled down on the breeze that was picking up.

Charlotte huddled inside her trench coat and the body armor Trip had insisted she wear, and slowly stood. "He should have been retired, enjoying his grandchildren. He shouldn't have died because some freak wanted to get to me."

She saw Trip's black-gloved hand leave his rifle and reach for her. But just before he touched the small of her back, he curled his fingers into his palm and tapped at the headset hooked to his ear instead. "How are we doing?"

A chorus of "clears" and one "nothing here" answered loudly enough for Charlotte to hear.

Captain Cutler buzzed in as well. "Easy, people. Keep your eyes open. We're not in any rush here."

But Trip apparently was. He moved a couple of steps along the trail Max had taken, then circled around to stand beside her again. His hazel eyes stopping scanning their surroundings long enough to land on her. "Are you ready to head back?"

With his truck in the shop, Trip had driven her to Mt. Washington in one of the team's SUVs, which was parked at the foot of the hill, while the others had followed behind them in an imposing armored SWAT van. It was parked around a bend, out of sight beyond a copse of trees, just like the other members of his team remained hidden in the trees and monuments around them.

"I think I've decided how I'm going to honor him." Charlotte murmured the announcement to the flowers and the sign and anyone who might listen. "I'm going to set up a college fund for all his grandchildren. I'll call the bank and our attorneys when I get home."

"Sounds like a good plan to me." He glanced toward the sky. "The storm's about to break. I can feel the dampness in the breeze. We should get home so you can make those calls."

But she wasn't ready to disturb this solemn, secure moment. "Could we stay for a while? Richard was always so patient with me—I don't want to rush my time here. I don't mind a little rain."

"A little?" That stern mouth eased into a grin. Trip's easy capitulation to her request reminded her more of the man who'd kissed her and less of the warrior standing guard. "We've had so much this spring, creeks are flooding, roads are closing—they're sandbagging the levees up by the river."

Charlotte discovered she could smile, too, with the subtle glimpse of Trip's humor. "Washing away is the least of my worries. I used to love playing out in the rain. I think when I was little, I thought I was combining bath time and playtime, meaning I could stay outside longer."

"Why do I get the feeling you were a real handful growing up?"

"Me? An odd duck is more like it. I just spent a lot of time in my head. I was always curious, always reading, always thinking. I suppose I did give my dad a few headaches when I wandered off on one of my adventures and lost track of the time. I didn't become any trouble until after high school."

She shivered and slid her fingers up to her rebuilt ear to finger the gold earring there, her thoughts automatically including prom night and the disastrous events that had changed her life.

This time, his black glove settled at the small of her back. "Chilly?"

"I'm okay." At first she stiffened at his touch, unsure of

its motive. Comfort? Protection? Keeping her focused on the conversation? Years of shielding herself from anyone outside her family made it difficult to resolve this growing fascination with Trip's passion and strength and almost poignant patience with her. He liked to touch and she... liked him touching her. But despite the fretful anticipation his sheer masculinity and straightforward desire seemed to have awakened in her, it took a huge leap of faith to admit she was developing feelings for this man she'd known for a week. Her body's instincts to seek warmth and shelter let her relax and turn her cheek into his chest.

But her mind, her emotions, insisted on holding something back. In some ways, she knew as little about men as she knew a lot about archaeology. Boys hadn't looked at her as dating material in school, and she hadn't looked at men in that way since. There was a security in being able to shut off her feelings, knowing that was one aspect of her life she could control—no one could mock or hurt her, no one could trick or abuse her. Yet there was a loneliness in that particular skill, too, and she was just beginning to wonder whether it left her in a more perfect prison than all her phobias put together did.

Trip's fingers tightening at the nip of her waist encouraged her to stay in the moment and continue. "I loved to read mysteries, solve puzzles. But I was just as interested in climbing trees and exploring whatever new places I could get myself into—a friend's attic, the museum's back rooms."

"So you've always been the explorer."

"It wasn't like I had any dates to keep me busy. I had my friends, my homework, my adventures...I guess I always did march to the beat of my own drum."

"High school's a tough place to be different, isn't it?"

Charlotte nodded against the rough weave of his vest

cover. She had an idea he was referring to his own experience about being labeled for his brawn and learning disability, rather than commiserating over her odd habits and plain looks. But he understood. Maybe more than most people, he understood why she'd made the choices she had. "That's why I was so excited about going to prom. It was my first date that Dad and some social event of his had nothing to do with. Landon Turner. He was a new guy in school my senior year—he had that whole swarthy Italian look going on."

"I hate him already."

She felt the first sprinkle of rain on her cheek, and while the initial drop startled her, she soon savored the cool trickles of moisture on her skin. "He had a soccer scholarship to play on the team with my friend, Harper. I'd been pining after Harper for years, but he never saw beyond the glasses. A buddy of mine, Donny Kemp—he was on the quiz bowl team with me—had asked me first, out of the blue—I didn't really know him, didn't know he even liked me—so I said I needed time to think about it. I guess I was still holding out for a miracle invitation from Harper."

"Sheesh, the soap opera of high-school relationships. I don't miss that."

She tiptoed her fingers up his vest until she found the warmth of skin above Trip's collar to cling to. "I'd been tutoring Landon, to help him keep his grades up so he could stay at Sterling instead of going back to a public high school. When he asked me, I thought it was as close to dating Harper as I was going to get so I said yes. And then I found out he'd done it as an initiation rite. One of the kidnappers had given him a hundred dollars to get me to the school, away from Dad and his security."

"What the hell kind of initiation involves getting you kidnapped?"

Charlotte flinched at the sudden sharpness in Trip's voice and he immediately released her.

"Sorry." He skimmed his hand over his face, but she didn't think he was snarling at the rain wetting his skin. "No wonder you don't trust men."

He turned away, muttering a curse, then startled her when he swung back around to face her. "Did Turner pay for his part in the kidnapping? Does he have any reason to come after you again?"

"He didn't come after me." Her guardian had returned in full force. How did a man turn his compassion and gentleness on and off so quickly? She hugged her arms around her waist, afraid of her own warring needs to run away or offer a reassuring touch. "Landon's prank was a cruel one, but he didn't know about the kidnapping. He testified on my behalf at the trial by identifying the man who'd paid him, and helped get the conviction. He was kicked out of Sterling Academy, and I think lost a couple of college scholarships. But the judge didn't file any criminal charges. He has no reason to want to hurt me now."

"Don't defend him." Charlotte backed away as Trip advanced, his suspicions overriding his patience with her. "If he didn't know about the kidnapping, then how did the kidnappers know about the initiation?"

"All the guys at school knew about the initiation dare. If I'd been more of a social creature, I would have heard the gossip, too. One of them must have let it slip somewhere, and the kidnappers paid Landon to make sure it was me he took that night." Talented though he was with his feet, Landon had never been the brightest bulb at Sterling. "He apologized, over and over. He used to call me..."

Every day. For months.

Charlotte. You have to forgive me. Charlotte? Answer me!

Oh, my God. Had she missed a connection between

Landon and her kidnappers? A connection between then and now?

Charlotte's heart rate kicked up a notch. Her breathing went shallow. She was going back in time. Slipping into the past. Remembering. "I want to go home."

"Honey, are you—?"

"Don't 'honey' me!" She whirled around, looking for Max. "Stay in the moment. Stay in the moment," she chanted. "Max?"

"Jones." Captain Cutler's voice buzzed into the radio, loud enough for Charlotte to hear the summons. "Is there a problem up there?"

"Charlotte?"

She put her fingers to her mouth and whistled. "Max!"

"She's on the verge of a panic attack, sir. Call everyone in. We're coming down."

Charlotte yelped at the big hand that closed around her arm.

But it wouldn't let go. "Look at me, Charlotte." He had her by both arms now, had hunkered down so she could see his face. "Look at me."

It was Trip. She knew it was Trip. But she was afraid. Afraid of the calls and the memories and the mistakes she couldn't save herself from. She blinked her eyes into focus. "I need to go home. I want to go home."

"Okay." His grip shifted to one arm and he gentled his tone as he towered over her. "I'm sorry I upset you. Stay in the moment, okay? Stay with me."

"I'm sorry, Trip. I must have pushed myself to be outside a little too long." She felt twenty-five pounds of furry warmth wedge its way in between them and sit on her foot. Max. Thank goodness. She reached down to stroke his fur, taking the edge off her panic. "Good boy, Max."

"You have no idea what a fighter you are, do you?"

"What do you mean?"

"You could summon the troops with that whistle." Trip pulled the dog's leash from her coat pocket and hooked him up. He rubbed Max around his neck and ears before pushing the leash into Charlotte's hand and straightening. "I'm the one who pushed you too hard. I thought Turner might be some kind of break on the case."

"You were just doing your job."

"I was being a jealous idiot and I scared you instead of helping." He held out his hand for her to take. "Let's get you home so you can make those phone calls about Richard's memorial, okay?"

She nodded, wrapping both hands around the leash, unsure what to make of his compliment or apology or the whole idea of a man being jealous over her.

Trip's gaze dropped to her fingers, understanding the unspoken message and accepting it. "And as far as Turner goes?"

"What about him?"

"Innocent or not, he'd better never show his face around me." Backed up by an ominous rumble of thunder overhead, his vow triggered a riot of inexplicable goose bumps across her skin. If they'd been sparked by her usual anxiety or the possessive promise in his words that tickled something new and uniquely feminine inside her, she couldn't yet tell. "Come on. Let's get out of the rain."

Although she hadn't taken his hand, he still put his fingers at her back to position her in front of him and lead the way down the hill with Max. He released her to tap on his radio. "We're heading back to the car. Bring it in, guys."

"That's a negative. Stand fast, big guy." Captain Cutler's crisp voice buzzed over the radio. Charlotte spotted the reason for the warning appearing from behind a mask of trees and doubling back on one of the cemetery's hairpin turns. Her eyes widened. Her steps slowed. "We've got an unmarked vehicle approaching on your six. White van, local plates."

"I see it." Trip's hand clamped down on her shoulder, stopping her beside a red marble headstone. "Let it pass."

Charlotte grabbed hold of the red marble, swaying as the van crept up behind the black SUV.

Her brain spun around inside her skull as Charlotte pushed herself up from the pavement. Where were her glasses? What was happening to her? Was she bleeding?

"Sir, it's slowing down." A woman's voice broke through the static in Charlotte's ears. "All I can see is the driver. One male. Sir, he's puttin' on the brakes."

But Charlotte was slipping back in time.

The screech of tires echoed through her aching head. What was going on? She squinted the blur of white into focus. A van. A white van. She tried to push up to her knees, but her head was so heavy. A yawning black hole opened in the side of the van. "Get up!"

Clarity kicked in a moment too late. There were hands on her, rough hands pinching and grabbing and countering every kick and twist she made. "No! Let go! Don't take me!"

"Shut up, Charlotte!" She flew through the air and landed in a heap on the dirty, rusty floor. She screamed as a hood came over her head and the van door slammed shut.

They were speeding away as a needle pricked her arm.

"Charlotte!"

Someone had pushed her down to her knees and shoved something warm and furry against her.

"Charlotte, you're all right—stay in the moment."

She fought inside her head to ground herself, to find her way back to reality. Her pants were wet. Something cold and wet was soaking into her jeans. Max. Max had his front paws on her shoulder and was licking her face. Her hands crept around his neck, hugging him tight. "Good boy. Good boy, Max."

"Stay in the moment," the deep voice beside her commanded. She took a deep, calming breath.

And then she saw the white van. "No."

It stopped at the bottom of the hill. They were coming.

"I won't go. Don't take me!"

He turned her bruised face into the stale bedding. "I'm tired of waiting for my millions. It's time to show Daddy just how serious we are."

And then she felt the cold scissors squeeze her earlobe. "No!"

"Charlotte!" the voice snapped. "Honey, I don't want to touch you right now. Listen to my voice. Stay in the moment."

"Trip?" She pulled one hand from Max's fur and reached out.

The driver's door opened and a man climbed out of the van. "Charlotte Mayweather?"

He looked right at her. He was coming for her. She backed away.

"I have something for you." He held up a small package wrapped in plastic.

Charlotte answered with a scream.

Chapter Nine

Ignoring the barking dog jumping at his legs, Trip threw his arm around Charlotte and twisted to put himself between her and the perp. He muffled her screams against his chest, pressed his lips against her hair and muttered every apology he could think of as he took her down to the slick wet grass and rolled his body over hers, waiting for the attack.

"Gun?"

"Remote?"

"Bomb?"

He heard the speculation over his radio, heard a slew of curses, then Randy Murdock's harsh, "Drop it! Get down on the ground! Now!"

"Madre de Dios!" Trip turned his head at the thick Latin accent and saw Randy's blond ponytail flying as she kicked aside the package and put the driver on the pavement. "I surrender! I surrender! *Por favor!*"

Murdock hooked her sniper's rifle over her shoulder, put her knee in the man's back and cuffed him. Captain Cutler pointed his gun at the windshield as Sergeant Delgado approached the rear of the van at rifle-point and swung it open. He paused, climbed inside, then jumped back out to the ground and flattened himself on the road to look beneath the van.

He could read the results in his team's posture even

before he heard Delgado's report. "Clear. The van's clear."

"He's clean," Murdock reported, rising after frisking the driver for weapons.

"Let me up." Charlotte's panicked screams had subsided to a hoarse plea. "I'm okay, Trip. I need to see him."

"Not yet." He got around the dog's frantic need to get to his mistress by grabbing him by the collar and pulling him down to the ground beside them. "Clear" wasn't the same as "all clear," and Trip had no intention of any surprises popping out to finish whatever the driver had started.

Captain Cutler lowered his weapon to a forty-five-degree angle and came around the van's front bumper while Sergeant Delgado turned his back to the van and circled, eyeing each direction along the asphalt and into the trees that dropped off to the bottom of the hill across the road. The captain nudged the plastic bag that had tumbled into the ditch with his toe, then knelt beside it.

The dog pushed against Trip's shoulder. Or maybe it was Charlotte. "I can't breathe."

Cutler holstered his gun. "No weapon. I repeat, no weapon." He plucked the bag from the water draining into the brick ditch and stood. "I've got one red-rose corsage with a note attached."

"A note?" Charlotte's breathy terror entered Trip's ear and went straight to the heap of guilt already twisting his gut. "For me?"

"Charming son of a bitch. Let's get this guy up," the captain ordered. "Do you speak English?"

"Yes."

"Did you write this note?"

"No, sir. No, I just deliver."

"Let's get you moving, too." Trip shifted his weight off Charlotte and rolled to his feet, bracing as he pulled her up in the same movement. "The RGK used a bomb when he went after Audrey last year," he explained, suspecting an apology alone wouldn't erase the wide-eyed shock behind Charlotte's glasses. "I wasn't taking any chances of a replay of that attack. And after shooting at my truck, I'm not waiting to see if he graduates to real bullets. Are you hurt? Are you with me?"

She had one hand on her ear, the other clutched tightly around Max's leash. Her eyes were transfixed by the van, but hopefully not focused in the past.

He'd protected her like the cop he was trained to be. But it was the man in him who cupped her cheek in his gloved hand and tilted her face up into the rain. "Charlotte?"

The rain splashed on her glasses, making her blink. Then some of the haze cleared away and she slowly shook her head. "I'm not hurt."

But she was still rubbing her ear. Had she hit her head on the way down? "Honey?"

He pushed her hand away and brushed aside her hair. Her earring was missing.

"Don't."

She jerked away, but he'd already seen it. The jagged line. The tiny white scars and stiff molded skin. She'd lost part of her ear and plastic surgeons had rebuilt it. No wonder she was so sensitive about him touching her there.

"Honey, I…" But the stamp of her features warned him she didn't want an apology. A quick scan up the hill a few feet led him to the gold earring. She snatched it from his hand and clipped it back on. "Are you with me?"

This time she nodded. She wiped the rain from her glasses and looked him in the eye. "The kidnappers took me in a white van. I was flashing back."

"I suspected as much." How could a woman he wanted

to reach for so badly not welcome his touch? He had to remind himself that protecting Charlotte wasn't about what *he* needed, and he curled his needy fingers into his palm. "Can you walk? Stick close. I intend to find out what this guy wants."

Trip tried not to read too much into Charlotte capturing his hand and holding on with both of hers as he led her down the hill. Yeah, maybe she was more scared of her stalker and the rest of the world than she was of him right now, but that didn't mean she wasn't still afraid of his big, bad self barging into her life and into her personal space.

He wasn't ready to let go, either. He raised his voice, not needing the radio to communicate. "What's in the note?"

Captain Cutler assessed Charlotte's condition before handing over the package. His curse matched the captain's. Charlotte didn't need to see this.

Don't despair, Charlotte. You'll be joining your old friends soon. Not even your new friends can stop the inevitable. I'm counting the days until we're together for the last time.

"A red rose with silver ribbons. That's the corsage I had at prom. I dropped it in the parking lot before I was abducted." Charlotte's hands pumped his. "What does it say?"

"Uh-uh."

The stubborn woman snatched it from his hands and read it, anyway. "Oh, my God."

He took the vile message from her and handed it back to the captain. "Our guy's a voyeur. He's around here somewhere, watching her reaction to this." While the captain dispatched Murdock up the hill to get the best recon of the cemetery, Trip pulled the pale-faced driver away from the van and turned him so Charlotte could get a good look at him. "You know this guy?"

"No."

"Señor, por favor." The stocky driver was younger than Trip had first suspected. He was guessing by the thickness of his accent that he hadn't been in the country for very long, either.

Trip pressed further. "He doesn't work for you or your family?"

"I don't know. He's not anyone I recognize."

"Please, sir. I work for the florist." He pointed over his shoulder to the road leading toward the cemetery's north entrance. "I deliver flowers to the Gonzalez funeral down at the chapel."

"The back of the van's empty," Delgado pointed out.

The driver turned to him, as if that proved his innocence. "I already go to the chapel. I'm on my way back to my uncle's shop now."

"Then you're taking the scenic route."

The driver frowned, not understanding Delgado's sarcasm.

Trip wanted answers. "What are you doing up here? With this?"

"The man. The man at the chapel—he give me fifty dollars to take this up the hill to the lady with the dog." With his cuffed hands the driver pushed the corsage bag away from him. "I give it. Please, *señor*—I good man."

The unexpected opportunity to put an end to this fueled Trip's adrenaline. "He could still be at the chapel."

Cutler nodded. "Sarge, take the car and check it out."

Delgado caught the keys Trip tossed him. "What are the chances he's still there?"

"If he's gone, then you find me footprints, tire tracks,

something we can follow. I don't like having a serial killer with so many ties to my team. And I don't think we're just talking about Alex anymore, are we?" His sharp blue eyes didn't miss a detail, darting down to the clasp of Trip and Charlotte's hands. "We're going to wind up having a showdown one of these days, and I'd rather we capture him before he catches us off guard."

Amen to that.

Delgado revved the engine and turned a U-ie on the narrow road, speeding down toward the chapel.

"I'll bag this and call the detectives." Captain Cutler adjusted the bill of his cap as the sky darkened and the rain changed from a few sprinkles to a steady downpour. He opened the van door and urged the driver to climb back inside and slide across to the passenger seat. "I'll keep an eye on this guy until we hear from Sarge, see if I can get any kind of a description out of him to back up his story." He nodded toward Charlotte, his face reflecting the same wary concern Trip felt. "Put her in our truck and stay with her."

Trip was anxious to get Charlotte behind the van's armored walls as well as out of view of the psycho-pervert who was behind this sick game. "I don't like the coincidence of that van showing up when we're here with Charlotte."

Cutler agreed. "Me, either. Who knew that you were bringing her to the cemetery?"

Charlotte seemed to startle from some deep thought when they looked to her for an answer. "I always tell Dad when I leave the estate. Laura and Kyle were with him in his office, meeting with the event planner they've been working with, Jeffrey Beecher. Bailey was there, too. My stepmother wants to host a fundraiser for the city's botanical gardens once all this rain clears."

"Plus there are the security guards and Detective Montgomery and whoever he's got watching the cameras to track Charlotte's every move there," Trip added.

"Well, that certainly narrows down the list of suspects."

The captain's sarcasm wasn't lost on Trip. "Believe me, you don't know what kind of traffic that place gets."

"Then I'd get her out of there."

"I would, too. Unfortunately, it's not up to me."

"Do the best you can, Trip. Trust your instincts—they're good ones. SWAT Team One will back you up as much as we can."

"Thank you, sir."

Trip was already turning Charlotte down the road toward the SWAT truck, keeping his chest aligned with her back and his eyes peeled as Cutler climbed into the white van.

"This way." He stopped her and pointed into the trees. "It'll be quicker if we cut through."

She stepped off the asphalt with him, but put on the brakes when she got a peek over the edge to the road below. "That's a pretty steep drop-off, and I can hear how fast and full the creek is running from up here."

"Yeah, but I hate being out in the open like this." Trip plowed into her back at the abrupt halt, knocking her forward, but catching her before she tumbled. "Anyone could drive by. I feel like there are eyes on us." He took advantage of his arm being around her waist and pulled her back against him, savoring the contact with her hips and thighs against his, needing it to feel she was secure. "It'll take us ten minutes to follow the road around, and if that sicko is here, you'd be in easy view the whole way. The shortcut will take us five and give us cover, if you're willing to get your shoes muddy. The trees should give us enough handholds to control our descent."

For a moment she relaxed against him, completing the

embrace. But then she was taking his hand, clicking to the dog and sliding down to the first tree. "I need to learn to keep myself safe, too. We're cutting through."

Four minutes and only one foot in the creek later, Trip was lifting Charlotte into the back of the SWAT van. Max just needed an invitation to join them, and after the dog hopped up and shook off, Trip closed and locked the door behind them. While Max found a spot on the floor to curl up and give himself a bath, Trip sat Charlotte on the bench that ran parallel of the center aisle and scooted past them to make sure the doors up front were locked. Then he secured the cage between the cab and the supply and command center of the truck. With inches of reinforced steel and no way to see in between Charlotte and her stalker, Trip finally relaxed his guard and breathed a little easier.

But the air inside the van quickly filled with the dank smells of mud and dog and grass stains on their clothes. And there was something warm and intimate about their bodies moving in the close confines of the narrow passageway. Charlotte's clothes were rumpled and sticking to every generous curve as she peeled off her Kevlar, but her cheeks were flushed with a healthy color and her eyes were bright with relief as she pulled off her glasses and reached beneath her black trench coat to find the hem of her blouse to dry her lenses.

As he stowed his rifle, three things hit Trip with stunning clarity. One, Charlotte Mayweather possessed a surprising beauty that was far more enticing than she gave herself credit for.

Two, Captain Cutler was right—he was feeling something for her more profound than guilt or some need to prove that her first impression of him as a man she needed to fear was wrong. He wouldn't be tamping down these warring needs of wanting to wrap her in his arms to shield her from everything she had to fear, and wanting to kiss that pursed mouth and uncover her layer by layer to get inside her if that was the case, right?

And three, as much as Charlotte's complexities both baffled and fascinated him, as much as he suspected her complete acceptance of him would finally give him the solace he sought to ease the physical and emotional hunger she'd awakened inside him, Trip knew he wasn't the right man for her. Not in the long run.

Charlotte needed Mr. Sensitive, not a hands-on kind of cowboy who wrestled her to the ground and dragged her through the mud and kissed her when she rankled him as he did. She needed someone well-educated and refined enough to live in her world, not a man who couldn't manage a cup and saucer and who took four months to read a book that a woman like her could finish in a week. She could use him as a cop, as the protector he was. But without the RGK in her life, she'd have no place for him—no use for a bull like him in her china shop of a world.

When he turned around and watched her fix her glasses and brave face back into place, that last realization hit him hard in the gut—and maybe closer to something a little more vital. He was falling hard and fast for the quirky heiress. But how the hell could the two of them together ever work?

"What?"

Smooth, big guy. Real smooth. She'd caught him staring, with maybe a little too much hunger and desperation stamped on his face.

He pulled off his gloves, shook off the excess moisture and stuffed them into his pocket. "Sorry I made you do the wilderness trek like that. I guess I've forced you to do a lot of stuff you're not comfortable with lately."

She shrugged off his apology. "Trust me, I'm happier being indoors and out of sight sooner rather than later."

"I'll get you home as soon as Captain Cutler calls with an 'all clear.'"

Her slight smile surprised him. "You're certainly an adventure to hang out with. I don't know that being soaked straight through to my backside is what I'd call fun, but about fifteen years ago, I'd have been all over sliding down that hillside and climbing the rocks across the creek. About the only dirt I get my hands on now is the dust at the museum."

"You know, you like getting dirty more than any reclusive heiress I know."

For one moment her eyes narrowed in a confused frown. And then she laughed. "So you've met a lot of us?"

"You're pretty when you smile, Charlotte."

And then her cell phone rang. Not the one Spencer Montgomery had bagged as evidence from the museum. Not the one Bud Preston had retrieved from the limo. The brand-new cell phone someone on her father's staff had picked up for her that morning was ringing.

The smile had vanished. "Maybe it's someone else. Like Audrey. We haven't talked since Alex put her under twenty-four-hour guard."

"She has the new number?" They both knew the timing was suspect after the note and van and corsage.

She pulled the cell from her coat pocket and stared at the blinking light. "It says 'Unknown Caller.' I have to answer it, don't I? That's what Detective Montgomery said."

Trip rested his hand on her shoulder and sat on the bench beside her. "Put it on speakerphone."

With a jerky nod, she answered it. "Hello?"

"Did you like my gift, Charlotte? Brings back fun memories, doesn't it?"

Trip snatched the phone from her fingers and spun away. "You better hope to hell you and I never come face-to-face, pal."

But while Trip seethed, the bastard didn't so much as startle. He breathed softly and then said, "Put Charlotte back on the phone."

"No."

"Then I'll call her again. And again. And again. On this number or another one. Until she gets my message personally."

As much as he wanted to hang up, Trip knew the longer they kept this psycho talking, the more chances they had at him slipping up and giving them a clue to his identity or location. But he didn't want her to hear this. He didn't want her to be afraid.

Trip felt four fingers curl beneath his belt at the back of his waist. Charlotte's unexpected touch took the edge off his protective anger. Did she have any idea how brave she really was? He dropped his arm around her shoulders and when she didn't pull away, he hugged her close. She curled her arms around his waist and answered. "I'm here. Why are you doing this?"

"You always prided yourself in being so smart, Charlotte. But it's driving you nuts that you can't figure it out, isn't it?"

"Is that the idea? To drive me nuts?"

"It's hard to keep it all together and move on with the life you want when someone else is calling the shots, don't you think?"

Her hair rustled against Trip's vest when she shook her head. "I don't understand. I've never done anything wrong. I've never hurt anyone."

"That's what you and your friends all claim. Yet one by one you've all denied me what I wanted, what I deserved.

I paid a terrible price for your betrayal. Justice is finally being served."

"My friends? You killed Val and Gretchen? You tried to kill Audrey?"

"I'm going to kill you, too, sweetheart. Make sure your boyfriend hears that." Trip could make out the sound of a finely tuned engine revving in the background. The perv was on the road, on the move. "No wealthy bitch will ever say 'no' to me again. I'm going to kill you, too."

Trip closed the phone and stuffed it into his pocket as soon as the call disconnected. Then he gathered Charlotte into his arms and squeezed her tight, feeling her shaking. Or maybe he was the one shaking.

But as Charlotte wound her arms around his waist and nestled under his chin, he felt his own fears dissipating, his anger hardening into something primal and territorial. "He's not going to hurt you, honey. I swear it."

"Because you've got my back?"

"Yeah." He tunneled his fingers into her rain-softened curls and buried his nose in their fragrant scent. "I'm calling the captain and then Spencer Montgomery. They need to know about this call. I think I can get a general idea what kind of vehicle he was driving from the sound of the engine."

"And tell Captain Cutler the man he has in custody isn't the man who's been calling me. The guy in the van has much too thick of an accent."

"Look at us, narrowing down the list of suspects." But there was nothing funny about eliminating one man out of hundreds of possibilities for the Rich Girl Killer.

"Trip?"

"I know. You want to go home."

Her fingers snuck up to his jaw and an answering heat pulsed to that spot. And then she touched his lips, lightly dancing over them with her fingertips as if trying to recall what they'd felt like pressed against hers. He groaned deep in his chest, his whole body aching to answer that sweetly curious caress. But she was leaning back, tugging at his chin, asking him to look at her. Easily and willingly done.

"Only if you're there, too. I know I keep freaking out on you, but I think I need you. Will you stay with me until this is over?"

The trust wasn't there in her eyes. Not yet. But he wasn't about to give her any reason to doubt him.

"Try pushing me away. This boy don't budge."

HIS HANDS WERE SHAKING as he tucked the phone inside his jacket pocket. What the hell? That conversation had lasted longer than the sixty seconds of toying with Charlotte that he normally allowed himself.

He'd lost his temper. That big bozo cop who thought he was on some personal mission to shadow Charlotte's every move had interfered with the plan and made him lose his temper.

The rear end of a semi loomed up at an alarming speed and he jerked the steering wheel to the left, not caring about the honking horn that warned him he'd cut someone off in the passing lane. He flew another two miles on I-435 before finally getting a glimpse of his own reflection in the rearview mirror.

"What are you doing?" he asked, reassured by the intelligence looking back at him. "Why are you letting them get to you again?"

Taking a deep cleansing breath, he slowed the car to a legal speed and merged with the traffic that would take him into one of the wealthiest neighborhoods in Kansas City, south of the downtown area near the Plaza. He was expected shortly, and he hated to be late. He might have to bite his tongue about some things for now, but in the end, he'd be victorious and they'd be the ones groveling for mercy.

He'd been beaten and talked down to, denied his family, rejected and overlooked because of those women. It wasn't right for a man to endure all he had. There had to be retribution. Someone had to pay—as dearly as he had—in order to restore the balance that his world so desperately needed.

As he slowed down for a stoplight, he reached across the seat and picked up his camera. He brought up his most recent pictures on the digital screen and smiled.

Nice. Spying the florist delivery van and putting it to good use while he'd been following her trip to the old man's grave had been a stroke of pure genius. The driver had been more than willing to help for fifty bucks. He might have driven up to Charlotte for free once he'd turned on the sob story about being an old boyfriend who wanted to show he still cared for his grieving ex.

"Look at the fear on your face, Charlotte." If her big armed buddy hadn't been there with the dog, she would have wigged out completely.

Having the cop join the conversation on the phone wasn't exactly what he'd wanted, but it was satisfying to hear the wobble in Charlotte's tone, even with her protector there with her. That meant he was well and truly inside her head now. Very nice.

When the turn signal for the next lane came on, he shut down the camera and carefully returned it to the pocket of the rolled-up coveralls in the gym bag beside him. He zipped the bag shut, then neatly arranged the handles so that they hung evenly on each side of the bag. For a moment, he contemplated giving in to the urge to pull his cigarettes from the bag's side pocket. But he would be meeting people too soon, and he couldn't afford to have the telltale scent of tobacco on him.

The light changed and he accelerated through the intersection, smiling at his success today, formulating the details for his next encounter with Charlotte. He had to get her alone to carry out the final phase of his plan. He couldn't risk her snapping out of her delusions. That meant taking care of the dog. And getting her away from the cop.

He drove over the bridge at Brush Creek, idly noting how the water was rushing near the top of the concrete walkways on each bank. Another few inches of rain, and parts of downtown K.C. could be blocked by flash flooding and closed streets. He could use that to his advantage. Yes, that might be exactly the best way to isolate Charlotte from her bodyguards.

His blood hummed at the sweet, sweet anticipation of his revenge. He wanted Charlotte Mayweather screaming and shattered and begging for mercy when he squeezed the life from her throat.

He smiled. Val dead. Gretchen dead. Audrey sequestered under lock and key. And soon, Charlotte would be dead.

The four women who'd ruined his life, who'd treated him as a second-class citizen unworthy of their time and consideration. He was better than that. Better than them. Soon, they'd all be dead and his hunger for their suffering would be appeased.

And then he could finally put his demons to rest.

Chapter Ten

"Another call?" Charlotte let her stepbrother, Kyle, hug his arm around her and walk her to his chair at the end of the dining room table. "How are you holding up?"

"I'm sorry." She patted his arm as he knelt beside her, then looked to her father, who was pushing away from the head of the table and hurrying toward her. "I didn't mean to interrupt your dinner. I just wanted to let you know that I was home and I was safe."

Her gaze automatically went to the big man standing in the archway between the dining room and foyer. Even separated from the group of family hurrying over to give her hugs and words of reassurance, he dominated the room with his steely eyes and alert, warriorlike stance. He moved aside only when the butler announced Spencer Montgomery's arrival and the emotionless, red-haired detective strode into the room to question her.

"There was a written threat, too," she added, a few minutes later, reading the details Detective Montgomery was listing in his notebook.

He nodded, clicking his pen and tucking it back inside the pocket of his blazer. "I got that and the flower from Captain Cutler. Plus, the name of the florist van driver. I don't think there's any reason to hold Mr. Gutierrez, although I did ask him to meet with one of our sketch artists to see if we can get a physical description of the man who paid him to accost you like that. We'll see if he shows up. His documentation was a little sketchy and," he glanced over his shoulder at Trip, still standing watch, "for some reason he's a little leery of the police right now."

Trip offered no apology. "We had no idea who he was. We weren't going to let him get to Charlotte."

And she, for one, was more and more glad that she did have SWAT Team One's personal protection. She offered Trip a quick, grateful smile, but turned her attention back to the detective. She was anxious to finish the report, get out of the sticky, muddy clothes that were drying against her skin and get to the soothing solitude of her rooms. "Someone is doing his damnedest to re-create every detail of the kidnapping. All I need is for that creep to actually put his hands on me and the nightmare will be complete."

Her father, hovering behind her chair, leaned over to kiss the crown of her hair. "No. That will not happen."

Her stepsister, Bailey, who'd been sitting kitty-corner from her throughout the interview, squeezed her hand. "Maybe we should postpone the garden party for a while, until all this blows over."

Spencer Montgomery eyed her straight across the table as if she was as airy as a piece of strawberry fluff. "This is a serial killer we're talking about, not the weather. It won't just blow over."

Bailey bristled in her pale pink suit, but met the detective's faintly condescending gaze with a tilt of her chin. "I'm talking about Char's comfort, not your investigation. She doesn't like large crowds of people, and I don't see why we should add to her stress when this situation is already difficult enough for her."

Trip added a grumpy echo from the doorway. "Finally, a voice of reason."

Bailey wilted under the one-two combination of the detective's glare and her mother rising from her chair to make her opinion heard. "Don't be ridiculous, Bailey. This garden party is your introduction with Harper as a couple to Kansas City society. I've taken Charlotte's eccentricities into consideration and scheduled it for one of those days when she's working at the museum."

Charlotte looked up at the handsome blond attorney with his hands resting on her stepsister's shoulders. "You're a couple?"

But her father didn't give either Harper or Bailey a chance to answer. "We've already discussed this. Detective Montgomery agrees that we need to maintain our regular activities so we don't scare off the bastard who wants to hurt my daughter."

Harper winked at Charlotte, but addressed himself to her father. "It was my suggestion, Jackson. Charlotte and I are friends from way back. Plus, Bailey was concerned."

Kyle spoke up from the buffet, where he was pouring himself a cup of coffee. "I agree with Bails. This party is a frivolous expense we don't need right now."

"I was worried about Charlotte, not the expense," Bailey insisted.

"I am, too." Kyle rejoined them at the table. "We don't need the distraction of any more people around the estate right now, do we?"

"Thanks, guys." Charlotte smiled at Kyle and squeezed her stepsister's pale hand. Bailey was quickly losing her rosy-eyed view of people—no doubt starting to feel like a pawn in the powerful man's world her mother had married into. And while Harper was saying and doing all the right things a solicitous boyfriend would, Charlotte got the idea that he was more focused on impressing her father, or even Detective Montgomery, than he was Bailey.

A decade had seasoned Harper's lanky good looks into a man who would turn any woman's head. With his family's reputation and bank account, he was definitely what society would label a catch. But as Charlotte studied his manicured hands and polished speech, she began to wonder exactly what it was that had made her think he was the god she'd crushed on so badly in high school.

The man standing in the archway had mud on his city-issued uniform and a scowl on his face. But she wasn't feeling so much as a flicker of interest in Harper this evening, yet Trip Jones stirred something deeper inside her.

True, she was a different woman now than she'd been in high school, before the kidnapping. Maybe that was the difference—Harper, while he cut a handsome figure in his tailored suit, seemed stuck in that boyish tendency to want to please anyone he perceived as more powerful than he was. Trip, to an annoying degree at times, didn't answer to any man or woman in this room. No one would ever mistake his brawny build and attitude as that of anything other than an intelligent, self-assured, full-grown man.

Those green-gold eyes were on her now, questioning her lingering perusal. But she felt no panic. There was something deep and intimate about the way he looked at her that thrilled a secret part of her that had been shut off for too long. Trip Jones was a man. He cared about her. He'd made no bones about the fact that he was attracted to her, that he wanted her in ways no man ever had before. She…believed…there was a bond growing between them that had nothing to do with stalkers and nightmares and keeping her safe. It was pretty heady stuff for an eccentric plain Jane to process.

No high-school boy had certainly ever looked at her that way. No high-school boy had ever kissed her or held her or sheltered her the way Trip Jones…

Charlotte snapped back to the conversation around her. No high-school boy...

It couldn't be.

She interrupted the discussion. "Harper, do you ever hear from your soccer buddy Landon Turner?"

"That's a name I haven't heard in a while."

Her father curled his fist around the top of her chair. "It's a name I never want to hear in this house again. Sweetie, why don't you go to your rooms. Let us sort this all out."

Trip took a step into the room backing her up. "She needs an answer to her question. Do you know what Turner is up to these days?"

Harper shrugged and smoothed his tie. "To be honest, we lost track of each other in college. I was at Harvard and...I don't think he got to play professional soccer the way he wanted. He was a scholarship student at Sterling Academy in the first place, otherwise, he couldn't afford it. And with all the delays and backlash from your trial, he lost his full ride to Westminster. I think he ended up at the university, or maybe even a community college. We ran in different circles by that point. I'm afraid I lost track of him."

That could explain the drinking and the endless phone calls alternately blaming her for ruining his life and asking her forgiveness. But had Landon outgrown his troubles and moved on with his life? Or had he somehow snuck back into hers, intent on taking the absolution she hadn't been able to give.

And if he had slipped back into her life somehow, could he have changed his appearance so much that, after ten years, she no longer recognized him? Was he here right now? Watching her?

A ripple of unease shimmied over her skin, battling with the anticipation she felt at finally having some plausible answers to identify the man playing this cruel game of terror with her. But she couldn't think here, she couldn't handle another minute of people and arguing and feeling so exposed like this. Charlotte pushed her chair away from the table and stood. "If you'll excuse me. I need to go."

"Of course, sweetie." Jackson hugged her tight.

Detective Montgomery stood as well. "I'll call you if I have more questions."

With a smile for the others, she squished in her wet tennis shoes across the room to Trip.

"Did you need something?" he asked, his voice terse.

Charlotte opened her mouth to ask him to wait until they got to her rooms to explain the idea percolating in her head. But his arm went out in front of her like a crossing guard's, stopping her in her tracks, and she realized he was talking to the man leaning against the wall near the hallway that led from the dining room to the kitchen.

Bud Preston brushed the rain off the shoulders of his Darnell Events Staff jacket, tonguing that ever-present toothpick in his mouth. "I'm just the hired help, sir—moving furniture in the rain. Gotta love my job. You wouldn't begrudge a man coming in out of the rain to use the john, would you?"

Charlotte nodded toward the hallway. "There's a restroom back there you can use."

"Go." Trip's warning was short and sweet.

Jeffrey Beecher walked in behind Bud, pulling off his clear plastic raincoat and tugging down the sleeves of his suit jacket. As soon as he saw his man standing there, he huffed with disgust. "Preston. Get back to work. I need all that iron garden furniture unloaded from the truck. And stick to the floor runners when you come inside so you don't track your mess through the house."

Bud turned and gave his employer a mocking salute. "Sir, yes, sir."

Trip's arm dropped once Bud disappeared into the kitchen. Jeffrey pulled a handkerchief from his pocket and removed his glasses to wipe them dry. "Sorry about that," he apologized. "Have they finished dinner yet? I have some details I need to go over with Mrs. Austin-Mayweather." He paused when he met them in the archway, putting on his glasses and wrinkling his nose when he saw the muddy streaks in Max's fur. "Did something happen?"

Trip slipped his arm behind Charlotte's waist and scooted her on past without answering. "Join the party. We're out of here."

As soon as she'd turned all the locks on her door behind them, Charlotte hung her wet coat in the closet. While Max trotted on past her to get a drink of water from his bowl, she untied her wet shoes and peeled them off her feet. Her socks came next. She peeled them off and dropped them on the rug as she hurried straight to the bookshelves across the room.

She heard the rip of Velcro as Trip removed his vest, but she forgot to even offer him a seat as she pulled out her high-school yearbooks and curled up on the couch with the stack of books beside her. While she warmed her toes beneath her legs, she opened up the first yearbook and scrolled through the pages.

A lamp turned on beside her, showering more light over her shoulder. "What are you doing? I figured you'd head straight to the shower."

She glanced up at Trip and back to her book. "You can use it if you need to. I wanted to look something up."

"I can wait until I can get back to the station or my apartment for some clean clothes." Her balance shifted as the sofa took his weight beside her. He picked up another book and thumbed through the pages. "High-school year-books?"

Charlotte nodded, finding the section of photos she needed. "Something that creep said. That none of us would ever say no to him again."

"I don't follow."

She trailed through the senior class photos with her finger, going down the alphabet. "I've only said no to two guys my whole life. One of them was Landon Turner when he asked me to forgive him for pulling that prank on prom night. And the other…" She squinted to be sure, then pulled off her glasses and held the page up to her eyes to see the long-forgotten face once more. "There. Donny Kemp."

Trip was a blur at this distance. "Your brainiac friend from the quiz bowl team?"

She tapped the photo as she handed him the book. "I turned him down for a date to the prom, and went with Landon instead." Turning him down for a date wasn't much of a reason for a man to threaten her like he had, but her choices for men she'd wronged were limited. "I have no idea if he still lives in Kansas City or what he looks like now. It's hard to picture him ten years older and probably looking a little less nerdy."

Charlotte nearly toppled over when Trip stood. When he strode to the door, she grabbed her glasses and hurried after him. "Where are you going?"

"Lock the door behind me. Don't open it for anyone but me."

"Trip?"

"I'm going to show this to Montgomery and have him track down Donny Kemp. Landon Turner, too. Maybe we can get his artist to age their pictures for us and see if you recognize one of them then."

"I didn't say Donny was the killer. He was always kind

of odd, but sweet." She hugged her arms around herself, hating that her revelation only raised more questions instead of offering answers. "And who am I to describe anyone else as 'odd'? And Landon was so...devastated when he found out what happened to me. He blamed himself for me getting hurt."

"Don't expect any sympathy from me." His voice was tough, but his fingers were gentle as he brushed a curl of hair off her glasses and cupped the side of her face. "They're leads, Charlotte. Something a lot more tangible and sensible than just waiting to catch this guy when he finally attacks and praying I'm not too late to stop him."

"GET OVER HERE, YOU goofy mutt!" Trip shouted, as Max trotted past the slobbery tennis ball he'd been so excited about just a moment ago and started nosing around the ground at the corner of the fence where he'd been trying to drag something through the ivy and chain links since they'd first come out for a morning romp. Pulling his new KCPD ball cap over his eyes to shield them from the morning drizzle, he jogged after the determined pooch. He picked up the abandoned tennis ball and gave the dog a playful swat on the rump. "Hey. Leave it."

Charlotte wore a bright yellow cap to match the brightly painted sunflowers that covered her ears. He still didn't think there was a thing wrong with the badge of honor she carried on the delicate lobe the doctors had repaired, but if she felt more comfortable hiding the scar, then he was content to let that vulnerable imperfection be a secret shared between them. Her skin glistened with raindrops and healthy activity as she ran up beside him, making it hard to imagine her as the skittish, reclusive heiress he'd first discovered in a storage room at the Mayweather

Museum. "Maybe it's a dead bird or ground squirrel that's gotten flooded out by the storms."

"Charlotte!"

She'd knelt down to shoo Max away and inspect the juicy temptation for herself through the fence. "I sure hope the farmers appreciate all this rain because I, for one, am getting sick and tired of it. I'm running out of dry shoes. Yuck." Her tone changed from curiosity to gross-out as she stood. "I don't want to touch it without gloves. I think Max has been eating it."

Trip squatted down to inspect what looked like a fragrant hunk of liver out of the garbage. Yeah, what self-respecting dog could resist that? He stood back up and handed off the tennis ball. "I've got my gloves in the SUV. I'll come around the other side to pick it up."

"Wait." She pushed the ball back into his hands. "You keep Max entertained—you've about got him tuckered out already. I'll go in and ask one of the staff to remove it. He doesn't usually get this much action when it's just me in the morning. I think he's having fun."

She was already heading toward the door. "All right. I'll dog-sit. But you come right back, understand?"

"Got it. Now throw the ball."

Trip hurled the tennis ball and grinned at Charlotte's delight in watching Max run after, then nearly do a backflip when the ball bounced off the fence and changed course. The door clicked shut behind her as she went into the house. Then he threw the ball again, purposely avoiding the corner with the meat.

It felt good to stretch out his muscles after sleeping on a couch that was entirely too small in a room that reminded him entirely too much of the woman sleeping in the connecting bedroom. Especially when a freshly washed dog had insisted on sharing the couch with him and his mistress didn't.

He pulled the ball from Max's mouth and scratched behind his ears. "You and I are learning to get along pretty well now. But I still prefer her curves over yours."

Max woofed a protest. Although his heart was willing, he really was getting tired. When Trip threw the ball this time, the dog pushed to his feet and loped after it.

He'd left Charlotte alone only for the hour it took him to drive to KCPD headquarters, where he could shower and get some fresh jeans in the locker room, and run upstairs to check on Spencer Montgomery's progress in running down her old high-school buddies. While Rafe Delgado had camped out outside Charlotte's door, refusing to let anyone—not even her stepsister, Bailey, with a late-night snack—enter, Trip had gotten Montgomery to share some information that was as unsettling as it was unexpected.

Landon Turner now lived in the small mid-Missouri town of Osage Beach, where he worked as a deputy with the sheriff's department and coached a prep league soccer team. A few calls by Detective Montgomery verified that Turner had not only been on duty in the Lake of the Ozarks area the past three days, but that he'd been on the scene of a multicar accident yesterday afternoon and evening when the RGK had been at the cemetery, spying on Charlotte's grief and paying an innocent man to help terrorize her with his van and a fancy flower.

As for Donny Kemp?

Trip wrestled with Max for a few seconds before tossing the ball again. At the same time, he was wrestling with exactly how he was going to share his suspicions with Charlotte.

While he took note of the dog's lethargy and waning interest in their game of fetch, Trip was more concerned about the best way to tell her that quiz bowl Donny seemed to have dropped off the face of the earth some five years ago. Montgomery had found no driver's license records, no tax statements, no prison record, no death certificate, nothing. Trip was a lot less wary of a man whose whereabouts could be accounted for than a man who'd simply ceased to exist.

As a law enforcement officer, Landon Turner could get access to the police reports and trial transcripts of Charlotte's kidnapping—right down to the last details that she hadn't even shared with him yet. Could Donny Kemp, if he was still alive, get his hands on the same information through another source?

A retching sound drew Trip's attention from his speculation. "Whoa, pal. Hey, you okay?" Max had stopped in the middle of the yard and was swaying back and forth as his stomach heaved in and out. Trip hurried to his side. "Serves you right for eating things that don't belong to you. You're not spitting up my hat you ate, are you?"

But when the dog stretched out on his belly and started getting sick again, Trip's teasing turned to real concern. "Easy, boy."

He didn't like the looks of the little pellets he could still see in the chewed meat. He laid a comforting hand on the dog's back and pulled out his pocketknife to remove one of the pellets. The thing crumbled into bits, but enough remained that he had a pretty good idea of what he was looking at.

"Son of a bitch." He wiped the blade in the grass and returned it to his pocket as the convulsions subsided. Although Trip had basic medic training to deal with human illnesses and injuries, he wasn't sure how much of that could be applied to canines. But rheumy eyes and another round of vomiting couldn't be good. If the Rich Girl Killer wanted to torment Charlotte, he couldn't find a crueler way than to go after her truest friend like this. "Oh, no you don't. Charlotte! Hey! Somebody!"

With a crummy sense of déjà vu, Trip unhooked the top buttons of his shirt and peeled the chambray off over his head. "Hang in there, boy. Hang in there."

He tore the sleeve from the body of the shirt and scooped up a sample of the meat and pellets. Then he wrapped the dog in the rest of his shirt, hoping the cooling temperature of his nose was due to the weather and not something more sinister. Weak as he was, the dog resisted the straitjacket effect of the shirt. "Easy. Come on, pal. I need you to be okay for your mama."

As he scooped the dog into his arms, the door from the house opened behind him and he heard Charlotte's sharp voice. "I'm sorry, Kyle. But it's not really yours to worry about, now is it?"

"I'm a professional money manager, Char. I'm just suggesting you show a little restraint."

"I know how to manage a budget, and I'm not spending anybody's money but my own…Max?" She was at Trip's side in an instant, her hands stroking the dog's head and calming him. "Maxie, sweetie, what's wrong? Oh, my God." She pulled her hand away from his muzzle with blood on her fingers. "Max!"

Trip didn't have a hand to spare to wipe that mess from her fingers or the time to give the words of reassurance that might erase the shock from her expression.

"Is something wrong with your mutt?" Kyle asked from the doorway, staying out of the rain and away from the trauma.

"Kyle! Towels, now," Trip ordered, not caring if it was a weak stomach or indifference that kept her stepbrother from helping out. Once he got Kyle moving, he stood, cradling the sick dog in his arms. He held out the smaller bundle in his hand and looked down at Charlotte's tearing eyes. Oh, no, no, no. This pooch had to make it. He wouldn't be able to handle Charlotte grieving over that loss. "You're not going to wimp out on me now, are you?"

"No." She tilted her chin and grabbed the sample without hesitation. "Tell me what to do."

She stayed right beside him as he carried Max to the door. "Get the keys to the SUV out of my front right pocket." They were in the house now, hurrying past a stunned kitchen staff. "Call your vet. Does he have an emergency room?"

"*She* does."

"Can you manage the dog and give me directions while I drive?"

"Yes." She took the towels from Kyle's hand as they passed the bathroom and quickened her step to wrap another layer of warmth around the dog. "What's happening?"

"I'm no expert, but I think he's been fed rat poison."

Chapter Eleven

Charlotte let go of Trip just long enough to step into the restroom and wash her hands. Then she was back in the tiny examination room, waiting for the vet to give her a report on Max's condition. Trip was her hero throughout the endless ordeal—from putting the siren on top of the SWAT SUV and getting Max to the E.R. in a matter of minutes, to never once complaining about her wringing his fingers off.

The hours of waiting were pure torture, but she couldn't be anywhere else right now. Max needed her. Sweet, silly, loyal Max, who'd already suffered through one disastrous prank, had been victimized again. Charlotte's hand drifted to her earring, reaching beneath it to touch the permanent mark of the violence she'd suffered—the mark that made her a kindred spirit with her beloved pet.

"That's why you chose Max, isn't it?" Trip's husky voice pulled her from her thoughts. He batted her hand away to tuck her hair behind her ear and trace his fingers around the delicate shell. "You both lost part of your ear because of someone else's cruelty."

Although his touch soothed, she squirmed away.

"You love him despite his flaws. In fact, I'd wager those imperfections are a big part of what makes him so special to you."

She tried to make a joke of it. "We're both a little shy of winning blue ribbons for our looks?"

But there was only heat and sincerity and maybe a touch of sadness in those verdant-gold eyes looking down at her. "You've both survived hell and know it's the beauty inside, the beauty you have to look for, that means something."

He threaded his fingers into her hair and dipped his head to kiss her ear. He was seeing her deformity. Touching it. She twisted her neck away. He didn't release her. After a patient pause, he brushed his warm lips over her ear again. "This is beautiful." She gasped at the ticklish contact and tilted her head. He hovered a few inches away, then kissed it again. "You're beautiful." This time she held her breath, held herself still beneath his healing ministrations, as he dragged his lips around the shell. She could only feel his breath teasing her scalp when he pressed his lips against the scar itself. "Max is lucky to have you."

"He's lucky to have you." She turned her head again, not to pull away from his touch, but to look straight up into his kind, caring, see-into-her-more-than-they-should eyes. "I'm lucky to have you."

His mouth curved into a rueful grin. "Hold that thought until we hear from the doc."

When he would have pulled away, Charlotte walked into his chest, seeking his warmth and strength. And for some reason she wasn't quite sure she understood, he wrapped his arms around her and gave them.

"He'll be all right, Trip. He has to be." She locked her arms behind his waist and snuggled beneath his chin. "He helped me get out of the house that first time. He helped me talk to you."

"Because the crazy mutt was eating my hat."

"No." She smiled at the understanding dawning inside

her. "Because he wasn't afraid of you. Because you were kind to him, I knew you...were kind. Not a bully at all."

"Well, then, I owe him one."

For ten years, she'd thought of home as her sanctuary, the one place where she could feel safe. But knowing some coward was there, under the very same roof, who could harm an innocent creature like Max—and have no qualms about killing him—left Charlotte floating in a landless sea of doubt and suspicion. No *place* was truly safe, and any sense of security that locks and doors and reinforced walls had given her was false.

But she was holding on to an anchor right now that gave her hands and her hopes something solid to cling to. Safety wasn't a place. It was a feeling.

What she felt for Trip, the love and trust that were growing inside her—the possibility he could be feeling some of that for her—*that* was the security she craved.

The only way to overcome her phobias was to deal with them, not hide from the things that triggered them. And the only way she could finally work her way past the craziness in her head was to take that leap of faith Trip had asked her to. It was up to her to prove to him—and to herself—that she could love and be loved.

But until she could figure out exactly how to do that, she'd simply hold on to Trip. For as long as he would let her.

A knock at the exam room door stopped her wandering thoughts. She quickly turned as the door opened and the lady vet walked in.

Trip's hand wrapped around both of hers. "Doctor Girard?"

The vet tucked her stethoscope into the pocket of her lab coat. "I have some good news and some bad news."

"Definitely the good news," Charlotte begged. "Please."

"The good news is—I think Max is going to be okay."

"Oh, thank God."

"Yes!" Trip scooped Charlotte up in his arms and lifted her off her feet, nearly crushing her with relief and celebration before letting her toes touch the floor again. "That's one stubborn dog. I wonder who he takes after."

"You, probably."

"Being as young and healthy as he is definitely helps," the vet agreed. "We got him the antidote within the twelve-hour time frame. He's still a little out of it, but he's resting now. He sits up in his kennel in the back room and looks at me every time I go to check on him."

Charlotte was almost light-headed with relief. "That's wonderful. May I see him?"

"For a few minutes. The main thing he needs now is rest and IV fluids to replace what he's lost. I'd like to keep him twenty-four hours for observation—just to make sure the toxin is completely out of his system and that there are no lasting side effects."

"Thank you."

When Charlotte hurried to follow, Trip's hand held her back. "Wait a minute. Doc, you said there was some bad news."

"Well, I suppose this is more for the police and animal control, but, after analyzing the sample from his stomach, I'm pretty sure this was deliberate." Charlotte's heart sank and her temper raged all at once. "For whatever reason, someone tried to kill your dog."

"YOU'RE SURE THIS IS what you want to do?" Trip dashed inside after Charlotte and closed the Mayweather Museum's steel back door. He swiped the rain from his face and hair, and paused to inspect the newly installed dead bolt. Once he was satisfied that the steel door was secured, he followed Charlotte into the warehouse with his toolbox from the SWAT SUV. "You don't have to talk to anybody at the estate if you want to hide out in your rooms. I'll make sure you're not bothered."

"That's the last place I want to be." She scooped up a handful of the yellow crime scene tape that had been cut down and tossed it in the trash can on her way through the museum to check the locks on the doors into the public area of the museum. "Wow, when Detective Montgomery said KCPD had cleared the scene, I guess I thought that meant they'd cleaned it, too. Look at those crates left open. And all this black dust?"

"The CSIs took a lot of fingerprints. All of them were excluded as ours or other museum employees. I'm guessing our guy wore gloves." No surprise there. Even one hint of DNA or a fingerprint and they'd have ID'd the RGK and put him away months ago.

Charlotte climbed over the table and the door to the storage room still leaning against it to look inside the room. She muttered a curse. "Nothing's been put away." She picked up one small box and set it back on a shelf. "Some of these items have lasted for centuries, but they won't last another day unless we take care of this mess."

He liked seeing her determined, excited, not thinking one whit about her fears, as she was now. While she might be trying a little too hard to stay busy to keep her mind off Max's near-death experience and their twenty-four-hour separation, Trip had a feeling he was seeing a glimpse of the woman Charlotte was meant to be. The one she would have been all along if greed and tragedy hadn't changed her life. This was the woman who chased dogs and climbed through the mud and kissed him as if she couldn't get enough of him when she wasn't too worried or frightened or overanalyzing things.

This was the woman he wanted—in every way a man could want a woman.

The boom of thunder overhead and the slapping sheets of rain and wind against the bricks from the storm outside shook him out of that sentimental vibe. Her mantra was to "stay in the moment." He'd be a better cop and a smarter man if he could remember to do the same.

The flicker of lightning through the windows high above them reminded Trip to double-check the switch box and electrical connections. If Charlotte was trusting him to bring her here and keep her safe, then he was going to ensure that every possible contingency for danger or panic was taken care of. Bad guys. Blackouts. Food. Floods. He had it all covered.

She set their sack of takeout dinner on the concrete floor beside her backpack and peeled off her black raincoat. She sprayed another layer of droplets across the front of Trip's wet T-shirt when she shook the excess water from her hair. "Oops. Sorry."

"I'm learning to expect that my time with you won't be neat and pretty, and that there's a fifty-fifty chance I'm going to wind up getting hurt somehow."

"I don't do it on purpose, you know. I'm just…" She reached out to wipe the water away, but he was already wet through to the skin. And either she was suddenly self-conscious about touching the pecs and nipples he unintentionally had on display—or she was feeling the heated intimacy of being alone here together as fiercely as he was. She stopped just shy of putting her hand on him before curling her fingers into a fist.

"A klutz?"

Her gaze darted up to his. "I was thinking *distracted*." She smiled nervously and picked up the sack. "There are some paper towels in the bathroom next to my office. I'll go get some."

A few paper towels and some Chinese takeout weren't going to douse the hunger that had been gnawing at him since Charlotte had asked him to bring her here. For the first time since he'd met her, she'd asked to be alone with him. She'd said the only place left where she could feel safe was here at the museum…with him.

That was a far cry from the woman who'd come at him with a sword and a rebel yell. Tonight felt almost like her version of a date—as if she wanted to be alone with him.

"Down, boy."

Charlotte had told him she had next to no experience with men. Her idea of being alone with him might be very different from what his randy hormones were thinking. So, ignoring the storm simmering inside his veins, he checked the gun and ammo clip on his belt, rechecked the doors and followed Charlotte into her office.

Trip quickly discovered that "office" was a relative term. Charlotte's work space away from her sitting room at home involved a desk and computer, yes, but there were also bookshelves, a long table made of a sheet of plywood over two sawhorses, stacks of crates, a workbench fitted with brushes, small picks, magnifying glasses and other small tools, a cushy dog bed and a beat-up end table where she'd set up their dinner beside a distressed leather couch with a blue-and-white quilt thrown over it.

"You sure there's room for me in here?" he teased.

She motioned him over to the desk chair she'd rolled up to the table and curled her legs beneath her to sit on the end of the couch. "It's perfectly comfortable when I work here late and need to take a nap."

He scooted between the worktable and desk. "Yeah, but I'm twice as big as you are."

"So you'll make it cozy in here." She smiled and he was helpless to do anything but what she asked. "Sit. Eat. Because after I make a couple of phone calls, I intend to put you to work."

Forty minutes later, Charlotte was on the phone to someone at the bank while he called in his location to Captain Cutler. A check outside the door showed him the sky was black, some of the lights were out in the downtown district and the rain was showing no signs of stopping. The weather report concerned Trip almost as much as hearing they were no closer to tracking down the identity of the Rich Girl Killer. After hanging up, he locked the door, did a quick check of the premises and ended up leaning against the door frame of Charlotte's office while she politely argued with someone on the phone.

"Well, no, that doesn't make any sense. Please do. I'll go ahead and start the endowment paperwork with our attorneys, but I'll tell them the check will have to wait until I hear from you. Thanks."

"Problem?"

Charlotte closed her phone and jotted something on a notepad before answering. "I wanted to talk to the bank before they closed about setting up the college fund for Richard's grandchildren. I figured endowing the fund with five hundred thousand would be enough to finance the education of all six kids, and others, if they come along."

"Half a million? I'm lucky if I have enough money to pay all the bills at the end of the month."

"Apparently, so am I." She pushed the chair away from her desk and stood. A tiny frown between her eyebrows reflected her consternation. "When I said I wanted them to draft a check for me, they asked if I wanted to transfer funds from another account so I wouldn't go below the minimum balance Dad set up when I inherited the trust fund."

Trip tucked his fingers into the back pockets of his jeans and shrugged. "Five hundred grand is a big chunk of money."

"I don't mean to sound crass, but…not for me. Not for Dad." She worked her bottom lip between her teeth as she checked the numbers she'd written on the notepad. "I'm careful about how I spend my trust fund because this museum and a few select charities are really important to me. I don't want to make a promise to them and then leave them in the lurch."

He looked at the notes she showed him, but on first glance they were just a jumble of scratches and backward figures to his tired eyes. "And you're sure you've kept accurate records?"

"To the penny. My father didn't make his fortune by not keeping track of the money he spends. And I learned from him." She tossed the notepad down beside her phone. "The bank is going to look into it."

"Have those attorneys look, too. Maybe someone at the bank has helped themselves to a little extra cash that they think you won't miss." Trip dealt with guns and bombs, protection details and hostage situations, not white-collar crime. "Larceny has never been part of the RGK's MO. He's about power and revenge, not money. So I don't think you need to worry that he's making some other kind of inroad into your life."

The wheels behind those intelligent eyes kicked into high gear. "You know, there have been a couple of anomalies with that creep coming after me. He wants me to feel the same fears I did when I was kidnapped, so he's recreated those events. The phone calls. The white van, the corsage. And Detective Montgomery said this guy had an obsessive-compulsive disorder—that he makes a plan and sticks to it, right?"

"What are you thinking?"

"I was never shot at during my kidnapping. No one stole any money from me. And no one poisoned a pet or hurt any animal I know of."

Ah, hell. Ah, double hell.

"There's more than one person trying to hurt you."

TRIP DIDN'T LIKE HIS next call to Michael Cutler any better than the first. With the possibility of not one, but two low-lifes out to hurt Charlotte, he'd agreed to put the rest of the team on standby alert. But with the spring deluge turning an overtaxed water system into the beginnings of a natural disaster, the captain had suggested that Charlotte would be safer if he kept her at the museum indefinitely, perhaps even through the night.

Trip opened his toolbox and then went to work replacing the hinges on the door he'd broken. He had the odds and ends he needed to piece it together well enough to rehang it in the frame until he could get to a proper hardware store. It was good that he had plenty to do to keep his hands busy.

Was he really worried about being cut off from backup? Not having the current stats on street closings if they needed to make a quick escape out of here? Or was he just antsy like a penned-up stallion at the thought of spending the night alone with Charlotte? Stretched out on that long, comfy couch. Together.

And having to be a gentleman about it.

He'd better start getting used to the idea of folding himself into that little office chair, instead.

"If you check your watch one more time, I'm going to get nervous," Charlotte observed as she held the door for him and he screwed it into place. They'd worked long enough for their clothes to dry stiff and uncomfortably, and for her to get a smudge of dust across her cheek. "Or should I be nervous?"

"Don't be." He buzzed the last screw in with his power drill and let the rain and thunder outside beat down on his conscience and fill the silence for a moment. "Captain Cutler said KCPD and the city's road crew have closed more of the streets around here."

She tested the door, seeming pleased with his handiwork. "We knew that. That's why the curator decided keep the museum closed for the rest of the week. Driving around this side of downtown could be a little dicey until the weather breaks."

He removed the drill's battery pack and put his tools away. "Cutler also warned me that Brush Creek and some of the area's drainage ditches have topped their banks. The bridges will be out of commission soon. Maybe we should have rethought coming here tonight."

"This building is airtight to control the environment of the pieces on display. Unless we leave the doors and windows open—"

"Which we won't."

"—we're not going to get any water in here."

Her arms were hugged tightly around her waist, an indicator she was picking up on some of his worries, but she kept her chin at that determined angle. She was trying so hard to keep this evening as normal as possible that it made Trip miss the barking dog and ancient broadsword just a little. With one finger, he wiped the smudge off her cheek, then lingered near the soft curls of her hair. "Just know, we may be stuck here until the rain stops."

"As long as you and I are the only ones stuck here."

He twirled his finger into a wayward curl and tucked it

behind her ear. "No one else will get in. No one will take you from me, I promise."

Charlotte's eyes widened behind her glasses. "Take me?"

Trip pulled his hand away, tamping down a Neanderthal-like burst of heat inside him. She so did not mean that the way his body reacted to it. He'd just made a slip of the tongue and, ah hell. "We'd better get back to work."

Thank goodness there were plenty of boxes to lift and tables to set aright—plenty of work to stretch his muscles and get himself too tired to think about Charlotte in any way other than her protector.

He was helping her put the shelves back into place inside the storage closet when she spoke again. "So I have to figure out who Donny Kemp is now?"

Right. Keep talking about the case. "He's Montgomery's main suspect."

She stretched up on tiptoe, lifting a padded box packed with an assortment of stone knife blades and arrowheads. "I don't think I've even seen him since the kidnapping. It's not like I go to class reunions."

Trip took the box and set it on the top shelf over her head. "If it's him, he's changed his name. That probably means he's changed his looks, too. Maybe by something as drastic as cosmetic surgery—maybe just by growing a beard or dying his hair or wearing colored contacts."

The scents of rain and ancient stone and Charlotte stirred in his nose as she faced him. "But all I did was turn him down for a date. And I'm guessing I paid more for that lapse in judgment than he did."

"Maybe something else happened to him that you've forgotten, or didn't know about because you had the kidnapping and trial to contend with." Trip moved out of the closet, unable to find another way to curb the urge to tunnel his fingers into her hair, to dip his tongue into her sweet mouth and consume her, when he should be thinking about nothing else but keeping her safe.

"I'm calling Audrey. Maybe she can remember something about Donny. Although I still can't imagine how a computer geek can turn into the Rich Girl Killer."

He jerked at the soft touch of her hand on the back of his arm. Yeah, that was the way to get past this crazy desire. Put *that* look on her face.

While Charlotte hugged herself and turned toward her office, Trip waited to follow. "We don't have to understand the how and the why right now. Let's just see if we can find the guy. Call Audrey."

"AND YOU'RE SAFE?" Audrey asked.

Charlotte peeked over her shoulder at the man sitting on her office couch reading a book. The white T-shirt and worn jeans that hugged every hill and hollow of his powerful body, along with the work boots and imposing black gun he wore on his belt, seemed so at odds with the thick paperback and sternly focused eyes.

His big hands made the book look small, as if it was a fragile thing he was handling with great care. Trip was such a physical being, too big for her cramped, intellectual's office, maybe too big for her untested heart and the curiously powerful need she had to be close to him. Yet she knew he would show the woman he cared about the same diligent attention and reverent care that he showed that book.

When she felt the blush heat her cheeks, she turned back to the phone. "Yeah. There aren't many people out in the city tonight. Dad's the only one at home I told that I was coming here. And Trip's with me."

"Then you're safe."

"I know." Although they'd talked through dozens of possibilities, nothing had brought them any closer to identifying who their former classmate Donny Kemp had become. But by putting their heads together, they'd come up with a disturbing pattern that left Charlotte more and more convinced that he was the Rich Girl Killer. "You're sure about Val not hiring him at Gallagher Security?"

"Once you started asking questions, I remembered her saying that. He didn't pass the company's psych eval."

"Go figure."

"Yeah. He thought he could use their old school connection to guarantee himself a vice president's job, but Val said he gave her the creeps. That fits your timeline of him disappearing about five years ago."

"And you beat him out for the summer internship at Harvard?"

Charlotte could hear typing in the background. Her ever-efficient friend was probably transcribing this conversation with plans to show it to her boss, the district attorney. "I'm sure it was Daddy's influence as an alum that got me the position."

"Another example of an influential, wealthy woman keeping him from what he wanted. No wonder he hates us."

"He's disturbed, Char. There's nothing rational about terrorizing and killing us."

"I wonder how Gretchen hurt him." Unfortunately, with Gretchen's death, that would be a much harder connection to follow up on. "I can see him being heartbroken if she rejected him. But me?"

"Maybe Landon Turner wasn't the first guy the kidnappers approached about getting you to the dance." She heard some more typing, and a reminder from Alex in the background that it was late and they needed to get some sleep.

"I'm going to do some more research into the men who abducted you. Maybe there's a link to Donny we haven't discovered yet."

"Don't do anything risky."

"With this guy hanging over me?"

"Huh?"

The next voice she heard was Alex's. "Good night, Charlotte."

She laughed. "Good night, Alex."

"Good night, shrimp," Trip hollered from the couch.

"I heard that."

There was a breathy interchange on the other end of the call that made Charlotte wonder which one of her friends had stolen a kiss. "Give me that."

Oh, to be so free and trusting with someone she cared about.

"Charlotte?" Audrey, apparently, won the struggle. "I can't wait until this is over and we can hang out again. I miss you."

"I miss you, too."

"If I get any brainstorm about where Donny is or who he's become, I'll let you know, okay?"

"Same here. Bye, Aud."

After hanging up, Charlotte looked through the window of her office into the shadows of the secured storage area. She felt oddly cocooned by layers of darkness and bricks and rain. She tried to summon the warning voices inside her head that normally sent her into fits of panic when she was away from home and something wasn't familiar to her. But the voices were sleeping. Or wising up. Home was no longer a safe place. The world wasn't a safe place. But here, in this room, on this night, with this man…

"Did you and Audrey solve all the world's problems?"

"Enough for tonight." She untied her high-tops and

kicked them off on her way over to the couch. Tugging the quilt from the back of the sofa, she folded her legs in front of her, pretzel-style, in the opposite corner, hugging the quilt's softness in front of her. "So you think it's best if we stay put for the duration of the storm?"

He bookmarked his page with his finger. "Are you okay with that? With some of the streetlights out, I'd rather not risk running across any flash flooding in the dark. And I don't want to miss spotting an enemy before he sees us. But if you want out of here before daybreak, I'll find a way."

She shook her head with a smile. "I'm okay. This weather is just as dangerous for you as it is for me. So's… the other."

"I'll find a way," he repeated. She believed him.

"No. This won't be the first time I've slept here. Though, admittedly, it hasn't been through the night. Or, with a man." He gave her a look that pricked a riot of answering goose bumps across Charlotte's skin. But when he turned back to his book, the excitement faded and she tried to blame the electricity she still felt sparking through her on the storm outside. "What are you reading?"

He held up J.R.R. Tolkien's *The Return of the King*.

"Sorry, I was on the phone longer than I intended. I didn't mean to be distracting."

"You weren't."

"But you've only turned a couple of pages in the last…" Charlotte sank back into the cushions as she heard the incredulity in her own voice. "I'm sorry."

If he took any offense at her comment on the slowness of his reading, he didn't respond. Charlotte knew books, loved books. And when the uncomfortable silence between them continued, she began to talk books.

"Has Aragorn led his men against the gates of Mordor yet?"

With a huff of breath that seemed to fill the entire office, Trip tucked a slip of paper into his book and set it on the table beside him. He startled her when he spun in his seat to face her. "I don't want to read."

"Just tell me to shut up. I guess I am a little nervous about staying here all night. The last time I didn't go home, I was being held—"

He reached over, grabbed her foot and dragged her clear across the sofa, until her knee was wedged against his thigh and the quilt was the only thing between them. "I want to kiss you."

Charlotte's pulse thundered in her ears. "What's stopping you?"

"Don't want to scare you off."

"You really think *you* can scare me more than anything else that's happened this week?" She brushed her fingers across the masculine stubble of beard on his jaw, and the sea of goose bumps returned.

He slid his hands beneath her bottom and lifted her squarely onto his lap so that she straddled him, facing him. "Scared yet?"

"No." Although she was trembling, she braced her hands on his shoulders, waiting for the warning voices to kick in, to tell her she wasn't ready for this. But the searing heat gathering beneath her thighs and in between was saying something very different.

Trip pulled the quilt from between them and tossed it to the far end of the sofa, pulling her close enough that she could feel his body heat through their clothes, but the soft rasp of cotton knit rubbing against the wilting crispness of her blouse kept them apart. He lowered his head, his warm breath fanning across her skin, his eyes targeting her mouth. "Scared?"

She slid her hands behind his neck and up against his golden-brown hair. "Not of you. Not of this."

He rested his forehead against hers and inhaled a deep, stuttering breath. His eyes were still on her mouth, his hands were roaming with aimless, grasping friction up and down her hips and back. "Cripes, honey. I want you. I want all of you."

His strong thighs were wedged between hers, leaving her open and vulnerable and aching to be filled. Charlotte felt her temperature rising from the inside out, or perhaps it was the outside in. She only knew there were sparks of lightning and swirling storm clouds of need building in the tips of her breasts and every pore of her skin. And Trip wasn't kissing her yet.

"Trip," she begged. "Please."

"I never want to do anything that makes you look at me with fear in your eyes again. That tears me up inside. I'd rather take a bullet than see you crying or afraid of me again."

In the raging awakening of desires denied and put on hold for too long in her life, a surprising voice of compassion whispered to her. He'd admitted, not that long ago, that she had the power to hurt him. Joseph Jones, Jr., might be big, bad and bossy on the outside, but inside, her brawny protector had a weakness. And if she'd hidden away from the world for ten long years because she'd felt too weak to face her fears, why should she expect Trip to willingly risk what frightened him the most after only a week?

Charlotte rose up on her knees and took Trip's face in her hands, looking him straight in the eye. "I'll tell you if I want you to stop, all right? If I get scared for even one moment—you'll stop?"

"Yes." Those eyes never lied.

Neither did hers. "Don't stop."

Trip closed his mouth over hers, tunneling his fingers into her hair to hold her lips against his when the force of his kiss pushed her away. Charlotte wound her arms around his neck and held on, opening her mouth to every foray of his tongue, welcoming his every touch.

When holding each other close wasn't close enough, Trip fell back across the sofa, pulling her on top of him. He kneaded her bottom, branding her through her jeans. Then his fingers slid higher, finding their way beneath her blouse, their calloused exploration striking heat against her cool skin. Her breasts pillowed against his harder chest, the ache in them eased by the contact, then stoked again as his hands began to move her up and down his body, creating a slow, delicious friction fueled by fiery kisses along her jaw and throat.

She was trapped in a torrent of hands and hardness and kisses and heat, with no outlet to ease the storm building inside her. Pressure gathered and heated in the heavy dampness between her thighs. And when her aching need fell open around the treelike hardness of Trip's thigh, she instinctively squeezed and rubbed, desperate for the release his body promised.

"Easy, honey," he rasped against her damaged ear, tenderly running his tongue around its delicate shell, arousing nerve endings that had never been touched this way before. "Easy."

As Charlotte moaned with frustrated need, he sat up, spilling her into his lap. He kissed her swollen lips, apologizing for the unwanted distance between them. His fingers moved to the buttons of her blouse, freeing the top two before peeling the whole thing off over her head so that he could pull her close and kiss her again.

Now she understood. He was delaying what she wanted, not denying her. A quick study in any subject, Charlotte reached for the hem of his T-shirt and tossed it to the floor beside her blouse. While he unhooked his belt and carefully removed his gun and badge to set both carefully within arm's reach on the floor beneath the sofa, she explored the responsive gasps and moans she elicited when she smoothed her palms across his taut male nipples, pinched one between her thumb and finger, eased its torment by laving it with her tongue.

"Charlotte," he growled with pleasure, flinching when she tasted the other nipple, shifting beneath her and letting her feel that he was just as powerfully aroused as she was. His hands moved to the clasp of her bra. "Careful what you ask for."

When the bra disappeared, he covered her with his big hands, squeezing, flicking his thumbs across each pebbled tip, testing the weight that seemed to grow heavier with every caress. Each touch sent a pulse of electricity straight to her weepy thighs. And when he closed his hot mouth over the first hard tip, she cried out his name as a lightning bolt of pure, raw heat sparked deep in her core.

"Trip?" Even as she clutched her fingers behind his head and held his mouth against her to ride out the exquisite torment, she was squirming, seeking, struggling to find that ultimate release his hands and mouth had primed her for. "Trip," she groaned.

"I know," he murmured against her breast. "I know, honey," he whispered against her ear. "I know."

He reclaimed her mouth in one hard, quick kiss and then put his skilled hands to use, deftly removing the last of their clothes, spreading the quilt beneath them, lying back on the sofa and stretching her on top of him. She nibbled at the edge of his square, unshaven jaw, marveled at the textural differences between her smooth legs and his harder male thighs, worked through an odd blend of excitement and trepidation at the pulsing length of his arousal nudging against her hip—as he pulled a foil pouch from his wallet and tore it open.

"I'm not on the pill or anything," she admitted, holding her breath and tilting her face up to his, worrying that he might have forgotten he was her first. Trying not to listen to a very old voice that tried to tell her she was plain and brainy and flaky and not the type of woman that a man like Trip would really—

"Shh." He hushed those doubts, twirling a wild curl around his finger and smiling as if he thought it was the most beautiful thing in the world. "Are you having second thoughts?"

She shook her head. "I never thought I'd be doing anything like this...that I'd want to. But I do."

He pulled her up to his mouth and kissed her softly, tenderly. "I'll protect you in this, too, honey. Trust me."

Charlotte had no idea how many pounds of strength and power were lying tightly leashed beneath her. But she wasn't afraid. This was right. Out of all the craziness and terror in her life, she knew this one thing was right. "I do trust you, Trip. I do."

Several slow, deliberate kisses later, and the storm was brewing again. Trip had sheathed himself and rolled Charlotte beneath him. He took the bulk of his weight off her with his elbows and entered her in one long, deep stroke, holding himself still inside her. Squeezing her eyes shut against the initial pain, the initial shock of this ultimate expression of intimacy and trust, Charlotte held her breath.

But he stroked her face, kissed the swell of her breast, kissed her lips, waiting with tender patience for the pain to pass, for her body to adjust to his size, for the pressure to build to an almost unbearable mix of frustration and anticipation. "Trip, please." She was feverish, panting, ready to burst. "Please."

"Look at me, Charlotte." He took off her glasses and set them aside, making one request of her. "I need to see your eyes."

She opened them wide, looked up into the purposeful determination and caring light she saw in his gaze. Trip nodded and began to move inside her.

And when the love and need became too much for her heart and body to bear, she wrapped her heels behind his thighs and buttocks, wound her arms around his shoulders and covered her body with the weight of his. With the roar of his release, he unleashed the storm inside her and pleasure rained down around them both.

Chapter Twelve

So the eccentric brainiac with the ear-piercing whistle had some distinctly feminine wiles lurking inside her, after all.

It was a dangerous one-two punch straight at Trip's heart that he was still mulling over as Charlotte nestled closely to his side and snored softly against his chest. She'd made herself as vulnerable to him as a woman could be, giving him the gift of her body and her passion. She'd been so curiously eager, yet so achingly innocent—bold and giving and…trusting.

Twice.

He brushed the toffee curls off her forehead and bent his head to press a kiss to the crown of her hair, grinning at the innate spirit of adventure that Kansas City's most reclusive heiress had unbottled these past few days he'd known her. An hour after he'd exhausted himself making her first time as perfect for her as he knew how, she'd nudged him awake, whispered a request into his ear, climbed onto his lap—and he hadn't been able to resist her.

He couldn't imagine two more different people than him and Charlotte. Yet he couldn't imagine being without her now.

Feeling her shiver in her sleep, Trip pulled the quilt up over her naked back, snugged her more tightly in his arms and listened to the storm quieting into a steady rain outside. The past few hours had been perfect moments sliced out of time. Isolated from the rest of the world, with thick walls and heavy locks and the weather itself keeping the danger stalking her temporarily at bay, they could talk and cuddle, read to each other and make love. The two of them together could work.

But what about life outside these walls?

What about when his job took him out on a late-night call to any corner of the city? What about when he wanted to take her out and introduce her to his friends and she was so terrified of the outside world that she wouldn't leave her rooms or this museum? What about when her father compared her PhD with his community college degree, or her trust fund with his government paycheck?

Once the Rich Girl Killer was caught and he knew she was safe, how did Miss Charlotte Mayweather and Officer Trip Jones work?

He wasn't smart enough to have the answers yet. He only knew that he'd give his life for this woman. She deserved to feel secure in her world and live whatever life she chose to lead.

And he'd give her his heart. If that was what she wanted.

Yeah, she already had that.

If.

THE CELL PHONE ON the desk was ringing.

Trip awoke, instantly alert, instantly aware of Charlotte's distress as she moaned and squirmed against him in her sleep.

"Make it stop," she murmured.

"Charlotte?"

Something wet and warm stung his skin. Ah, hell. She

was crying. She was dreaming some damn-awful nightmare and she was crying.

Trip sat up, pulling her into his arms and gently shaking her awake. "Charlotte? Wake up, honey. It's a bad
dream."

"Stop. Make it…"

The phone rang again and suddenly she was awake. She
pushed her hair off her face and tugged the quilt up over
her breasts. Her eyes were narrowed, searching, as if she
was disoriented and surprised to find herself naked, her
body tangled up with his.

"Charlotte?" *Please don't be afraid of me. Please don't
regret what happened. Please don't give me that look.*

She whirled around as the phone continued to ring.
"What time is it? Where are my glasses? Is that him?"

"Right here." He handed her her red glasses, scooted
off the sofa and picked up his shorts as he looked at the
phone. "It's almost three in the morning. Here."

He handed her the phone and she shied away. "Is it
him?"

Trip shook his head. "It says 'Kyle.'"

"Kyle?" Her fear transformed into shock. Her posture
relaxed and she reached for the phone, verifying the same
name he had read. "Why on earth would my stepbrother
be calling me at this time of night?"

Trip quickly dressed and rearmed himself with his
Glock and spare 9 mil magazine, not liking the snippets
of conversation he could hear on this end of the phone.

"Where? Brush Creek Boulevard and Hazelton. Got it."
Trip laid out her clothes and politely turned his back as she
followed his lead and got dressed. "Why did Harper let her
leave by herself? I'll see what we can do from here. Yes,
I'll tell him."

As soon as she set the phone on the desk beside him,

Trip turned to see her zip up her jeans and, button by button, cover up those beautiful curves and the memory of how responsive they'd been to his every touch. He hated the grim line of her mouth that was still pink and swollen from the abrasion of his five o'clock shadow and hungry kisses.

Something was seriously wrong in Charlotte's world and Trip didn't waste words. "What is it?"

"Apparently, my stepsister, Bailey, was out on a date. She was driving home in this weather and her car stalled out crossing a flooded street." She sat to pull on her socks and red tennis shoes. "Either she's trapped in her car because of the water or she's scared to get out because of the neighborhood and the blackouts—I don't know. He said she was pretty upset and hard to understand."

"She should call 9-1-1."

Charlotte tied her second shoe and stood. "Kyle did."

Trip blocked the door. "Then what does he want from you?"

"It's only a couple of blocks from here. We can get to her before the emergency vehicles or Kyle can. At least keep her company until help arrives."

"*I* can keep her company. You're staying put." He left the office, pulling out his own phone. "Give me the address. As soon as I phone this in to Captain Cutler, I'll go."

"She's *my* sister." She quickened her pace to hurry after him. "Trip, think about it. It's the middle of the night, she's wrecked her car, she's all alone—you might be a little... scary."

"Wrong choice of words."

"On first impression. I meant what I said before. I'm not afraid of you now. Damn it, Trip." She grabbed his arm and asked him to stop and face her. "Are you telling me you didn't change your mind about me, too?" She had him there. "You're probably still not too sure when I'm going to wig out on you next, are you?"

"You're right. With you, I never know what to expect. I just know it's going to be interesting." He liked the idea of leaving her alone and unprotected a little less than he liked the idea of her being out in the open with him, anyway. "Put on your coat. And this."

He pulled the Kevlar vest from the hook where it had been drying and strapped it around her chest and back.

"We'll make this as quick as we can. You stay right beside me and do whatever I say the moment I say it. You're still my first priority, understand?"

She nodded. Smiled. Tugged on his shirt and pulled him down for a quick, surprising kiss. "Thank you. For everything."

THIS WASN'T RIGHT. Where was the damn dog?

He moved to a different position on top of the Mayweather Museum's roof and used his scope to follow the couple hurrying hand in hand through the rain. He sat back for a moment, needing time to sort things out.

His plan was to shoot both the bodyguard and the dog. Then Charlotte would be easy to take. She'd trust him dressed like this. With her boyfriend on the ground, bleeding to death, she'd be happy to see him.

He went back to his original position and scanned the back of the SUV. Had they left him there? Was the dog inside the building? It would be easy enough to get inside again, but that would mean changing his plan, altering his timetable. And he was ready to strike. Tonight. His hands itched with the need to close around Charlotte's throat.

But he'd always been so careful about his plans, so precise. He couldn't stand details that were out of place.

But the opportunity was here. The time was now. She'd be all alone.

He released his breath, calmed every muscle, picked up his duffel bag and followed.

TRIP WAS SOAKED TO the skin and feeling like a rookie again. When Captain Cutler and Sergeant Delgado and even that gung-ho newbie, Randy Murdock, arrived, they'd call him twenty kinds of fool for walking into an exposed, indefensible scene like this one.

If someone wanted to ambush Charlotte, this was the perfect setup. It was a lot easier to be seen than to see from this vantage point. Abandoned streets. No lights for two city blocks. High-rise hotels on one side of the creek and adjacent roadway, two- and three-story shops and apartment buildings on the other—with plenty of open space in between where anyone with bright lights and a four-wheel-drive transport could reach them.

"Are you sure this is Bailey's car?" he shouted over the roar of Brush Creek hitting the concrete abutment on the underside of the Hazelton bridge and swirling past the silver sports car pinned between the bank and the bridge's outer wall.

"It looks like it. I don't know her license plate, though."

"Stay put."

He left Charlotte up on the road where the water was only ankle deep and waded into the rushing flood current with his flashlight. Testing each step to make sure he wasn't washed on down the creek, he approached the bobbing vehicle from behind, gritting his teeth against the abrasive sound of steel grinding against concrete. The water was pushing against his hips by the time he fought his way to the upstream side of the car.

"Is she in there?" He heard Charlotte's shout like a faint echo.

He shined his light inside the car. "No. It's empty."

He swung his light around, peering through the dimness of rain and shadows to see if he could spot any foot traffic on the sidewalks or streets. Deserted. Dead. They were the only souls out on a night like this.

"Is there any way to know if someone else could have picked her up? Her boyfriend, maybe? What the…?" The feeling of dread turned to fury as Trip's light hit the floor-board beneath the steering wheel. He flipped the steel flashlight in his hand and busted through the passenger-side window.

"What are you doing?" Charlotte shouted.

His eyes hadn't deceived him. The two-by-four wedged beneath the accelerator told him this was a trap, that the wreck had been staged, that the woman he loved was in mortal danger and he might be too late to keep her safe.

He plunged toward the higher ground, waving Charlotte back to the apartments across the street. "Get back to the sidewalk! I want you out of sight right now!"

"Trip?" She was frightened by his warning, but she was moving.

He stumbled once in his haste to get to her and swallowed a mouthful of gritty water. He spit it out and floated a few yards off course before he found his feet again. "Call your sister right now."

She had her phone out, was dialing. "Now you're scaring me."

"I don't think anyone went into the water in that car. It's a setup. Move."

It *was* a setup. Only Charlotte wasn't the target.

Yet.

Trip spotted the subtle movement in the darkness on the

roof of the apartments. He angled his light and caught its fleeting reflection off the lens of a rifle scope. "Run! Get back to the museum! Don't stop until that door's locked behind you!"

He reached for his gun.

But the bullet tore through his shoulder and knocked him back into the rushing water before it ever left his holster.

"TRIP!"

Stay in the moment. Stay in the moment!

Charlotte stood frozen long enough to see him disappear beneath the surface of the water and for something darker to bubble up in his place. Blood? Oh, God.

"Trip!"

Rain smudged her glasses and tears blurred her vision, leaving her blind to the buffeting assault of noise around her—racing water, drumming rain, distant footsteps, her pounding heart. She needed Trip. Needed to get to him. Needed to help.

What the hell was going on? Was that a gunshot? Was Trip hurt? Was he dead?

She swiped the water from her glasses and scrubbed the tears from her face. She took one step off the sidewalk. Took a second and a third toward the rushing flood. The grinding crunch of crushing metal grated against her eardrums.

Bailey's car groaned as the rising water freed it from the bridge and carried it silently downstream.

"Oh, my God."

The water had taken Trip, too. She was paralyzed with fear. Alone. In the open. Trip was gone and she was helpless.

People can change. You want to change. You can do something about it.

Trip's words from the day of Richard's funeral rang in her ears. For ten years, she was trapped and afraid—helpless to face the world. In the span of a week, a friend had been murdered, and her nightmares had become a real, living thing. She'd met a man, made love, fallen in love… and refused to lose him.

She could change. She had changed.

Trip Jones had her back. And, by God, she was going to have his.

She pulled out her phone. She could call his captain, Michael Cutler. They were already on their way after Trip's call. But she'd tell them to hurry. Hurry! Get SWAT Team One here—they'd know what to do. Only, she had no idea what the number was. Idiot. Call 9-1-1.

A doorway opened and closed in the darkness behind her.

Run! Don't stop!

"Charlotte? Charlotte!"

Someone was shouting her name.

Run!

Charlotte's body reacted even before her brain fully kicked in. She took off, moving her legs. She stumbled at first, and the weight of the Kevlar threw her off balance and she landed on her hands and knees in the flooding street. But just as quickly as the water soaked through the vest, coat and clothes to chill her skin, she pushed back to her feet. She lifted her heavy wet shoes and jogged, stretching her legs, picking up speed. And then she remembered she damn well knew how to run and took off—splashing, speeding through the dark and the rain.

"Charlotte!"

Don't look. Run.

One block. Two. Turn.

The floodwaters that covered the sidewalks grew shallow, then disappeared by the time she crossed the street to the Mayweather's back entrance. Her lungs burned. She was cold. She was scared. She skirted the Dumpster and entered the alley lot.

And skidded to a stop.

Her mouth dropped open, she was breathing hard. For one split second she flashed back in time.

White van. Danger. "Don't hurt me…"

She started to mouth the words that had haunted her since that fateful night ten years earlier.

But she blinked the rain from her eyes, blanked the memory from her thoughts. She stayed in the moment.

Yes, there was a van parked in the alley next to Trip's SUV. But it wasn't white. And the man climbing out of the passenger side and hurrying toward her wasn't her enemy. "Kyle!"

Charlotte ran forward to meet him. She threw her arms around his neck and hugged him, reassured to see the familiar face. "Thank God. Have you heard from Bailey? She wasn't in her car. Please tell me she got out okay, that she's someplace safe."

Kyle patted her back, then left a brotherly arm around her shoulders as he started to walk. "Bailey's at home. She's fine."

"Thank God. I was so worried. We need to get help, Trip's hurt. Someone shot him. I'm not going to believe he's dead. I can't lose him." She took several steps with Kyle, then stopped and twisted away from his arm as the initial rush of relief cleared and his words truly registered. "Wait a minute. Bailey's at home? Why didn't you call me? Trip risked his life to save her. Why didn't you call?"

Kyle's blue eyes squinted against the rain. "Someone shot your boyfriend? Lucky break for me."

"What?"

"Get in the van, Charlotte."

And then she saw the gun in Kyle's hand. And the bruiser in a security guard uniform sliding open the van's side door. Along with the uniformed man behind the wheel, they were all waiting. To take her.

"No!" She backed away, tried to run.

"Get in the damn van!" But rough hands grabbed her, kicking and screaming, picked her up off the ground and threw her inside. Once the door slammed shut, Kyle turned down the collar of his raincoat and sat on an overturned crate, facing her while his silent, oversize friend bound her wrists and ankles with duct tape. "You've already made this more difficult than it needed to be, so be a good girl and shut up."

When déjà vu should have kicked in at this re-creation of her kidnapping, it didn't. She was too angry at her stepbrother, too worried for Trip—too different a woman from what she'd once been to not want to fight back. She was firmly in this horrid moment, and fought back with the only weapon left her. Her words.

"You're the copycat—the one who's been aping the Rich Girl Killer, trying to drive me over the edge into crazy land. Why?"

He pulled a handkerchief from inside his coat and wiped the gun dry. "You can't keep spending your money, Charlotte. Because it's not there. I haven't put it all back yet. And Jackson can't find out."

"This is about money?"

"Yes, damn it! Millions and millions of it. These fine young men work for a friend of mine and are here to help me get what I owe them."

She flinched at the tearing of her wet skin beneath the tape. "How about asking for a loan, Kyle? Why resort to this? Why kill a man?"

"I didn't kill anybody. Yet." He slipped the gun into his pocket and pulled out a long scarf. "I'm just being resourceful. I thought I could take advantage of all your paranoia and the way you kept flipping out with this Rich Girl Killer after you. I asked Jackson to have you declared incompetent—to give me legal guardianship over your trust fund."

"You stole money from my trust fund?"

"It's called embezzlement, Char. I tried to live up to Jackson's faith in me, but all my investments went belly up. So since you never pay any attention to the family business, I took your money to hide the losses and repay the man these two work for."

She eyed thug one and thug two and got a pretty good idea of what was going on. "A criminal? You got involved in something illegal and lost Dad's money and stole mine to hide your mistake?"

Kyle tossed the scarf to the man with the tape. "But you keep giving it away like it's water. There's no more to give away, Charlotte, you crazy bitch. I can't afford to lose my job or Jackson's support."

"Or get on their bad side?" Thug one was wrapping the scarf between his fists. "You don't think killing me is going to turn Dad into your enemy?"

"Me? But don't you see the brilliant setup? The Rich Girl Killer is going to murder you. I copied everything he was doing to you—I intensified it by shooting at you when you were stuck in the middle of all those people, on display for the public and press. I poisoned your stupid mutt. It's all leading up to your death at the hands of a notorious serial killer. I'll be sure to say something nice at your funeral."

Should she tell him that the RGK's MO was to strangle a woman with his hands, not use a ligature like a scarf? "Did you kill Richard?"

"No." Kyle tapped the driver's seat in some unspoken signal. "But that day at his funeral, I saw how you reacted when he contacted you. I upped the ante by pushing you harder to crack."

"I'm saner now than I've ever been, Kyle. More grounded. Looks like you failed at that job, too."

Rage reddened her stepbrother's face and he rose up, swinging his arm through the air and backhanding her across the face and sending her glasses flying. Charlotte fell to the floor of the van, her mouth tasting like copper, her head ringing. "You crazy Daddy's princess. You screwed up your life, but I'm not going to let you screw up mine." Kyle glanced over his shoulder to the front seat. "I don't want to do this here. Drive."

"I can't."

"What do you mean?" Kyle moved behind the driver's seat.

Thug one took his seat on the overturned crate to spy out the front, as well. Charlotte spotted a blur of red and rolled toward them, praying they were her glasses. Victory. But as she put them back on her face, her success was short-lived.

"Run him down. We don't need any witnesses."

What? Despite the bonds on her hands and ankles, Charlotte scrambled to her feet to look through the windshield, too. Her heart sang and sank all at the same time.

Trip.

He was standing at the end of the alley, his chest heaving in and out with every breath, soaked to the bone. Blood was turning the left shoulder of his white T-shirt crimson. He stood with his legs braced apart, his right arm raised in the air, with his gun pointing straight at them.

"Drive, you idiot!" Kyle shouted, stomping on the driver's foot atop the accelerator. "He can't play chicken with a speeding vehicle and win."

The van kicked into gear. The tires spun on the wet pavement, then found traction and lurched forward. Charlotte tumbled to the back of the van, screaming all the way. "No!"

TRIP STARED DOWN THE van. His muscles were shaking after a swim and a run and the sudden demand to be still. His chest ached with every breath, and he was guessing the bullet that had hit his shoulder had nicked a lung as well. His left arm no longer screamed in pain, but hung numb and, for the moment, useless at his side. He never wanted to be this wet again. But the rain was a good thing. It had masked his approach, and the chill of it hitting his skin kept him awake, alert, when every drop of blood seeping inside and out was pulling him toward sleep.

His gaze drifted once to Kyle Austin—now he understood why he'd never liked that guy. But then he turned his attention back to the business end of things and focused all his attention on the driver. *That* was his target.

He'd seen the scuffle in the van, had raged at the knowledge that Charlotte was the one being harmed. But he knew his training, knew what he had to do.

One man alone didn't take on an entire army. Wounded and outnumbered, he'd be of no use to Charlotte if he charged that van. A smart warrior used his experience and his surroundings and whatever skills he could to obtain and keep his advantage.

He was the biggest, baddest cop on SWAT Team One— the immovable force who held his ground and intimidated his enemy. He had hands that he'd learned over the years were good for a couple of things—fixing what was broken, making what was needed, protecting what was right and loving a woman. Loving his woman.

"I've got your back, honey."

The tires squealed on the wet pavement. By the time the stench of burnt rubber teased his nose, the van was racing toward him.

Trip stilled his hand and squeezed the trigger.

"No!" CHARLOTTE SCREAMED as the van hurtled toward Trip. Milliseconds flashed by like eons. "Move!"

She heard a gunshot. The windshield cracked and the driver slumped forward. There was another gunshot and another.

"Get him out of there!" Kyle yelled.

The van lurched from one side of the alley to the other, careening off the bricks, narrowly missing a power pole. Every time Charlotte made it to her feet, she was thrown to the floor of the van.

"Get him!" Kyle had a hold of the steering wheel now, and Thug one tried to pull the dead driver out of the way. "You son of a…"

The van picked up speed. Charlotte was on her feet. Kyle turned the van straight toward Trip.

"No!" She hopped forward, then threw herself at Kyle's back, knocking him into the dashboard before he could get into the driver's seat.

The van veered to the right, Trip flew into the air and they slammed into the trash Dumpster and skidded to a crashing stop. Charlotte hit the floor one more time, but the Kevlar protected her from the crate and flying debris that threw her into the van's side door.

She was woozy for the first few seconds her world was still, her stomach roiling from the killer carnival ride. Her body was bruised, but as soon as her head was clear, she shoved aside the debris, ignored the moans of her step-brother and abductors, and pushed open the side door and tumbled out.

"Trip?" She clawed at the duct tape, but it held fast. So she crawled to her feet and hopped around the Dumpster. "Trip!"

He was lying in the middle of the road, scraped up, bleeding. His leg was twisted at a grotesque angle, telling her it was broken. But he was alive. She saw his chest heaving for breath, watched him trying to push himself up onto his right arm, heard him groan in agony and fall back to the pavement. "Charlotte?"

"Trip."

As she fell to her knees beside him, she heard the screech of brakes and a trio of clipped, angry shouts.

"Get a bus here, now! Murdock, van! Sarge, I want those men in handcuffs, now!"

Charlotte leaned over her fallen hero to wipe the rain from his eyes, nose and mouth, and to press a gentle kiss to his scraped-up jaw. "I thought you were dead."

"Not yet, honey." Two long blinks and the fading focus of his handsome eyes revealed just how badly he was hurt, though. His fingers brushed against her thigh and she reached down, taking his hand between hers. "Are you hurt? Did they hurt you?"

Three dark figures swarmed past her. "I'm okay. I'm scared again. For you. But I'm okay."

"Engine's off!"

"Drop your weapon!"

"Get on the ground! I said get down!"

"Go, captain—we've got it covered."

Michael Cutler was suddenly kneeling down on the opposite side of Trip, taking a quick assessment of his injuries and calling it in on his radio. "Officer down, I repeat, officer down. Gunshot wound. Vehicular strike. Where the hell is that bus?"

He immediately pressed his hand against Trip's shoulder, and Trip winced with a curse.

"Gotta stop the bleeding, big guy." The captain pulled a knife from his belt and reached across Trip's chest to slice the tape from Charlotte's wrists. "Are you hurt, Miss Mayweather?"

She shook her head. "Trip saved me. If they'd taken me away in the van...they were going to kill me."

Was the captain smiling? "I didn't think he'd let that happen." Then he was by-the-book serious again. "Open your eyes, Jones. Stay with me. I need a report."

Trip's eyes slowly blinked open. "Yes, sir."

Rafe Delgado knelt down beside Charlotte. "That looks like a bad break. We'd better not move him."

"You squeamish, Miss Mayweather?" Cutler asked.

"No."

"Good." He grabbed her hands and placed them over the bullet wound on Trip's shoulder, pressing them down the way he had. "Feel how hard I'm pushing? Keep that same pressure there—no more, no less." He shrugged out of a backpack and pulled out a first aid kit, ripping open a couple of giant gauze pads. "What's the situation, Delgado?"

Rafe reached down and braced Trip's other shoulder to keep him from twisting with the pain. "Easy, big guy. You know, you're supposed to jump out of the way when a vehicle comes speeding toward you."

Trip nodded. "If there wasn't a lady present, I'd be flipping you off."

"Sarge?" the captain prompted.

"Bus and backup are en route. We've got one dead body and two perps handcuffed on the ground. One of them tried to take out Murdock. He won't be fathering children for the next month or so."

"Ouch." Trip grinned, but his eyes were drifting shut again.

She felt his blood seeping through her fingers, tears burning in her eyes and spilling over. "Trip? Don't leave me now, sweetheart. Don't leave me."

With a jerky movement, he lifted his hand and wiped the tears from her cheek. "Don't do that, okay? That'll really kill me."

Then his hand flopped down against her leg and his eyes drifted shut. "Trip!"

"Get the blanket out of my truck," the captain ordered. "He's going into shock."

Trip murmured between his lips. "I got your back, honey. I told you I did."

"I know."

"I love you."

She knew that, too. "And you say I'm crazy."

Chapter Thirteen

Trip checked the clock on the wall and wondered how much longer he had to listen to Rafe Delgado and Randy Murdock debate who should be given the credit for arresting Kyle Austin and his surviving band of would-be kidnappers—SWAT Team One or Spencer Montgomery?

The persnickety detective had probably been hassling Charlotte with questions about that night at the museum. Was there any connection to the Rich Girl Killer beyond the obvious copycat crimes? Did she see who'd shot him? He hadn't. All he could identify was a man on the roof with rifle and scope—his guess was the RGK. His guess had become Montgomery's leading theory when the lab's ballistics check proved that the bullet the doctors had taken out of Trip's chest didn't match the handguns they'd taken off Kyle and his goons.

Who was there to protect her from Montgomery? Or family members and staff she shouldn't trust? Who was going to play fetch with her dog and keep her company in those lonely, isolated rooms where she didn't belong?

Nineteen hours. Nineteen hours without seeing Charlotte, and all these yahoos would tell him was that she was fine. That she looked good. That she'd asked about him.

He'd been through surgery, had been hooked up to this pulley contraption to keep his set leg level and elevated.

His leg itched like crazy inside its cast, and the stitched-up holes in his left arm and lung ached whenever he moved too far one way or the other. The nurse had offered him another round of painkillers, but why would he want to be drifting in la-la land when he could be refereeing a conversation between these guys?

"Look, guys." Murdock and Delgado stopped their bickering and Captain Cutler set aside the magazine he'd been reading in the corner. "I appreciate you coming to check on me and all—"

Captain Cutler strolled to the bed. "The doctors say you're here for a week, that you'll be off for rehab for a good three months, and that you'll need light duty for another month after that. I figure you can man the dispatch desk or drive the truck for us."

Delgado scoffed. "Hey, that's my job."

"I'm losing my team by attrition here. I'm going to wind up bringing Kincaid back from paternity leave early or promoting someone new to the team, and I haven't got this one trained yet." He winked at Murdock.

"Should I be insulted?"

"No, you should leave," Trip suggested. "You should all leave."

"My point is…" Michael Cutler was a man used to giving orders, not taking them. From anybody. "You've been beat up pretty bad, big guy. I want you back on my team. But I want you in one piece."

Trip's frustration waned for a moment. These really were good people, good friends. "Are you being mushy with me, sir?"

A light flashed out in the hallway, and all at once there was a buzz of conversations and another couple of flashes, and altogether too much hubbub for a place where patients were supposed to heal and get some rest.

Michael Cutler squeezed Trip's good shoulder and grinned. "I don't do mushy. I'm stalling for time."

His friends stepped back as the noise outside in the hallway grew louder. Then a couple of familiar faces popped through the doorway. "Hey, shrimp."

Trip smiled as his best friend, Alex Taylor, came forward to shake his hand. "Good to see, big guy. I'm tellin' ya, if I'd have been there, you'd still be in one piece."

"Oh, so now you think you're funny?"

"I think you missed me."

"Settle down, you two." His fiancée, Audrey, leaned over and pressed a kiss to his cheek. That explained the flashing cameras. Pretty heiresses who'd gone into hiding because a killer wanted them dead tended to draw a crowd when they went out in public. Trip tucked away the wistful thought of Charlotte and fixed a smile on his face. "We brought you a present." She turned to the door. "Okay!"

The scrabbling of paws on the hospital's slick linoleum floor might be the second-best sound he could have heard right then. "Max!"

The black-and-tan torpedo ran into the room and launched himself onto Trip's bed. "Whoa. Hey. Ow. Good to see you, buddy. We survived, you and me. We survived."

It took a moment to wrestle the mutt down to his good side, accept a friendly lick or two and then inspect the red vest he was wearing. "Certified Therapy Dog?"

Captain Cutler whispered an order. "And now, we leave the room."

Audrey clicked her tongue and took Max's leash. "C'mon, boy. Aunt Audrey is going to find you a snack."

One moment, his hospital room was in chaos, the next—it was serenely perfect.

"Hey, Trip."

Charlotte Mayweather stood in his doorway. Her beautiful hair curling around her face, her high-topped tennis shoes on and her eyes smiling, beautiful, behind her red glasses.

"Get over here."

She ran to his bed, was far too cautious about winding her arms around his neck, and gently kissed him. Screw that. He was hungry, he was needy, and his eyes were inexplicably tearing up. Trip snatched her around the waist and pulled her right onto the bed with him, claiming her mouth and pouring out his love and feeling with his one good hand that she was well and truly here with him and she was all right.

When he let her come up for air, she touched his cheek, wiping away a tear. She stretched up to press the tenderest of kisses against his brow. "Don't do that sweetheart. It tears me up inside to see you hurting."

She smiled wisely, gently throwing his one phobia back at him. "I'm okay, Trip. I just needed to see you. And now I'm okay."

"God, I missed you." He grabbed a handful of her jacket and pulled her close again, kissing her cheek, kissing her neck. Her hands were on his face and in his hair as she returned the assault, kiss for kiss. "I was so worried something would happen to you. KCPD arrested your stepbrother, but the RGK is still out there." He kissed her hair, kissed her ear. Stopped himself short. "Hey, look at these pretty little earrings." He pulled far enough away to look her in the eye. "They're beautiful. They fit your ear perfectly."

"It's the new me. You said I could change. And I'm changing." She turned in the bed, adjusting her position so that she could lie beside him, with her head on his shoulder and her hand splayed possessively at the center of his chest. "I'm not hurting anything, am I? I know I have an unintentional habit of—"

"No." He draped his right arm behind her back and claimed an equally possessive handful of her beautiful bottom. "Nothing hurts with you here like this." A moment passed before he frowned and asked, "How did you get here?"

He felt her smiling through the thin cotton of his hospital gown. "Audrey and Alex drove me."

"I meant, this isn't your home or the museum. You've got Max with you, but, you're out in the world." He pressed a kiss to the crown of her hair. "You okay with that?"

She nodded. "It's a little scary. I'm not ready to drive myself yet or dive into the Plaza crowd when they turn on the lights Thanksgiving night. But I'm fine. I knew my driver, knew my destination—and I was so lonely without you. Like I said, I'm changing. I feel stronger now. I don't want to be a shut-in anymore. I want to live. And love."

"That makes two of us."

They lay together for several minutes, and Charlotte's bravery and simple willingness to break free from her mental bonds to be with him healed things inside him that no doctor could touch.

"I hear you've got some time off coming up," Charlotte finally whispered. "Any plans on how you're going to spend it?"

"Any suggestions?"

She snuggled closer. "How about going on an archaeological dig with me? Unless I uncover another King Tut, I'm guessing the press won't follow me into the middle of nowhere. And we'd be overseas, beyond the reach of Donny Kemp or whatever he's calling himself now."

"The middle of nowhere can be a scary place."

"Not with you around. Nothing is too frightening for me to handle when I know you'll be there to have my back."

"I always will," he promised.

"Digs can be pretty remote. It might be just you and me. Alone in a tent."

"Will it be dry there?"

"We can go to a desert dig."

"Please. One sleeping bag?"

"Yes."

Fantasies did come true. "Where do I sign up?"

"I love you, Trip." She pushed herself up to seek out his eyes. "I may be a little flaky around the edges, but I've never been a liar. I'm *not* too flaky, am I? I mean, not too much for you to handle, right?"

"I see myself as kind of a 'Charlotte Whisperer.' I got you out of that house, didn't I? Got you to stop attacking me with archaic weapons and kiss me instead." He leaned forward and touched her lips to prove his point. "I think I can handle you."

"Are you sure you want to?"

"You are one of a kind, Miss Mayweather." Trip smiled and pulled her close. "And you're all mine."

Epilogue

The man showed his identification to the guard, emptied
his pockets of anything suspicious and signed the chart
to be admitted to the visitation room at KCPD's Fourth
Precinct detention center.

He walked past a young pregnant woman and the lowlife
in the orange jumpsuit who was lecturing her across the
table. Other than the guard at the door and the man he was
visiting, they were the only people in the room. Good.

Once he spotted his quarry, he straightened his tie and
lapels and headed to the table at the far side of the room.
He slid onto the bench on his side of the plastic table and
studied the weak-jawed coward sitting across from him.

"Who are you?" Kyle Austin asked. "My court-
appointed attorney? You look like an attorney."

He reached beneath the knot of his tie, into the lining
of his suit and from the underside of his watch, and calmly
began assembling his gift out of sight from the room's
security cameras.

"Hey, c'mon, man. I'm as glad to get out of that cell as
anybody, but I don't know you."

"Really?" he finally spoke. Compulsion had cleared his
mind, left him focused on his task. "I thought you claimed
to know me quite well. That I served as some sort of inspiration for you."

He pressed the pad into the palm of his hand and glanced down at the drop of poison glistening off the sharp tip of the attached needle, carefully avoiding pricking his own skin.

His father and uncles had taught him well. They'd taken him all over the country, all over the world, to learn their craft. They'd beaten him senseless when he hadn't learned it right. So he was very careful, very correct, very precise in every task he set for himself now.

"Wait a minute, are you…?"

"I believe your stepsister knows me far better than you do."

"The RGK?"

He held out his hand and Kyle was already instinctively reaching across the table to shake his hand the way any man would. He took Kyle's hand, pricked his skin, held on tight when the other man flinched so he wouldn't waste a drop of the precious potion he was injecting into him.

Kyle Austin was already feeling the effects. His joints were locking up, his breath was constricting, his heart was stopping.

The visitor stood, pulling out his handkerchief to hide the device and wipe the trace of the other man's blood from his hand.

"Never interfere with a plan of mine again."

* * * * *

Engaging Bodyguard

DONNA
YOUNG

To Kate Stevenson, Rhonda Kramer
and Shannon Godwin.
For your guidance, your faith and your infinite
patience.
Thank you.

Chapter One

The sky was a flat black, the air dense with the promise of snow. Distant laughter sliced through the cold; on its heels came a spattering of cheers and clinking crystal.

Cain MacAlister tossed off a double shot of hundred-year-old Scotch, embracing the bite on his tongue, the burn when it hit his gut.

He didn't believe in happily ever after.

Hell, he didn't believe in happily ever anything.

Cain settled into the terrace shadows, enjoying the darkness that stretched around him. He poured himself another drink—three fingers high this time—from the bottle he'd grabbed from the bar.

His mother had certainly outdone herself with the reception. Politicians, celebrities and the world's wealthiest packed the ballroom in honor of his sister Kate's wedding. He'd even noted a royal or two. None, however, outshone the newlyweds he'd left twirling around the dance floor, laughing and hugging, oblivious to those watching.

Mr. and Mrs. Roman D'Amato.

The wind—driven upward from the Manhattan streets—snatched at Cain's shirt collar, its icy fingers flexing in the night air.

Unhurried, Cain leaned back against the wall, welcoming the chill from the cement when it penetrated the thin layer of his tuxedo. As the days approached the end of March, the weather tended to hang on to the colder temperatures of the Atlantic. But the bitter cold, the razor-sharp cuts of the wind, simply assured his solitude.

He set the liquor bottle onto a nearby ledge just as a muffled *thwump* hit the air. *Careful,* a warning whispered—its hum vibrating through his Celtic blood. Cain straightened, his stance predatory.

A clump of snow falling?

Maybe.

His hand slid over the Glock nestled in his shoulder holster, only to stop mid motion, the polymer cool beneath his fingertips. Hearing nothing, he shifted forward until he detected the faint scent of cigar smoke. Heavily spiced, unmistakably Cuban.

With a grunt, Cain let his hand drop from the pistol. "Joining me for a celebratory drink, Jon?"

"No." Jonathon Mercer, the director of Labyrinth—an elite branch of the CIA—stepped from the darkness into the fringe light of the ballroom's French doors. In spite of his sixty-odd years, Jon was a strong, broad-shouldered man with a shock of white hair and features so sharp, he looked as if he'd been hewn from granite.

With a jab of his cigar, he pointed toward Cain's glass. "Isn't that a bit much, even for you?"

"Not tonight." Cain had been weaned on Scotch.

Both men knew it would take more than a few shots to put him under the table.

"It won't bring Diana Taylor back," the old man bit out, his tone surly enough to spark an argument.

Cain brought the tumbler to his lips. "You're right." In one gulp, he drained the glass, using the alcohol to blur the memories of long hair the color of polished mahogany, the laser-blue eyes that were quick to flash with intelligence and, when spurred, passion.

"Damn it, Cain. It's been three years. Diana's murder was unavoidable. No one could've anticipated that car bomb."

"Let it go, Jon." Diana had been petite, delicate in nature as well as build. She'd deserved a better…what? Cain caught himself. Death? Life? A better fiancé? An ache pulled somewhere under his heart, but this time he didn't pour another drink. Tonight, even the bite of whiskey couldn't fill the emptiness.

"Not until you let *her* go." When Cain didn't answer, Mercer tried again. "Look, I might have been only her boss, but I cared for her, too," he said, his tone edged with irritation over the admission. "Not only was she the best damned profiler we had, but she was a hell of a woman."

"Your point?"

"Labyrinth is Black Ops. You've worked for me long enough to know the game. Hell, in the last ten years, you rewrote the damn play book." Mercer took a short puff on his cigar. After a moment, he glanced over the balcony to the hazy glow of the city street seventy floors below. "She understood the risks of the job, Prometheus," he murmured, his voice rough, sandpaper against sandpaper. "We all do."

"Do we?" Cain ignored the use of his code name and set his glass on the ledge by the bottle. Living with the grief had become easy, but the emptiness? He'd found that words, no matter how sympathetic, couldn't fill the void that entombed him.

"What if she *had* lived? What then?"

"We'll never know will we?" But Cain knew. "And what about Diana's grandmother? Did she deserve to die with Diana?"

"There are always casualties."

"And if it had been Lara, Jon? What if it had been your daughter burning to death?"

Mercer's blue eyes became twin shards of ice, but the man didn't answer. Cain suspected he couldn't. "Forget it." Cain said, even though he knew they both wouldn't. Ever. "You didn't come out here to play counselor. What do you want?"

Mercer sighed, admitting defeat. "Peace and quiet." He leaned his hip against the balcony railing and unbuttoned his coat. The wind caught at the front tails, slamming them against the cement until metal jingled. Frowning, Mercer patted his jacket, then reached in the pocket. "This was the closest I could come to both."

"Lucky me."

"I thought so." Mercer's hand froze. "What the hell?" He pulled out a small, white envelope and ripped it open. Several coins spilled into his palm. "Damn it!"

"Quarters?" Cain asked as another warning whispered from the far recesses of his mind. In the space of one heartbeat, Cain palmed his gun.

But he was too late. Two muffled pops hit the air, so close together each sound almost blended into one. Mercer jerked, then took a step back trying to recover. His features slanted with shock.

Cain grabbed for Mercer, his fingertips snagging the older man by his tuxedo lapels preventing him from tumbling.

"Jon." Deftly, he lowered Mercer onto the mosaic tile, using the cement railing for cover. Cursing, Cain unbuttoned Mercer's coat. The air between them clogged with the metallic scent of blood. Gut-shot. Two perfectly placed holes—an inch apart—tattooed his stomach. "Stay with me, Jon."

For a brief second, Cain tilted his head, obtaining a clear view of the highrises, stories of glass and steel, flanking their hotel. The shot could've come from any one of a hundred different places. Although unlikely, the possibility remained that whoever had taken Mercer down was out there, still observing.

Mercer drew a shallow breath. "The coins…a warning." The words were barely audible, forcing Cain to place an ear by his friend's mouth. "Find Diana."

"Diana?" Disbelief ripped through Cain, tearing his heart wide open. He grabbed Jon, fisting the lapel this time. "Diana's dead," he demanded in a harsh whisper.

"No." Mercer shoved the coins into Cain's hand— warm, sticky blood now coating the metal. "Hiding."

Mercer's eyes fluttered shut. "Shadow Point. Do…it."

The coins dug into Cain's palm, his jaw tightened.

Diana alive? His mind raced, calculating the possibilities, searching for reasons.

Finding none, the betrayal settled deep, merging with rage, filling the void.

If Diana *was* alive, he'd find her.

Then after?

She'd better run like hell.

Chapter Two

The asphalt path—wet and salt-ridden—dulled the rhythmic slap of Celeste Pavenic's running shoes. She tried, unsuccessfully, to concentrate on the sound and ignore the fatigue burning behind her eyelids, leaving them gritty and sore.

In the distance, Lake Huron bellowed. Its ice-ridden waves hammered the rocks, agitated by the strength of the northeasterly wind.

Feeling the same restlessness, she doubled her pace. Her muscles screamed in protest, her lungs dragged in the frost-bitten air, but she only pushed harder. Under her sweatshirt, Lycra clung to her damp skin—and to her gun, its holster snug against the small of her back.

God, she hated running.

Dodging patches of ice, Celeste veered past a rusted pipe gate, where a No Trespassing sign banged an unsteady rhythm in the wind.

She turned onto the lighthouse's gravel road, more snow than pebbles, and navigated the steep incline that spilled out to the keeper's cottage—now a small museum for the summer tourists.

Several yards beyond, the lighthouse's lone, white-washed column of stone appeared stark and haggard against the craggy rocks of the point. A few windows dotted its walls, all framed with emerald-green shutters, vivid enough in the dimming light to soften the harshness.

She circled around the side of the tower, stopping only when she reached its weatherbeaten door. With one last step, she collapsed against the pine then gracelessly slid to the ground.

On her knees, she sucked in long, deep jags of oxygen and waited for the blood to cease pounding through her temples. Overhead, the seagulls cried, their evening rant somehow soothing now that she'd finished.

Every day, for the past three years, she'd forced herself to run five miles. Never the same route, never the same time, but always five miles.

And twice a month she rewarded herself with a visit inside the lighthouse. With a slight shift of her head, she took in her surroundings. Pleased that she was alone, she slipped a piece of strong but flexible plastic from her sock and shoved it into the lock. Once placed in contact with the metal, Celeste counted to ten while it expanded, shaped then hardened into a key.

After having lost her other key earlier in the month, Celeste grinned over the fact that once again she had access to the tower, access that was usually limited to the county's historical society.

With one twist, the shoved open the door.

After another quick check, Celeste entered, then shut it behind her and ran up the hundred-odd feet of iron spiral stairs.

Solace. That was her reward, if only for a brief moment in time. She stepped through the steel trapdoor of the lens room and outside onto the iron walkway.

Waves rushed in, crashing against the rocks, then retreating in leisure—one piling on top of another, making it difficult for the gulls as they dipped and skated over the water, searching for their dinner.

Celeste leaned forward, her palms spread on the railing. Thin shafts of daylight pierced the curtains of clouds that hung low over the slash of gray lake. She angled her face into the sun's rays, attempting to absorb some of its warmth, chase away the evening chill that had already seeped her bones. This was her time, her moment of peace when she shut out the world. She breathed in the heavy scent of pine and decaying sand reeds, tasted the moisture—letting the familiarity untwist the knots deep within her belly.

"So it's true."

Celeste swung around, her feet braced, her fists high ready to swing.

Eyes the color of pewter and just as cold caught hers, stopping her heart, stopping her dead.

"Cain."

He stood only a few steps away, his shoulder resting against the door's trim, the lean lines of his face set as firm as the stone behind him.

"Hello, Diana."

The name sounded foreign, it had been that long. Her fists dropped to her side, but they didn't unclench.

"It's Celeste," she corrected. Wary, her gaze drifted over his worn jeans, black shirt and black leather jacket, noting the violence that rode the unyielding lines beneath. "Diana died a long time ago."

"Celeste," Cain drawled, testing, his tone a rough wool that slid over her, its texture abrasive with anger.

The anger should have frightened her. But these last years had been too desolate. Her dreams too vivid.

"Pavenic, right?"

His eyebrow rose when his gaze rested on her hair. Automatically, her fingers touched the short, feathered ends, now sweat-dampened and plastered to her forehead. In the past, her hair had lain in long, easy waves past her shoulders. It had been Diana's one vanity—and to Celeste a potentially deadly encumbrance.

"That's quite a name."

"It's more than a name, Cain. It's who I am." His hair, she noticed, was the same thick mane of black pitch. Once professionally tapered—it now hung in disarray, roughened by the wind. Not long enough to be shabby, but wild and untamed enough to tempt a woman's fingers to dive deep, to feel its soft tickle against her palm.

When her own palm did just that, Celeste's throat went dry. She wanted to look away, but it had been so long. Greedily, she drank in the lean muscle, long bones and breadth of shoulder in one slow pull. He was a man who commanded attention, and sometimes with it, respect—but more often, caution.

Her gaze drifted to the dark ends of hair curled

around the collar of his jacket. They added a savage edge to the aristocratic slant of his cheekbones, making them seem stronger, unbending—defining the confidence beneath. The kind of confidence that came with rigid beliefs, heritage and years of discipline.

A warrior.

And at one time, she thought, her warrior.

"How did you find…" her voice trailed off. Emotions swirled in her. Fear, anger, confusion were only the few she could identify. Through it all, she realized only Jonathon Mercer could've sent Cain. And for only one reason. "Jonathon?"

"Dead." The word was clipped, business-dry—not surprising considering Cain had delivered it.

Duty first.

She'd known, of course. A split second before she saw the shadows flicker in the iron-gray of Cain's eyes. Still, the grief sliced through her, razor-sharp. She wanted to double over, rock back and forth to keep the pain at bay, but knew from experience neither would help. Death was final. Nothing changed that.

"How?" she asked, her fists now clenched for a different reason. "Who?"

"Murdered. Double tap to the stomach."

She waited, wanting more. When he didn't offer, her fists rose to hip level, her knuckles turned white. "The details, Cain. Give them to me."

"You mean, other than the fact that you're in hiding? That you might be in danger?" He lifted a negligent shoulder. "I have none. Jonathon died too quickly."

Her muscles loosened, but only slightly. Celeste

believed him. If Jonathon had been forewarned, he would've contacted her. "I don't suppose if I tell you to go, you'll do it?"

"Not until I get some answers."

He deserved them, she knew. And much more. She'd taken part of his life from him—for the right reasons—and left him grief in its place. No one had that right, but she'd taken it anyway. Just as she'd do again, if it meant keeping him safe.

"I half expected plastic surgery."

Startled, Celeste frowned. "Your mother would've made it…difficult." Cain's mother, Christel MacAlister, specialized in reconstructive surgery, mostly with children born with deformities. But as an expert in her field, she ranked among the top in the world. Celeste hadn't wanted to risk the possibility she'd find out. "Even with thousands of plastic surgeons in the world, I still didn't want to risk the possibility that Christel—"

"I suggest…" He hadn't raised his voice, but the icy tone sent shivers down her spine. "…we don't discuss my family right now."

"The intention was never to hurt—" She caught herself, tried to loosen the guilt that seized her chest. "Besides, Shadow Point is far enough off the beaten track, surgery didn't seem necessary."

"How far off the beaten track can you be when Olivia Cambridge lives down the road?" His laugh was harsh, steel scraping stone. "Having the president's mother within a few miles must bring a tourist or two."

"Some. More soon," she admitted, suddenly unsteady with doubt. Angry that she'd been with him only a few moments and the inadequacy had returned, clutching her gut. "When the Cambridge Auction begins. I've been here since…for quite a while and never had a problem."

"Olivia Cambridge doesn't know who you are then." It was a statement more than a question, but she chose to answer it anyway.

"You mean, she doesn't know that I was the lead suspect in her grandson's murder?" She shifted, unable to ease through the pang of regret. "Yes, she knows."

"And President Cambridge?" Cain straightened and studied her, his eyes flashing like finely brushed silver. "Does he realize you're living in his home town?"

Celeste was first to blink and hated herself for it.

"No," she bit out, her jaw hurting with the effort. "It's complicated. Too complicated for me to explain."

"Complications I can handle. Lies…" He paused. "Not so much."

"The lies go with the job. Your job. And I haven't asked you to handle anything. Not in a long time." When his gaze caught hers this time, the arrogance flashed, then disappeared—but not before it ignited her temper. "I'm not going to start now. Go home, Cain. I don't want you here." When she tried to walk past, he snagged her arm. Little shots of electricity, sparked. His fingers flexed as if he'd felt the sting too.

"Jon's dead. What you want or don't want doesn't concern me." Oh, his stance was deceptively casual and emphasized the force of his chest and the leanness of his hips. But she was no fool. Not anymore.

She shook him off, then stepped forward, a scorching storm of anger driving her until they were almost toe to toe.

"God, you haven't changed have you?" Celeste asked rhetorically.

He was taller than most, certainly much taller than her. Just shy of a foot, she remembered. But it took more than height to intimidate her. "I did what was necessary."

Surprise caught his features, if only for a millisecond. If she hadn't been watching she'd have missed it. Diana had never taken a stand against him.

Good, she thought, better for him to know now she'd changed.

"Necessary for who?" Cain prodded.

"For everyone." Faking her death might have been drastic, but she still believed the reasons held fast.

She had to. Or she'd have gone insane.

"Does that include Grace, too? Or do you have her hidden somewhere?"

The insult plunged deep at the mention of her grandmother, a mortal wound, as had been intended. Her composure slipped, but her stance didn't. "She died in the explosion."

"Yet you survived."

She hadn't wanted to. The high-pitched screams of terror. Her grandmother's hands clawing the window, the sweet sickening scent of burning flesh mingling with the more rancid odor of burning hair.

Fixing a sneer on her face, she pushed away the nightmare. She'd changed her identity in order to find Grams' killer. Walked away from her past. Except for the ring, she admitted, feeling the metal warm and

comforting against her skin, its sapphire hidden between her breasts.

Both the ring and the name Pavenic—a surname of
Romanian gypsies—had given Celeste courage. And
with it, a new life.

"Survival is a matter of perspective," she answered,
her words clipped, her control back in place. "You
wouldn't understand, Cain."

"That's where you're wrong, *Celeste,*" his voice
dropped, his smile glacial enough to freeze her blood.
Without warning, he grabbed her shoulders and hauled
her to him. "The last several years provided me with an
enormous amount of perspective."

"WELL, WELL, what do we have here?" The man's question slid through tightened teeth, its vicious edge lost in
the shrill whistle of the wind.

He shifted his position, leaning farther back against
the boulder, leaving him a line of sight through the
crowded pines. His thumb moved over the dial until the
high-powered scope brought both Prometheus and the
woman into view. Satisfaction rolled through him. The
fact that Prometheus had appeared in Shadow Point
so soon hadn't surprised him. When an outcome is
planned, there is little to be surprised over.

He studied the woman, noting the way she stood, her
back straight, her features defiant—enough to make his
finger tighten on the rifle's trigger. The cold metal urged
him to apply more pressure, but he controlled the impulse with little effort.

A bullet maimed, even killed. Both ways brought pain.

But not the excruciating pain she would soon endure.

Not for the money. Or his reputation.

Merely because of the pleasure.

For three months, he'd known she'd die. And during that time, he'd savored the taste of her death as he would have a fine merlot. His lips twisted, their slant feral. A soft, subtly sweet—blood-red—Merlot.

For now, he'd watch, indulge his curiosity. If she and Prometheus hadn't joined forces over Mercer's demise, they soon would. Incentive—if the correct incentive— tempted even the most cautious. And the coins…well, that was just pure genius.

He considered the possibilities. His plans weren't so set that he couldn't adjust them a bit. For the time being, he'd increase the stakes just a little. After all, he had a point to make.

Lachesis…Prometheus…

Even together, they were no match for him.

"LET ME GO." Blue eyes, now diamond-hard, met Cain's unflinchingly. The movement turned her features into the dimming sunlight. Except for the stubborn chin, her face was a perfect oval, framed by short, disheveled wisps of honey-colored hair.

Familiar enough to feed his rage. Feminine enough to make him resent it.

"I don't have the answers you're looking for," she insisted. "And if I did, why believe anything I'd say?" She glanced away for just a moment. Enough to tell him that dealing with the truth of that statement was still a struggle for her. "I killed the president's son."

"It was never proven."

"That's just semantics. Alive or dead, we both know I'll never be truly free from suspicion." Her tone remained cool and unattached, with no trace of self-pity. "So why trust me?"

"Oh, I don't trust you, sweetheart," he said, knowing his grip must be hurting her. But he refused to care. Refused to give in to anything but the rage. "Not any farther than I could bury you." He brought her closer until her gasp warmed his cheek, leaving no room for the wind to weaken the floral scent that clung to her hair. But it wasn't enough. Not for the past years of hell. God, he'd almost wanted her to be maimed, scarred, half dead—anything to show she'd reason not to contact him. But instead, he'd found her running, her body trimmed with feminine muscle, sleek and compact—her skin flawless and flushed pink. Vibrant, beautiful.

"No." She'd whispered the word, but only after his gaze had dropped to her lips, catching their slight tremor.

"Why?" he snarled, more to himself because he found no satisfaction in the fear that quivered her chin, brittled the blue of her eyes. "Tell me."

"It wasn't your problem."

The agony of the past years surged into fury and disbelief, heating his temper. Revenge was not only sweet, it was justifiable. One hand snaked out, gripped her hair while the other held her in place. He wasn't gentle, couldn't have been if he wanted. She slammed into him, her gasp of denial hovering just below his mouth.

A bullet splintered the wood pane behind his shoulder, cutting off Cain's retribution with a jerk of his head.

In unison, they dove around the curve, hitting the iron walkway hard. "Go!" Cain shouted in her ear but she was already moving, crawling around the curve.

He grabbed his gun from its holster. Holding it barrel up, he tilted his head and peered over the low wall that surrounded the lamp room. "The shot came from the trees." His words were curt, snapped out over another burst of gunfire.

"This isn't your battle, Cain." Celeste reached down, snagged the small 9mm from her back, ignoring the trembling in her hands. Damn it, she'd left him because of this. She tried not to think of how close his mouth had come to hers—the overwhelming temptation to close the distance herself.

"That's where you're wrong. It became mine the second those bullets hit Mercer's stomach." Another shot ricocheted, this time mere inches from Celeste's ear. Cursing, Cain pressed her farther onto the iron walkway. "Keep your head down!"

In the summer, the windows around the lighthouse were curtained during the day to eliminate the sun. Otherwise, the lens became a giant magnifying glass strong enough to start fires in the surrounding scrub. Unfortunately for her and Cain, the county's historical society removed the curtains for the winter. The open panels of glass would make them easy targets for the sniper.

She nodded in the general direction of the woods. "That second shot came from the top of the trail, about sixty yards. He's got us pinned."

He glanced through the metal railing, judging the

distance. His eyes met hers. Cold-hard slate clashed against azure hued steel. "So we jump."

She assessed the hundred-foot drop, only sparing a brief glimpse at the water pounding the rocks and sand below. "I see you haven't lost your warped sense of humor."

"Now sweetheart, you know I prefer the term *dry,*" Cain answered, the sarcasm deadly.

Simultaneously, they fired off several shots into the closest bank of trees. The glass panel exploded over their heads, Cain grunted. "Nothing humorous about this guy." He released the empty magazine, then shoved it into his coat pocket.

"He's playing with us, Cain."

"And he's alone. Wouldn't be any fun otherwise." Cain shoved a new magazine into his pistol. "How many clips do you have?"

"One more," Celeste admitted. She fired while he reloaded, knowing twelve bullets wouldn't give them much time.

"Even if we had a hundred, our range is much shorter." He snapped the buckle from his belt. "Up for a little rappelling?" Encased in the metal was a long thin wire-like cable and miniature grappling hook.

"Is that safe?"

"Worried?"

Yes. "Curious."

He quirked his eyebrow then, she saw the twitch at his lips. She found herself wanting to see him smile and that annoyed her.

Quickly he uncoiled the cable. "Kate's latest project.

Synthetic spider silk. Stronger than steel cable, flexible like nylon."

Celeste knew who Kate was of course. The female version of Cain, with raven hair and slate-gray eyes. She'd met Doctor Kate MacAlister, now D'Amato, briefly at a dinner party for some Washington senator, long before she'd met Cain actually. Damn smart, she remembered—and that from nothing more than a shake of hands, and a few polite sentences.

A world-renowned scientist, Kate was the youngest of the over-achieving MacAlister siblings, Cain being the eldest with their brother, Ian, filling the middle.

Celeste glanced at the ground before slipping her gun back into its holster. "You have a hundred feet worth of twine in there?"

"Twenty," he corrected before refastening his belt and hooking the end of the rope to the railing. "Enough to get us to the first window below." Within seconds, he'd removed his coat and handed it to her. "The leather will protect you better against flying glass. Use your heels to kick in the window."

"And the stray bullets?" Keeping low, she shrugged into his jacket. She caught the scent of leather, soap and moisture—as if he'd just bathed in the icy waters of Lake Huron. An overwhelming urge to snuggle into the warmth surged through her.

"Won't touch us if we do it right." Quickly, he threaded the wire into a makeshift harness between her legs before clipping it around her waist. "It's weighted to hold me plus another two hundred pounds."

His gaze raked over her. "You've lost weight. Almost too much."

"But you haven't lost that MacAlister charm," she murmured. At five foot three, Celeste never had tipped the scales much over a hundred and fifteen pounds, but secretly, even she admitted it'd been months since she'd come close.

"You'll be okay." He reached into the pocket of his jacket. A second later he handed her a pair of dark leather gloves. "Once you get through the window, undo the cord and I'll pull it up."

"Thanks," she retorted, not bothering to hide her derision. Instead, she studied the width between the iron railings.

"Don't worry. At my count of three, throw yourself over. I'll cover you."

"And who's going to cover you?"

The hitch in her voice caught his attention. His eyes narrowed. "I'll take care of that, too."

Always the hero. And if he got hurt? What then? Annoyed by the fact that she cared, she slipped on the oversize gloves, the inside pelt still warm from his hand. Her skin tingled but not from nerves. Not this time. "I don't—"

He captured her chin, his fingers firm. "Gypsy, do what you're told."

Her heart stumbled. She caught it in a gasp. Gypsy. She hadn't heard the endearment since their weekend together at his cabin in Colorado, when he'd whispered it, hot and moist, against her ear.

The same weekend he'd proposed.

Cain turned her toward the railing, making sure she was balanced in her crouched position. "One…two…three!"

Gunfire exploded around them. Celeste threw herself at the railing. The hard edge of metal hit just under her ribs, causing her to catch her breath. A searing pain stabbed her side, and she cried out. Suddenly, a hand curved the back of her thigh and hoisted her over the railing.

Rapid fire struck the barrier nearby. A bullet hit Cain's pistol, knocking it from his hand into the water below. Cursing, he curled himself around her, and flung them both over.

The cable shuddered and then tossed them into the wall of the lighthouse. Cain grunted as he slammed into the concrete, back first.

"Hold on." His breath tickled the slope of her neck where her shirt had ridden down. Nerves dried her throat, nothing else, she told herself. If they weren't hanging eighty feet from the ground she probably would've found the situation humorous. He gripped her waist, but Celeste wasn't sure how strong a hold he had. She closed her eyes briefly and prayed.

Twisting, Cain flipped them around. With his feet braced against the wall, he used his upper-body strength and tucked her into the curve of his chest.

"Cover your face." Cain grabbed her gun from its holster. The pistol exploded two rounds. Glass shattered.

With one sharp kick, the window frame snapped. Seconds later, they landed inside.

Despite the chill in the air, drops of sweat tickled the damp skin between her shoulder blades. Senses alert, her gaze scoured the inside of the lighthouse.

Framed by the spiraled stairs hung five hundred pounds of iron. The clockwork weight-driven mechanism had been designed like a cuckoo clock with gears, cable and a large spool. Once the keeper rewound the cable onto the spool by crank, the weight lowered inch by inch into the tower, causing the clamshell-like lens to turn.

"This is the guy who killed Mercer." Cain grabbed her hand and pulled her down the stairs behind him. "And who planted the C-4 explosives in your car." When he stopped at the bottom, she nearly collided with him. "Am I right?"

"I think so. And my guess is he's really pissed off now that he's found out I'm still alive."

Another spray of bullets had him checking out the window, her gun still in his hand. "Just for the record, he's not the only one pissed off about that."

Before she could answer, Cain hit the door with his foot. Wood splintered, then slammed against concrete. Bullets strafed the lighthouse, catching them in the doorway. Celeste dove behind a nearby log, then felt the hard impact of Cain's body beside her. Bullets sprayed the sand around them. Cain fired back, targeting the ridge. "He hasn't moved.

"Give me my gun," she demanded, then took off his gloves and shoved them back into his coat pocket.

"I'm the better shot." He nodded toward the keeper's cottage standing halfway between them and the edge of the woods. "Run on three. I'll cover." His fingers hit the air. "One…two…three!"

Celeste flung herself over the log and hit the ground in a roll, coming up only yards from the small brick

cottage. Gunfire raged around her, peppering her path.
Adrenaline surged as she dug into the sand for traction.
It sucked at her feet, weighing them down. *Too slow.*
You're running too slow. She dug harder until her calf
muscles burned. Suddenly, Cain tackled her from be-
hind, carrying them both several feet through the air.
They hit the ground, a yard from the cottage wall.

Bits of frozen sand scratched her eyes. She tried to
blink the sting away, spit the grit from her mouth. "I
would've made it," she snapped, then tried to wiggle out
of his hold. Cain's body tightened, she felt every line,
every rigid muscle. Cursing herself when her body softened in response.

Cain hissed. In one fluid motion, he stood and positioned himself flush against the wall. "Only because he
was toying with you." Cain's face shifted into tight lines.
"Do a better job next time." His gaze caught hers, the
message clear, before returning to survey the path.
"There's a cluster of rocks ten meters ahead."

She fought the twinge of panic. "Damn it, Cain. If this
guy is Jonathon's killer, did it occur to you that he wants
me and that maybe, just maybe, you might be in the way?"

"That's the plan." He handed her the gun. "Do you
think you can cover me?"

"Try me." Celeste gripped her gun tightly, her sweaty
palm slick against the steel. For two cents, she might just
shoot him and his condescending attitude. With a shove,
she reloaded her weapon, satisfied when the clip snapped
into place. "I'd take the bike path to your left, it comes
out behind the ridge. Might give you an advantage." She
nodded toward the path, nestled in the trees across about

twenty feet of sand to their left. "But you'd better run fast. I've only got a few rounds left," she snapped and scanned the beach, not totally convinced this sniper was alone. "And I might shoot you by accident."

"Then aim at the sky," Cain ordered before he hit the ground running toward the woods. "And stay put."

With a precision that belied the tremble in her fingers, Celeste emptied the clip into the ridge as the dense pines swallowed him whole. In the distance, rifle fire strafed the woods in response.

She scoured the terrain until her eyes ached. But the shadows grew longer, their depths murky.

Nothing.

Adrenaline fed her. That and fear. After all this, she couldn't lose him now. Wouldn't. With grim determination, Celeste darted after Cain, empty gun in hand.

Understanding one way or another, she'd pay.

Chapter Three

"What the hell were you thinking?" Cain met her at the top of the trail, his rage palpable.

"I don't know," she snapped, her tone sarcastic, her nerves crackling from the adrenaline that came from picturing Cain dead. "Maybe that you'd get your ass shot off if I didn't back you up."

His eyes narrowed at the cussing. In the past, Diana had never cussed. Well, that was just too damned bad, she wasn't Diana anymore. The sooner he realized that the better.

"And how would you manage to save my *ass?* By pitching your pistol at a rifle and taking it out?" He grabbed her hand and dropped some cartridges into her palm. "Fifty-caliber. Think you could've stopped one of those?"

"At least I had something." Her chin tilted in defiance, her fist closed around the metal, hoping to gain some control. Now wasn't the time to tell him she'd never been on the wrong end of the gun.

"I had something too." Within a blink, a knife appeared in Cain's hand and in the next breath it was sheathed once more inside his sleeve. So he still carried it. A present from her; in its high-carbon steel she'd had engraved the word *Prometheus*.

An engine gunned in the distance. Cain bit out a curse. In unison, they bolted toward Cain's Jag, parked a few yards away, as Cain punched the car remote, unlocking its doors. "He's headed north toward town," Cain yelled.

"Don't tell me—your little voice?" She reached the door, then jerked it open and was caught off guard when the scent of leather hit her. She hesitated, but only for the second she needed to forestall the nausea. A reaction she'd dealt with ever since Gram's death. Ignoring his lifted eyebrow, she asked, "Is that voice of yours still foolproof?"

"It didn't tell me you were alive." Celeste scrambled in, just as Cain slammed his door and turned the ignition. Tires squealed as he stomped on the accelerator. "Press the white button under your seat."

When she did, a slim drawer slid out, its contents two 9mm Glocks and a dozen clips.

When she quirked her brow, he answered. "The car is a prototype."

"Your sister keeps busy, doesn't she?" Celeste grabbed both pistols, checked them and handed him one.

"She's pregnant. As a scientist, developing safeguards channels her mothering instinct into something productive." He placed the Glock on his lap.

Celeste caught the thread of pride that ran through his statement. The sibling bond. A pang of envy tightened her stomach. Being an only child, she'd never experienced that kind of closeness. "You mean, now that she's pregnant, her maternal instinct is to find ways to protect her brother from harm."

"Exactly."

"And Roman? Is he still in the business now that's he's going to be a father?" The importance of the question resonated through Celeste.

He shot her a look. "For a dead woman, you're pretty well informed."

When Celeste didn't answer, he said. "Roman retired from the agency once he married Kate and now he runs my company." For years, Cain's company, MacAlister Securities, had served as a cover for both Cain and Roman. Now it seems the job had become a legitimate one for Roman. Kate wouldn't have to worry about being a widow.

"And the car?"

"It's loaded with the latest detection and satellite systems. All reinforced with special plating." He downshifted to take a particularly nasty hairpin turn in the road.

Bombproof. He didn't say it, but she understood. The upgrades had been a direct result of her death. "It wasn't you he'd wanted, Cain. Remember, I'd been driving your car for a month."

"Trying to analyze me?"

Celeste's eyes skimmed the wedge of trees on both sides of the road, spotting nothing except the flash of roadside mailboxes passing by. "It's my job." She propped her elbow on the door rest, and tugged at her hair, not caring if she left the strands in disarray. "We almost had him."

"We might not be out of luck yet." He nodded toward his mirror. She caught a dark green sedan maneuvering behind them. When it signaled to pass, Cain automatically slowed a bit.

"You think he waited off the road somewhere for us to pass?" Celeste noted the tinted windows just before it came abreast of theirs.

Cain tightened his grip on the steering wheel and shifted the Jag into high gear. "Hold on!"

The sedan slammed into Cain's side, catching the Jag's back panel. The impact threw Celeste sideways.

The sedan hit again, this time holding tight against them and forcing Cain onto the right shoulder of the road. Bullets pinged their car. Cain hit the gas and jerked the wheel, sending them into the oncoming lane but keeping them in front of the sedan. "Close your eyes, Gypsy."

"Don't tell me—" Celeste caught sight of a semi truck, two tons of chrome and steel, bearing down on them with its horn blaring and called herself an idiot for not taking Cain's advice. "Watch out!"

Chapter Four

"Trust me." Cain downshifted and hit the road's left shoulder. "I've got it under control."

Shots hit the back windshield leaving several webbed cracks in the glass. Celeste ducked, a major feat while her eyes remained glued to the sedan closing the distance. "I hope so, because he's coming again."

"Grab something!" Cain roared.

He didn't need to tell her twice. Alarm shot down her spine, pooling at its base. Celeste grabbed the dashboard seconds before Cain plowed through some roadside mailboxes.

When the Jag hit the pavement, he wrenched the steering wheel and hit the brake, sending the car into a nasty spin. Celeste's cry drowned under the screech of tires.

Cain jumped from the car, his gun appearing in his hand. He slammed the door shut. "Stay down!"

It wasn't until later she realized she'd ignored his order again. Cain crouched, his gun low, deliberately waiting. Her heart threatened to explode. She hit her seat belt release, grabbed her gun then scrambled out her side, using the car as a barrier.

Her breath came in shallow, quick gasps as the sedan bore down on them. Systematically she and Cain fired, emptying their guns into the car as it sped by.

"Get in!" Cain leaped back into the Jag, his expression dark with an unreadable emotion as she followed. He hit the accelerator and gravel flew, pelting the car.

But when they rounded the next curve, the sedan had disappeared. Too many side roads and winding driveways all covered with snow that effectively blocked any dirt from kicking up made it impossible to determine his escape route. Cain skidded to a stop, his eyes searching, knowing that in the darkness, the chase was useless. He jammed the car into Park.

"Next time." Cain's expression hardened. Only the systematic flexing of his fingers on the steering wheel told Celeste how angry he was.

"Are you crazy?" Fury drove her. That and terror. He'd done it, she thought. His indifference to danger had taken her beyond control. Later she'd figure what do about it, but for right now she'd use what wits she had left to yell. "Do you think those bullets were made out of marshmallows? One of them could've hit you and you'd be dead. Even I know you don't stand out in the middle of a road and let some idiot use you for target practice."

"Bullet-proof." Briefly, Cain tugged at his shirt before dismissing her without a second glance. "I know what I'm doing."

"You've got to be kidding!" Celeste squeezed his arm, maybe a little harder than necessary, but she didn't care. It annoyed her he'd said the words so casually. The lean muscle beneath her fingers flexed, showing its strength, forcing her to concentrate on the material. She wouldn't give him the satisfaction of flinging herself into his arms, holding him tight.

Not while she was bawling him out.

"He could've been firing armor-piercing bullets," she admonished, using the shirt as a pretext to assure herself that he was all right. The cotton material appeared no different from any other.

She glanced down. "The jacket, too?"

"Yes." She should've known when he'd insisted she wear it at the lighthouse earlier.

"The lining is specifically woven with a newly developed bullet-proof material. Kate has been working on a process for some time." He flipped the jacket's collar back and forth. "The weight difference in the cloth is minimal." His knuckles brushed her cheek, sending a cascade of goose bumps over her skin. Her reaction just fed her anger.

"Another MacAlister gadget?" Intuitively, Celeste knew Kate wouldn't be happy about Cain's recent stunt either. "It's probably the only way she can counter your heroics."

"It holds a ninety-percent effectiveness rating," Cain commented, unaware of Celeste's thoughts. "Enough to put the odds in my favor."

She let the ten-percent difference slide because she had bigger fish to fry. "What about your head? Last I heard *stupidity* was many things, but it wasn't bullet-proof."

"A calculated risk. If he wanted us dead now, he wouldn't have given up so easily at the lighthouse."

Cain grabbed his cell phone, pressed the key pad and put the receiver to his ear. "And he would've hit me with at least one bullet just now. He took Jon Mercer out from eight hundred yards with a double tap to his stomach."

"That's a big if." His indifference pushed her into rage. "And here's another. If a ricochet had hit you by mistake, you'd have been just as dead."

Cain held up his hand to stop her tirade. "Ian, I need a make. Dark gray. Taurus. License plate Charlie, Tango, Alpha—that's all I got."

Cain's younger brother, Ian, was an ex-navy SEAL. Jon had mentioned to Celeste that he'd resigned his commission. Obviously, he was working for Cain. "I don't believe this. The next time you stand up in the open against an armed assassin, I'll help Kate make you an armored straitjacket."

She'd muttered the words, but he heard.

"Hold on, Ian." He reached over and caught her chin. "The next time you don't stay when I tell you to, Gypsy, you'll have the opportunity. Because I'll lock you up tight in a little room right next to her lab."

Celeste slapped his hand down, telling herself she'd do the same to Cain when this was finished.

"Ian, the car's probably stolen, but let me know. I want this guy." Cain's eyes narrowed into twin blades of tempered steel so sharp they left Celeste no escape as they sliced through the car. "Let's just say, we played a little chicken today."

With those words, she hugged herself, finally understanding what he hadn't told her. This went beyond finding Mercer's killer, beyond duty.

This was personal.

"It was a draw."

She heard the promise in his answer.

"This time."

ON THE RIDE back to town, Celeste managed to temper the swell of anxiety that rose through her. It wasn't the killer who scared her, not overtly anyway. She wasn't stupid—she knew the man was dangerous—but she'd waited too long to let a simple warning from him make her bolt.

No, the killer didn't frighten her half as much as Cain did.

Logic dictated they join forces to find Mercer's killer, but she'd discovered the hard way that logic sometimes didn't matter.

"What the hell was Jon thinking?"

Irritated, she didn't pretend not to understand the question. "Maybe that I could take care of myself."

"You're a profiler, not a trained undercover operative."

"You make it sound like it was an assignment. Or worse, one that I had asked for."

"Look, Jon saw something in you. Something no one else did. I won't deny that." The both knew that during her mid twenties, she had shown a natural talent for profiling. Enough that one of her professors recruited her into the FBI's program in Quantico, Virginia. Within a few years, at the urge of President Cambridge, Jonathon had approached her to join Labyrinth.

"I quit Labyrinth right before the car bomb. Jonathon didn't have much say in my decision."

"He told me at your gravesite. Look…" Cain sighed.

"I can't change the past. Or my decision to stay in Colombia while you were under investigation for the Bobby Cambridge murder. But I'm here now." He cocked his head, arched an eyebrow. "Want to talk about it?"

Celeste would've gone with the quick, decisive no response. The one she'd repeated a thousand times. Mostly to a set of government psychologists whose job it had been to determine her sanity.

Except that she'd caught the quiet understanding that shadowed his features.

How many times during her ordeal, had she wished for this moment? How many times, with her spirit nearly shredded by lies, had she begged God to bring Cain to her rescue?

But he'd chosen to stay on assignment, even when Mercer had sent for him. Knowing Cain, she hadn't expected anything else. Loving Cain, she'd hoped for more.

Shame snapped her spine to attention. Pride kept it straight. He hadn't come then, couldn't, but still she had hoped. "They prepare you in training, condition you for possible capture and enemy interrogations." She gripped her hands, concentrating on the tinge of pain rather than the echoes of humiliation. "They just never tell you that sometimes, they turn out to be the enemy themselves."

"I wasn't your enemy, Celeste." His grim tone only deepened the sadness of the memory. "I was on the verge of a major arms bust, people were going to die, if it hadn't been vital—"

"You'd have been with me." Her voice sounded strained even to her ears. "I understood that."

"Did you? Mercer told me you wouldn't let him explain why I'd decided to stay." She studied the stone-hewed features beside her. When his mouth tightened, she caught the slight gesture only because she was looking so hard. She suspected he didn't care whether she observed him or not and that the grim line was more for her benefit than because of his thoughts.

It was amazing, she thought. Indifferent, even stoic—the man still dripped sex. But it had always been that way, ever since the moment she'd first met him years before.

"You were on assignment, Cain. The details of that mission wouldn't have changed the outcome of my situation. Or my career with the agency."

Ironically, the same career that had brought them together, she mused. Roman had set up their first meeting at MacAlister Securities, on a case Celeste could no longer recall clearly. Cain had arrived in a tuxedo. He'd been on his way to some kind of reception, she remembered, but she'd caught the sudden shift from indifference to curiosity when Roman introduced them. It wasn't until his hand brushed hers in a handshake, that time had slowed. Ever so slightly, he'd caressed her wrist, catching the flutter beneath his thumb. When his eyes had caught hers, their smoky depths swirled with hidden promises—promises that had sparked a fire deep within her belly. And others, she found in the deeper, calmer layers of gray that warmed her heart.

With a single phone call, his schedule had been rearranged, his dinner engagement forgotten. Suddenly their brief encounter turned into an intimate supper, the wine to an expensive bottle of champagne. The hand-shake to feather-light touches and responding sighs...

"Labyrinth or not, Jon should've placed you under protection—"

"Someone high in the ranks contracted this killer. No one can be trusted."

"I could've damn well protected you."

"Your choice," she snapped, then immediately regretted it. "Look, it was better that you didn't. You would've hidden me away, then gone after him yourself."

"Damn right."

"And you would've died. No one was safe with me, Gram's death proved that. I insisted on disappearing alone." Celeste felt her anger rise and tried to beat it down. "I didn't give Jonathon a choice."

"And he's dead."

"That's it, isn't it?" It wasn't the words that caught her attention, but the animosity underneath. "You're angry. But what are you angry about, Cain? That you decided to bring down an arms dealer rather than hold my hand through an investigation?"

"The investigation was standard procedure. The car bomb wasn't."

"So it's because Jonathon didn't tell you I'd survived."

"Not Jon. You."

"I'd already decided I wasn't going to marry you. Telling you I was alive made no sense."

When he didn't deny it, she said, "You think it was an easy decision?"

"Which? Breaking the engagement or not letting me know you were alive?"

"Both." Celeste answered, allowing the bitterness to filter through. "You didn't love me. The engagement was a mistake that I had no intention of compounding by involving you in this mess."

"Engagement or not, you shouldn't have run from me." This time the rage was there, simmering under every syllable, thickening the air between them. "You should've damn well run *to me* for help."

"And what could you have done that Jonathon hadn't?" she asked with disdain, not waiting for an answer. Cain hadn't denied her accusation that he'd never loved her. The realization made her throat ache. "One of these days you're going to trip over your arrogance, Cain."

"Tread carefully, Gypsy. Because my arrogance isn't what you should be worried about right now."

But it was too late for that. The fear, the injustice, the years of guilt converged on her in one fell swoop, overpowering any thought of prudence. She leaned in, wanting him to see what he'd stirred in her—how much she resented it. "You know why, you weren't told? Why you weren't brought in to protect me after Grams died?" Her finger hit his bicep with each question, not caring when she found steel beneath, her emotions no more under control than a runaway train.

"No. Why don't you tell me."

Determined to, she missed the flash of heat behind his eyes, the threat in his tone. "It's because the mission was on a need-to-know basis. And for once, MacAlister, you weren't on the list."

He jammed the brake, bringing the car to a dead stop

on the roadside. The force threw her forward, then snapped her back like a rubber band. Before she could react, he'd hit the clip of her seatbelt, caught her shoulders in a vice grip and jerked her to him. Her heart slammed into her ribs, her teeth knocked together.

"Damn you!" Then his lips hit hers, punishing. No love, no desire.

A reckoning—to her, for the agony of what she'd put him through, and to him, for allowing himself to suffer.

Not what she'd remembered, not what she'd realized she wanted. Desire bubbled, touched off by the heat of temper, like molten lava that had been waiting a century to awaken. With it, came the quakes of uncertainty, the tremors of fear.

Don't make it worse, she told herself. Don't make it genuine.

His mouth shifted, as if sensing the surge of emotion. The tempest settled into something deeper, but no less dangerous. Just more confusing.

She wouldn't struggle.

As it turned out, she couldn't.

With a few strokes of his tongue against her lips, the confusion became curiosity, the curiosity, yearning. All within a heartbeat. Her mouth opened on a gasp as the hunger slammed into her emotions, hurling her off balance.

Then he pushed her away. But not far enough for her to feel safe. She jerked back, crying out when her head smacked the window. She blinked, angry enough to say something, cautious enough to hold her tongue.

He gunned the engine, taking out his rage on the machine. Without a word, she settled into her seat, aware of the nearness of his body, the deafening silence.

The persistent sting in her scalp didn't register until he turned onto the road. But she didn't rub away the pain. Instead, she hugged her chest, tight—the ache in her heart hurting far worse.

"Here." Cain reached into his jeans pocket and withdrew five quarters. "We were at Kate's wedding reception. Jon had joined me on the hotel balcony to smoke a cigar just before he was shot."

"Brand new." Celeste moved closer, hating the nervousness that crept in, and glanced at the backs of the coins. The State of Michigan. "All identical."

"All in an envelope inside Jon's pocket. No prints, of course. Nothing but Mercer's name. Laser printed." Cain paused long enough to slide a glance her way. "These were a present from Jon's killer."

Celeste nodded. "It's his trademark. Which means Jon's killer would've been at the reception disguised as a waiter, a guest. Anyone," she reasoned aloud. "If the coins had been slipped into his pocket any earlier, Jonathon would have discovered them and would've notified me or taken better precautions."

"Possibly." For a moment, Cain's gaze didn't leave Celeste's face, unnerving her. What did he think he'd see? Carefully, she schooled her expression.

"Either way, the hit man was making a statement."

"No, not a statement," she corrected, then took the quarters and examined them one by one in the light of the window. "The coins tell us that the killer knew I was in Michigan before he shot Jonathon. He was issuing a challenge."

"Lucky for him I'm listening then."

"It wasn't luck, Cain. If I'm right, this guy knew exactly which buttons to push to bring you here."

"Then we'll just have to start pushing back."

"Define *we*," she countered.

"*We* don't need to be lovers, Gypsy. Or friends." It was a statement of fact. Spoken bluntly. "We just have to be in agreement. Either I'm in or you're out."

"Meaning?" She shifted, instantly alert, unwilling to be caught off guard again.

"It would only take one phone call for me to arrange for your protection," he challenged.

"Which, defined by your terms, isn't really protection, but more like…imprisonment," she replied, her jaw clenched. Cain never threw out idle threats—the fact his taste still lingered on her lips was proof.

"Can't fool you. But then I've always said you were good at your job." Cain downshifted to avoid a squirrel in the road, not surprising Celeste. "If I think it's for your own good, I'll have men here in less than an hour with an arrest warrant."

"I'm sure there's a compliment somewhere in there," she answered derisively, not willing to give him the satisfaction of knowing she caught the grin that played over his lips.

Jerk.

"Even if you could trust them, Cain, it would be impossible." Having her arrested that quickly would take resources that Cain didn't have access to—

She jolted with the realization. Jon had only been dead a day, but it was still feasible. She'd heard the rumors, even before she'd left. Nothing overt, just the whispers. The great Prometheus. The only man who could take over the reins of Labyrinth when Mercer retired. "You're the temporary director, aren't you?"

"The jury's still out," he answered, seemingly unsurprised by her comment. "Mine and theirs."

"You'll take the job." She moved away, suddenly needing the distance a few inches put between them. "And the truth is, you *should* become the new director. And Jon realized it."

"My coming here had nothing to do with being director and everything to do with Jon's murder and you."

Cain maneuvered the Jag onto Shadow Point's main street. The wind kicked up, rattling the wooden signs of the storefronts. Celeste caught sight of the white clapboard buildings, most painted the previous summer, some showing signs of movement inside.

Not a surprise, even for Saturday night. For the last week or so, most owners spent hours after closing preparing for the Cambridge Charity auction, knowing the town would receive an early influx of tourists.

"Do we have a deal?" His access to information made it impossible for her to object and they both knew it.

"On one condition." She pointed out the car window to the few people on the sidewalk. The residents' easy acceptance, their unabashed friendliness, had soothed her shattered soul, then eventually, had won her heart and her loyalty. "See them?" Her index finger tapped the window, not caring that she left smudges on the glass.

"There's a good chance they're in danger and don't even know it. I refuse to let that happen."

"It wouldn't happen if we put you somewhere safe." He parked in front of her store and shut off the engine.

"No. He'd find me, Cain. Then other people would get hurt in the process." *You.* Celeste deliberately faced Cain, her back straight, her jaw tight. "I want Mercer's killer found. I want the guy who thinks he can take pot shots at me and get away with it caught. Then I want you far away from me as soon as possible. Agreed?"

After a long, torturous moment, Cain punched a button and unlocked the door. "Agreed."

"Partners," she muttered, not bothering to hide her annoyance as she followed him onto the pavement.

"Not quite." He slipped the keys into his pocket before giving them a careless jingle. "You're not experienced enough."

"What?"

His comment rankled. Or maybe it was stubborn line of his lips.

"This isn't up for debate." He took in the damage to the Jag, then he pointed to the barely dented metal. "You're still in trouble. If he knows where you run, he knows where you live."

Trouble she could handle. Cain, she wasn't so sure about. Celeste eyed the minor dents and scratches. Obviously, he'd told her the truth about the car having reinforced plating. Just like its owner. Celeste watched him for a moment. "How did you know to find me at the lighthouse?"

"I followed you." The negligent lift of his shoulder

seemed almost too casual. "Which is why we're going to relocate you."

"I'm not leaving my home. I have responsibilities."

Cain froze, his eyes murderous, startling her. With a long glance at her stomach, he asked, "What responsibilities?"

Chapter Five

"What? You think I have a baby?" The quiver in her belly stayed out of her voice, just barely. Celeste couldn't deny that in those first weeks, she'd hoped, even prayed for what might be.

Then later she'd dreamed, knowing it would never be.

"Relax, Cain. My responsibilities include the feline kind. My cat, Pan."

"A cat is portable."

"My antique business isn't." He raised an eyebrow. She quirked hers right back.

Diana Taylor had taken pride in not being tied down to anyone or anything until she'd met Cain. She'd lived from hotel to hotel, never forming roots. A gypsy, he'd called her until it had become an endearment.

"I see."

"No, you don't, but that's okay." She jabbed her thumb at the Jag's back window. "Shouldn't we move the car to the alley?"

"No," he said, not bothering to follow her gaze. "If anyone asks, tell them a flock of irate seagulls attacked us."

"Oh, for heaven's sake." She folded her arms to keep from shaking him in frustration. The man was turning her into a loon. "No one's going to believe that."

"It doesn't matter whether they believe it or not." He tugged on her coat sleeve, pulling her along the sidewalk. "It's time to eat and talk."

"Fine." She clutched her collar together, giving in to a sudden need to protect herself. "You eat. I'll talk."

"I believe, Gypsy, we're finally communicating."

"If you think this is communicating," she copied his dry tone, pleased with herself when she succeeded. "We're in for a rough time."

DIANA *had* changed. And the evidence proved to be her business, Cain decided.

The sun had lost its intensity, sliding farther toward the horizon. Within an hour it would be dark. Already heavy with the promise of snow, the evening breeze tugged at their coats and nipped at their ears.

Diana's store stood alone in a two-story building at the end of town. Only the whitewash and green trim showed any similarity to the other stores which stood in a long curvy tail bordering Main Street.

Cain noticed the sign first, only because of the squawk of the hinges as it swung in the wind. "A Touch of Serenity. Is that just your store's name or a goal?"

"It's my home."

A home, he knew, she struggled to keep. It had taken very little effort to pull her financial records. Within hours, Roman had given him a detailed report of her bank accounts—which held barely enough for her to live on.

A line of benches marched along the boardwalk, all black wrought iron with green slats of wood, all flanked by sandstone flowerpots and all strategically separated by matching garbage containers.

Except in front of Diana's place. Her porch was subtly different. *Cozy* came to mind, startling Cain. With a bay window for its backdrop, a swing bench hung to the right of the door while two rockers sat on the left flanked by wooden barrels, big enough to hold a morning coffee or a set of feet for a lunchtime nap.

"A little cold to be sitting outside, don't you think?"

"I like to rock." She glanced at the bench before putting her key into the lock. "On a good night when the stars shine, I like the cold, too."

Cain almost grinned at that, remembering a time when the slightest breeze would send Diana into a fit of shivers. A woman couldn't change that much.

It only took one glance at the inside of her store to prove him wrong.

If *cozy* described the porch, the warm, Victorian charm of the store put *cozy* to shame.

He'd known it was an antique store, and he'd been in many, shopping with his mother, dragged along by his sister. Both were antique fanatics. But Cain had never seen one like Diana's.

Couches and chairs—some in pastel florals, others in jewel-colored velvets in blue, green and gold— crowded the floor, setting off the dark grain of the hardwood. Groomed and overstuffed, each piece set to draw the eye to the softer tones of vintage oak, mahogany and cherrywood furniture nestled nearby. Fragile lace throws and hand-crocheted doilies covered every piece.

"Nice place, Gypsy." An oversize stone fireplace stood to the right, waiting patiently with fresh logs to light.

Celeste threw the dead bolt, punched in her ten-digit code, and waited impatiently for the red light to beep. "You sound surprised."

"Considering that only a few years ago, the idea of staying more than a month at one particular hotel got on your nerves, yes, I am surprised," he admitted.

"I told you before, that was Diana, Cain. Not me. I enjoy collecting pieces of the past for my customers."

Simple solution, for someone who has to live without one, Cain thought. "You got the full security package, didn't you? Motion, heat, the debugging sensor. Not top of the line—not even close—but workable."

"Jonathon insisted on the security." Her voice remained even. "I insisted that it wouldn't be one of your systems." She flipped on the overhead track lights. They cast a soft, easy glow across crystal decanters and stained-glass lamps, leaving one's mind with a nostalgic sense of the past. "If our killer shows up, we'll know it."

Cain caught the light scent of rose and talcum that was Diana's grandmother.

Another deliberate reminder?

She yanked off his coat and tossed it onto a hundred-odd-year-old oak chest. Her mouth thinned. "I've brought home a guest, Pan." Eyes a few shades lighter than Diana's own blue ones studied Cain from the top of an eight-foot-tall antique library shelf.

The sleek black cat yawned in response, a full, wide yawn that allowed his pink tongue to unroll leisurely from his mouth.

Celeste smiled wickedly at Cain. "He doesn't seem impressed."

"That makes two of you," he mused. "Had him long?"

"Since I moved in. He came with the place. I found him in the storage room while I was unpacking." She held out her arms and Pan jumped into them. "I realized soon after that I enjoyed his company." Cain watched intrigued as Celeste rubbed her cheek against the cat's head, then whispered something soothing in his ear.

Pan jumped from her arms and she laughed. "My company he takes in small doses." For a moment, she watched Pan relocate on the bay window's overstuffed cushion and stretch out. "He has his own entrance through the stock room for his midnight prowls. An old dryer vent near the floor. It's no bigger than his head, so I don't worry too much about someone else squeezing through." With a shake of her head, she said, "Sometimes I really envy his independence."

For a response, Cain sauntered over and scratched Pan between the ears. "Hello, cat."

With a long, lazy purr, Pan flipped over on his back and started batting his paws at Cain's hand.

Celeste frowned over the male bonding.

"Any other…friends I should know about?"

"You never used to play games, Cain. I'm sure within seconds after locating me, you had Roman do a background check."

Cain straightened, ending his game with Pan. "Only

what we could find out through data bases." Cain's tone
was tolerant as he eyed a small musical figurine on a
nearby lace-covered table. The statuette was of a young
woman rocking a small, sleeping boy, his head snuggled
against her shoulder. He picked up the figurine and
wound the key. The low tinkling of a lullaby filled the
air. "I like this."

Handcrafted in Italy, the figurine was a favorite of
hers too. Actually, she loved it. So much, she'd been
tempted to keep it herself. But why did the fact he liked
it too suddenly anger her?

"There's no special person in your life right now?"

"No one." Her chin tilted enough to show off the stubbornness. "Loving someone would only risk their life."

A yowl mocked her from across the room. "Shut up,
Pan."

Cain cleared what might have been the beginning
of a laugh from his throat. "I take it he doesn't want
to be excluded."

"Most likely," she lied, conscious of the flush that
invaded her cheeks.

Cain studied her for a moment but Celeste didn't
back down. She had nothing to hide when it came to relationships. The fact that she'd wanted to ask him the
same thing, but couldn't without being obvious, only
added another layer to her frustration. "Do you want to
hear about this killer or not?" she asked, becoming
downright angry when the bite in her question only
raised an amused eyebrow.

"Isn't that why we're here?"

"I thought so until a moment ago." Now that she was

committed, she wanted to get the job done and get Cain out of her hair. "It started with Bobby Cambridge's murder. More accurately, it started on the day of the kidnapping. Bobby was on his way to a private summer day camp with the usual security detail of Secret Service agents."

Celeste replayed the scene in her mind as her hands kept busy rearranging white roses in a fluted vase. Long-stem roses were the one extravagance she indulged in. "Except one had turned greedy."

"Frank Bremer," Cain responded. "Weapons special-ist turned agent after a stint in the military and FBI. A loner. No close friendships, no letters from home. A man who decided to take care of his own retirement."

Celeste's eyes narrowed with suspicion before she continued. "After pulling over for feigned car trouble on a deserted part of the highway, Bremer killed several agents in cold blood, then took off with Bobby."

"Risky," Cain acknowledged. "But Bremer had the element of surprise on his side."

"Exactly. And who else would know Secret Service procedures better?" she asked rhetorically, her hands stopping as she got lost in relating the facts. "He ditched the car for another hidden nearby. By the time back up arrived a few minutes later, he was long gone."

The warmth of the store did nothing to diffuse the cold pit in her stomach. She'd gone over this a hundred times. Still, it never got easier. "It was simple at that point," she said. "Bremer had cut out the tracking chip implanted behind Bobby's ear and left it crushed on the pavement. A few hours later, he made his demands, short and to the point. Then ditched his phone.

"Our guys weren't so smart." Celeste frowned. "After agreeing to the drop-off, the FBI, Secret Service and everyone else involved tried to pull a fast one."

Cain nodded. "Bremer found out—presumably through a phone call from you—went back and killed the kid, then himself. Unusual, but understandable considering we would've hunted him down."

The memory of her grabbing Jonathon, trying to convince him Bremer hadn't worked alone, flashed through her. It was her persistence that had turned their suspicions to her. That and the record of Bremer's number on her cell phone. "It was the official version, yes." Annoyance chewed at her throat, forcing her to clear it. "But not the correct one."

"Okay," Cain said, and then leaned a hip against a nearby sideboard. "Why don't you tell me your version."

"The correct version, you mean."

He folded his arms. "Your version."

The attitude angered her more than the words. "Frank Bremer was smart. He wanted untraceable cash, old bills in small denominations. If they'd even thought about using the standard tricks like dye explosives or tracking devices in the payoff bag, he would've killed Bobby. A helicopter was to drop the money into the Potomac at his specified location with no surveillance. Most figured he would show up in underwater gear and snag the money. But the Feds screwed up. Broke their deal."

Cain's mouth flat-lined. "We don't negotiate with terrorists, even when the president's kid is involved."

"I know, I took National Security 101," Celeste responded derisively. "The FBI kept a twenty-four-hour watch on the drop point. Bremer supposedly found out about it and never showed."

"He'd been updated on all the latest surveillance equipment." Cain crossed his ankles, seemingly relaxed. Celeste knew better. The lines of his body might have eased, but underneath, the muscles remained tense, alert. "Other than the record of his cell number on your phone, there was no evidence of a breach from the inside."

"But it's there. Somewhere." It wasn't easy under Cain's penetrating gaze, but she held her ground. "The point is, by the time the good guys realized Bremer had outmaneuvered them, Bobby was already dead and someone had left Bremer's phone number on my cell. And that someone contracted the hit on Bobby."

"Okay, so Bremer never showed at the drop," Cain continued, obviously aware of the details. "Instead, he went back to the cabin where he'd stashed Bobby and killed the boy with an injection of sodium pentobarbital, then shot himself in the head. End of story, tragic but not unusual in kidnapping cases. Most victims die within the first forty-eight hours—Bobby lived twice that long. And from all accounts, Bremer had treated him well. Some say the boy never saw the end coming."

"My argument exactly and one that ended up biting me in the butt later." Celeste struggled to keep any emotion from underlining her words. "I was on the case from the moment Bobby was kidnapped. I'd insisted on it." If she'd just been less confident, and quicker at putting the pieces together…

"I'm surprised Jon approved the assignment, considering the fact that Grace and Olivia Cambridge were friends."

"He had no choice once President Cambridge requested my help," she said, waving the comment off with her hand.

"So how did Bobby's treatment help your theory?"

"Frank Bremer would never have treated Bobby kindly." She ran her fingers impatiently through her hair. "During his assignment to Bobby, he wasn't friendly or unfriendly, just indifferent. He never complained about the detail, but his associates said that a few weeks before the kidnapping there was always a thinly veiled undertone when he talked about the kid—which wasn't often. Deep down, I'm sure, Bremer considered anything other than protecting the president a step back in his career." Celeste paused, knowing the next portion would burn like salt in wounds yet to heal.

"Don't stop now, Gypsy," he prompted softly. "You're on a roll. After Bremer was assigned to Bobby..."

She nodded, using the few seconds to gather her nerve. "From here it gets a little complicated. Bobby was a sensitive kid. Shy. Introverted. A problem when you happen to be the president's youngest child and your family is continually under the microscope. It only got worse when his sister, Anna, went off to college that first year they were in the White House. The fourteen-year age difference between them made her more of a caregiver than a sister. The same year Anna started college, he started kindergarten. Losing her only added to the stress of facing the attention alone. On his first day of school, Bobby freaked out. To calm him, Olivia gave him an angel coin."

"What kind of coin?"

"A good-luck coin. A Frenchman by the name of Dupré designed the coin in the late 1700s and carried it in his pocket—always," she explained, suddenly aware of the floorboards squeaking. She stopped pacing. "One day, having fallen out of favor with the king, Dupré was arrested. Legend has it that he prayed to his guardian angel—which he'd imprinted on one side of the coin—to save him. Or he could have used it to bribe the guard. Either way, the next day he was set free and the coin became a symbol of good luck."

"A talisman of sorts."

Celeste nodded. "For years, Bobby never went anywhere without that coin in his pocket. It became his security blanket. He'd almost rubbed the image off by using it as a worry stone."

Celeste jammed her fists into her stomach. She'd seen Bobby when they'd found him—had insisted on it. He been sleeping, his body—gangly, with pointed shoulders—tucked endearingly under a NASCAR comforter, similar to those that a thousand boys his age owned. His blond hair was mussed, like that of most ten-year-olds when they are sleeping. The soft spikes of hair were damp against the flushed cheeks—still warm even in death, from dreams of racing, flying jets and space ships.

"Cain, they found the coin in his hand. When Bobby died, I'm positive he wasn't holding the coin. Someone placed it in his right hand later. Deliberately. Bobby was left-handed."

"It only supports the theory that you had profiled Bremer and instructed him exactly how to leave the boy."

"An assassin, not a kidnapper, targeted Bobby. No one could have saved Bobby. By the time I realized it, I'd been set up and Bobby was already dead."

"Only you believed that."

"Cain, Bobby wasn't abused during his captivity. He wasn't restrained, he was well-fed and clean."

Even gripping her fingers together couldn't hide the fact that her hands shook. Cain shifted, fighting the urge to hold her, knowing if he did, she'd fall apart before she could purge the memory. So he did what was necessary, what he seemed to be good at lately. He pushed her temper.

"The FBI experts said only a woman would be that sensitive to the kid…which was one of the things that indicated your involvement."

Chapter Six

"Circumstantial."

He shrugged, satisfied when her eyes fired with anger. "If you say so."

"I do." She started pacing again, but this time the tempo had picked up with determination, her eyes shooting cobalt sparks. Having been raised in a family with Scottish tempers himself, he couldn't miss the flash of fury or the reluctant admiration he felt because of it.

"You're right, Cain. There was no evidence of struggle during those last four days of his life. That showed Bobby trusted his caretaker. At least enough not to fight him. Bobby was the kind of kid who'd have needed constant reassurance from someone he believed in. And since I was with Mercer and a half dozen other guys pretty much during the whole episode, it couldn't have been me."

"Another possibility is that Bremer could've fed Bobby some story—that they were in hiding from some danger, maybe." Cain reasoned. "Gained the kid's trust."

"That scenario doesn't work. Remember Bobby was

an introvert and Bremer had been with him for several months prior to the kidnapping. During that time, there was no friendship, no closeness—only mutual toleration. Top that with the fact Bremer cut up Bobby's ear to get the chip, he wouldn't have trusted Bremer, even if he'd tried to become friends."

"So you're saying it had to be someone new. A Ted Bundy type who was able to gain Bobby's trust almost immediately?"

"Exactly. Almost like a good cop–bad cop ploy."

"With Bremer playing the bad cop," Cain responded grimly.

"Unknowingly, of course. The autopsy showed no outward injuries aside from his ear, not even marks on Bobby's wrists to suggest he was bound. It also indicated that his last meal was a fast-food hamburger and fries. Bremer wouldn't have jeopardized his plans by buying Bobby his favorite meal."

"He could've changed his appearance. Shaved his head, worn a fake goatee."

"All the possible variations of disguises had been sent out over the media and Bobby's disappearance launched the biggest manhunt in two centuries, twentieth and twenty-first. Yet, no one recognized him when he bought the meal? Not likely." Celeste snorted, raising another eyebrow from Cain. God forbid if Diana had done that, she thought.

And because of that thought, she almost did it again. "Remember this guy was FBI at one point in his career, so he wasn't stupid." When Cain grunted, Celeste ignored the insult to the Bureau guys and continued.

"Every fast-food outlet within a hundred square miles turned over their security tapes. Not one man fitting Bremer's description ever came near one of their buildings that day.

"The autopsy also showed Bobby had been given a sleeping agent in his food before the barbital injection. Bremer would've shot him. Not loaded him with drugs before killing him. He had no reason to. A bullet is fast, simple. Military." She let her words sink in. "And Bremer wouldn't have taken the time to make sure Bobby's lucky coin was in his hand first."

"So you're telling me this other guy either did all of this to set you up—or he had a loving heart and killed Bobby in the least traumatic way possible."

"No, our killer doesn't have a heart or a conscious," she insisted, recalling that she'd made the exact same statement to Jonathon. "Bobby Cambridge's death was a foregone conclusion."

A knot of tension throbbed at the base of her neck— a nuisance she refused to give in to. "My being set up was a last-minute thought, triggered simply by my working the case—a case where this killer's client got cold feet and decided to take matters into his own hands. Otherwise, they would've have set me up with more than just one phone call on my cell. Either way, it was imperative the operation looked like a kidnapping."

That's what infuriated her the most, the wasted time, the useless words. The endless strategizing by the kidnap experts that had led them nowhere while Bobby's life slipped through their fingers like sand. "This guy was kind to Bobby just because that's his style. He meticulously researches his victims. Then he kills in the manner he decides fits the victim's profile. It's his trademark.

"Gabriel knew which Secret Service agent to seek out."

"Gabriel?"

"A nickname I gave him." She studied Cain in her peripheral vision and waited. The familiar feeling of inadequacy roiled within, but stubbornly she squelched it. She'd stand by her profile, no matter what Cain MacAlister thought.

"Okay," he drawled. "Let's say there was another player, someone who paid Bremer to kill Bobby. Why wouldn't this Gabriel turn it into a real kidnapping and take the money before he murdered the boy?" he prodded.

"Because Gabriel's a professional. Someone had already paid him for the job, most likely two or three times the ransom amount. He never wanted the president's money. Probably understood better than Bremer that the chances of seeing the money were infinitesimal. He needed a patsy to pull off the actual kidnapping."

Her mind raced through the details again. "He may even have masterminded the whole thing with very little input from Bremer. Just think, if Bremer hadn't died, right now he'd be the most wanted man alive—the man who murdered the president's ten-year-old son. There wouldn't have been a place on this planet he could hide. Gabriel couldn't afford to let him live. Bremer signed his own death sentence the moment he agreed to the kidnapping, he was just too arrogant to realize it."

"And since they believed that you were the accomplice, the FBI had no reason to look farther."

"The didn't have enough evidence against me and they had to let me go."

"Which is when, like Bremer, you became a liability once you were released."

"So the question is…who paid Gabriel?"

"And why?"

"If we find the who, we'll know the why."

Celeste noted Cain's *we* but didn't let it go to her head.

"So why the nickname Gabriel?"

"The angel coin." In her mind, it was a simple correlation. "I connected it to Gabriel the Archangel."

"The angel of mercy," Cain murmured. "If what you say is true, his motivation wasn't kindness."

"Still…" Celeste looked at Cain. "In his own twisted way, Gabriel kept Bobby away from the ugly."

"How about some food?" Celeste crossed the hardwood floor, her heels thudding her irritation with short, staccato beats. "My apartment is this way." Pointedly, she walked to the storeroom. "I have two entries, one from the store and another from a stairway at the side alley."

The stock room, a long, flat area that ran the width of the store, held very little merchandise. Mostly assorted lamps, a chest and two chairs, all with bright yellow tags marking them as layaway items.

"I don't believe in a lot of surplus."

A closet door, or so it seemed, graced the side wall. Beyond it lay a short flight of stairs that led to the second-floor apartment.

When they reached the top of the stair, she stabbed

a series of numbers into the security keypad. Once the alarm beeped, she opened the door.

Cain had expected an extension of the store. What he got was a surprise. The apartment was designed with a great room and a small hall that led to the two bedrooms and bath.

Simple. Uncluttered.

But then again, how cluttered can an apartment get when its furniture consisted of a Nautilus, free weights, sparring bag and treadmill?

A gymnasium, right down to the dull white walls and scuffed hardwood floor. She'd thrown in a brown corduroy sofa, threadbare on the arms and so mangled any decent flea market would have rejected it.

On the kitchen counter was a microwave and a portable television. A radio sat on the floor near the weights, filtering a sultry jazz throughout the room.

As long as Cain had known her, Diana had left music on twenty-four seven—for company, she used to joke.

But the scent that lingered was flowers and earth. Not roses and talcum. Because he could, he inhaled deeply. "Don't tell me—you're going for the featherweight championship this year," Cain mused.

"No, downstairs is home. This is my workspace."

"Still, I have to admit the right combination of chrome and iron does the heart good."

"Because Grams and I died, my inheritance went to several designated charities and everything that was Diana's stayed behind." A decision she'd made not realizing at the time the immense relief and freedom that had come with it.

"What happened to my mother's engagement ring, Gypsy?" The question slid out of nowhere. During her days of being interrogated, she'd learned those questions were the worst kind.

"I don't know," Celeste answered slowly, cautious of the minefield being laid. "After I left the letter breaking our engagement at your apartment, I forgot to leave it, too," she explained, feeling the lie as it slithered over her tongue and knowing the self-hatred that would follow. "It was lost when the car exploded. Flung from my hand most likely. It was never recovered."

"How did you survive the blast?"

Celeste closed her eyes, briefly, knowing he deserved an answer, but undecided on how much she deserved to hold back. "I'd been upset. Too upset to drive."

"Because of the investigation?"

"Yes, mostly. I'd only been released a few days before and still hadn't really recovered." Restless, Celeste went into the kitchen and turned on the water. "Grams talked me into spending some time with her. Do some shopping, maybe see a play. Just excuses to get away." After filling the kitchen basin, she slid in the few dirty dishes she'd left from lunch. "We were in your apartment parking garage. I had just dropped off my letter to you. I realized I'd forgotten to leave the ring, so I grabbed it from my purse and was going to run it upstairs. Grams insisted on driving."

Celeste smiled at the memory as she swiped the sponge over a sandwich plate, rinsed it and set it in the drainer. Even at seventy, her grandmother had refused to give into Father Time. "She'd wanted to get behind the wheel of that Porsche ever since you'd given me the car. I wasn't in any shape to drive and I had just enough humor left to let her."

Nausea cramped her belly.

"Just that once," she whispered, knowing if she'd said no, Grams might have survived. A bowl slipped from her fingers and shattered on the floor. "Damn it!"

"Gypsy, it's not your—"

"Yes, it is." She spaced out the words, more to convince herself than him. "Don't you even dare think about offering me sympathy. I don't want it."

She wanted to take her comment back, but the hard planes of his face told her it was too late. Instead, she grabbed the wastebasket beside the kitchen door.

"Anyway…" Kneeling by the counter, she began tossing pieces of glass into the garbage. "I grabbed the ring, threw my purse on the front seat and shut the door. I hadn't taken more than one or two steps past the car when she must have turned on the ignition."

Celeste sat on her heels and abandoned all pretenses as the memories rushed back. "The explosion blew me clear." She remembered the vicious body slam of heat. "Grams screamed. I raised my head from the pavement and saw her trying to get out, her hands…"

She shook her head trying to dislodge the sounds. "I must have passed out. Jon told me that the heat was so intense, it set a few more cars on fire. No one could get close for a long time. Later they found me under a pickup truck. Apartment Security records showed only my signature. And since Grams' body was burned beyond…" She cleared her throat, forcing the images back. "The firefighters automatically assumed Grams was me. By the time they found me, I was covered in blood from a head wound. Before they figured out I was more than an innocent bystander at the wrong place at the wrong time, Jon had worked his government magic and I had died from the head trauma."

"How long were you in my apartment?"

"Grams and I were there a half an hour. No more. Just enough time to write the note and take my things." Ignoring the trembling of her fingers, she finished picking up the glass.

"Giving the killer plenty of time to rig the Porsche."

"He used the ignition to detonate the gas tank."

"Is that why you hesitated at the Jag this morning?"

"Yes. It's also why I don't own a car." She shrugged. "Cars give me a bout of nausea. It usually passes in moments. A reaction from the explosion."

"It wasn't your fault, Gypsy."

She rose to her feet, furious with herself for letting her guard down, if only briefly.

"And Olivia?"

"She and Grams had been friends since Radcliff, remember? When Bobby disappeared, Olivia and I became quite close through the whole ordeal. She never believed I was involved."

By the time Celeste had snagged the broom from the pantry, swept up the splinters of the bowl and put it all away, Cain had set the last dish in the drainer to dry.

"I don't think I've ever seen you in the kitchen," she said, once they were finished. Unsettled, she tried to match this man to the one who'd been her fiancé. "Who are you?"

"I'm just a man, Celeste." He sat at the table and leaned back, watching her with hooded eyes. Lifting a shoulder negligently, he added. "Not much more to it."

There it was again, the detachment he'd shown when they'd dated. Only now, it plucked at her tightly strung nerves. Before, she'd just respected his privacy.

God, she'd been so naive.

"But there is," she argued, not quite putting her finger on the cause of her frustration.

His eyes captured hers, the gray in them smoky, the murky depths somehow reassuring. "Just ask me."

"I don't understand—"

"You can trust me." His tone dipped, touching off a sensitive chord somewhere deep within her. "That's what you want to know, isn't it?"

Automatically, she started to shake her head, only to stop in midmotion when she caught sight of his expression. Lord, he was arrogant. "Trust isn't just given." Nevertheless, something compelled her to do just that. She sat down and gripped her knees under the table. What was it about heroes that made you believe in them?

Heaven knew, she didn't want to.

"Gypsy," Cain covered her hand, his thumb stroking the soft pad of her palm. "How did Olivia discover you were alive?"

Aware the subject was no longer focused on Cain almost made her laugh. That had been the standard in their conversations. She'd ask a personal question, he'd deflect. Sometimes, it reminded her of a sparring match. One Cain always won. "I asked Jon to hold a funeral for Grams and me."

Celeste yanked her hand back, not wanting the sympathy the contact would bring. "God, it was awful. When my mother died, I was barely old enough to remember. I never thought…" She took a deep ragged breath, trying to dislodge the knot from her throat.

Born fatherless, Celeste had been dragged from city to city by a mother who'd been pampered all her life and followed any man who caught her mother's eye. At age five, Celeste's world had abruptly changed when her mother had died in a car wreck with another woman's husband. Within hours after her mother's death, Celeste had been placed in the care of her grandmother.

"I waited hours after everyone left, before I went to say my goodbyes." Petite, white-haired with a will made of tempered steel, Grace Taylor had once been a New York debutante. A loving, yet possessive woman, whose harsh ways had forced a daughter away. Once she'd gotten custody of Celeste, she'd refused to let her granddaughter repeat the past. She'd hired the best tutors and nannies, keeping Celeste always within reach. Secluded. "In spite of everything, I loved Grams.

"Olivia saw me at the cemetery. I didn't know she had a meeting with the cemetery director about our headstones. The man wanted to show her a statue near ours. You can guess the rest." Celeste smiled. "She almost fainted at my feet but recovered herself just in time to avoid giving my identity away to the director."

"The fact that Olivia's your friend doesn't absolve her from suspicion."

"I know. But this goes higher than her. Higher than you realize. We can't trust anyone."

"Including the president."

"Yes, especially him. Emotionally, Robert killing his son would be a leap. But logically…" Abruptly, she turned away, looking across the room, seeing nothing, Cain was sure. Her profile revealed the battle within. "God, why didn't Jon just take my secret to the grave?"

"Did you choose your alias or did Jon?"

"What?" Her head snapped back.

"You heard me."

"I don't have an *alias*."

In Cain's work, he'd used a hundred different identities through the years. Forgotten more than he remembered.

"Celeste Pavenic is who I am. Other than finding Bobby's murderer, my past doesn't exist."

"Everything from the past?" He saw her chin thrust forward, her eyes narrow. He would have been amused by her response, if he hadn't tuned into the fear behind the defiance. Been annoyed by it.

"Everything."

"I'm from your past." His statement hit the air with the heavy thud—a gauntlet thrown to the ground. And damned if he didn't want her to pick it up.

"Exactly."

The buzz of Cain's phone cut her off. "What is it?"

"Hey, boss."

"I'm nobody's boss," Cain replied, his harsh tone born from frustration with Diana more than from his brother Ian's flippancy.

"We both know Roman only accepted Mercer's position temporarily to give you time." Ian grunted. "But when you're running things, you might think about acquiring me before I change my mind and retire, too. This contracting thing could get old, you know."

It had only been a few weeks since Ian had resigned his naval commission, so Cain took the flippancy in stride. If his brother did anything outside of government work, it would be running their family business. The old man would love that, Cain thought, absently. It was a known fact that the youngest son of Quentin MacAlister had the gift for making great whiskey. "What do you have for me?"

"You were right about the car. Stolen last night from a couple on vacation. Rental."

"Okay, so what else you got?"

"There's been a rash of B and E's in your area."

"Burglaries? Go on."

"The police breakdown is on its way. Check your PDA. Looks like someone's been busy. There have been six break-ins in the last few weeks. Some businesses, mostly residential—all high-income targets. Nothing's surfaced on the street yet." There was a pause.

Cain heard Ian's fingers fly over his keyboard.

"In every case, they've used advanced tech equipment to gain access. Stuff only available to the upper echelons of the government." Ian's concern filtered over the phone. "I'm sending a list of projected targets with the report."

"Robberies?" Diana murmured the question.

Nodding, Cain grabbed the unit from his pocket. "Send the report, Ian."

After a short pause, his brother responded, "Here it comes. Notice the two topping the list."

As the data filled the screen, Cain zeroed in on the obvious.

"Olivia Cambridge," he noted. "The family mansion is located fifteen minutes from Shadow Point."

"She arrived at Shadow Point a few weeks back. Earlier than usual. Could be the auction but it's not her usual pattern." It was common knowledge the president's mother spent the colder months in Palm Beach. "I don't like it, Cain. My muse is talking." There was a pause. He let the words hang in the air. "The connection is too coincidental. And in my experience, an answer this clean usually stinks to high heaven by the time it's all over."

"Hell, it already smells," Cain added. "Mercer's shooting is tied in. I want that connection found, Ian. And while you're at it, get me more on Olivia Cambridge's charities, her bank accounts and who hangs out in her social circle here. There's a leak somewhere and Olivia Cambridge might lead us to it."

"Got it."

"And Ian…"

"What?"

"Be discreet. The president wouldn't be the first to sacrifice family for political gain. And I'm not so sure about his mother. Both are at the top of our list along with Vice President Bowden and the rest of the legislature. And until they're all cleared, we don't want anyone getting suspicious."

"Don't worry, brother. Discretion is my middle name." Ian's tone hardened over the possibility that the president might have killed his own son.

"How about the warehouse? What have you got on that?"

"I sent you the inventory. Looks like Mrs. Cambridge and her pals are storing some pretty pricey items for the charity auction."

"Get me the security schematics on the warehouse, the Cambridge estate and any other estates listed. Pull in favors if you have to."

"You'll have it by tonight. Roman's already working on it. He also said to watch yourself or there'll be hell to pay from Kate," Ian warned. "The pregnancy has left her hormonally challenged and this time he says you're on your own."

"I'll handle her if the need arises."

"What about Diana? How are you handling her?"

For some reason the question grated. "It's under control." But Cain's little voice was nudging him, laughing at his confidence.

"I see." The pause between the two words left no doubt what his little brother was thinking. Cain didn't bother correcting him. "She's there."

"Yes." It was a statement not a question, but Cain chose to answer anyway. "Anything else?"

Ian took the silent order to move on. "Yes." This time the pause was longer. "Lara's getting impatient."

"Only impatient?"

"If I didn't know you better, I'd think you find this situation amusing." Ian's sigh held a comical edge. "She doesn't like me keeping her in the dark like this, Cain. Hell, she just doesn't like me. Compound that with the fact that I'm stopping her from finding her father's

Engaging Bodyguard

killer—well, let's just say certain parts of my anatomy are at serious risk."

Cain almost smirked over the younger man's concern. Or the lack thereof. "You're tough, you can handle her," he responded, deliberately withholding sympathy.

"Hell, some things are just beyond the call of king and country. Since you trained her, you know she won't hesitate to maim me if she thinks I'm in her way. Which I am." Satisfaction rolled over the phone.

"Keep her pacified, Ian, but don't underestimate her. She was my best protégé," Cain ordered. "Right now, I don't have time to deal with a grief-stricken operative."

"Can I use brute force?"

Cain had recognized long ago that Ian was attracted to Jonathon Mercer's daughter. He wondered if his brother realized it yet. "Only if necessary. Lock her up if you have to. Just keep her out of my way. And call me with any updates." With that, Cain snapped the phone shut, not feeling the least bit bad about hanging up.

"Lara wants a crack at Jon's killer?"

"Yes, but I've enough to worry about, without having—"

A knock exploded through the room, making Diana jump. Quickly, she reached for her pistol then crossed to her apartment door. But before she could grab the knob, Cain was there, his hand flat against the wood.

"Ask who," he mouthed soundlessly.

"I was going to," she whispered harshly, her glare shifting to the trim black metal pistol he held—barrel up. "Who is it?"

"Jim Lassiter, Miss Pavenic." A throat cleared. "Can I have a moment of your time?"

Cain slipped the weapon back into his waistband and stepped partially into the room's shadows, his curiosity sparked by the unexpected visit. Understanding he might need the local law, Cain had run a background check on Sheriff Lassiter before arriving in Shadow Point.

He recalled that Lassiter, a widower in his late forties, had retired as a captain from the Detroit Police Department's Homicide Division. Two months prior, he had the accepted the position as the town's sheriff when no one local had anything even close to his qualifications.

After following suit with her weapon, Diana opened the door. "Hello, Sheriff." Her smile, Cain noted, was somewhat rigid, but her voice remained steady. "What can I do for you?"

"I'm sorry to disturb you, Miss Pavenic. But an hour ago, a drag race occurred on the road outside of town. I have a witness, a truck driver, who says one of the vehicle was a black Jaguar. It nearly ran his rig off the road." The sheriff pushed back the brim on his Stetson, uncovering a dark, receding hairline. "You were seen getting out of that same Jag here in town. Now, I have some pretty angry people wanting to get replacement on some damaged mailboxes."

"I understand—"

"Hello, Sheriff." Cain stepped beside her, opening the door wide to accommodate them both. "The car's mine." The hand Cain extended was grasped immediately. "I'm…Miss Pavenic's fiancé, Cain MacAlister. Sorry about the damage. I got carried away when some fool challenged me for my space on the road. When it got out of hand, I stopped my car, but the other car had already disappeared," Lassiter released Cain's hand. "I was going to report the incident but you beat me to it.

"Of course, I'll pay for the expenses." Cain removed his wallet from his pocket and handed the sheriff a business card. "Call that number and talk with my partner, Roman D'Amato, and he'll take care of everything."

After a glance at the card, Lassiter tucked it into his coat pocket. "Most of the folks will accept this. Others might not…" He shrugged. "Let's just say I know firsthand that some people aren't as amicable to strangers." He hooked his thumb through a front belt loop.

"If they don't accept it, have them contact me here. I'll take care of it." Casually, Cain slipped his arm over Diana's shoulder. "I'm hoping not to be categorized as a stranger around here for much longer. Isn't that right, sweetheart?"

"What?" Her gaze flickered, before she recovered, bestowing upon Cain a look of absolute adoration. "Oh, yes." She shifted her gaze to Lassiter. Her hand patted Cain's stomach, her fingers digging into its muscles as she snuggled deeper into his right side. Cain was sure the sheriff didn't notice. "I'm sorry, honey," she demurred with a laugh, before turning to Lassiter. "I'm still not used to the idea of being engaged."

"Well now, most folks didn't even know you were dating." Lassiter commented, his voice holding a hint of speculation.

"We met through mutual friends." She smiled. Still, Cain noticed the lines tighten at the sides of her mouth.

"I guess congratulations are in order." The sheriff's friendly manner didn't quite reach his eyes.

"Thank you. I'm a very lucky man, finding someone as special as…Celeste." Cain let his arm drop until his hand rested on the soft curve of her hip. He pinched her backside lightly. Immediately her fingers flexed, then relaxed against his stomach.

"Have you folks set a date?"

"Not yet," Cain answered first. "We're still working out the logistics with my family."

"MacAlister." The blue eyes studied Cain in a new light, his eyes drawn once again to the card. "As in MacAlister Whiskey?"

"Guilty," Cain acknowledged with practiced ease. "My father's company."

"I read about it in some financial magazine. Saw your picture." He grinned. "Caught my eye because it's my favorite brand."

"I'll tell my father you said so. He appreciates the feedback."

"You do that." Lassiter tipped his hat. "And since you're willing to provide restitution, I'll let you off with a warning. Call it an early wedding gift. Just see that it doesn't happen again."

"Thanks," Cain said, and slid his hand into the soft curls at the base of Diana's neck.

With her sharp intake of breath, Lassiter glanced up.

"Maybe you could come over some night for dinner," Cain suggested, keeping his tone casual.

The sheriff hesitated, then bobbed his head until his chin disappeared into the thick collar of his coat. "I'd like that. Hell, I'm getting tired of diner food—" He tipped his hat low onto his forehead. "Excuse me, Miss Pavenic."

Lassiter extended his hand once more to Cain. "Congratulations again on your engagement."

"Thank you, Sheriff."

Cain watched the other man leave before shutting the door.

"You can stop now," she snapped and tried to side-step his hold.

"I could," he stated, refusing to drop his arm. "I'm just not sure I want to." He pulled her body closer, noting when the heavy lashes that shadowed her cheeks flew up in surprise.

"Gypsy." He drew out her nickname, enjoying the taste of it against his tongue. Sweet, he thought, too damn sweet to handle the bitterness in him. Nonetheless, he cupped the back of her neck, urging her closer. He noted a small flicker of alarm, right before her eyes deepened into cerulean pools. He gentled his touch, no longer surprised over his concern for her.

Unable to stop himself—not wanting to stop himself—Cain studied her clean-scrubbed features, following the graceful line of her face until his gaze rested on the slightly moist tendrils of hair that clung to her forehead and cheeks.

"Consider this…" he challenged softly, enjoying the minklike texture of her hair against his skin. He leaned in, allowing his mouth to hover above hers. "Redefining the term *we*."

Chapter Seven

The kiss itself was gentle. Only a butterfly dusting against her lips. Still, Celeste's heart trembled.

"What are you doing?" Her voice, rough, blended with the muffled roar cresting in her ears. But it was the fire in his eyes that set her trembling. His voice dipped seductively, strumming a chord deep within her long and hard, until her toes curled.

"Satisfying your curiosity." The warmth of his breath tickled, then excited. "And mine. Isn't that what you wanted?" Sparks of electricity raced up her arm, leaving her skin tingling. When his thumb rubbed the pad of her hand lightly, she couldn't control her sharp intake of breath.

"Pretending we're a couple…" The impulse to bury his fingers in the damp curls, to draw her face up to his, increased the hammering in Cain's blood. He struggled to keep his expression bland. "…simplifies things."

"Simplifies—" The word came out in a squeak. She cleared her throat, obviously trying to gain some control over her anger. The action drew his gaze to the small, erratic pulse at the base of her neck increasing his craving for that spot—sweet and fragile—under his mouth. "Can't you be honest with me for once?"

"You first."

When Cain's gaze caught and pinned hers, any thought Celeste had of fighting disappeared under a surge of longing. His free hand skimmed her jaw before slipping around to cup the back of her head. The small hairs on her neck stood.

"You want honesty?" He leaned closer until his breath tickled her cheek. Without a thought, Celeste shifted her mouth to taste the warmth on her lips and he captured her in a slow, shivery kiss. There was a cautious intimacy in the way his lips caressed hers. The kiss spanned three years of yearning, of deprivation that started in her heart and grew until it overwhelmed her soul, leaving her body throbbing.

"This is honest, Gypsy," he whispered after his mouth broke away. He nibbled her lower lip, the curve of her jaw.

"No," she disagreed, but in spite of herself, Celeste waited, her breath locked in her throat, the anticipation making her heart race. "It's a weapon."

Cain absorbed the insult, accepting the lie for what it was—an act of self-preservation. He stroked the soft skin of her neck with the tip of his finger. Her lips trembled and Cain's blood raced. Enough that when her lips parted as if to say something more, he moved closer. The slight switch in positions fanned his desire, touching off a high-pitched hum throughout his body.

Shock rippled over her features, telling him she felt it, too. But the fear remained in the widening of her eyes.

His body tightened, every muscle rigid with awareness. The attraction was there—flash-fire hot. After everything she'd been through, everything she'd done, she
still wanted him. He'd bet his sanity on it.

"Stop it!" Her words exploded between them, a little
breathless, more than a little desperate. Taking a deep,
unsteady breath, she stepped back, startled when Cain's
hand fell away. He let her go, using the time to bank his
desire, to silence the hum.

"I have no idea what game you're playing." Her
hands went to her hips, though a charming flush invaded
her cheeks. "But I'm not interested."

"This isn't a game, Gypsy." Regret, finely edged and
razor-sharp, sliced through him. "And you *are* interested. But I agree, this situation is complicated enough."
When she didn't respond, he wasn't surprised.

For a moment, Celeste hadn't thought it'd be so easy.
And for a moment, she didn't want it to be.

"I want guarantees," she insisted, albeit weakly.

"Go ahead," he folded his arms, evidently unconcerned and more annoyingly, unaffected.

"Don't think I'm going to be like Lassiter." Celeste
glared. "He used your father's reputation to size you up.
Right about now, he's wondering how I met you for real
and how long you'll be staying."

"You're going to have to trust me on this," he ordered.
"And not go off half-cocked."

As usual, his features remained impassive. She'd
spent her life on the fringe of society. Over the years,
she'd learned to observe, to read people from their
actions, voice inflections, facial expressions. But she'd

never been able to read Cain MacAlister. "I'm not the one in this room who's the self-appointed protector of mankind, Prometheus."

"We're not talking about me."

"Good thing, because we could definitely talk about some control issues, couldn't we?"

Cain sighed. "Why don't we stick to the reason we're here."

"Fine." On stilted legs, Celeste led him to her second bedroom. The smell of fresh paint lingered in the air as they entered, a by-product of the pristine white walls.

"So tell me more about this killer," Cain said.

"Personality wise?" She switched on a nearby lamp. "Detached. Unaffected."

"Your typical antisocial type?" Cain's eyes narrowed against the low amber light filtering the room.

"Actually, he's extremely sociable and very comfortable moving around in elite circles." When Cain stepped behind her, the room seemed to close in on Celeste. She flipped on additional lights, hoping to widen the space. "Otherwise, he wouldn't have access to the people he's targeting."

"Okay, so how did you hook him?" In one long sweep, Cain's gaze took in her office. Or what she'd always thought of as her office.

"A few months ago, the killer left the first series of coins."

"First series? How many all together?"

"Including Jonathon's, four."

"Nothing showed up because—"

"At my request, Jonathon made sure it didn't."

"I believe you're beginning to impress me, Gypsy." His gaze skimmed over the wallpaper—only it wasn't paper, but photographs—that covered one wall. Some were of Bobby, some were of his family and other Shadow Point residents. Others were of people who were no longer alive—their few smiling portraits framed by pictures of their corpses—some were riddled with blood and gore, others not. Spattered atop and in between lay a rainbow of Post-it notes. At one time, these people had been strangers to Celeste, but not anymore. Over the last few months, she'd become intimately familiar with these individuals and their backgrounds.

Cain let out a low, easy whistle. "If anyone but me saw this, they might think you were a serial killer. Or at the very least, a very sick individual."

She had to agree. Other than the photos, the room held little more than a cheap particle-board desk, a swivel chair and a computer. Somehow, she couldn't bring the coziness of her store into something that contained such evil. He scanned the photographs. "You're sure this is a man?"

"I'm sure. Men posture differently, physically as well as mentally. I'd say we're looking for a Caucasian male in his prime. Somewhere in his forties. Any younger would make it difficult for him to mingle with that kind of crowd. Any outstanding features, like a mole or scar would've been surgically removed. No habitual behavior. Easier to switch identities that way."

Cain grabbed his cell phone from his pocket and punched in a number. With a decisive "Call me," Cain snapped the phone shut.

"Money, his reputation, that's what drives him." She glanced at the pictures on the wall until she came to Bobby's. "How he kills, that's just…a diversion." She smoothed her hand over the photograph, absorbing the familiar ache. "Mercer believed me from the beginning, but with no proof, he wasn't going to take it to the president. We'd already decided to continue investigating. My death made it easier."

"And Olivia Cambridge?"

"After she spotted me at the cemetery she contacted Jon and insisted I move to Shadow Point or she'd blow my cover. She knew I'd continue the investigation and wanted firsthand knowledge.

"Jonathon took a risk and I stayed here to make my dealing with her easier."

Cain nodded, but continued to scrutinize the other photos. "And Jonathon kept your presence here in Shadow Point a secret."

"Yes."

"President Cambridge wouldn't have been the first leader in history to kill a family member to ensure his position. Sympathy goes a long way with the American public during election years. However, when I suggested the theory to Jonathon, he didn't agree. If his death is connected to these others, you can be sure it's a paid contract. I just don't know who the client is or the why."

"He can't kill all of us," Cain argued.

"That's my point. He could if he wanted to. I'm betting whoever is paying him has found an access to all of our files."

"A government official?"

Celeste nodded. "Or another operative." The Labyrinth files were classified. Even the president had restricted access unless he required contact.

"Jon wouldn't allow the records—"

"And as you've pointed out before, Cain, Jonathon's dead. Besides, this guy doesn't waste his time. He wouldn't be playing with the coins if he wasn't already getting paid to kill these people," she replied. "He's meticulous—pays enormous attention to detail. Everybody knew Jonathon always stepped outside alone to smoke his cigars.

"I'm betting that the coins started showing up because he'd realized I survived the explosion." Edgy, Celeste opened a small fridge under her desk and grabbed a bottle of water. Absently she offered it to Cain, but he shook his head. "If I had to speculate on the two highest probabilities…" She pointed the bottle in the general direction of the photos. "…when he tries to kill us, he's going to do it in such a way that he'll show off his skill, his cunning, or he'll set us up for another murder."

"Or both."

"That, too," she admitted easily. "Cain," she warned, "don't underestimate this guy. His reputation is everything. He doesn't make mistakes. In his business, if he did, he'd be dead."

"You forget, I'm in the same business."

"I haven't forgotten." She started past him, but his arm came up to block her retreat. For an instant, she thought the muscle flexing against her breast might have been deliberate.

"Still enemies?" His eyes slid over her face, questioning. But it was the purr behind the words that stroked her heart, set its tempo faster.

"Uncomfortable allies," she tossed back. Heavens, she'd never trusted anyone except Grams before Cain. Never really understood that trust took on a different meaning when dealing with passion—or love for that matter. Not that she had a lot of experience with either.

Oh, she'd had the typical clichéd affair with one of her professors in college. Not because she'd found true love, but more because she thought herself sophisticated enough to deal with sex. But when that professor found another willing student to add to the notches on his bedpost, she bowed out gracefully, not caring, but not liking the bad taste the situation had left in her mouth.

From that moment, she'd avoided any kind of involvement…until Cain. He released inhibitions in her that she'd never known existed and a love she never thought herself capable of.

So now, when desire sharpened his granite-like features, a succession of small electric charges exploded at the base of her spine.

In another place, another lifetime, Cain could've been the lover she desired, the husband she dreamed about. "Cain, I—" Celeste stopped, not knowing what to say.

"It's all right, Gypsy." He dropped his arm, turned toward the photos once more. "So Gabriel works alone?"

With a bit more steadiness than she was feeling, Celeste swung away, not sure what to think of the abrupt change in Cain. How could someone turn off emotion so quickly? Especially when her own roiled within.

"For the most part—yes. Partners are dangerous, unreliable," she said, setting her bottled water onto the desk. Water would only aggravate her already fluttering stomach. "Gabriel tracks his victim's life, learns their habits then kills them. Obviously, he decided we're important enough to study."

"So, like you, he profiles people."

"Yes, to put it simply."

"And the coins are just his way of keeping our attention."

Celeste rubbed her temples tiredly. "The coins appeared a couple of months ago—on the body of a man by the name of Doctor Alejandro Longoria."

"Spanish." Cain took a moment to place the name. "Expert in plastic surgery. Spoke at a seminar here in the States just before he died. Interpol suspected he'd been killed by an unsatisfied customer."

"He was. I believe one of his patients, possibly a surgery gone wrong, hired Gabriel to kill Longoria."

"His face was shredded—his heart cut out. All with his own scalpel."

"And all the facial incisions were precise, as though the killer had been following a map or—"

"Copying the same incisions made on his disgruntled customer."

"Five Georgia quarters were found in his coat," Celeste explained. "Their emblem consisted of a peach, an oak tree and a banner with three words. Wisdom. Justice. Moderation. The authorities didn't think it unusual because Dr. Longoria was known to be collecting them from Americans who passed his way."

"But you disagree."

"Do you remember when Supreme Court Justice Miles Rokeach died?"

Cain grunted, disgusted. "Someone breached his yacht, most likely from under the water. Easy enough. Pay off a crew member, arrange for a predetermined location, then kill the contact with the rest of the crew. The authorities didn't find the ship for several days and the crew members were gone. Most likely thrown overboard."

"The authorities found Justice Rokeach and his wife dead inside."

"And you believe your assassin left the Georgia quarters in Longoria's coat as a clue," Cain prompted, unwilling to use kid gloves on Celeste. "That's pretty vague. So far the only connection is the word *justice*."

"And the southern state of Georgia," she countered, obviously not intimidated. "Don't you see? After rendering them unconscious with a stun gun, the killer stripped them naked and sealed them in the cabin. But not before he'd left a canister of hydrogen cyanide gas behind. He rigged a timer to allow both of them to regain consciousness before the canister detonated. They were found dead by the door."

"I heard the rumors. A white supremacy group backed the murders in protest over the judge's religion. He was Jewish."

"Exactly. And in their nightstand ashtray lay five state quarters. New Hampshire. The Old Man on the Mountain."

"Mercer?"

"The president had nicknamed Jonathon Old Man."

"Again you're stretching, Gypsy."

"And he's dead."

Celeste caught Cain's gaze. "I've tracked Gabriel back four years. Men, women, children. Diplomats, mob figures, the cartel. I can't be one-hundred-percent positive, but all were hired hits, all were killed with Gabriel's flair. None with coins until after Bobby's death."

"Why the coins? And why now? Because of your report on the coin left in Bobby's hand?"

"It fits. Otherwise, why not a note, a memento, like jewelry or a flower?"

"It's all been done before."

"Exactly. Not original enough."

"Speaking of jewelry, Gypsy…" Cain paused, watching her face. "How about telling me the truth about my mother's engagement ring?"

"I told you—"

"No more lies. I realized when Jon told me you were alive that you might have kept it. You see, I placed a homing device in it with a fifty-mile range so when I tried to find you I turned it on. I got no response. Not until this morning, that is."

"That's how you found me so quickly at the lighthouse." She took a deep breath. "You actually kept track of me with a homing device."

"No, it was a precaution. One I never used."

"I guess we've both lied, haven't we?"

At some point Cain had become important to her again. The actual moment it had happened didn't matter. It disturbed her more that he had.

"I guess we have."

Deep down, she realized she had even started hoping

that she'd found something with him again. Something special. But how could that hope survive when she disagreed with everything he stood for—or expected.

"This isn't going to work." Not the mission, not the relationship, she thought. She'd figure out another way to trap Gabriel. She bit her lip to keep it from trembling. No one besides Grams had ever cared enough to protect her. But Celeste didn't fool herself. Where Grams protected out of love, Cain did it out of duty.

Unfortunately, Celeste wanted—needed—love. Not protection.

Cain caught her by the elbow. She closed her eyes, resisting the temptation to turn into the comfort of his arms. How pathetic could she be?

"Leave me alone, Cain." Her lids fluttered open, unable to hide the entreaty.

"No. You've been alone too long already."

"Stop playing Freud." She bit back the urge to kick him in the shins. "What are you going to do when this is over? If we aren't dead that is."

"I'll leave." His answer was gruff. "Because it's for the best."

When she thought she couldn't care any more, hurt any more, his confession proved her wrong. "Whose best?"

"In the past, I might have protected you the wrong way. And I'm sorry for that. But I did it for the right reasons. Left with the same situation, I'd do it again. And while I'm here, no one is going to hurt you. Not Gabriel. Not his client. No one. I'll make sure of that."

And who is going to protect me from you? she wondered silently, already knowing the answer. The answer didn't matter because she understood that it was already too late. When Cain left, he'd be taking a part of her with him.

"Come on." He hugged her to his side. "I'm still hungry."

Celeste snuggled deeper under his arm, understanding what was beneath the words—what he hadn't said. He cared for her. "Are you suggesting that I feed you?" she asked, not in the mood to deal with her rioting emotions.

"No. I'm telling you to."

Even though his expression hadn't changed, Celeste knew he was joking. She wasn't in any mood for that either. "Then you'd better ask nicely or so help me—"

"Please?"

The shock of that one softly spoken word smacked the breath from her lungs. But it was the smile that came with it that almost brought her to her knees.

"I've got vegetable soup," she whispered, forcing her feet to keep her balanced. "Canned."

She'd forgotten how blatantly sexual his smile could be. The flash of white teeth, the slight tilt of his lips that hinted at some unknown male secret.

He leaned down and kissed her, catching her gasp of surprise with his mouth. Laughing, he did it again before using his free hand to guide her through the doorway. "You remembered my second weakness."

She looked up at him, fighting the desire to touch the dark stubble on his jaw, to kiss the hard line of his lips— lose herself in the strength of both. Quick to tease. Tender. Romantic. This had been the man she'd known.

The one who'd swept her off her feet, discovered her passion. It was the other part of him, Prometheus, who had broken her heart. "Cain—"

"No more questions for now." He touched his finger to her lips, then inhaled sharply when she kissed it. "First we'll eat, then we'll worry."

"Not so fast," she mused, knowing he did it deliberately. Dangled that carrot. "What's your first weakness?"

His hand drifted up to caress the nape of her neck.

"Obstinate gypsies."

THE DINNER was relatively easy. Cain ended up fixing it while Celeste took a shower.

Dressed in a light blue turtleneck sweater and jeans, she sat down with him and ate a grilled cheese sandwich and canned vegetable soup. Two cans, Celeste corrected, since Cain wasn't satisfied with one bowl.

"You're not cut out for this job, Celeste." Cain leaned back, and wiped his mouth with a napkin. "You should be teaching or raising a family."

"That's funny coming from you."

Cain stiffened ever so slightly, enough for Celeste to realize how harsh she'd sounded. When he stood, she caught his hand, gave him a small squeeze. "I'm sorry. I didn't mean that."

Before he could answer, the radio switched songs, catching Celeste's attention. "Hear that?" she asked. The radio played a familiar Nat King Cole melody.

Cain nodded.

"It was one of Grams' favorites," she whispered, not wanting to ruin the peacefulness of the moment.

"You miss her terribly, don't you?" He whispered, too, but the words came out rough, whiskey-soaked.

There'd been a time when passion had deepened his words, not sympathy.

"Yes. But I've missed you more."

For a moment, time slowed. His hands slipped up her arms bringing her closer. "For what it's worth, Gypsy, I've missed you, too."

His gaze caught her, now silver pools of molten diamonds. It was too easy to get lost in the way he looked at her—in the way he made her feel.

Shifting, he backed her up to the wall. The cold pine went unnoticed as the heat of his body eased between her legs.

"Please, I don't want…" Not when she felt this raw, this vulnerable. She shook her head, unable to finish.

"That's the problem." He caught her chin with the tip of his finger. The muscles quivered just under her jaw, but this time it wasn't from fury. "I do."

Chapter Eight

Cain braced his forearms against the wall on either side of her head and sank deeper into the embrace, using only his hips to force her flush against the wall. His mouth dropped to her ear, grazing the delicate curve of her lobe. A sharp nip, a light stroke of his lips turned the quivers into a violent flux of tremors.

Desperate, Celeste turned her head away, realizing her mistake instantly. He swooped to nuzzle her neck. His warm, damp breath raised goose bumps everywhere his lips skimmed. She wedged her hands between them but instead of pushing, they held on as memories stirred.

"Cain." His name came out quick, riding another gasp of pleasure. "I'm afraid."

"Ah, Gypsy." His hand slipped under her sweater and around to her back, tracing small, lazy circles at the base of her spine.

His fingers should've been icy, but they weren't. Hot flames of desire licked at her skin wherever he touched.

"I'm the last person you should be afraid of."

The warmth of his palm cupped the curve of her

waist. His thumb brushed gently against the small in- dentation just above her hip. A thick, liquid heat flowed, forming a whirlpool low in her belly. With a moan she arched, grinding against him, trying to ease the sensation.

Somewhere in the distance, she heard a slight buzzing. It took her a second to recognize the gentle slide of her jeans zipper. Instinctively, she gripped his wrist.

Turning her hand, he pressed a kiss to her palm. His tongue darted out to trace a delicate crease. A groan es- caped her. His nostrils flared at the sound, but it was his gaze that changed her mind. The gray irises had sharpened to silver lightning, telling her exactly what he wanted.

A sense of urgency drove her. She couldn't have stopped her response, even if she'd wanted to.

And it pleased him. Very much, she realized. There was that maddening air of arrogance surrounding him again, but this time it seduced her.

Slowly, his hand slipped under her sweater again, this time lifting it, exposing her to his gaze. A flutter rose through her chest, swelled in her throat. His hand slid across her taut belly, his fingers icy but his palm fiery hot. Her breath caught with the snap of her bra's front clasp.

"Beautiful," he murmured. He eased the cup of her bra aside and gently outlined her breast with his finger- tips, tracing the curves with infinite care. The caress spiked the currents of desire already racing through her. Her breasts swelled and she shifted closer, hoping the erotic strokes of his fingers would ease their ache.

His knuckles brushed the ring hanging from her neck, sending it skittering across her breastbone. She

gasped. Her eyes met his and the possessive heat in
them made her tremble.

"I'm glad you kept my ring," he whispered.

But when he drew away, Celeste heard a whimper,
surprised that it had come from her.

"Hold on," he coaxed, the seduction melting over her
like warm butter. He flipped her around so that her stomach pressed the wall, his pelvis bumped against the crevice between her buttocks. When she groaned, he pushed
again, straining. The intensity ripped through her, savage.
"When we were on the rope…" He pulled down the neck
of her sweater, just enough to graze his teeth down the side
of her neck. "I wanted…needed to do this."

"Yes." With slow deliberation, she rubbed, eliciting
a hiss against her ear. "Me, too."

Slowly, he turned her back, lifting her legs up around
his hips, his mouth slanting over hers, fusing their passion, blurring her thoughts.

"More," he demanded, his voice raw, his body rigid.
He guided her hand under his sweater. "All."

Hair, thick and coarse, tickled her palm. A delicious
shudder heated her body, causing her fingers to curl, her
throat to hum.

His muscles quivered then bunched beneath her
touch. His heart skipped a beat. Power surged through
her. The hum she held escaped in a satisfied purr.

Tentatively, she moved her fingers, this time brushing
her nails lightly across his chest, remembering with deliberate slowness his pleasure points. She smiled when
a long, deep groan rasped against her ear.

His thumb brushed the hard peak of her breast.

But it wasn't enough. Unable to use words, she pulled at his shoulders, trying to bring him closer. Still, his touch was light, painfully teasing and totally in control.

A moan of frustrated pleasure slipped past her slightly parted lips. His mouth covered hers, this time dominating more than persuading. Her emotions whirled and skidded. She grabbed his hair, holding him, holding on, mindless to everything except the edge of desperation that crept between them.

Cain broke away, his hand fisted in her hair, his teeth at her neck, feasting. "Diana—"

Celeste froze.

"Stop!" She pushed away, her hands hitting his chest, demanding release. Nausea whiplashed through her. "Stop it, you bastard!"

Abruptly, Cain released her only to grab her arm when she started to fall. "Damn it! You're making it sound like I just betrayed you by whispering another woman's name. You are Diana!"

"No, I'm not!" The tears were there, swelling before she could blink them away.

"From where I stand, lady…" he ground out the words as his gaze raked her body. "You most definitely are."

Once again, Celeste found herself hauled closer, held by both shoulders, her eyelashes almost brushing his. It was beginning to be a habit with Cain, she thought angrily, then stopped. Shock rippled through her.

The lighthouse, the car and now. All three times he'd grabbed her in anger. No kid gloves. No fragile care. Cain would never have done that three years ago. He'd never grabbed Diana like that. Always in control, always even-tempered.

Angry, irritated…even in the midst of passion, Cain always maintained control.

It was a sobering thought. She'd been just as guilty as he about comparing now to the past.

"Cain, I'm—"

"So am I, *Diana.*" Slowly, he let her slide until her feet touched the floor. "So am I." He turned away, the disgust underlining his movement. "I'm going to sleep on the couch. Tomorrow, we'll check out Olivia Cambridge."

Celeste didn't argue, understanding by his rigid stance that he was beyond listening. Maybe even beyond caring.

Still, for a split second, if he had lifted his arms she would've fallen into them, placed his heart beneath her cheek and wept.

Another sobering thought.

Silently, she walked to her room and quietly closed the door.

Chapter Nine

Detroit, Midnight

The wind whipped icy shards of snow and bits of garbage across the deserted pavement of Michigan Avenue. Only the neon lights of the strip clubs and adult bookstores revealed signs of life as they glowed like dim beacons above the heads of a few prostitutes huddled in doorways. Obviously, it was easier to freeze to death than to face their pimps with empty pockets.

Gabriel eased the dark green sedan to a stop in front of a triple-X theater where a lone hooker guarded her territory. The marquee cast a jaundiced glow over the entrance, accenting the woman's sunken eyes, the hollowness of her cheeks.

She'd been talking on her cell phone when she caught sight of his car. Quickly, she finished the conversation and placed her phone in the small beaded purse hanging at her side.

Come here, the man urged silently. He pressed a button to lower the tinted window on the passenger side. A blast of frigid air rifled through the interior, but he enjoyed the sensation. The ride into the city had been long and stuffy.

After darting a glance up and down the street, the prostitute brushed her blond bangs away from her forehead—only to have her fingers snag in the uncombed strands.

He waved to her and fought a sting of impatience when the woman hesitated, wobbling slightly on her stiletto heels. His hands tightened over the steering wheel when indecision crossed her face.

After a moment, she straightened and took several shaky steps forward. Her bare legs, protected from the elements by only a purple micro-mini, drew his attention. Even in the darkness, he noted the deep bruising around her feet and ankles. Confident there'd be track lines by the marks, he relaxed his hands.

She stuck her head through the open window and gripped the edge of the car with trembling fingers. The smeared mascara around her bloodshot eyes gave her a ghoulish look. "Hey, baby, wanna party?"

Up close, he noticed the harsh creases set in the planes of her face and estimated her age at around thirty. This line of work tended to age women rapidly, so admittedly, he could be off by five years or more. But the pale, almost translucent skin told him that the slight twitching of her shoulders and arms wasn't from the cold weather. This woman had already had her fix for the evening.

"I'd enjoy a party," he murmured and unlocked the car.

She slid into the seat and immediately the distinct scent of wet dog and stale cigarettes permeated the air.

Not bothering to tug her skirt back into place, she provided him with a glimpse of her merchandise as he pulled away from the curb.

He felt, rather than saw, her glance over his suit. "Are you a cop?" Her voice was husky, reminding him of Janis Joplin.

He allowed his lips to form a cultured smile. "No, just a businessman."

"Hmm." Seeming satisfied, she relaxed against the upholstered seat. "Well, businessman, I get a hundred bucks an hour for straight sex. Anything fancy or weird boosts the rate to three hundred." She looked at his leather gloves as he turned the steering wheel. "I'm not into pain, so no whips or handcuffs."

The light at Woodward Avenue turned red and the driver stopped. "How about…" he drawled, before letting his gaze move suggestively over her emaciated body. "…I pay you in crack."

Greed flickered across the pinpoint pupils of her glazed blue eyes. "Now you're talking, honey." She leaned into him, letting her hand drift over the zipper of his pants while her tongue licked the thick red gloss covering her upper lip. "Or you could pay me in cash and we share the groceries."

"Better yet, I'll show you a drug that will take you flying and we don't party at all." Gabriel slipped his hand behind her neck and pricked the skin under her ear with a small needle.

Surprise, then fear flitted across her face before she fell unconscious against his shoulder.

With little effort, he shoved her back onto the passenger seat. The small drug dose, combined with the other substances in her body, would be enough to kill her soon enough.

After turning south on Woodward, he checked his rear mirror, satisfied when no car appeared behind them. He pulled to the curb, cut the engine and lights before reaching for the woman's purse and snagging her cell phone. Careful not to put his mouth too close to the receiver, the man punched in a number.

"Hello." The male voice was hoarse from sleep.

"I received your request," the man stated, casually studying the snowflakes landing on the windshield. "So talk."

"How did you get this number?" The tone was enraged, all traces of sleep gone. "Only my family has access to my private line."

"That's not important. What's important is that you broke our agreement. You weren't to contact me so soon." Flicking a glance at the unconscious woman, he added. "Your message proved inconvenient."

"It couldn't be helped. I hired you to do a job. One that may be in jeopardy." His client took an agitated breath. "With the news of Jonathon Mercer's death, the security assigned for our target has been restructured."

The man relaxed. "There was always that possibility. The government tends to get jumpy when one of their own is killed."

"I want you to be prepared. Nothing can go wrong." His client's agitation grew with the demand.

"I've agreed to the job, I'll make the hit. There'll be no interference."

"Just make sure of it. There's too much at stake."

"So you have said, many times." Indifferently, the man leaned over and checked the woman's pupils, then her pulse. "By the way, my fee has doubled."

"Doubled? After you screwed up with the woman, I don't—"

"Celeste Pavenic is a minor…hiccup. She'll be taken care of when I'm ready, not before. As you said, added security means a greater chance of discovery. Hence, a need for larger risks. If you don't like it, find someone else." He started to hang up.

"All right. You'll get your money."

"I'm sorry, I didn't hear you," he replied and slapped the prostitute's face. There was no reaction.

"I said, you'll get your money."

"Then I agree." The man shifted back into his seat. "You'll do as before. Deposit the payment to the same account. Half now, the rest when the news hits the wire."

"It'll be done tomorrow."

And moments after the deposit, the money would be transferred through several different accounts until it reached the correct one overseas. "Do not inconvenience me again." Sharp steel edged each word. "Or the deal's off. Understood?"

"Yes. Yes," the other man replied, his drawl growing thicker with his impatience. "There will be no more contact between us. Just take care of business. You understand?"

The man in the car disconnected, tempted to take the imbecile's money and not do the job. He drove along the Detroit River until he found an acceptable area. The snow and wind sharpened off the water. The long, bellowing gusts had left the road deserted. He leaned over the woman and pushed the door open. Not bothering to get out, he shoved her onto the roadside and watched her roll a few feet. "*Au revoir, chérie,*" he said, as he tossed the purse out. Seconds later, his calling cards followed. He watched the silver glint against the snow, then reached for the camera in the glove compartment. "Say cheese," he quipped, then pressed the button.

As he closed the door, he replayed the telephone conversation in his mind, then spoke aloud as though the man on the other end were sitting beside him. "Tomorrow afternoon, my friend, you will learn of the dead prostitute. What I wonder is how you will explain the presence of your private number on her cell phone?" He settled against the leather seat for the long trip home. "Now *that* will be inconvenient."

CAIN LAY on the couch, understanding immediately when the worn cushions gave way—comfortable, comforting—why the piece had avoided the garbage dump.

But soon her scent clouded around him. He'd done his best to ignore it after she'd stepped out of the shower, smelling as if she'd rolled in a meadow of wild flowers.

Another change. Diana had been upper Manhattan, her scent more stylish, classy and serene. Restless, he stood and watched Pan pad out the kitchen door, most likely to start his nightly prowl. Cain soon started stalking the apartment himself. Checking windows, doors.

He caught sight of the weight bench and automatically loaded up the bar, although he was impressed at the sixty pounds she'd left there. Celeste Pavenic was as far from Diana as Manhattan was from the Rocky Mountains. Earthy, simple—strong. Although not as Rambo-strong as she thought she was.

Rhythmically, he lifted the weights. Damned if she wasn't impressing him. Scaring the hell out of him, too.

Cain had vehemently argued with Jon over her acquisition into Labyrinth. She'd been too raw, too delicate to survive out in the field.

But there was more to it. At Quantico, Jon and Cain had observed Diana through a two-way mirror. Dressed in a trim, navy-blue suit with a skirt just high enough to show a little too much thigh, and hair long enough to keep her femininity intact, she could've been a corporate poster girl.

But surprisingly, it was the air of efficiency that drew his attention. She leaned over a desk, her hand resting lightly on the shoulder of a redheaded man whose face was nothing more than an explosion of freckles. They both scanned the computer screen in front of them, pointing at data, deep in conversation.

Then, almost as if she sensed their presence, her head tilted just enough to study the mirror. The man continued to talk while she continued to stare. After a moment, she smiled, a soft serene tilt of her lips, before allowing her associate to pull her attention back to their discussion.

The impact of that one look, calm as a glass-covered pond, settled the frenzied storm in Cain. He'd spent years dealing with scum, mucking around in places where only the foulest creatures bred.

She'd became his beacon, an oasis amidst the chaos.

His decision to seduce her came at that moment, however, it had taken months for him to arrange the meeting through Roman. Then, for four months he'd courted her, leaving his seduction until the end.

She'd surprised him. In Cain's mind, gypsies had always been tall and sultry. After one weekend in his cabin, she had shattered that image forever. The memory of her sighs, soft and fluttering with uncertainty, still haunted him—how her heart had raced with each caress, how her moans of erotic pleasure had turned into demands for release. And when he hadn't obeyed right away, how she'd risen to meet him, naked and passionate, her skin slick with heat, her body pliant—her heart open.

Then he'd proposed.

He'd offered her passion, comfort, protection—if not love. And when she'd needed the protection, the comfort…he'd had no choice about leaving her. Another operative, Jordan Beck, had been captured and left to die in the bowels of Colombia. Cain had been his only line out.

As a satellite operative, Diana should never had been in real danger, the interrogation should've been routine.

But she'd stuck to her theory after the boy's death. Not once had she broken under the endless grilling.

For days, they'd kept her at a table, pounding her with questions. But while her answers never changed, Diana did. Her voice hoarsened to sandpaper, her features sharpened and her cheeks hollowed. Given little sleep and even less food, she'd taken it all with dignified grace, defying their allegations. All the while, he was sure, silently grieving for the dead boy.

Guilt twisted his gut because even knowing what he did now, he would have made the same choice.

"Cain."

She'd whispered his name from across the room, but the underlining desperation smacked him square in the gut.

Slowly, he set down the weights.

She'd changed her clothes. A man's plain white T-shirt hung to her knees over a dark pair of sweatpants and fleece scuffs on her feet for added warmth. No makeup, her hair in feathered disarray, she looked more like a teenager than a grown woman.

"I know its not fair for me to ask this, but…" She stopped in mid-step, poised to turn and run. "Oh, hell."

Cain had been around her enough now to realize she only swore when she felt cornered or off balance.

But he wasn't paying attention to the words, as much as to the need reflected in her eyes. Not desire, but reassurance.

"You see, so much has happened, and it's been so long since…" She dragged a hand through her hair, telling him she'd been doing the same for probably the last half hour. "Damn it, I need…"

Without a word, he scooped her up in his arms, recognizing his own restlessness as a desire to hold her. It was time to stop denying them both.

She sighed and melted into him, but it wasn't until her arms encircled his neck that his own body settled, for once content.

Gently, he brought her back to the couch. Sinking in, they lay curled, her back snug against his chest, her head tucked safely under his chin. Slowly he rubbed, enjoying the texture, the smell. Needing to comfort, needing that comfort.

The rightness seeped in, catching him off guard.

Little by little, the layers of muscles relaxed. His, hers. Until she sighed again, then his arms tightened. "How long has it been, Gypsy, since anybody's held you?"

"Jon did, once. When we said goodbye. A big bear hug. It felt good. Other than that, no one since our weekend in your cabin."

"And Grace?"

"You know Grams, she loved me, but she wasn't one to…" She stopped and shook her head. "Cain, I didn't leave you because of the choice you made. I agreed with it."

"I know."

"We would've never been happy. Not really. Funny thing is, Jon saw it, too. He sat me down like a father would, to ask me if I was sure about being married to you."

"I could see him doing that." He sighed, not liking the raw feeling invading his chest at the mention of Jon's name.

Without thinking, he started rubbing the hollow between her shoulders, where he suspected the muscles refused to unknot.

"Mercer recruited me, you know. In fact, he recruited both Roman and me just as we were finishing our final year at the Naval Academy. Roman because of his diplomatic connections, and me—well, let's just say I proved I could handle myself even back then. That, along with the MacAlister name, caught the government's interest."

Cain breathed in her scent, no longer fighting the impulse, absorbing it easily. "When I started with Labyrinth, I began distancing myself from my family, friends. Partly because of the lifestyle and, of course, because of the risk. At first it was difficult, but over the years, with each mission, it became easier and easier until I couldn't break free, didn't want to. The scum of it eventually sticks to you like thick crude oil, to the point where you feel you'll never be clean."

"You can't change who you are, Cain."

"You did."

"No, I was no more than a lump of clay, molded into who I was told to be. Rather than take the risk I might be my mother, I became nobody really."

The carefulness of her statement, squeezed at his heart. He absorbed that too, as he did her scent, but this time, not so easily.

"You were always Prometheus. You probably came out of the womb with fists raised," she said.

He felt her smile against his arm and enjoyed the humor. Her humor.

"Jon recognized that in you, Cain."

"Maybe."

"Definitely." She leaned back and stared at him for a minute. Her face pale, like smooth milk glass, making the blue of her eyes softer—a rich sapphire velvet. Still, he noted the small lines of fatigue etched around her eyes and mouth. Remorse shadowed his conscious. He'd done that.

"That's why I let you believe I'd died, you know. It was the only way to protect you," she whispered.

Foolish, stupid even, but Cain still felt the slight

warming beneath his heart. In her position, he would have done the same.

"I didn't think you'd grieve too much, because I knew you didn't love me, not really, Cain. But your sense of duty to protect—engaged or not—would have made you stay."

"I understand." And it frightened him, that he really did understand. And more importantly, forgave. "You did what you felt was necessary."

"I was still clutching your mother's ring when the firefighters found me." She turned back, snuggled in deeper. "I kept it because for a long time it was my lifeline. But now…" She took a huge, shaky breath that trembled against his chest. "If you want it back…" The courage was there more than ever in that one simple offer.

And the love.

It was the latter that tugged on him—the deliberate, gentle tug of the inevitable. And God help him, in that moment he slid, slow and easy, into its warmth. "No. Keep it. It's yours." Needing more, though not sure why, his hand eased over her arm, grasped hers, palm to palm, fingers locked. *It has always been yours,* he mouthed the words silently against her hair.

She shifted her head until her cheek lay over his heart. He felt moisture dampen his shirt and recognized the tears for what they meant. The fact that she'd trusted him enough to let go humbled him, making his tumble that much more amazing, and that much more terrifying.

He'd taken on the Mafia, drug cartels, rogue agents and terrorists. Fearlessly, systematically. But for the first time, Cain tasted uncertainty.

After a while, the rhythmic breathing against his forearm told him she'd fallen asleep.

Gently, he cupped the back of her head, holding her to him. He placed a soft kiss on her brow, let his thumb caress the silkiness just under her ear.

The T-shirt's tag had flipped, sticking out of the neckline, Cain recognized the brand as his favorite. One that was no longer manufactured.

She'd taken his T-shirt from the cabin with her.

"You sure pick the damnedest time to go soft on me, Gypsy." Amused and frustrated, he closed his eyes—knowing he wouldn't find rest so easily. What the dregs of the world hadn't managed in over a dozen years, fate had handled in less than twenty-four hours.

A tiny gypsy had brought Prometheus to his knees.

A HIGH-PITCHED WHINE hit the air like a raid siren. Cain hit the deck, one arm protecting, one hand reaching for his pistol.

"A fax?" Celeste struggled off the couch, her eyes blinking away the sleep. "Jon is the only one with this number. Not even Olivia has it."

By the time they reached the second bedroom, a paper lay in the machine's slot.

"A photograph." Her fingers trembled, her face paled to white linen. But when she looked at Cain her eyes were ice-blue and steady. "Score one for the bad guys."

With a curse, Cain snagged the picture.

It showed the clear lines of a woman lying in the snow, her eyes open, the pupils flat and lifeless.

Cain scanned the picture until his eyes locked on the

lower right corner, knowing instantly why Celeste's hand had begun to shake.

According to the time stamp, the picture had been taken less than three hours prior.

"She's dead." Celeste leaned against the wall and looked up at the ceiling, trying to check her emotions. The soft tick, tick of a watch was the only sound echoing through the room.

Automatically she glanced at Cain's watch and froze. "Your watch is digital."

"Yes. What has that—"

"Shhh!" Celeste swung around, her eyes searching.

When Cain stepped closer, her hand held him back. "Bomb." They both started searching then, but it Celeste who found it.

"The fax machine."

"Get out of here, Gypsy," he growled.

"No!" She rounded on him, snapping fingers impatiently. "You still carry that penlight?"

When Cain didn't move, Celeste yelled, "Damn it, Cain. You may have handled my death by reinforcing your car against explosives, I handled it by learning how to disable them. Give me the light. Hurry!"

Cain reached into his pocket and pulled out his keys, then disconnected the penlight. He punched the red button, turning on the light. "Leave the black button alone."

"Why?"

"Because it triggers a laser. I sure would hate like hell for it to touch an explosive."

"Good call," she agreed with derision and directed the light to illuminate the underside of the fax machine.

The bottom had been removed from the machine to allow several small squares of a clay-like substance to be tucked up underneath the casing. Celeste shifted, feeling a thin sheen of sweat form on her brow. "Get out, Cain. He's got this thing loaded with C-4 explosives."

"Not on your life."

Hearing the hard edge on his statement, Celeste didn't waste any more breath, and instead pointed the light into the paper feeder. She saw it then, an analog wristwatch fastened to the back inside corner. The feeder triggered the watch to start its countdown. They had a minute at most. But worse, wires ran across and down each seam. "Damn it! He's rigged the whole thing so it can't be opened."

She jerked him away. "Let's go!"

They both hit the apartment door, scrambling. Halfway down the outside steps, they jumped the railing.

The store shattered, windows and frames exploded, showering them with splinters of glass. Instinctively, Celeste covered her face and sprinted blindly, held tight in Cain's grip. Before she could think, a second explosion—its blast hot and angry— shoved her into Cain and pelted them with wicked blows of wood and cement.

"YOU'RE LUCKY, Miss Pavenic. Just a bad sprain." The paramedic, a thirty-something-year-old blonde who'd look more comfortable holding a surfboard in his hands than a stretcher, finished bandaging Celeste's right ankle. "You should be as good as new if you take it easy for a few days and ice it every so often to keep the swelling down."

"Thank you." The throbbing had eased into a dull ache with the light compression of the wrap.

The paramedic stepped to the side and started putting his supplies away. "I understand your refusal to go to the hospital right now, but I would have it checked within the next few days."

"I'll be fine." Slowly, she slid off the back of the ambulance, testing her leg. "See?" Earlier, the paramedic had given her his jacket to stave off the biting wind. Now, she zipped it until the collar closed around her neck. She managed a tentative smile as she limped away from the ambulance, grimacing at the sharp pain only after she'd turned away.

Cain appeared at her side, and steadied her with his hand cupped at her elbow. "Going somewhere?"

"I've nowhere to go, or haven't you noticed?" Cain had foregone a coat, still wearing only his shirt and jeans to protect him from the cold. Other than a few facial cuts, he showed little evidence of their ordeal.

"What do you have on the woman?" she asked, knowing Cain had spent time on the phone while she'd been checked over.

"A Detroit prostitute by the name of Joyce Raines." Cain paused. "Age thirty-two. No relatives, no permanent address—other than her pimp's—and no worldly possessions except a cell phone—again, paid for by her pimp. Ian's hit a snag with the phone records."

"What snag?"

"There are no records," Cain spat. "Phone company doesn't understand how it happened, of course.

Roman's on it now. He's checking for back doors—it's only a matter of time before he finds something."

Celeste knew Roman's expertise lay in computer technology. "Could be our missing link. Whoever set me up used the cell phone to do it. I'm betting it's no coincidence. Whatever happened on that phone call might have cost Joyce Raines her life."

"Quamar's come up empty in Detroit. No witnesses, no leads. Other than her drug addiction, Raines led a sad, uneventful life." He handed her his PDA to read the details herself.

Quamar was also heading up to Shadow Point, something Cain had decided to keep to himself for now. It certainly wouldn't hurt to have someone else around to help keep an eye on Celeste. Cain couldn't ask for better back up than Quamar Bazan. Mercer had recently contracted Bazan for Labyrinth after the ex-Mossad agent had helped Cain save Roman's and Kate's lives the previous year.

"Joyce Raines." Sorrow shadowed Celeste's eyes, dimming the blue. She took another look at the PDA, but not before Cain saw the muscle flex in her jaw. Had he ever cared for people that much? "Just another statistic, isn't she?"

"Whatever she was, Gypsy, she didn't deserve to be murdered."

"Did you notice the list of items that are being held at the warehouse for the Cambridge auction?"

"Yes." Not for the first time, Cain noted the strength beneath her strained features, her pale skin.

"I think we should take a look."

"Not we. Me."

"You?" Celeste's temper flared, but Cain watched as she managed to control her exasperation, just barely. At this rate, Cain decided, it would take her years to master the technique. However, he found it intriguing that in spite of her experiences, she still wore her emotions out in the open for everyone to see.

"I'll decide if I'm going, Cain. Not you," she said. "Gabriel is upping the ante with that bomb. He wants to see just how much we can endure, if we're smart enough to survive his tactics or scared enough to run. I'm not going to let him win, not when we've come this far."

"I'm taking you to my place." His hand tightened, halting their progress, his eyes catching a black shadow by the porch.

"Cain, what quarters did they find on Joyce Raines?" Celeste stepped forward, then froze. Her whole body started to quake.

"Kentucky." Following her gaze, Cain understood. "My old Kentucky Home."

Chapter Ten

The bastard had left it just for her. Only a few feet away from the front stoop of the store. Close enough to the burning building so it wouldn't be missed. Far enough away so the fire wouldn't touch it. He'd even dropped a blood-red bow from her shop on the body as if it were a gift.

She took another shaky step forward, her anguish palpable. Still several feet away, she reached out to touch the mangled animal. Cain stopped her, clasping her trembling hand within his when what he really wanted was to gather her close and take away the torment he saw in her eyes.

"I should've realized Gabriel would target..." the rest of the sentence caught on a sob.

In the background, a police officer's camera flashed systematically, catching onlookers for future scrutiny. Just in case the bomber wanted to enjoy his show. Soon, Cain knew, they'd take pictures of the cat. Something he wanted to avoid her seeing.

There was little blood around the carcass, which

meant whoever had killed the animal had done so somewhere else. Maybe inside the store. Cain looked up at the blaze as the firefighters fought to control it. The fire had climbed as high as the treetops, the flames stroking the blackened sky. A small crowd of people had formed—some neighbors, most strangers—forcing the deputies to push them back to a safe distance.

"I'll take care of it," Cain responded, gentling his voice. Looking again at the heap of raw meat, he forced himself to remain objective. Only a slight tremor of his jaw gave away the fury that brewed under his calm surface.

The cat had been decapitated, the head left by its partially skinned, mutilated body. The guts had been thrown like discarded streamers over the steps and sidewalk. Amidst the gore near the tail lay five quarters—all North Carolina, all flashing brightly against the black fur.

Gabriel had wanted her to be able to recognize her friend, and leave no doubt about the torture he'd suffered.

Cain pulled her to his chest, and forced her face away from the gruesome sight. "I'm sorry." This time the comfort came naturally to him, like breathing. Trouble was, he wasn't sure he liked this new side of him. The hate had been easier to handle.

A sob escaped her, muffled by his clothes. Lightly, he soothed her, his fingers tracing long lines of comfort up and down her back. "It's over."

Another sob, this one a vicious jab just under his heart, a heart he'd thought long ago had stopped feeling anything.

Celeste drew a shaky breath. "I can smell him even

through the smoke, Cain." Fur soaked with blood had a distinct scent. Sour. Tinny. Heavy. The grief raked her from toes to chin, laying her wide open to its pain.

"I want him autopsied. Tonight." Slowly, she straightened, stiffening her spine to keep from crumbling into a ball. "If Gabriel left something behind, even the tip of an eyelash, I want it found." She sidestepped Cain, to get a closer look. To remember every detail. Bile rose in her throat. She tasted the acid before beating it back down.

"I'll talk to the deputy."

She glanced at the burning building, though she no longer cared about her lost possessions. No longer cared that the rose and talcum that was Grams was gone forever with the ashes and smoke.

"Miss Pavenic, I think I might have found something that belongs to you."

Both Celeste and Cain turned as Sheriff Lassiter approached them.

A worn Stetson, a sheepskin coat and his long, easy gait only accented the sheriff's small-town persona. Not an easy feat considering that until a few months before Lassiter had been a city boy.

In his arms, he held a bundled rescue blanket, but it wasn't until he'd almost reached them that Celeste heard the angry hissing.

Pan!

With a cry, she reached for the cat, hugged him tight. Her fingers smoothed the damp fur while she instinctively counted the heartbeats beneath.

The answering mew, although irritated, sounded

healthy. Celeste offered a prayer for the animal on the ground a few yards away that hadn't been so lucky.

"Thank you, Sheriff," Celeste swallowed the knot of tears, that clogged her throat. "I don't know what to say—"

"Part of the job," Lassiter replied, shrugging. "I found him under the Dumpster in the alley. Put up quite a fight when I went after him." Lassiter pushed back the brim on his Stetson, and smiled gently. "If I were you, I'd keep a close track on your pet from now on. He's probably down a life or two."

"Probably, but thank you anyway," Cain answered, shaking the sheriff's hand and then nodding toward the blaze. "Have you found out anything yet?"

"The firefighters say that the flames caught hold of the lamp fluid stored in your stock room. Only took seconds after that." Lassiter looked up at the two-story inferno and scratched the stubble on his cheek with his knuckles. "They haven't figured out what caused the explosion though. Could have been a gas leak. Could have been arson."

Cain slipped his arm behind Celeste's shoulders. When she tried to shift away, his hand curved her hip, stopping her.

"I hope you all don't mind if I ask a few questions." Lassiter tilted his head in the direction of the fire. "Like why someone would want to burn you out?" His lips flatlined. "Or leave a mutilated cat on your doorstep?"

"A burglary gone wrong?" Cain suggested. "We've heard there have been several break-ins lately.

"You did?"

"News travels in small communities. Especially bad news."

Slow to answer, Lassiter's gaze shifted from Celeste to Cain, intense and curious. "A mutilated cat adds a new twist, don't you think?"

"That's the problem. We don't know what to think, Sheriff." Celeste answered, cutting off Cain. The slight pinch on her hip told her he wasn't happy about it either. "The building exploded. Other than that—"

"Frankly, I'm amazed we got out alive. Once the explosion hit, we were running," Cain interrupted. "We gave our statements to your deputy."

"He told me." Lassiter paused long enough to rub the back of his neck. "You know, I've only been in town a little over two months, and I've seen more action here than during my last six months in Detroit. Whoever's behind these burglaries is leaving one hell—" He coughed, covering his slip. "Is leaving a mess."

"Any leads?" Celeste asked casually.

"None. Despite the mess, the places have been clean. No evidence. The trouble is that robberies rarely happen in Shadow Point, so people don't have security systems or surveillance. Most don't even lock their doors at night."

Celeste stiffened in defense of her neighbors. "Most have lived here all their lives and don't feel it's necessary."

"Yet, you did," the sheriff speculated. "Didn't you, Miss Pavenic?"

"Yes, but I haven't lived here my whole life, either."

"Funny though, them firefighters over there told me that someone would've had to be pretty savvy to breach your alarm system. Now, why would a thief target a store with a security system, when another with a dead bolt is just a block away? And why would he break in while you two were enjoying your dinner upstairs?"

"I'm not an expert, but maybe this particular one preferred a challenge."

"Maybe," he agreed, but his narrowed eyes said he didn't. "But why isn't your system set to notify my office when it's breached?"

"I felt safe enough that the extra precaution didn't seem necessary, Sheriff."

"Next time, you might want to consider it."

"Next time, she will," Cain responded easily, intentionally cutting off the sheriff's questions. "But for right now, I think we both need to regroup."

Lassiter paused, then nodded his agreement. "I'm sorry about your store, Miss Pavenic. But I promise you, I'll get to the bottom of this." He turned away, only to swing back again. "Do you folks have a place to stay?"

"We haven't decided—"

"She'll be staying with me," Cain said, then slid his hand into the soft curls at the base of her neck. "I've rented a place just south of town. Your deputy has the address."

Her arms tightened in surprise. Pan screeched and struggled to get free. When one claw found it mark, Celeste gasped.

Smoothly, Cain grabbed Pan and bundled him into the rescue blanket. "I'll keep an eye on her," Cain said, keeping his tone casual. "And the cat."

On cue, Pan popped his head out from between the blanket's folds, and Lassiter scratched him between his ears. If he thought it strange that Cain had his own place already, he kept it to himself. "That's good to hear."

"Once your investigation is finished, I'd be interested in knowing how the burglar got through the security system," Cain admitted easily.

"I can't make any promises." Lassiter glanced back at the roof engulfed in flames. "Looks like it's gone now, but I'll let you know what we find. Meanwhile, you folks be careful. I'm not convinced this is the end of things."

"We'll keep an eye out for anything out of the ordinary."

"I appreciate that." Lassiter nodded and turned away.

Celeste watched the sheriff amble towards his patrol car. "He didn't believe us," Celeste murmured, then rubbed noses with Pan, letting the warm velvet fur reaffirm that he was safe.

Cain's mouth twisted wryly. "Maybe we should have gone with the seagull story."

"First Grams, then Jonathon, now my store and Pan." She scratched Pan under his collar, eliciting a purr. "He's destroying everything personal to me. We need to warn Olivia Cambridge, Cain."

"Not yet, Gypsy. Not until we know for sure she's not behind all of this."

"We can't take the risk—"

"I'll make sure we boost her security a little bit, to cover our bases."

There was a loud crack, like thunder. Celeste jerked around just in time to see her apartment collapse into her store. Cain squeezed her into her side, reassuring her.

The gesture made her chest constrict.

"Cain, I want Gabriel," Celeste said, trying not to think of the blazing mass behind her. Instead, she concentrated on the coins and the stray cat that lay cold on the ground next to them. "I want back in my store first thing in the morning. If Gabriel left anything behind, I want to know."

"There's a lot of hours between now and the morning," Cain answered grimly. "I think we'd better put them to use."

"I agree," she said, this time taking comfort not from the *we* but from his arms. For the moment she was safe.

"Cain," she whispered, suddenly overwhelmed with the realization of what he'd done for her. Of how this evening could've ended.

"Hmm?"

A firefighter yelled. Another raced past. The savage looks on their faces told Celeste she'd lost everything.

Celeste gave herself a second or so to allow the words to unclog from her throat. She glanced up at the swirling snowflakes that danced in the wind above their heads. The more unfortunate ones were caught in the flames, their split-second sizzle echoing in the night air. "Thank you for saving my life."

"I haven't saved it yet, Gypsy."

She saw the cold determination cemented on Cain's features.

And loneliness took on a completely new meaning.

"No more, Celeste. You're done."

"Don't you ever get tired of bossing me around?"

"I wouldn't have to, if you stopped letting your emotions cloud your thinking. You're injured and that makes you a liability in a situation like this."

"You're not the team leader here, MacAlister." Exhaustion tugged at her, but she refused to give in. It had taken another half hour for the fireman to contain the fire. Once they had, Celeste and Cain had left. "I'm a trained operative," she added, ignoring the fact that her ankle still throbbed.

"A trained operative who spent all her time in satellite offices with very little field experience."

"The quarters were a message for me. You and I both know that the odds are he'll show up at the warehouse tonight." She thought of the North Carolina coins. "The airplane on the quarter? The airfield by the warehouse?" Her laugh ground to bitter dust in her throat. "Gabriel's not even trying to challenge us now."

Cain flicked off the headlights and slowed the car to a stop. The warehouse was a converted hanger located on the north edge of town, just past an old airstrip. The steel building sat a couple hundred yards back from the road with only some floodlights in the distance marking its position.

Still, she was annoyed when Cain switched off the ignition. "We could probably creep a little closer, don't you think?"

"What I need you to do can be done from here where you'll be safe." He glanced into the rearview mirror and saw Pan lying stretched on the seat licking his paw. "Besides, you have Pan back there to keep you company."

The cat stopped in midstroke, mewed, then continued his onslaught. Celeste ignored him, knowing the cat was biding his time. He didn't like being cooped up any more than she did. "How am I going to be any help here?"

"Look, Celeste, I need you to watch my back while I place the security cameras." Cain dropped the magazine of his gun, checked it, then slid it back into place. "Will you do that for me?"

"Fine." She spat out the word and permitted herself a withering stare. He was lying of course, but when he put it that way…

She folded her arms, furious at her vulnerability. The problem was, she was beginning to wonder if there was anything he couldn't do by himself.

Cain punched a few buttons nearby. "Let's see what we're dealing with."

A circular screen blipped. Within seconds of inputting information, a schematic of the warehouse superimposed itself over the original diagram. Cain used a small toggle to guide the tracking until it focused on the different areas. With a few taps on the keys, he zoomed in. "If we've jumped to the wrong conclusion and these burglaries are just a coincidence, then we've only assisted Lassiter in getting his guy. No harm, no foul."

"We're not wrong," she argued, still irked that he'd won.

Two white figures appeared on the monitor. "An RTI?" Remote Thermal Imaging Systems, used to track a person's body heat by satellite. She'd seen many like this one during her career with Labyrinth but always in surveillance vans, never in cars, let alone a Jaguar.

Celeste tapped the screen. "You've got two guarding the warehouse. I'm betting private hires looking for extra cash. Not any big threat for the great Prometheus." Celeste leaned over the screen, almost bumping heads with Cain.

"Don't tell me you're worried?" When his eyes found hers, the eerie green of the computer screen cast a sharp and very dangerous edge to his features. "Don't be." He held up a miniature camera, the size of a tack. "Planting the cameras is easy. In and out. Thirty minutes max."

"Why can't we just tap into the warehouse cameras?"

"Unreliable. I prefer my own."

"Easy or not, watch yourself." Her request drifted in a hushed whisper between them, thick with tension. "I've never lost a partner," she said.

"You've never had a partner." A sensuous light passed between them, and its implication sent unwelcome waves of excitement rolling through her. "Not like me anyway."

"Yes, well…" She cleared her throat, pretending not to be affected, before glancing again at the console. Both guards had remained stationary—one at the back of the building, the other in front. They looked like small white globs.

How dangerous could white globs be?

"Here." He handed her a small piece of flesh-colored, gum-like substance. "There's a small transmitter in the center."

"I've used them before. It amplifies my voice with vibrations so no one else can hear me but you. And vice versa." She took a moment to adjust to the foreign feeling of chewing gum in her ear. "If I think you need help, I'm coming in."

"Not unless I give you the okay. Agreed?" Cain took an identical one and placed it in his left ear.

She nodded toward the two guards on the screen. Let Cain think what he wanted. "Don't hurt them."

He quirked his eyebrow, an action she was becoming familiar with. "They're not the bad guys, Gypsy. I promise they won't even know I'm there. Just keep an eye out. The guards will patrol the grounds on and off. Even if Lassiter doesn't understand the coins' meaning, he's smart enough to beef up the patrol cars in the area. I'd like to avoid a run-in with a trigger-happy lawman."

"Watch out. He's rigging the bombs with analogs on purpose. And the access too. If he's planted a bomb in the warehouse, it'll be rigged to the door as well as a clock. You can almost bet on it."

He tipped her chin up. "Don't worry, I'll come back to you."

Maybe it was the words he used or the stress of the day. Either way, Celeste felt her emotional barricade give. Burying her face in his neck, she breathed a kiss against his skin.

Slowly, he pulled her to him until her face turned upward. "You pick the damnedest times to go soft on me, Gypsy." His mouth descended to hers. "We might just be by a bed next time." The last of his statement was smothered in a series of slow, shivery kisses.

"Don't be too sure," she said, when she finally came up for air. A small lock of hair curled against his forehead. Not thinking, she brushed it back into place with trembling fingers. The gesture was familiar enough to make him pull back. Celeste masked her hurt, realizing it was okay for them to kiss, but he wouldn't allow anything remotely connected to caring. Heroes didn't become involved.

But she wasn't a hero.

"Be careful," she whispered, talking to an empty car. He'd already slipped into the darkness. It unnerved her how quietly he moved, because it reminded her of who he was—and more importantly—that he couldn't be anything else.

Pan's high-pitched meow broke into her thoughts. She glanced up to see him take a swipe at the windshield. "Don't start complaining."

Sitting on the dashboard, Pan looked at her, his black lids half-closed, his manner superior.

"I could let you go, but I'm not going to. So deal with it."

With a short, spiteful meow, Pan jumped to the back of Cain's seat. His fur spiked into little spears of hair, while his nails dug into the leather.

Celeste glanced at the small, puncture marks dotting the upholstery. Normally, she would've scolded him, but tonight she figured he was justified. "Feeling better?"

Far from it, she decided dryly, when the cat shifted slightly and flicked his tail.

"Gypsy." Cain's voice rumbled softly in her ear. "I'm in. Where are the guards?"

She studied the screen. "They haven't moved from their positions." Her eyes darted once again over the white figures. "I'm not reading you, Cain. Are you wearing an implant?"

"Yep. Otherwise, I'd be part of the crowd."

Celeste was familiar with the thermal diffuser chips, but never had needed to use one herself. Mostly because they were permanent, surgically inserted under the skin.

"Just let me know when their positions change. They should be making rounds soon. Until then, stay alert."

"You and I both know I'm too far away to do any good," she said while she scanned the darkness. "Wasn't that your plan?"

"No tantrums, Gypsy. I need you to keep up your end of the job. I don't like surprises."

She glanced at Pan. The cat was just putting the finishing touches on the upholstery. Grinning, she noted several additional holes in the leather. Childish? Maybe. Satisfying? Definitely. "My tantrums are the least of your worries." She scratched between the cat's ears in reward. "You just keep your end out of danger," she warned. "And I'll look out for the rest."

Having tired of his game, Pan settled into her lap and, from the satisfied way he licked his paw, seemed content.

"Gypsy, check camera one for me."

As she watched, the screen divided itself into a tic-tac-toe board. The top right block flickered then focused on one of the warehouse aisles.

"It's working," she acknowledged, her eyes searching for movement among the boxes and shelves.

"Copy that."

She studied the screen, then the outside. Cold fingers of fear stroked her spine and her muscles tightened against the sensation. She eased her gun from its holster and set it on the driver's-seat cushion. Cautious, she pressed farther back into her seat and waited.

IT TOOK one bullet from Gabriel's silencer to shatter the floodlight, blanketing the warehouse entrance in darkness. He paused next to the building, waiting patiently, listening. After readjusting his night goggles, he glanced down. The guard's lifeless body lay at his feet.

With very little effort, Gabriel shoved the dead man's back against the wall. The slap of his skull on the concrete echoed softly in the night air. Gabriel scooped up the flat-topped security hat and placed it back on the guard's head. The dark brim covered the small, symmetrical hole that tattooed the middle of his forehead—leaving the impression that the guard was asleep.

Swiftly, Gabriel tossed the man's gun, phone and other items into the brush before accessing the security panel, noting the age and uselessness of the system. Why is it, he thought, most people think things will never happen to them until they do? Thousands of dollars of merchandise in storage, protected only by some floodlights, a few cameras and an antiquated infrared system—the minimum equipment required by their insurance company.

He glanced again at the dead man. "They're making it too easy for me." He traced several wires, discovering someone had rerouted the main circuits. "Well, well."

After grabbing a small black canvas bag from the ground, he slid a six-inch blade from his arm sheath. With one swipe, he severed the wires. The interior lights blinked, then disappeared. The cameras went dead.

He slipped through the door and crept past some larger crates, tempted by the opportunity to torment his adversary. "Come out, come out wherever you are," he whispered, finding enjoyment in a game he was never included in as a child. "Whoever you are."

"GYPSY, give me the guards' positions."

Fifteen minutes. Celeste's heart pounded. Cain had planted half the cameras in less than fifteen minutes. Another half dozen cameras and he should be out of there.

"They haven't moved—"

The warehouse lights winked, then darkened in the distance.

Cain swore. "Gypsy, listen to me." She heard it, the worry. "I want you to stay—" A sharp buzz pierced her eardrum. She cried out, her hands tearing at her ear until the transmitter dropped into her lap. Someone had jammed the frequency. Her eyes locked on the screen, immediately taking in the two fading white blobs, and then a third, burning bright and moving unhurriedly toward Cain.

Gabriel. It had to be.

Desperately she tore apart the car, looking for a flashlight, night goggles, something to help her maneuver in the dark—only to come up empty-handed. The man had fifteen million gadgets but not one lousy flashlight.

Gun in hand, Celeste pushed open the car door and slid out, wincing when her injured ankle tried to take her weight.

Without a sound, Pan shot out through the open door.

"Pan!" she whispered harshly, but she was too late. The darkness swallowed him whole. "Stupid cat," she muttered, forcing herself not to worry. The wind flogged her, each icy lash cutting deep to the marrow of her bones. She glanced again into the night and clamped her jaw down on a frustrated scream.

In her mind, time accelerated, devouring precious seconds before she reached the first guard in front of the warehouse doors. She squatted, tested his pulse. None. She searched him for a flashlight, frustrated when she found nothing. Didn't anyone use one anymore?

She saw them then, the glint of metal in the moonlight. After scooping up the coins, she shoved them into her jeans pocket, not caring about anything except Cain's safety.

Hurriedly, she stepped over the body and slipped through the open door.

As shadows shifted—some merging, most separating into shapes—Celeste moved farther into the building, heading in the general direction of Cain's last location.

The size of two high-school gymnasiums, the warehouse was packed from front to back, bottom to top, with shelves, all overloaded with packaged goods. Most, she imagined, for the auction, others being held in storage for local businesses.

Pistol raised, the grip slick against her clammy hands, Celeste crept forward. So that is what caring for a man did to a woman? It makes her stupid with nerves. Carefully using the wooden crates and boxes as a guide, she worked her way through the maze of shelves.

A whoosh of air was her only warning.

A hand gripped her hair, jerking her head back. Fingers dug viciously into her scalp and cold steel bit her neck, cutting off her cry of alarm. "Drop the gun, Celeste." The knife blade pressed harder, its blade cutting her skin. "Gently."

Celeste felt the sting, the warm trickle of blood over her collarbone. Her gun slipped to the floor with a quiet thud.

"Or should I call you Lachesis?" The whisper taunted her, sending abrasive waves of fury over her.

"It's ironic really, don't you think? Lachesis being the Fate who determined the length of a mortal's life."

"If I had that kind of power…" she rasped, his vileness crowding her, suffocating her. "You can bet you would've never lived past your first breath."

Gabriel laughed, a grinding of vocal cords. "I must say, my night goggles certainly provide a nice advantage. I can see why Prometheus is smitten." He pressed closer, his chest to her back until she heard his black heart beating under her ear. A clammy sheet of moisture coated her skin, but she forced her mind to focus.

"Are you and Prometheus enjoying my game—"

Celeste relaxed, dropping her weight into Gabriel. When he caught her, the blade shifted away. She slammed her elbow into his ribs causing him to hiss and his hand to slide.

"Cain!" She ducked, aiming for Gabriel's groin. Within a fraction of a second he recovered, catching her punch, twisting her arm viciously until she cried out.

"Bitch!" He shoved her, chest first, to the floor and dug his knee into her spine. "Do that again and I'll break your back." The darkness disguised his features, but she'd remember the inhuman edge in his voice forever.

The warehouse emergency light flipped on, its red glare momentarily blinding her. Gabriel swore and threw off his goggles. Celeste hoped the shock of the light had blinded him, too.

"Looks like you got lucky. Tell your boyfriend to take better care of you. It isn't time for you to die. Not yet." A needle pricked the nape of her neck. He released her arm and stood. "But soon."

She tried to see him, tried to grab for the weapon lying only inches from her face, but a sick, malevolent numbness spread throughout her body. It was almost as if her circulation had stopped, leaving her muscles disengaged from her mind.

Seconds later—or maybe even minutes, she couldn't be sure—she found herself floating, cradled in massive arms. A fog, dark and thick, crept in, narrowing her peripheral vision. She tried to blink the mist away.

It was hard to make out more than the size of the man, but Celeste knew he was huge. An accomplice?

"No!" The word came out hoarse, so low she couldn't be sure he'd heard her. Talons of fatigue clawed at her, dragging her into a dark abyss. Struggling against obscurity, she tried again. "Cain!"

"Shhh. I am Quamar Bazan, Cain's associate. He is unharmed." The soft Mediterranean accent rumbled deep within his chest, a lullaby against her ear. "It is you we need to worry about."

Cain. Not harmed. With a sigh, she stopped fighting the crushing weight of fatigue, allowing her mind to drift with only one thought—if she didn't die now, Cain would certainly kill her later.

A SOFT, TWO-TONED WHISTLE floated to Cain. His muscles flexed but didn't relax. Softly, he whistled his response.

Cain heard nothing, not even the soft rub of shoes against the concrete before Quamar joined him, holding an unconscious Celeste to his chest.

"Is she okay?" The question came out in a short, savage snarl. Celeste's scream still echoed in his head, triggering the terror in his chest. Even as he'd hit the emergency lights, raced toward the sound—he'd known Gabriel had her, would hurt her. Known that he would be too late.

"She is fine. I checked her pupils and her pulse." Quamar shifted until her face tilted toward Cain. "It appears he drugged her. Fast-working, but harmless."

Fresh blood smeared her jaw. Cain moved the jacket collar a few inches, revealing the cut on her neck, a vivid red against her pale skin. Another reason to bring Gabriel down, he promised himself. Then he wiped some of the blood with his thumb, relieved when her pulse beat strong and steady beneath.

His eyes lingered, stroking her cheek, until he heard his friend clear his throat.

He jerked back, catching himself. "Get her out, Quamar," he ordered. "Take her to the cottage. And when you get there, see if these cameras can give us an image on the portable, although I'm sure they won't. I didn't have time to place any in this area. Check with Roman, too. He's monitoring from headquarters." Cain scanned the warehouse. "Our friend is long gone. I'm going to finish with the cameras, in case he decides to come back. I'll clear out before the law gets here or call them if they don't. It will give me time to…" He glanced at Celeste, his jaw tight, his eyes fixed. "…think."

Quamar's gaze flickered, sliding from Celeste to his friend. His broad lips widened with pleasure, his teeth gleamed, bright against his dark skin. "So you have become human after all, Prometheus."

"Don't worry," Cain ground out, not bothering to misunderstand. "I'll get over it."

Chapter Eleven

"Are you better, Miss Pavenic?"

Celeste angled her head, the closest she could come to a nod without having it implode. It had been a good five minutes since she'd come around, but she still didn't feel strong enough to move from her reclining position on an overstuffed blue-paisley couch.

"Do you have any aspirin?" She willed the parade of cannons to stop discharging inside her skull.

As he made his way to the bathroom, Celeste noted his tailored black slacks and black crew-neck sweater. Did everyone in this business, except her, have money?

Neither his clothes nor the confines of the cottage minimized the size of the man. He returned and dropped some tablets into her palm. She murmured her thanks and closed her eyes out of self-preservation. If she looked up at the man, her neck would stretch and her head would probably fall off before her gaze reached his chin.

"Is there anything else you need? Something to eat, perhaps?"

The thought of food touched off a wave of queasiness. Quickly, she swallowed the pills with the help of some warm tea. "No, thank you…" What did he say his name was? "Quamar." She frowned, struggling to find the whole name. "Quamar Bazan."

"You have a good memory, Miss Pavenic." The words were low, the accent heavy—and surprisingly soothing.

"Please," she murmured, wishing the aspirin would take effect. "It's just Celeste." The dread she'd felt earlier tried to reassert itself. Agitated, she rubbed her temples.

The man merely inclined his head as he poured more tea into her cup. "Then I insist you call me Quamar."

"All right, Quamar." She tried to smile. "How long did you say before Cain would arrive?"

"Soon. But there's no need to worry, he's in no danger."

Cautiously, she nodded her assent. "Cain. He's your friend?"

"Yes."

Celeste sighed, settling back against the couch. "And here I thought he didn't have friends," she quipped, only half-serious. She inhaled deeply, catching the light, spicy scent of the giant. Exotic, masculine. Pleasant.

"I never said he considered me a friend. Only that I considered him one."

She peered at him from beneath her lashes. "He must. He trusts you enough to bring you here. Trust doesn't come easily to him."

"Nothing comes easily to him except his job."

She acknowledged the truth of Quamar's statement. "You know him well." Deliberately, she took in the room, noting Cain's strong presence. Not his physical presence, although she caught a glimpse of his coat on the wall rack and newspapers on the table, but more of how the air was charged with him, like some sort of static electricity.

Startled, Celeste realized she'd come to rely on his energy. "Somewhere along the line, Cain's work became his life."

"Perhaps you should ask him why." He rose, the teakettle in hand, and walked to a light-paneled wall. He flipped off a switch leaving the room in a soft amber glow that emanated from the kitchen.

"Perhaps I'm afraid to hear the answer," she murmured.

Pine trimmed the stone-hewed fireplace, updated to burn gas, and accented the quaint cottage. Only a few feet from the couch, the muted hues of the fire mingled with the light, both complementing the cozy lines of the furnishings and the hand-cut ribs of the barrel-vaulted ceiling.

Like many cottages, there was a small but serviceable kitchen, a booth-style table, and a bathroom on the opposite side by the bedroom. All clearly visible from her position on the couch.

Unlike most cottages, computers and surveillance equipment took up one corner. Scattered in piles lay gear and apparatus—some under counters, more stacked on top.

"You've come prepared." Quamar's graceful motions surprised her as he walked to the kitchen and reached into the cupboard for a small first aid kit.

"A precaution." Quamar shrugged, returning to

where she lay and sitting down on the coffee table beside the couch. "One of many."

Celeste watched him glance at the work station, monitoring the high-tech systems. Computers, radar tracking, satellite imaging, closed-circuit monitors—some she recognized, the use of others she didn't have a clue about.

"If you have to work—"

Quamar's gaze returned to hers. "I have set up the portable monitors but Cerberus is monitoring through a satellite feed, allowing Prometheus and myself a little more freedom to accomplish our mission."

"Cerberus?" It took Celeste a moment to remember. "Cerberus—that's Roman D'Amato. I remember." She nodded her head. "Cain has him watching the warehouse?" She asked, suspecting the answer before Quamar spoke.

"Yes." Slowly, he tilted her chin up exposing her neck. "The wound is paltry, but needs cleaning. Do I have your permission?"

"Yes." The throbbing ebbed, and Celeste managed to sit a little straighter. "The portable monitors are new. Are they another of Kate's inventions?"

The antiseptic wipe soothed the sting of the cut. The gentleness of Quamar's fingers soothed the tension everywhere else. "Doctor D'Amato is an extremely clever woman," he explained.

Something in the man's tone—some pride, a softness that seemed more than casual—caught Celeste's attention. "Does Cain know that you're in love with his sister?" She almost bit her tongue off when the question slipped out. She must be more exhausted than she thought because she usually wasn't so unfeeling. Or maybe Cain was rubbing off on her.

But Quamar surprised her with a grin before bandaging the wound. "You must be very good at your job."

"Lucky guess." Uncomfortable with the quizzical glint in his chocolate-brown eyes, Celeste focused on the smooth lines of the giant's bald head.

Something about the man conveyed trust, gentleness. She decided to be honest. "Look, I'm sorry. I'm not usually so callous. Your feelings for Kate D'Amato are none of my business. My only excuse is that it's been a long day."

"We all have our secrets." Then, with a chuckle, he sat back and studied her for a moment. "It is hard for one not to love Doctor D'Amato. Yet, because of this love, it is easier to accept that she has found happiness with a close friend."

"Is it?" she murmured. Celeste had known Cain would eventually love another. Even while she'd hoped as much, during the late hours of many nights, the despair haunted her.

"Prometheus hasn't realized that you still love him, has he?" After grabbing the first aid kit and wrappers, Quamar took them to the kitchen.

"No," she said, too startled by his question to offer any objection. "How did you guess?"

"Probably the same way you did." His laugh was marvelous—a thick, warm comforter to snuggle under on a dreary day. "It was not hard. Your eyes burn with a blue fire at the mention of his name. A fire that is not created from just anger or frustration."

"With me it's never been a question of love, Quamar. But acceptance." She did love Cain. "Too much has happened. Our pasts are too tangled. We've both changed." The admission came hard to her, and not without pain.

"Will you tell him?" Quamar asked, seemingly busy with his task, but Celeste wasn't fooled.

"That I love him?" She questioned, proud of herself for not letting the show pain through. "Probably. Will it matter?" She asked rhetorically. "Probably not."

His features gentled with concern. On most men his size, the expression would've appeared ridiculous, on Quamar it was genuine.

"We have an unpleasant history." Celeste sighed, her mind sweeping back through the years.

"And here you both are—how did you put it?" His smooth forehead creased as he struggled for the word. "Tangled." His mouth curved, victorious. "You are both still tangled."

"But in a different way," Celeste admitted. "An entirely different way."

Quamar nodded. "But when a person is tangled, there are only two options. Take the time to straighten the knots, or cut themselves loose, quick and clean.

"You do not have much time to decide." He nodded toward the kitchen window. "Cain has arrived. And…" he added as his eyebrow rose speculatively, "…if I am not mistaken, he appears extremely agitated." Quamar glanced over his shoulder. "You might want to consider cutting loose, Celeste."

When she frowned, Quamar laughed. "At least you would have a knife for protection."

CAIN PARKED and cut the engine of the Jag. In the distance, a dog barked, then after a second, came a few answering howls. For a moment, he listened, trying to find something to calm the storm within him. But in his mind's eye, Celeste lay unconscious in Quamar's arms, the red gash on her neck, her body limp.

The anger surged, fed by impatience and—damn her—fear. Celeste had managed to worm past his emotional barricade and left the need for reassurance throbbing in him. Reassurance that she was safe.

He glanced at the cottage, following the pointed peaks of its roofline to the clapboard siding and small-paned windows. The knowledge that she sat just beyond the glass did little to help.

On the surface, he appeared to be in complete control, even relaxed. But a caged tiger prowled within— held back with a fragile lock.

"Let's go, cat." Pan yowled as Cain pulled him from the passenger seat into his arms. "I don't want to hear any complaining." Cain shoved open the car door with his foot and stepped out into the cold night air. "You're going to owe me some leather, and I don't mind taking it out of your hide."

CELESTE DISMISSED Quamar's observation. Cain furious? Even if he was, he'd control it. He wouldn't allow himself to be so human. She stood though, wincing only a little over her stiff ankle, refusing to face Cain any other way. What she expected was indifference, even a scathing lecture on her incompetence—not that she would've tolerated it.

What she didn't expect was the rush of relief that hit her when Cain filled the doorway.

Quamar had told her Cain was safe, but until she saw it herself, she hadn't truly believed him. She caught the back of the couch for support and drank in the raw sexual vibrations, the rugged windblown features—the angry determination. She knew, ironically, that if he were to change, he wouldn't be the man she loved.

"I found your cat by the warehouse." Cain dropped Pan to the floor, showing disinterest when the cat scooted under the couch by Celeste. "You should do a better job of keeping track of him."

"I should—"

"Yes, you should." It ought to have been charming— just the thought he had rescued Pan, Celeste fumed. But then he'd had to open his mouth and ruin it.

He glanced at the monitors. "Anything?"

"No. Gabriel disabled the cameras," Quamar answered and shrugged on his down jacket. "I doubt he will return."

"Then we try again," Cain said. "Follow me." Before turning, he pinned Celeste with narrowed eyes. "You stay here."

Not waiting for an answer, the two men stepped outside. Celeste prickled with anger, forgetting her earlier worry almost instantly.

"I'm not your pet, Cain. And I'm tired of being told to stay." When she pushed the door open, both men turned in unison, like two vultures spying prey. Celeste took an involuntary step back, halted and stood her ground.

"I don't think you want to mess with me right now,

Gypsy." Each word was spoken low, each syllable drawn out.

She stiffened at the challenge. "Really?" She moved with a definite purpose, choosing to ignore her limp. The night air lashed out at her, piercing her shirt, leaving her skin a blanket of goose bumps. She crossed her arms, more in defiance of the man than the weather. "I'm not messing with you, I'm working with you," she responded tightly, annoyed when she couldn't stop the piercing shrillness of her comment. "You tend to forget that." God, he'd not only turned her into a loon, but a shrewish one to boot.

Quamar tilted his head back with a low, rumbling laugh. "I will head to the Cambridge mansion. It seems you have your hands full here. I will contact you if I discover anything."

"The mansion? To do what?" Celeste knew she'd be safer if Quamar stayed, but she refused to think of that now that he was leaving. She was not a puppet in this mission, to be pulled this way and that, whenever it appealed to Cain. If she hadn't warned him, he would've been knifed at the very least. And for once she'd like to see a little gratitude, damn it!

The slam of the car door brought her abruptly out of her thoughts.

"Quamar's going to scope the estate, see how secure it is." Cain watched as she rubbed her arms. "We can give Olivia a little more protection, without jeopardizing the integrity of our investigation."

"Why aren't we going with him?" she demanded, biting down on the urge to let her teeth chatter.

"I trust Quamar to take care of business." Cain's face tightened. "And as I pointed out before, you're injured."

She reached up and yanked the bandage off her neck, barely holding back a wince. "It's nothing more than a scratch."

"And your ankle?"

"I've run on worse," she countered, defiant, until a ripple of shivers ruined the effect.

Cain's eyes narrowed. "Get inside, Celeste. I don't need you to catch pneumonia on top of everything else."

"Don't worry about me."

"I wouldn't if you followed instructions."

"Instructions? Or orders?" With a huff, she limped past him, grateful to be back in the warmth of the cottage. "I told you, I can take care of myself."

"You're wrong." The chill in his words dropped the temperature inside to zero.

Cain locked the door, then lounged casually against the frame. "I told you to stay in the Jag." His comment was low, even lazy, but he didn't fool her. Not anymore. In the soft light of the room, she saw what she'd missed outside in the darkness.

Although his stance seemed relaxed, his eyes had narrowed into two slits of tempered steel. And she understood instinctively, if she moved, they'd slice her in half.

Quamar had been wrong. Cain wasn't angry, he was enraged. Containing a sudden surge of panic, she glanced at the doorway behind him and gauged her chances.

"Go ahead, try it," he taunted, crossing his ankles. "I'd like nothing better."

"You'd have come after me under the same circumstances." Silently calling herself a fool for not heeding Quamar's warning—for depending on Cain's innate self-control—Celeste stepped back, putting a little distance between her and the storm she saw raging in him. Somehow she knew, a simple grab and shake wasn't going to do him this time. "Admit it."

"I needed you monitoring the cameras," he countered evenly.

"Quamar said Roman was monitoring them, too."

He eased away from the door then, and took a step toward her, stalking her. "You didn't know that."

"I didn't know a lot, it seems." Her chin went up, as anger brought her a surge of courage. "You take risks all the time. I have the right to choose when and if I'll do the same."

"Wrong again."

She flung her head back, annoyed by the fact that she had to in order meet his gaze. "How was I supposed to know Quamar would show up? Why aren't you screaming at him?"

"Because…" He removed his jacket and tossed it onto the bench seat. "*He* followed my orders."

"You knew?" Of all the unbelievable… "How? I was with you every minute today, Cain."

"He and I made arrangements while you were dealing with the paramedic." Blood pounded in his veins, straining every muscle, every fiber of his being. Emotions he'd kept in check for an eternity rose to the surface.

When Celeste threaded her fingers through her hair in agitation, the movement caught his eye. Somewhere in that split second, he decided. This time, it would take more than simple eye contact to reassure him that she was unharmed.

"And you were going to tell me about these arrangements…when?"

"I wasn't going to tell you at all. Since he was wearing a non-thermal implant, you'd never have known the difference."

"I could've shot him!"

"*Not* if you had stayed in the car." Ever so slightly, he moved closer. Although they were still inches apart, she could feel the heat of his anger burning through her clothes, singeing her skin. "You made the wrong decision and risked your damned life because of it."

Celeste tried another step back, but her bottom hit the end of the kitchen counter. The dimensions of the room had shrunk in the space of seconds.

"Hold it!" She brought her hand up between them, regretting her action almost immediately when he caught her fingers.

"I did once," he murmured, then moved in, closing the distance, his eyes now smoky slits. "More than once. A thousand times, I've held back with you." He pinned her, imprinting his hard, long body against hers. "Not this time."

Her heart fluttered. If she didn't tread softly, she'd lose more than just this argument.

She'd lose herself.

"Look, I'm sorry you're upset with me for being in the warehouse, but nothing happened." She tried to maneuver away, but the edge of the counter bit into her back.

"Nothing happened?" A vein in his throat bulged, and

her eyes widened in fascination. How could she ever have thought this man lacked emotion?

"You're damn lucky." He gripped the counter on either side of her. "You could've been killed." Celeste watched his shoulders and biceps flex in an effort to maintain his temper. "Quamar was there to cover my ass, and instead he had to save yours. Dammit, we almost *had* Gabriel. I should strangle you just for that." His breath exploded in a hiss. "And for scaring the hell out of me."

"No!" Alarm skittered up her spine. Without thinking, she flung herself forward, shocking them both as her arms tightened around him. "Don't you see? I had to help you," she murmured and buried her face into his chest. "When the transmitter went out, and the guards were dead, what did you expect me to do?"

"Trust me." Cain's arms automatically jerked around her, gathering her closer. His anger dissolved with the pain in her admission. He stroked her hair, catching the familiar scent, using it to reassure himself she was safe. At least for now. "I expected you to trust me."

"He might've killed you," she whispered, her shame seeping through. She leaned back and Cain saw the sheen of tears. "I couldn't do anything else." Cain caught her sob against him and kissed the top of her head. She took a shaky breath. "I love you."

It should have stopped him. A wounded admission like that would've stopped him before. Hell, a thousand things would've stopped him before. Things like integrity, duty—simple decency. But not one of them was going to now. He'd known that when he'd locked the door. He'd known it the first time he'd kissed her. Hell, he'd known it the moment Mercer had uttered her name.

With a touch of his finger, Cain tipped her head back. The room's lights set the honey-gold of her hair on fire, drawing him like a moth to its flame. Gently, as if haste might destroy the moment, Cain ran one knuckle down the delicate curve of her throat, stopping briefly to feel the hitch of her breath.

"So beautiful." He dipped his head until his lips rested by the fragile shell of her ear. "You have only a few seconds to say no," he whispered, checking his control, before giving in to the temptation to taste.

A gentle finger touched his lips, cutting off his words. "Shhh." The word was carried on a sigh so soft it was almost a prayer. "I want you, Cain. Even if it's just for now."

The tightness in his chest—a tightness he hadn't realized existed—eased. He didn't like the fact that her decision was that important to him. Meant so much.

The change in the way Cain held her was subtle, but Celeste felt it. His arm flexed against her back, his hips shifted slightly away. She glanced up at the taut skin of his cheekbones, sharpening the angles of his face while the gray in his eyes swirled, twin hurricanes.

"Cain?" Her hands froze against his chest, paralyzed with fear. Not fear of the war waging within him. But fear of his withdrawal.

No! Her mind screamed. *Don't be the hero. Not now.*

Chapter Twelve

Celeste grabbed his head, tugging his hair, pulling him down. Her lips pressed against his, clumsy in their haste. The resistance was there, the way his mouth flattened against hers. But she would have none of it. She loved this man with every fiber of her being, and if all she had was this moment, so be it.

Boldly, she stroked the grim line of his lips with her tongue. She teased the corner of his mouth as he'd done to hers so many times before, only to pause long enough to nip sensually at his lower lip.

With a growl, he cupped her bottom and lifted her, holding her tight against him, leaving her feet to dangle inches above the floor. His lips opened over hers, capturing them with a tender fierceness that melted her bones into a waxy goo.

"Let me show you what seduction is," he murmured hoarsely. Without losing contact, he placed her on the counter, bringing their eyes almost level, and stepped between her legs until his arousal rubbed against the apex of her thighs.

Her surge of victory was brief, flitting away under the sudden onslaught of desire and nervousness. She'd freed the beast, but now what would she do with him?

As if he understood, he eased back, his gaze a soft caress. Gently, as if not to frighten her, he outlined her breast through the cotton of her shirt, each stroke of his finger setting off a burst of electric jolts through her. With a moan, she gripped the counter.

Cain felt her shudder, her hesitation. With deliberate movements, he skimmed the line of her spine, enjoying each shiver he set off. When he reached the base, his hands curved around the flare of her hips, lifted the T-shirt over her head and tossed it aside.

His gaze fastened on his ring hanging between her perfectly shaped breasts, blue ice against hot silk. A primal need burst through him.

With the tip of his finger, he traced the silver chain, fascinated as the goose bumps tripped over her skin. He let out a grunt of satisfaction that spanned a hundred years of his Scottish heritage.

"Cain." The raw plea came from deep within her, drawing his attention to the erratic rise and fall of her chest.

"No silk lingerie?"

With a jerk of her head, her eyes found his. "That was Diana."

Reverently, Cain rubbed the fabric of her bra between his finger and thumb. His hand hovered over the front, his knuckles deliberately brushing the swell of her breast, enjoying the contrast of the soft cotton and silky skin. "You make simple white cotton sexy, Gypsy."

Celeste's nipples tightened. A moan escaped her lips. "Wait!" The request came out more than a little frantically as she slipped off the counter. Cain deliberately allowed her body to slide against his until she touched the floor, causing another series of tremors. His or hers, he couldn't be sure. "My decision."

Riveted in place, Cain watched as she walked to the middle of the living room, dressed only in her bra and worn sweats. She pulled the drawstring loose, letting the waistband hang low on her hips, dipping slightly to reveal a hint of the shadow between the soft curves of her bottom. When she stood straight, her muscles flexed with a natural grace that made him taut with desire.

"My seduction," she whispered.

The serenity was there but still undermined by lines of tension as she slipped off her shoes and knelt on the sheepskin rug in front of the fire.

She closed her eyes against the heat of his gaze. Even from a few feet away, he caught how her fingers shook then fumbled slightly before releasing the catch. Slowly, she gripped the bra and pulled it away, freeing herself.

The silence was deafening, except for his own uneven breath. He stayed, mesmerized. Her breasts glowed like peach-tinted cream, the nipples dark, dusty-rose buds. She inhaled until her breath caught in her chest, exposing the delicate lines of her rib cage. The memory of her arching beneath him made his loins ache.

On a soft cry, her hands flew up in embarrassment, her eyes blinked open.

"Don't." His order was low, raspy—a man in pain. "I want to look."

His steady gaze, edged with passion, bore into her. With a shaky breath, he watched her drop her arms, leaving herself fully exposed.

The warm, burnished blush of the fire cast golden shadows, catching Celeste in a muted halo. The radiance made her skin appear delicate—almost translucent.

Graceful, strong.

He slipped the first button of his shirt free before he realized what he'd done.

Still, desire gnawed at him as his fingers hovered over the next button. He wanted to resist the pull, the urge to be with her. Hell, he might as well resist the urge to breathe.

Restlessly, Celeste ran her hand through the rug, caressing the supple surface. Cain's body grew heavy, aroused, spellbound by the sensual innocence that flowed from her. The second button slid undone.

"Cain?" Her request, though whispered, was simple.

With one tug, he freed his shirt from his jeans. A few seconds later, his shoes and socks lay on the floor.

He grasped the shirt fabric and yanked. The last three shirt buttons popped off. They hit the hardwood with a bounce and a rattle, causing her to freeze.

Before she could react, however, Cain was behind her, curling his body close to hers. When she relaxed, a surge of satisfaction rushed through him. He slid the bra off her shoulders and down her arms, letting his fingers trail over the silk of her skin. Only then did he reach for her, skimming the outside of her breasts before stroking the tips with his thumbs. He'd been the last to see her this way—burning with desire, aching with need. No other man had touched her since him. Like a double-edged sword, the thought brought satisfaction and with it, finely honed pain.

"You cast a spell over me, Gypsy. A curse, maybe."

Celeste's senses heightened with each word—forcing her to take a long, deep breath. A spell? Over Cain? A different form of excitement tripped down her spine.

She felt the brush of his shirttails against her sides, the warmth of his naked chest against her back. Hair, rough and sensual, tantalized the points of her shoulder blades, causing them to flex in greed, wanting more.

She slid her knees together to bring him closer, allowing his thighs to tighten against her in a ritualistic dance. No words were needed. Not here, not now.

He guided her hands to her belly, splaying them under his. Gently, he drew her back into him as he dipped then cradled her with his hips. As the hard length of him prodded her bottom, she shivered and gave in to the urge to rub.

She felt his hiss of pleasure on her neck, and layers of goose bumps spread. Then, deliberate fingers eased her sweats down, trailing in its path until they caught on the thin material of her panties. The deep, throaty entreaty triggered small tremors along her nerve endings, giving her a sense of power she'd never experienced before. Slowly, almost as though he was waiting for her to protest, he maneuvered her hand down the flat planes of her stomach, under her waistband, to the apex of her legs where her underwear was already moist with anticipation.

"White cotton?" He whispered, with a hopeful note underlying the question.

Her heart pounded, jumping from her chest into her throat, leaving her unable to manage more than a short, jerky nod. With gentle fingers, he guided her until they both massaged the ache building beneath the sable curls.

Flames of desire scorched her skin as they licked their way up and down her limbs. Automatically, she started to part her thighs, allowing more access.

"That's right, open for me, sweetheart." Her head fell back against his chest, as his fingers dipped and stroked. "I'll take care of you."

Take care of her?

"No!" She gasped, trying to harness some control even as she sagged farther into him. She tugged her hand free and turned into his arms. She fisted her hand to keep from stroking his fevered skin. "I want—"

"Me, too," he growled wickedly. "So let me." He took advantage of her hesitation to slip his hand under her sweats, his fingers traced the valley between her buttocks. Celeste's eyes closed, her head rolled to the side with a whimper. Wave after wave of longing swelled over her at the unexpected caress.

Cain captured her mouth, his tongue thrusting, plundering—savage in its intensity. For a moment she gave in to the rawness of the possession, the turbulence of his passion as it swirled around them.

He tried drawing her to him again. Immediately her other hand joined the first and pushed, breaking off the kiss.

"No," she panted, more than a little desperate. "I want more—"

His lips covered her nipple with a primitive possessiveness that left her weak. Long, liquid lines of desire traveled from her breast to her belly, only to settle like warm honey between her thighs. Heavens, she loved that feeling. She let her fingertips slide over his nipple hoping to create the same sensation for him and was rewarded when a groan rumbled deep within his throat.

"I want control," she said, surprised at the rawness of her voice. She realized that more than anything in her life, she wanted to seduce Cain, the way he'd seduced her at his cabin—making her mindless with passion, making her fall in love. "All this time, you told me I needed to trust myself. But you were wrong, Cain. I needed to discover myself." She took a deep breath. There was still a chance for her to grow whole again. Something she'd never had as Diana.

He drew in a long, ragged breath then lowered them both back—catching her against him as they settled onto the sheepskin rug.

"I'm an equal. Yours. Quamar's. The people here in Shadow Point." The admission came from the darkest pit in her being. "I'm someone who matters." *I'm someone worth loving.*

Cain tilted her chin up until their eyes met. He kissed her lightly, tenderly, before laying his head back onto the rug.

"Good." She blew the word out on a long breath. Before her courage caved, she bent forward until their bodies touched. Slowly, she slid upward, hearing the hitch, the hiss just before her lips touched his ear. "Let me know what you like," she murmured, then she nipped his ear.

"That's a good start." Cain's face remained rock-hard, his features giving nothing away. He stroked her neck, tracing its delicate curve with his thumb.

Her pulse leapt under his caress. "Don't," she said, jerking back. "It's my turn."

"Okay, sweetheart." He shrugged, but Celeste wasn't fooled. When he locked his hands behind his head, the veins popped, the muscles bulged. She smiled with wicked delight, more than up for the challenge he'd just presented her.

Pleasure purred through her at the thought of taking Cain to his breaking point. "I think…" She deliberated a moment as she sat up, wiggling just a little across his groin. "I want to kiss you."

She trailed a delicate finger over his stomach, satisfied when it clenched beneath her touch. "Here." She stopped at his waistband and unsnapped his jeans. She tugged on the loose end of his shirt. "Comfortable?"

When his gaze fastened on her bare breasts, her heart nearly stopped but her nipples tightened. "Gypsy—"

"My turn," she said a little bit shaky, before standing. She didn't risk a glance in his direction. Nonetheless, she felt his eyes burn her as she slowly slipped out of her pants and underwear. It had been easier years before. Cain had always taken control.

Her courage had come from the heat of the moment. But now…

For a second she just stood there, lingering—not to tease, but because her legs wouldn't move. When her gaze finally caught his, there was an untamed, almost ruthless, flare of passion in the gray depths. She was surprised she was able to stand under the blast of heat, but in a blink it was gone, replaced by a hooded, almost sleepy gaze. Which somehow, Celeste decided, was just as dangerous, if not more so. "Man, Cain, you're sexy."

Her tone was like raw silk whispering over his skin.

Hell, Cain groaned silently, she'd barely touched him. But the words…desire thrummed in his veins, thick and hot.

Once again she straddled his waist, this time with her back to him, giving him an unhindered view of her beautiful derrière. His fingers flexed with the urge to cup the round curves, stroke the sensitive skin again. With one slow scoot she moved down onto his stomach. He could feel the brush of her minklike curls against his navel, smell the scent of her arousal. Cain locked his fingers together in a fierce battle for control.

When she unzipped his pants, he arched his hips, more in reaction to the butterfly touch of her fingers than to help her along. With one gentle shove, she pushed down the pants and briefs to his thighs.

He heard her gasp as his erection broke free of its restrictions. When she hesitated, leaving his jeans still halfway down, he knew those same fingers were going to flutter over his arousal.

Her breath hitched, her body tightened.

"Gypsy," he warned, his voice raw, his body desperate for a few seconds of reprieve. If she touched him now, there was a good chance he would embarrass himself. "It would be easier for me, sweetheart, if my jeans were completely off."

She looked over her shoulder, her expression sultry

and determined. Somehow, Cain sensed, her nervousness had disappeared, drowning under a waterfall of self-confidence. That in itself made this sweet torture worth it.

A moment later, she tossed his clothes aside, leaving them both naked. She faced him then. "Ready?" she asked, desire smoking her words. She crept forward, brushing, sliding until she was astride his chest.

His body throbbed, his heart pounded. Still he didn't touch her, but the effort cost him, as small drops of sweat beaded at his temples.

Taking a lesson from Cain, Celeste traced a small pattern on his biceps before moving to the inside of his elbow. When his muscles flexed then bunched in response, she couldn't stop the female satisfaction that rolled through her.

Riding that wave, she leaned down and parted her lips a mere inch away from his mouth until their breath mingled, hot and moist.

He was tight and aroused beneath her. She'd never felt more powerful in her life, more sensual.

Or more fragile.

"Cain." She chewed his bottom lip just a bit. A growl rumbled deep within his chest and triggered soft vibrations against her thighs. Celeste moaned and sank against him. He smelled of sex now, hot and sinful. "Kiss me."

Cain's mouth covered hers, his tongue thrusting, his hands still locked behind him, his arms straining with the effort to keep his shoulders in the air. Celeste gripped his hair, holding on, devouring the spicy male taste that was him.

Sheer willpower saved her. She pushed against his

chest, not willing to give up her advantage. Still, when he eased back onto the rug, she slid her tongue over her lips for one last taste. Pleasing her, pleasing them both.

"My turn?"

The rawness in the question made her body hum. He'd asked—not told—and hadn't realized it. Secretly thrilled, she shook her head.

"No," she said, her eyes brilliant.

But Cain was on fire. Their kiss surged his body into an exquisitely painful arousal. He tried to concentrate on something else, to undermine the need. When her lips brushed his neck, all thoughts spontaneously combusted.

"I like the taste of you," she whispered against his collarbone before trailing smaller, more delicate kisses across his chest. "Spicy, dangerous." Her tongue swirled around his nipple, and desire clawed at him, causing him to arch slightly from the floor. Where in the hell had she learned that?

Cain felt, rather than saw, Celeste shift down onto his thighs, her hands trailing behind her hot, little mouth as she moved. When she stopped, he could hear her breath grow heavier as she studied his arousal.

"You're so beautiful," she whispered, reverently.

Cain ground his back teeth, willing his body to obey his mind. Willing his mind to ignore what his sweet Gypsy was about to do.

Neither worked.

Her lips brushed the very tip of his arousal.

"Gypsy," Cain moaned, just short of demanding—for her to stop or continue he wasn't sure. Didn't care.

She'd heard him, he knew, but had ignored the plea,

intent only on her exploration. She shifted her weight until she lay lengthwise on his legs, her hips automatically gyrating against him as she moved.

Cain closed his eyes against the desperation rising in him.

Her fingers, cool and slender, cupped him, her thumb stroking the soft skin underneath. He felt the ring's cool metal as it drifted over his heated skin. His body shook, grasping at the slippery edges of control, discipline—anything.

"They feel like velvet. Soft, thick velvet." Her breath hitched. Then her lips touched them.

Cain shot up with the force of a missile, his hands still locked in place. That was his mistake. Because just then he watched her mouth, still swollen from his kisses, close over the length of him—moist, warm, sweet.

A moan rose from the very depths of his being, only to explode from his lips in a burst of longing.

Celeste looked up, her throat constricting at the almost feral look in Cain's eyes. A whimper escaped her lips, low and harsh—helpless as her core contracted in painful need.

"Cain?"

His eyes burned, he gripped her hips. With one fluid motion he hoisted her in midair, waiting for her to look at him. When she did, she gasped at the primal heat, the fierce possession and reveled in it. Roaring her name, he impaled her. She cried out with pure animal pleasure.

He surged forward, touching the very tip of her womb, touching the very tip of her heart. Emotions overwhelmed her. His, hers, both. Fever-pitched, she raked her fingers along his stomach, demanding he appease her monstrous yearning. He pulled out then plunged back in. Flesh inside flesh. Tight, hard. With one final cry, her body clenched, shuddered then exploded, her climax consuming her.

Only then did Cain give into his need. With another deep, almost savage, thrust, he came, shouting her name once more—the passion eradicating all but one last coherent thought.

Mine.

Chapter Thirteen

Quamar Bazan cursed silently at the damp weather that stole the heat from his blood. He adjusted his dark knit cap, pulling its edges over his ears. During his life, he'd spent many evenings in the cold, for the Sahara without the sun was like a bitter woman—frigid and steadfast in its vengeance against man. But when that same man gazed upon stars that blanketed the desert sky, well…

One glance told him no stars would appear anytime soon over Shadow Point. Allah was allowing nature a darker path tonight. So be it, he thought. The time would come when he could once again return home to the desert and his people.

In the distance, the dull roar of the wind rushing through the trees caught his attention. It is the way, Quamar mused. Life sometimes hastens on its path, stirring up man and nature along its way.

He slipped over the eight-foot stone wall surrounding the Cambridge estate. Pulling a cigarette-size tracking stick from his backpack, he hit a button to extend the prongs and stuck it into the ground under some bushes. On the tip, a small satellite dish beeped its activation, ready to feed perimeter readings back to Cain and headquarters.

Quamar grunted as he grabbed another. Concealing the sticks along the property boundaries would make it unnecessary for him to breach Olivia Cambridge's mansion. Quamar preferred it that way. He had no desire to disturb an old woman from her sleep.

Slowly he made his way across the area, his pattern a simple, direct line, his senses alert for patrolling guards.

He smiled in the darkness, a secret smile, as he swept through the brush soundlessly, measuring the distance, watching the reading feed into the small computer in his palm. Even though Quamar acknowledged the necessary equipment, he found more pleasure in the simple nomadic life of his tribe.

Unlike Prometheus and Cerberus.

His friends, Quamar had learned over time, did nothing simply. The concept was foreign to their driving nature. Why should love come to them any differently?

The scent of tobacco drifted through the air and Quamar slipped into the shadows just before the heavy step of a boot cracked a nearby branch. Quamar shook his head in disgust as he watched the red glow of a cigarette bounce through the night air as a guard passed by. It seemed Prometheus was correct. Breaching the mansion would be child's play, especially to someone of Gabriel's caliber.

Deciding he'd given the guard enough time, Quamar stood, checked the grid and gauged the next perimeter point.

Mid step, the pain him hit like an ax, cleaving his skull from crown to chin. Quamar dropped to his knees. He absorbed the shock and tried to stand. Another swing of pain—this time leaving stars—jagged with razor-sharp points—bursting behind his eyes. Bile thickened his tongue, even as the ground rose to meet him, cold and hard like a slab of concrete.

Through it all, Quamar felt the wind, its soft edges hastening past.

Then he felt nothing.

THE MOON broke free of the clouds, holding off the soft hues of dawn. A thin streak of light trailed across the walls, giving Celeste her first real look at the bedroom. She was surprised to find that it was nearly wall-to-wall king-size bed—sturdy pine with yards of breathing space and lots of wood.

In what little floor remained open sat a large oak dresser, a matching nightstand—and beige. Beige comforter, beige curtains—she tipped her head over the side of the bed—beige carpet. All understated in their elegance, and all accented with rich, earthy-brown walls. Simple, masculine.

Celeste gazed at Cain, who sprawled across most of the bed, his arm trapping her waist. Sometime during the night, he'd pushed away the warmth of the covers, leaving the sleek lines of his body naked to the cool air that danced in the room.

He'd had called her Celeste. Not Gypsy, not Diana, but Celeste. In his sleep, he moved his arm. His hand cupped her breast. From top to toe, goose bumps ran amuck, and in their wake came a series of slow, sweet shivers. She bit her lip, suppressing the sigh that threatened to slip past.

Even while he dozed, she sensed the barely controlled power that lay coiled in long, lean muscles. The man was a contradiction in terms. Lethal yet safe, powerful yet gentle.

Her gaze skimmed over the scars that patterned his back. Celeste ached to know what had happened, but she'd have to ask. And something she'd seen before in Cain's eyes—dark, wicked shadows—had warned her not to. He would never risk sharing that much of himself with her.

Cautiously, she touched one of the hard lines. A knife wound that hadn't been there the last time she'd last slept with him. A disfigurement that came with a history—one that ran much deeper than the skin, one that ripped through the soul, leaving unfathomable ramifications.

A past that had created the man.

She adjusted the down comforter, tugging the trapped corner from under her waist and pulling it to her chin. Sometime during the night, Cain had carried her to bed. The heat from their lovemaking had dissipated, leaving her slightly vulnerable and chilled.

No undying declaration of love would follow their lovemaking, now or ever. Even though the realization hurt, she didn't blame Cain this time. She'd taken the chance, had known the consequences. And in her heart, she knew she'd do it again.

Just as she knew he wouldn't.

A fist pounded the front door, startling Celeste. In an

instant Cain was awake, his feet planted beside the bed, his gun leveled, his body naked. "Stay here."

He pulled on his jeans, only pausing long enough to zip them, swearing when the attack on the front door continued.

As Cain stepped from the bedroom, Celeste grabbed one of his sweaters lying by the bed—time permitting only accessibility, not modesty—and slipped it on, grateful when the hem fell just past her knees. Seconds later when she joined Cain, Sheriff Lassiter was standing on the porch, his face blotchy with irritation, his frown turning his eyebrows into one bushy line. White plumes of breath puffed from his mouth as he talked, reminding Celeste of a spotted dragon.

"I want some answers, MacAlister."

A very angry dragon.

"It's five-thirty in the morning, Sheriff," Celeste responded. "Couldn't this have waited a few more hours?"

"No, it can't." The blue eyes, now rimmed with black fury caught hers over Cain's shoulder. "The car your fiancé raced against yesterday was stolen."

"It makes sense," Celeste said, then glanced surreptitiously at Cain. "Kids probably joy-riding after boosting a car."

"I would agree, but this car had more than a dozen 9mm slugs embedded in it. You wouldn't know anything about that would you?"

"No, we don't," Cain said easily and leaned against the doorjamb, his body blocking any movement of the sheriff's to step inside. "Why don't you ask the truck driver who spotted us racing?"

Celeste's hand slid easily over the warm skin of Cain's back until she hit the cool metal tucked safely in the waistband of his jeans.

"I wasn't asking you, MacAlister." Judging from the early hour, the sheriff's shadow of whiskers and red-rimmed eyes, Celeste figured on that top of everything else, the sheriff wasn't happy about the extra work hours he'd probably put in. "Let the lady answer for herself, if you don't mind."

"I do mind. The lady has been through hell in the last ten hours." Cain's arm tightened on her waist, drawing her to his side. She leaned in and allowed him to support most of her weight.

"I don't know about any bullets, Sheriff," she stated.

"No one's made any threats to your person in the last twenty-four hours? No one, let's say, who might want to torch your store?"

"Even *if* someone had," Celeste replied carefully, "I'm sure you can appreciate that we don't want to accuse anyone without proof."

"Since it's my job to investigate arson, I believe that's my call, isn't it?"

"I think—"

"I'm sorry, Sheriff," Celeste inserted, when Cain took a step forward. Her hand stopped him in mid-stride. "I'd hate to see what the media would do if they got a hold of my name and Cain's connected with unsubstantiated charges of arson."

"Look. Don't talk to me about the media," Lassiter snapped. "The day hasn't even started and already mine is in the crapper. I'm not much in the mood for games.

Besides your fire…" He jerked his thumb in the general direction of town. "I finally nabbed the burglar who's been ripping off people. Except I find out that not only has he killed two security guards out at the old airstrip, but, as we speak, Olivia Cambridge is lying on a slab down at the morgue with a broken neck. Strangled with her own damned necklace."

Horror slithered through Celeste, coiling deep in the pit of her stomach. Cain's body tightened, ever so slightly. Celeste felt it only because she was still against his side. "Olivia Cambridge is dead?"

"Stone-cold." Lassiter shoved his hat back on his head. "And the media you're so worried about won't be interested in you. In fact, I'm sure that every reporter within a two-thousand-mile radius is racing here to get the scoop on the president's dead mother. Can't keep something like that a secret. The only consolation is that someone put a bullet in the guy before he escaped."

"Who?" The question came from Cain, short and flat.

"The guards. A partner. Who the hell knows? The guards were firing at shadows when my deputies got there. Olivia Cambridge was lying in her study, dead and our killer was lying out on the lawn, bleeding a river from a head wound—jewelry spilling from his pocket."

"What time?"

"A little over two hours ago." Lassiter's eyes slanted, suspicious. "Why?"

"She must've interrupted a robbery," Celeste guessed, realizing that the sheriff hadn't mentioned any coins. Either he was keeping it a secret or there hadn't been any.

Maybe Quamar—

"I've seen stranger," Lassiter responded, his gaze resting pointedly on Celeste. "Like the fact…" He switched his attention back to Cain. "…that only a few hours before, Miss Pavenic's building was torched. And let's not forget the mutilated cat left on her doorstep—and, by the way, preliminary forensics have found nothing on that."

"The timing could be nothing more than a coincidence," Cain answered, his tone and his expression both smooth as glass.

"I don't believe in coincidences. Not in my jurisdiction. Especially when a foreigner who looks like a reject from the World Wrestlers' Foundation, ends up shot on the president's mother's front lawn."

"A foreigner?" Celeste made her question seem nothing more than casual curiosity. But a deep-down dread twisted the muscles of her stomach.

"A male, approximately six-six, late thirties to early forties, bald. Nationality undetermined. No identification, of course. In his car or on his person. That would make my job too easy." He paused for a beat. "You two wouldn't know him by any chance? Or you've maybe seen him around town? Or in that stolen vehicle?"

"No." Cain's answer was short, clipped.

Quamar? Shot? It took all Celeste's willpower to squelch her reaction. "You said he didn't die…"

"Not yet. But he is in surgery. Airlifted to Saginaw. Lucky for him some of the best surgeons in the country work from that hospital. But if he survives the night, I'll be surprised."

There was nothing they could do for Quamar, not

right now—except pray. One glance at Cain's rock-hard features, told her he'd concluded the same.

"Damnedest thing I ever saw," Lassiter continued, pulling his ear. "Whoever this guy was, he came prepared. He was wearing a knit cap that seemed to deflect most of the force of the bullet." The lines in Lassiter's face deepened with uncertainty. "I don't know about you, MacAlister, but I've never seen a hat, other than a military helmet, that could stop lead. I've sent this one to the lab for a breakdown of the material. If that cap was made here in the United States, I'll find out where."

"How about the security tapes from the estate? Do you have them?" Cain asked, seemingly unconcerned.

Lassiter grunted in disgust. "Useless. Somehow, he managed to breach the outside security system, then jammed the cameras. Found a whole bunch of electronic gadgets on his person and in his car. But all we got on the film is static. By the time her personal guards noticed and reached Mrs. Cambridge, it was too late. Seems they were paying too much attention to the Red Wings game and not enough to the monitors. Complacent bastards."

"What's going to happen now?" Celeste asked, already working through the possibilities herself.

"You're kidding right?" He snorted. "The news is slowly leaking out in town which means the media won't be far behind. I imagine once the president gets the message from the governor, who I notified a while ago, he'll be flying in to see to his mother. They'll put a cap on the information going out. They've already shut down the airspace within a hundred square miles of

Shadow Point. Besides the Secret Service, I'm sure he'll be bringing the FBI, CIA, Merchant Marines—and anyone else he can think of to interfere with the investigation. And all I can do is wait for the circus to begin."

"I'm sorry we couldn't have been more help, Sheriff," Celeste offered, hoping to end their conversation.

"But you can, Miss Pavenic. Both of you can." His gaze encompassed them both. "Don't plan on leaving the area anytime soon. I've a feeling that somehow the fire last night ties in with the murder. And I might have more questions later."

"We're not going anywhere," Cain said easily.

"Good." Lassiter removed his hat. He hit it against his thigh, knocking off a thin film of snow before stepping off the porch. "And to think I left Detroit for this."

HER FURY had faded more quickly than she'd thought it would. Only grief mingled with the ache of self-contempt remained, thrumming quietly yet insistently. "I should've seen it coming." Celeste moved away from Cain and dropped into a blue gingham chair. She pictured Olivia, slender and frail, only a little bit taller then Celeste herself. At seventy-six, Olivia would never have had a chance in a fight with Gabriel. "Quamar—"

"Roman's checking into his status, Celeste." But Cain's voice was grim, his features arctic-cold. Whoever had shot Quamar would pay, Celeste was sure. "When he knows something, we'll know something."

After the sheriff left, Cain had called Roman. It seemed Quamar hadn't laid enough satellites to give them a good reading on what had happened to their friend.

"The sheriff didn't mention any quarters." Tired, she rubbed the tension from her temples and studied the ones she had retrieved from the guard at the warehouse. She handed them to Cain. "All New York with the Statue of Liberty on the back."

"Olivia?"

"Maybe," she acknowledged. "But why not leave more by her body?"

"Lassiter could've been withholding the fact they found more coins."

"Possibly, but I don't think so," Celeste said. "Not when he already has his suspect nailed. He'd mentioned the jewels, why not the coins? Especially when he would've put them together with the quarters found by the dead cat?" Celeste shoved her fingers through her hair. "Quamar must've come across Gabriel after Olivia Cambridge was murdered."

"Or Gabriel took him down right before." Cain pocketed the quarters. "*If* Gabriel is the burglar."

"It's logical. He sets a precedent with the other robberies, then kills Olivia under the same circumstances."

"To make her murder seem unplanned?" Cain frowned. "Are you saying she was the target?"

"She certainly could've been, but why play the game with us if he took care of Olivia himself?"

"He wouldn't have," Cain said. "Which means—"

"She wasn't the contracted hit." Celeste started pacing. "But the bait."

"Meaning her death was setting a trap for the real target."

"Don't you see? It makes sense. If you kill Olivia

Cambridge, whose attention are you going to get? Besides the media's, I mean."

"You're telling me Gabriel wants the president's attention?"

"He wants more than that, he wants the president here." Celeste stopped pacing, pausing long enough to sort through the facts. "Olivia's murder certainly exonerates the president as a suspect. No advantage will come for his career through the death of his mother. That makes him the victim." Her tone hardened, determined. "Gabriel wants the president. I don't know the hows and the whys or even the when. But the where will be here. An unanticipated trip to Michigan makes the president vulnerable." Her eyes caught his, absorbing strength from their tough, steady gaze. "You have to make the president listen. Tell him to stay away."

"That's simple." His sarcasm wasn't lost on Celeste. "After all, his mother's murdered with a Labyrinth operative found half dead on her front lawn. And to top it off, the woman who conspired to kill his son lives in the same town. A goddamn nuclear bomb wouldn't keep him away."

"You have to try."

"I need hard evidence, Celeste."

"You won't have it." Her chin hitched only slightly when she continued. "Most people thought President Cambridge wouldn't run for a second term after his son's death—that he'd roll over and die from grief. Instead, he got angry. Turned some of it toward me, but more importantly, he turned the rest of the anger against terrorists and other organized crime. The man's not going to back down. You know that, I know that and Gabriel knows that. If I'm right, Gabriel's counting on it."

"I see where you're going with this, Celeste, but you're speculating all of this—"

"The most logical reason to kill Olivia Cambridge is to bring her son to Shadow Point. With his father buried here, the president isn't going to allow his mother to be buried anywhere else. It's a guaranteed point of contact. One predetermined by Gabriel." She stood, suddenly restless. Or maybe she'd just felt like a sitting duck in the cottage.

"And if you're wrong?" He'd asked the question calmly, but even so, Celeste felt a piercing chill.

"It wouldn't be the first time." She sighed. "But right now, this is all I have, and we're running out of time." Lord, she wished he'd do something. Berate her because she wasn't finding a definitive answer, wasn't doing her job. Scream at her.

Take her in his arms and lie to her that everything would be all right.

Anything as long as he did it with some kind of emotion.

"You need to stop him, Cain. The possibility that I'm right is too high for you to ignore me. Tell him that somehow I was involved with his mother's death." She rubbed the goose bumps from her arms, wishing it was just as simple to rub away the past. "That I'm on the loose, that his life is in danger."

"I'll decide what's right for the mission."

He didn't touch her. Didn't kiss her. Rejection stiffened her back, tensed her muscles. She wouldn't beg. Not for his forgiveness, not for his love.

Cain knew what she wanted, saw the appeal shadowing her face. He rolled his shoulders, resisting the urge to answer her silent plea, sure that if he did, she might be able to convince him to use her.

He'd done it so easily in the past, but now...

"I'm taking a shower." He tipped her chin up, ran a finger underneath finding comfort in the smooth, softer skin that hid there. He couldn't remember any other time he'd felt so beaten up. "Eat something. There's toast. Once I'm out of the shower, we'll go to the Cambridge mansion for answers." He kissed her forehead. He gave himself that, knowing it had to be enough for the moment. "We'll figure this out, Celeste."

He'd used *we* again. At least there was that, she mused as she slipped back into the bedroom. Not love, not even lust anymore. She had no doubt that only duty remained for him—that and the need to protect her.

She heard him start the tap running, and then the door to the bathroom closed. The quiet decisiveness of the sound triggered one simple question.

Just how long would that feeling last?

THE WATER was hot, abrasive. Deliberately so, to keep him focused.

Celeste was starting to trust him. The revelation brought neither anger nor shock—just acceptance. And the knowledge left him vulnerable.

The ring of his phone broke into his thoughts. With a curse he cut off the water, swung back the curtain and reached for his cell where he'd left it on the sink.

But he was too late. Celeste had a cup of coffee in her hand and was already holding the phone to her ear.

"Jon!" Her face went linen-white, her hand trembled. "No, I'm fine. Yes, he's been…I'm glad you're…" Cain stepped toward her when her voice died. "Here's Cain."

"Celeste!" Cain swore when she turned her back to him and walked away, her hand in the air, telling him to back off.

"Damn it, MacAlister. What's going on?" The hollow echo of the retort told Cain he was on a speaker.

Cain watched Celeste walk into the bedroom. With jerky movements, she started pulling on her sweats, his white T-shirt.

"From what we could tell, you had suffered an abdominal wound—" Cain told Mercer.

"Not about my injuries, damn it." Mercer cut him off. "If you're still angry about Celeste being alive, get over it. I want a status report."

"I'm sure Roman's told you—"

"I did." Roman's voice boomed from the background. "He wants your version."

"And Quamar?"

"Still in surgery, Cain." Roman answered again, the concern in his voice raw. Roman and Quamar's friendship was rock-solid, dating back to when an Arab rebel unit had targeted Quamar's tribe. Roman had helped save Quamar's people and earned the giant's loyalty. "I'll let you know as soon as I know something."

"Tell me what the hell is happening, Cain," Mercer rasped.

It took Cain less than two minutes to bring Mercer up to date.

"And Celeste—why in the hell did she sound shocked? You didn't tell her I was alive, did you?"

"No," Cain's answer came after a moment, but the anger was there. Live wires snapping in the air.

"You'd better deal with it." Mercer paused. "Damn it, it feels like my belly's on fire." The words came out on a grunt of pain.

"Have you talked to the president?"

"Damn fool," Mercer answered, his irritation back. "I tried to convince Cambridge to delay his trip to Shadow Point, but some damned idiot named Lassiter promised to release Olivia's body to the embalmer. The autopsy was simple and to the point. She died from a crushed windpipe. The broken neck came after. They're waiting for the toxicology report but expect it to come back negative."

"Cain," Roman inserted. "Cambridge's people have already made arrangements for the funeral to take place later this afternoon. Couldn't get him to reconsider the location either—something about the family plot being sacred."

Mercer coughed. Swore. Then coughed again. "I didn't agree, of course. But there's no talking sense to him this time. Especially since his advisors are pushing the schedule. Figure the sooner the better. So far, they've been able to apply some pressure and stopped the press dead in their tracks, but they can only hold them back for so long."

"If they deal with the situation immediately, there'll be less damage control later," Roman added.

"Air Force One is due in Saginaw soon, Cain." Mercer continued. "All other details are being kept under wraps for security purposes. Even the FBI won't know when he hits town until he does."

"No other way to persuade him?" Cain asked.

"Would you listen to anyone if it had been Christel?" Roman inserted quietly.

Cain ignored him. "Jon, Celeste believes Gabriel will make an assassination attempt. I agree."

"We all agree, damn it," Mercer bit out. "Did Celeste fill you in on everything?"

Mercer's question seemed innocent, but Cain wasn't fooled. Jon was searching for some type of reaction.

"Yes."

"Good."

"But we can't use her as a reliable source," Cain responded, although he'd already planned to provide an extremely detailed report. He wanted the case well-documented with Celeste's history and current involvement. This time he'd make sure she'd be protected from any future recriminations. "Not yet, anyway."

"I agree." Mercer's sigh was long, weary. "The president wouldn't listen to her even with evidence to back her up. This is personal."

"Obviously, the man is not himself," Roman commented.

"Not himself indeed," Cain acknowledged, then after a moment added, "Not surprising, considering someone is systematically murdering his family."

"At least he's not bringing Mora or the girl, Anna. No sense in putting the First Lady and their daughter in jeopardy too. The only one accompanying him is Vice President Bowden." Mercer replied.

"Risky." Cain didn't like it. Having two heads of state in the same place at the same time was just asking for trouble. Too much of a temptation for fanatics.

"Damned stupid," Mercer bit out. "And after Robert got over the initial shock that I was alive, I told him that. But president and vice president have been friends for years, and Bowden felt they needed to show a unified front. Terrorist threats or not. He spouted some Southern rhetoric about dignity and courage." Mercer's voice hardened. "I didn't buy it. Personally, he knows it's a good publicity move if the reporters do get wind of the situation. The man's as slippery as those damned water moccasins he was raised around."

"Jon," Cain said. "Is Cambridge planning to tell anyone that you survived the assassination attempt?"

"No, not until I officially take command again." He grunted. "Roman's in charge until further notice."

"Did Cambridge at least beef up the security, Jon?"

"Yes, but over Bowden's protest. Besides the president's permanent attachments, they're bringing up the Detroit branch of Secret Service." Mercer snorted in disgust. "The vice president didn't want any changes that would alert the public to the murder."

Both Cain and Roman knew there was no love lost between the vice president and the director of Labyrinth. Although he had no proof, Jon had always believed that Bowden maintained his own agenda—one that didn't necessarily take into consideration the best interest of the American people.

"The problem is, Bowden has a valid argument," Mercer admitted. "Damned Secret Service tends to trip over themselves during these unplanned stops. If they can't get their security measures in place a month in advance, they might as well send out an invitation to every crackpot in the country."

"We added our own little mix," Roman interjected casually, but Cain wasn't fooled. "Ian and Lara are on their way," Roman explained. "They're posing as Secret Service agents. One on Cambridge, one on Bowden. But even then I don't know if it will be enough."

"Lara? *She* knows you're alive?" Cain swore. "Who authorized the change in assignment?"

"I did." Mercer interjected just as harshly. "You shouldn't have told her I was dead, Cain. She could have been informed. No reason not to trust her."

"It wasn't a matter of trust," Cain argued. He knew that Roman, as Labyrinth's acting director, had the final say in this decision. "It was a matter of her temper. She's emotionally involved—wants to avenge her father." Cain's jaw tightened. "You felt you owed her this?"

"No. I felt *you* did." Mercer's voice sharpened into finely honed steel, showing the hardened structure of the man beneath, the man who had survived years of jungle warfare. "And she isn't the only one who's on a crusade." He paused, letting his barb hit home. "Or am I wrong?"

"Let's just hope you're not dead wrong," Cain responded tightly.

"Cain," Roman cut through the tension. "Kate sent you a special present with Ian. She's says you're to use it or she'll come there personally, pregnant or not, and kick your ass."

A warning edged Roman's statement and Cain understood it. Kate wouldn't be the only one doing him physical harm if he caused Roman's wife undue stress while she was pregnant.

"What's Ian bringing?"

"Some of Kate's smoke screens. The ones that filter high winds and stay put." Roman's smirk came over the line loud and clear. "And if I know your sister, probably a whole arsenal of other gadgets. Plastic explosives, some acid rope."

"You two need to be on your guard," Mercer interrupted. "Whoever wiped the records clean on that prostitute's phone had high connections. Even Cerberus here," the older man said, his voice roughening with exhaustion, "couldn't find them. I'll expect you to keep me apprised of the situation."

"Cain," Roman's voice came over the phone. "Before we let you go, have you found out anything else on this Sheriff Lassiter? I came across a glitch in his file, as though someone had been screening the data just prior to his move to Michigan."

"Other than his being suspicious about our involvement in Celeste's fire, nothing out of the ordinary."

Cain tightened automatically, finding Celeste sitting on the bed, her delicate features serene. More Diana than he'd seen in the last twenty-four hours. Quietly, she listened, her long, soothing fingers stroking Pan, who lay curled in her lap.

"I don't like it. I started digging deeper into the files,

running a check on everyone who'd be at the funeral. Someone changed information on Lassiter's file. I missed it on the first check, because of the security path. The method is similar enough to the hooker's cell phone records to make me suspicious."

"It's enough to question him. Get on the phone and have Lassiter detained at his office. We're on our way," Cain replied. "If what you say is right, there's a good chance he could be Gabriel."

"I want that bastard out of commission before Air Force One touches Saginaw's tarmac," Mercer ordered.

"I'll take care of it."

"One more thing," Mercer said, his voice grim. "I've put Celeste through hell, all in the name of patriotism. She doesn't owe me anything, especially loyalty. I don't take something like that lightly. Anything happens to her, I'll hold you responsible. Got me?"

Cain's eyes narrowed as he studied Celeste. "If anything happens, Jon, there won't be enough of me left to hold responsible."

If he hadn't turned away, Cain would have caught her wince.

Chapter Fourteen

The Sheriff's Department was small, simple in its furnishings. Metal chairs, metal desks. Tan linoleum floor. One window to each wall, some of their blinds at half-mast, most closed.

Nothing to distract from business, except for an occasional plant. Most of these were artificial, Celeste realized when she studied the bent palm tree in the back corner.

Certainly, there were no pictures of family in evidence. Not because the people who worked here didn't have family, Celeste deduced, but simply because there was no room. Every available space held stacks of papers or hanging bulletin boards.

One lone desk near the door survived the clutter, only because it held a tall, tarnished coffee urn, with enough dents to make her wonder about its efficiency. The heavy scent of burnt coffee grounds hung in the air.

"Can I help you folks?"

Celeste took in the blue suit, matching necktie and white shirt. The guy had Agent stamped all over him.

Secret Service and FBI people crowded the office,

some on computers, most on phones. It was hard not to conclude that they'd found a base of operation.

"I need to talk to Lassiter, where have you got him?" Obviously, Cain had pegged this guy as a no-nonsense, by-the-book agent.

"And you are?" The man was in his mid-forties with muddy brown hair cropped short enough to necessitate the use of a barber every week, but not enough to hide the dusting of gray. Tall and lanky, she thought, Jimmy Stewart with a Brooklyn accent. And, by the look from the shrewd green eyes, the man in charge.

"MacAlister." Cain flashed his identification.

"Sam Garrett. Detroit Secret Service." The muscles relaxed, just enough to appear comfortable, but the eyes remained sharp. "I've been waiting for you, MacAlister. Seems you have some friends in pretty high places." He turned his piercing gaze on Celeste. "And you are?"

"Celeste Pavenic," she said with care. It had been a gamble for her to come, but she'd insisted. Her face had never been made public, never reached past the White House. These might be Detroit agents, but within an hour, Washington Secret Service will be all over Shadow Point. By that time, she hoped, it wouldn't matter.

"I'm Mr. MacAlister's associate." Celeste held out her hand, something neither man had done. "I wish we could've met under less urgent circumstances, Agent Garrett."

He grasped her hand firmly, shook once and let go. "Well, to tell you the truth, I don't quite know why we are meeting, ma'am. I was just told when MacAlister here showed up, I was to give him access to Lassiter. But I find myself…curious—"

"Roe, get the hell out of here. Find that son of a bitch, MacAlister. I want answers. Now!" Lassiter's voice cracked like thunder through the office.

"That would be your friend," Garrett informed them, poker-faced.

A college kid came out from the back room. Sandy-haired, with a basset hound's brown eyes, his face flamed in red. "Agent Garrett, the sheriff is pretty pissed—"

"Roe, this is Mr. MacAlister." He nodded toward the young man. "Deputy Rowan Cash." Without waiting, he waved his hand toward Celeste. "I believe he and Miss Pavenic would like a short conversation with the sheriff."

"Not her. Just me."

Cain caught the stiffening of Celeste's body and grabbed her arm. He nodded toward a scratched-up door with Lassiter's name plate glued to it. "Is it empty?"

"Yes," Garrett answered, his brows raised.

Cain glanced at Celeste. "Stay in there and wait for me."

"I'll do no such thing."

"You're not watching this interrogation, Celeste."

"Try and stop me."

"Agent Garrett," Cain addressed the other man, but his eyes stayed locked on Celeste's. "Miss Pavenic is a civilian with no identification. She is under my protection, most likely from the man you know as Sheriff Lassiter. We believe he might be an assassin whose intention is to kill both her and the president." His eyes flickered over Celeste at her gasp.

"I'm making a formal request that you keep her under

security in Lassiter's office, with a guard posted at the door until I get out of the interrogation. Is that clear?"

"Crystal." Garrett nodded toward Roe. "Deputy Cash, stand guard over Miss Pavenic until Mr. MacAlister tells you otherwise."

"Yes, sir."

When Celeste turned toward the office, twin blue lasers sliced through him, but it was the desolation behind them that caught his gut. He'd pay for this later, but at least for Celeste, there would be a later.

Celeste slammed the door shut behind her with a tightly controlled shove. Garrett let out a slow whistle between his teeth. "Hell, MacAlister, I just met you, but the parting shot that lady just sent you—well, any other man would be a shriveled pile of garbage on the floor."

"I've handled worse."

The lift of Garrett's eyebrow told Cain he doubted it. "If that's the case…" Lassiter bellowed out another stream of curses. "…your man in there should be a piece of cake."

When Cain stepped into the interrogation room, he expected Lassiter to lash out at him. What he got was a long, dismissive look.

"What the hell do you think you're doing, arresting me?" Lassiter demanded to know, leaning back in a metal chair, his wrists resting on the matching table in front of him.

"Shut up, Lassiter." Cain's little inner voice was working overtime. "Tell me why anyone would be messing with your government files."

"How the hell should I know?" Lassiter glared at

him. "Maybe someone doesn't want me looking at things too closely. Maybe someone wants me out of commission." Lassiter snorted. "Maybe someone wants you chasing your tail."

Cain swore, because the comment hit too close to home. "It takes more than just one goddamn phone call to put you in jail, Lassiter. Your files have been changed. At a level too high for me to believe you're not—"

Cain blinked, running through the facts in his head. Without a word, he turned on his heel and headed for Celeste. When Deputy Cash saw him coming, he quickly stepped out of the way.

"What the hell is going on, MacAlister?"

"I don't know." Cain shot his answer to Garrett from across the room. "But I'm going to find out." He shoved the office door open, knowing before he did that his little voice had been right.

Celeste had disappeared.

Chapter Fifteen

Cain roared when he saw the open window. But it wasn't until he saw the sapphire ring sitting on the desk that he felt the swift slice of fear.

He snagged the ring, its metal still warm from her skin and swung around.

That's when he saw it. On the wall—a newspaper photograph of Jim Lassiter receiving an award. A little leaner, a lot more hair, the sheriff stood proudly erect next to chunky brunette Cain guessed to be his wife.

He glanced at the date. Seven years before. "Damn it!"

Cain grabbed Cash by the shirt and shoved him against the wall. "How long?"

"I don't know." Roe's Adam's apple bobbed—to the point where Cain almost shoved it down the boy's throat. "I didn't hear a thing."

"Damn it." Garrett's hand gripped Cain's. "Let the kid go, Cain. It's not his fault."

Cain swore and let his hand fall away, ignoring the deep ragged breaths from Cash. "Go release your sheriff," he ordered the deputy before turning to

Garrett. "Issue an all points bulletin on Celeste Pavenic. I want her picked up now."

"DAMN HIM!" Celeste veered off the main street into the alley, needing the air, the space to think—not caring the wrath she'd face for climbing out the office window. The wind slapped at her, streamers of ice pricking against her cheeks. Cain had no damn right telling her to stay this time.

Cain had made his point brilliantly. With Lassiter in jail, her role in this mission had ended. Jon was alive. And between him and Cain, they'd take care of the president. That was all that mattered, Celeste reasoned, trying to convince herself.

Not the fact Cain had withheld the truth even after they'd made love.

In bed they'd played at being equal. In careers, he wanted her to sit while he took care of things. Kept her safe, a token partner in a locked room.

No, she corrected. A nonperson in a gilded cage.

Diana.

The truce hadn't lasted long between her and Cain. But the fact was, it had lasted much longer than she'd expected. It had taken the phone—its ring signaling the next round.

On the ride into town, there'd been no words left—only stony silence. In the past twenty-four hours, she had tried logic, persuasion—and when neither worked—temper.

She gritted her teeth, acknowledging her temper hadn't quite lifted. Stubborn idiot, she thought and kicked a small stone, vaguely registering its clank against a Dumpster.

If Lassiter hadn't called Cain a stupid son—

Celeste froze, remembering the tone with which Lassiter cussed at Cain. She replayed Gabriel's curses right along with it.

It wasn't the same.

Celeste turned on her heel, the fear slipping through the temper, its edges teetering on real terror. "It's not Lassiter, damn it," she said aloud.

A hand grabbed her arm, a second later cold steel touched the back of her neck. "You figured it out too late, Miss Pavenic."

"TIME TO WAKE UP, Goldilocks." The words slid into the mucky haze. The timbre coaxed, even soothed, but when she tried to focus, it floated from her, leaving only confusion.

And the cold.

The chill slithered in and gnawed her limbs with sharp, icy teeth. From beyond the haze, she heard a low moan and realized the pitiful noise came from the back of her throat.

She tugged at her arms wanting to cross them for warmth, but her wrists were too heavy to lift.

"Wake up." Stars exploded behind her eyes. The impact threw her head to the side, jarring her neck. Pain shot through her jaw, up to her temple and burst through the top of her head. She cried out, but the sound was feeble, hollow. Blood seeped across her tongue—its sharp, copper bite mingled with the rancid taste of adhesive, gagging her. With effort, she swallowed the foulness back and forced her eyes opened.

"It's about time you came to," the voice quipped, its low, caressing tone contradicting the stars that continued to rake the inside of her skull.

Celeste blinked, until her vision cleared enough to focus on a curved iron railing. Deliberately she forced her gaze up, following the spiral of wrought-iron steps.

The lighthouse.

She struggled to rise, fighting off the last of the drug-induced fog. Cold metal bit into her wrists, throwing her off balance onto her side.

"Don't bother. You're handcuffed."

Celeste jerked her eyes toward the source, only to hear coarse laughter come from behind her. Celeste remembered that same laughter in the alley, then a sharp prick of a needle in her neck.

"Remembering?" He patted her shoulder, pleased.

She gauged from the shadow lengths that it had been a few hours since he'd kidnapped her. Gabriel wasn't stupid. He'd stripped her down to her T-shirt and sweats, left her barefoot, then positioned her strategically so that no one could see her if they peered in through the lower window.

"You're no lightweight, though. I'll give you that. It took almost the same amount to *kill* the prostitute. But she was already flying high on heroin." He leaned close to her ear. "Enough about her. Let's talk about…me." His laugh sent her skin crawling. "I suspect you'd like me to formally introduce myself."

The man who stepped in front of her looked more like a lawyer than a cold-blooded killer. He was no taller than six feet and the sun streaks in his shaggy blond hair under his knit cap were too strategically placed to be real.

With the black goose-down parka, he could have been mistaken for a yuppie jogger....

"How's your ankle feeling?"

Nausea slipped through her, thick and oily. She'd seen him before.

The paramedic at the fire.

"I see you're surprised." His lips were wide, but not overly thick, with only a hint of cruelty beneath his smile. "Maybe even a little disappointed?"

Celeste curled her fingers in her palms, trying to contain her rage.

"I wouldn't be so hard on yourself. After all, I've been at my profession much longer than you've been at yours." He crouched, putting his face mere inches from hers. No heavy beard line, no defining bone structure. An ordinary stranger who passed by on the street.

"It's amazing what roles a person can assume when he has access to the appropriate credentials. A definite flaw in our society now that we've become so advanced in our technology."

He stood, then stepped onto a nearby crate, jumping a little to test its strength before returning to Celeste's side. "You, of all people, would understand that, Miss Taylor."

He pointed to a thick eyehook impaled into the circular stairs above her head. "I'll have to position you soon, but first I wanted to thank you for making my job easier this time around."

Celeste tested the handcuffs.

"I suggest you use your intelligence." He reached over and caught her chin, his nails cutting into her jaw.

"It's been quite a game, hasn't it, Celeste?" With a knowing look, he released her, then threw a second crate on top of the first. The second he didn't test. "But it's not quite over yet."

A tear escaped down her cheek.

"Crying won't help." With his thumb, he smeared the drop, allowing his nail to scrape her cheek. The brown irises of his eyes remained empty, lifeless as stagnant water. "I've watched many cry. Men, women, children. In the end, they still died. Some sooner." His shoulder lifted indifferently.

The sting from the scratch fed her contempt, showing him the tear wasn't from fear but rage.

Gabriel's face tightened. "Defiance won't help you, either." Slowly, he slipped the thick noose around her neck. The rope lay heavy against her collarbone, then squeezed her windpipe as he pulled.

"And it certainly won't stop your death." He dragged her like a dog on a leash across the granite to where a large wooden lever protruded from the floor a few feet away. The rope's coarse fiber dug into her skin and her airway spasmed, but Celeste forced herself to remain passive, understanding that if she didn't move, she wouldn't strangle.

"See that switch? Here's where the final moments of the game come into play." He lifted her until she stood on the box, then tied the rope end through the eyehook. "I believe it's called Sudden Death." He wobbled the crates, causing Celeste to catch her balance. "As you can see your position's a bit precarious, so listen up."

Gabriel eased the knot—just. Air rushed in, burning her windpipe.

"I've given you enough rope so that if you jump and kick just right, you might hit the lever and stop the weight. Of course, you'll snap your neck—therein lies your choice."

"And if you miss?" He strolled over to the light-house's clockwork weight. "Don't worry, because un-derneath is an explosive—nitroglycerin—to make things a little more interesting. I love interesting, don't you?" He tugged on the chains. "Once the weight hits... well, you get the picture."

A violent shiver wracked her body—from cold or fear, she couldn't be sure. Celeste shifted, trying to keep her blood flowing into her arms.

"Oh, if you're hoping Prometheus will save you..." Gabriel started toward the door. "...so am I." He opened the door. "In fact I'm planning on it. You see, I've rigged the door to set off a remote detonator."

"Of course, to help you, he must succeed in killing President Cambridge for me. Otherwise, I won't tell him where to find you."

Cain? Kill the president? She shook her head. Never.

Seeing the gesture, Gabriel smiled. "Oh yes, he will." His eyes grew hooded, almost languid. "You thought you understood me? Understood the type of person I am?" He leaned against the wall, his arms folded. Lights and shadows harshened his features, showing them chiseled by years of butchery. "I played you from the word go.

"If *I* killed the president, I'd have to disappear permanently. Having someone else take the credit allows me to fade into the background for a while, then resurface at my leisure. This time there'll be no signature with the kill. No political statement to link me in any way."

Celeste understood. Gabriel had deliberately tied himself to a certain trademark all these years so that at the right moment, all he had to do was drop the trademark—go against type. No one would suspect.

"Nothing personal against you or Cain." He gave a thin, dangerous smile. "To make the ruse believable, I needed the best—Prometheus."

Celeste clenched her jaw, her body aching from the immobility. Her ankle throbbed from taking her weight.

"I read his government file. Found his vulnerable spot. You."

Celeste stiffened. That meant someone else had accessed Mercer's records and passed the information on to Gabriel.

"Once I realized you'd done me a favor by not dying the first time, Jonathon Mercer became my trigger and you became my bait. I'll bet you didn't know you were in Cain's file, too." Gabriel's tone was like ice. Celeste felt its chill slide into her and freeze her blood.

"After all, who could be more pathetic? A woman who was once Prometheus's lover and whom the president blames for the murder of his son?" He chuckled, the cold disappearing instantly. "Yep, a plan just can't come together any better than that."

His words were meant to wound, but they didn't. She was no longer the woman he described. No longer pathetic and weak. And she wasn't going to just roll over and die while Cain's life hung in the balance.

"It takes the weight almost three hours to lower completely. So you've got some time." He glanced at the noose around her neck, then pushed the lever. The gears clicked rhythmically in the air. "I disengaged the lamp, so no one outside will notice anything different. I don't want anyone disturbing you. Don't disappoint me, Celeste."

THE MESSAGE was blunt. The paper taped to his windshield. "Meet me on the ridge alone—or the Pavenic woman's dead. You have one hour."

The snow and sand should've crunched under his footsteps, Cain made sure it didn't. What little sun there was had disappeared. The fog thickened leisurely, encouraged by the lint-gray clouds that hung low over the horizon. In the past, the lighthouse lamp would've been activated, its solitary signal flashing in quick, short series—casting a warning out over the water.

Cain saw the silhouette of a man by the edge of the ridge, one foot resting on a small boulder, his back to Cain.

That in itself was meant as an insult.

Cain didn't care.

"Did you know that every lighthouse is set on a different flash sequence?" The voice floated across the distance. "To help the ships passing to chart their course." He shrugged when Cain made no comment. "Too bad ours isn't operational. Looks like it's going to be a bad day for the ships." The man glanced over his shoulder. He was just a few inches shorter than Cain, dressed in a dark parka with the hood up. What wasn't covered by the hood lay hidden beneath a ski mask. "But a good day for a burial. Don't you think?"

"What I think is irrelevant."

"True." Gabriel studied the lake, his hands in his pocket, his head to one side. "Did you know the word *Prometheus* means foresight?"

Cain didn't blink, didn't move—didn't buy into the act. "I'm not here to share tidbits of trivia."

"No, just making an observation." The man chuckled before stepping toward Cain. Without a word, Cain raised his arms and Gabriel patted him down, looking for weapons, recorders. They both knew he could take his time. He was in charge, the one in control.

But Cain was patient. This game he knew, understood.

Gabriel stood, satisfied Cain was clean. "I'm assigning you a labor."

The Greek term for task was not lost on Cain. "You want me to ensure your assassination of the president succeeds or you'll kill Celeste." The wind blustered about, gusting with fury, spraying mists of snow from the frozen edge of the water. Still, the force of nature dimmed in comparison to the rage building in Cain.

"Actually, *you're* going to kill the president. Today at the burial."

Cain mentally shrugged. It could've been either scenario. "And if I don't, Celeste dies."

"And in considerable pain."

Cain's stomach clenched at the comment, but outwardly he showed no emotion.

"You don't seem surprised."

"Very little surprises me." Cain forced his jaw to

relax into a deadly smile. "Besides, you left the coins on the guards at the warehouse. Lady Liberty is Celeste. Or am I mistaken?"

"The Cambridge burial takes place in an hour." Gabriel laughed at Cain's raised eyebrow. "My client keeps me well informed. But it leaves you very little time to make arrangements to attend—if you haven't already."

"And if I can't?"

"You could always ask your brother, Ian, to sneak you in."

Cain allowed astonishment to flicker in his expression and Gabriel grunted with satisfaction. "Don't underestimate me, MacAlister." The brown eyes narrowed dangerously. "I haven't gotten where I am by being sloppy. Your choice is simple. You can kill the president and save the woman. Or they can both die. I'd just have to disappear for a long time. Not something I want to do, but sometimes sacrifices are necessary."

"If they die, you wouldn't be able to go deep enough to hide from me."

"I wouldn't hide from you. I wouldn't have to." Gabriel's tone went arctic. "Didn't I mention you'll be dead, too?" The man shrugged, changing moods like a chameleon. "Frankly, I could've killed you several times—the lighthouse, the car chase—even on Main Street in broad daylight."

"Instead, you kept me interested."

"And we both know that protecting the Pavenic woman did the job. The woman has made you careless."

"Or maybe I figured the woman would lead me to

you and allowed myself to be played." He lifted a negligent shoulder. "After all, here we are."

"Certainly a possibility. But somehow I don't think you wanted it to go this far." Gabriel shifted, his eyes narrowing on Cain's bland expression. "You understand, there's no reason for all of you to die. I'm not getting paid for that."

"And the bottom line is money."

"Of course." Gabriel's tone remained matter of fact. "I leave all that patriotic crap to you heroes." He glanced up as small flakes of snow began to fall. "Now, I have Celeste in a somewhat perilous position. If you don't kill Cambridge by the time he leaves the cemetery, you won't have time to save her."

"I'm listening."

"It's simple. Even for you. Get near enough to kill him. The *how* is your choice."

"And his Secret Service kills me."

"You're a smart man, Prometheus. Utilize your brother. I don't care. My client wants Robert Cambridge dead. Whether you survive or not doesn't interest me."

"Tell me who hired you."

"I would except my next client might frown on the fact I can't keep secrets."

"You could rely on repeat business." Cain shrugged off the urge to attack, to see Gabriel's blood flow. "After all, you murdered Bobby Cambridge for this client, too. Didn't you?"

"Did your girlfriend tell you that?"

"She didn't have to. It's logical."

He tipped his head back and studied Cain's face for a moment. "Maybe."

Cain didn't flinch. There were different ways to play chicken. "Very few men could've pulled off that kidnapping and gotten away with it."

"Now you're flattering me."

"Someone wants Cambridge out of the White House. A mental breakdown over the death of his only son should have—would have—brought most men to their knees. Unfortunately for you, Cambridge has a will of iron. The kind forged from years of war and service to his country."

"Yeah, he's a regular patriot."

"And that leaves you only one choice now, doesn't it?"

"Not me, my friend. If it had been up to me, I would've killed the whole family. Been more profitable."

"Why the statement? Why not kill him in an accident?"

Gabriel's lips thinned into a feral smile. "My clients have bigger egos than we do, Prometheus. They prefer flash to subtlety. I please them when it suits me. Or when the money's right. This time it happens to be both."

"When I kill Cambridge, I'm just supposed to take your word that you'll free Celeste."

"You have no choice." Gabriel paused, feigning astonishment. "You aren't suggesting that I might not be trustworthy, are you?"

"It takes a high-ranking contact in the government to forge law-enforcement files and erase phone records."

"You have no idea," Gabriel said coolly. "I've left evidence with my client. It shows you and your friend

Bazan's involvement in not only Olivia Cambridge's murder, but the Pavenic woman's also."

"Evidence I'm sure they'll find once I kill Cambridge."

"Only a small challenge for someone of your caliber," Gabriel reminded him. "By the way, I have front-row seats at the burial today. So I'd better see lots of blood when he dies. That way there'll be no doubt." With one last glance at the lake, he walked past Cain. "Remember, the woman has only a few hours left. Don't disappoint me."

After a couple of steps, he stopped and faced Cain one more time. "And Prometheus. When you report back to Mercer, speak kindly of me, would you?"

THE SHADOWS grew long and jagged, creeping forward like the Grim Reaper. Raw fury fed what little strength Celeste had left. She yanked on her restraints wincing when the steel gnashed her wrists, shredding more of her skin and leaving the warm, steady trickle of blood on her palms.

She shifted her feet, giving her bad ankle a respite and automatically easing the throbbing in her calf.

The gearbox stood beside the lever, while inside, the steady click of the mechanism ticked its countdown.

FOREST HILL CEMETERY was larger than most would expect for such a diminutive population. Fortunately for security purposes, it was also located past the western edge of town and fairly isolated by a small forest. Hence the name, Cain thought wryly. Rows and rows of cement markers, various shapes and sizes—all pristine, most bare of flowers—stood serenely behind a five-foot wrought-iron fence that stretched around a four-block radius.

Just as Gabriel had predicted, Cain had no problem securing an invitation to the burial service. The problem would be getting close enough to the president to kill him.

His eyes skimmed the perimeter from behind mirrored sunglasses. In one glance, he spotted a dozen state troopers patrolling the area, others in sniper positions. The Cambridge family plots were located in a lavishly manicured garden beside the cemetery's mausoleum. Lassiter, along with several deputies and a few agents, were positioned on the roof of the weathered building, their rifles sighted on the spectacle below.

A damp, murky mist shrouded the hills, providing a dramatic backdrop to the discreetly plain but large drum-shaped mausoleum that stood alone amidst the cluster of pines and dormant maple trees. Constructed of cut limestone and covered with leafless brown vines, the mausoleum appeared nearly black with age. Two curved staircases, ornamented with various religious symbols, flanked opposite sides of the double oak doors, winding from the ground to the roof's flat surface.

President Cambridge stood near the newly dug, oversize grave. Oversize, Cain decided, to match the opulence of the more weathered gravesite of the president's father.

Snow dusted the ground and the scent of fresh, wet dirt hung heavily in the air in spite of the wind that gusted and swirled around them, stirring coat tails and flapping pant legs in its wake.

President Cambridge was tall, distinguished in a charcoal-gray overcoat with a subdued shirt and tie. His brown hair, peppered with gray, was cut tastefully close and neat, and although time had thickened his chest and waist, at fifty-five, the man was the epitome of elite.

Beside him, stood the slighter, shorter vice president, his thinning straw-blond hair standing at attention in the wind. Bowden's long, sleek Armani overcoat showed a peculiar contrast to the president's less showy attire.

There was a third man at the head of the gravesite. A slightly hunched, plump man in his late fifties. He was dressed in black, a white strip of cloth displayed in the open collar of his coat.

"We are gathered here in prayer for our dearly departed sister," the reverend intoned, raising a gloved hand toward the suspended mahogany casket while the other held a small, red Bible. "Olivia Ruth Cambridge."

Of the Secret Service, nine men and one woman surrounded Cambridge and Bowden. For a moment, Cain studied his brother, the largest of the dozen Secret Service agents. Ian, opposite in looks from his siblings, had cobalt eyes, hidden at the moment by sunglasses, and their father's chestnut hair, cropped militarily short.

In the distance a wail sounded, like a baby crying. Cain bit back a curse, knowing better. Pan was cheerfully shredding the rest of Cain's leather upholstery and letting everyone within earshot know it. At first, Cain had thought about leaving the damned cat behind, but for some reason he couldn't. Pan was the only thing Celeste would have left after this mess. Now, as the howling continued, he wished he'd thought harder about it.

Cain caught Lara Mercer in his peripheral vision. Slight in build and of average height, she wore the standard black Secret Service suit and still managed to stand out from the other agents. Her hair flashed red even with the lack of sunlight. She'd bound it tightly to the crown of her head, accenting her refined features and bringing out the riot of freckles on the otherwise flawless skin. But Cain knew that under those freckles existed a competent operative…when she curbed her emotions. Efficient and reliable.

Removing his sunglasses, he gave the signal, hoping that for this mission, she'd stay that way.

Lara and Ian slipped their hands into their pockets. Cain braced himself when they pulled out their fists and watched as the coffin was slowly lowered into its hole. With a flick of his wrist, Cain hit the detonator on his watch.

Simultaneously, three sheriffs' cars, no more than two hundred feet away, exploded. The ground shook, the Secret Service yelled as they dove for Cambridge and Bowden.

Chapter Sixteen

Chaos hit Forest Hill Cemetery.

Smoke bombs exploded, mingling with the rich, dark clouds from the burning cars. Ian and Lara had taken care of the protection detail—leaving them in thick, green curtains of smoke that defied the wind currents.

Behind Cain, shots sounded, the distinctive pop of specialized bullets from Ian's and Lara's guns. The veterans screamed for coverage while the less experienced scrambled in confusion and others coughed—their eyes red and tearing, their throats clogged with the smoke. Several agents lay at Cambridge's feet, unmoving, leaving their chief vulnerable.

Grimly, Cain launched himself, tackling the president and propelling them both into the grave.

Cain heard the grunt of pain, the whoosh of air as Cambridge landed back-first onto the casket. The instant Cain's knife filled his hand, he buried it, hilt deep, into the president's chest. He heard the squeal, the sharp intake of breath. A sound that had almost become a litany for death during Cain's years with Labyrinth. Only this time, a good man exuded the noise. He pushed that thought away and pictured Celeste in his mind. Without hesitation, he yanked the blade clean, then forced himself to bury it again.

Blood flowed, covering his hands, slicking his grip. The smoke dissipated and still he stabbed, only stopping when the president no longer moved. He left the knife embedded as bullets peppered the hole. A flash of heat stroked his side. Without checking, Cain knew the bullet had gone clean through.

With one hard shove, Cain pushed Cambridge off the coffin and onto the dirt beside it. Then he disappeared on the opposite side, wedging himself between the casket and the dirt wall. Fire lanced his ribs. He glanced down at the wound then, saw where the blood darkened his shirt from hip to rib. With cold indifference, he pulled out his gun, and glanced out the hole.

"Get going!" Ian shouted as he dropped to the ground next to the grave. Breathing heavily, he reached down and grabbed Cain's forearm and pulled. Cain came up, his weapon firing. Bodies littered the ground. "They'll stay unconscious for at least ten minutes, but no more than twenty," Ian advised, before dropping his clip and jamming another into his pistol.

Vice President Bowden threw himself into the hole and covered the president with his body. Neither brother looked twice at the man.

"Lara's got Lassiter's men pinned from behind the building." Ian tossed Cain a spare pistol and watched him tuck it in his waistband. "I'll cover you from the front. Be careful," he warned. "Those bullets aren't real.

They're knockout pellets." Ian glanced at the roof as another shot exploded by his feet. "That friendly fire is from our minister," he spat sardonically, pointing to the top of the mausoleum. "I'm betting he's your man. One shot and I can take him down."

"No. Unconscious doesn't help me find Celeste."

"What's your plan?" Ian scanned the perimeter for Lara. She was crouched behind one of the larger grave markers a few yards away, systematically shooting the agents and troopers with the pellets.

"You distract Lassiter's men." Cain nodded toward the roof. "I'll do the rest."

Ian quirked his brow. "What's your backup plan?"

Cain's eyes met his brother's. "If I fail, make sure he does, too."

"My pleasure," Ian promised, his face set.

Cain took the mausoleum stairs in four long, strides. Gunfire whizzed past him as he hit the cement roof, rolled and palmed the smoke bombs. He squeezed each as he came up and whipped them at the deputies. Smoke exploded on the roof. Cain fired Ian's pistol taking down the remaining three men, but lost sight of Lassiter.

His wound burned and the blood-soaked shirt stuck to his skin, but Cain ignored both. From the opposite wall, Gabriel stepped forward, gun raised. "Like I said, Prometheus." He pointed his pistol toward Cain's wound. "The Pavenic woman has made you careless."

When he tries to kill us, he's going to do it in such a way that he'll show off his cunning.

Celeste's words collided with the truth of Gabriel's and fury darkened Cain's peripheral vision to a tempered black. In one fell swoop, all the emotion—anger, betrayal, guilt—he'd buried for the last three years poured out in a torrential storm and filled his head with a blinding red haze.

"Make it count, you son of a bitch, because I will." Cain threw his weapon away and advanced, his hands swinging loosely at his sides.

Eyes narrowed, Gabriel tightened his finger on the trigger, his aim focused on Cain's forehead.

The pistol discharged as Cain threw himself sideways. He felt the burn of the bullet's heat across his ear. Insane with rage, he lunged toward the killer, dodging the gun suddenly wedged between them. Its handle dug into his ribs, grinding cartilage. He hissed with pain, then smashed his forehead into Gabriel's face. The other man absorbed the hit with a grunt, but the shock loosened his hold. The gun flew from his fingers, over the wall, and clattered on the pavement below.

With his hands free, Cain tackled Gabriel but the other man was ready. He met Cain halfway. Their bodies slammed shoulder to shoulder. Cain's back teeth knocked together and he tasted blood. He grabbed Gabriel by the neck and squeezed. "Tell me where she is or I'll kill you now."

Gabriel's hands locked on Cain's wrists, but he didn't make any attempt to free himself. "Kill me and you kill the woman. Let me go and she still has a chance."

"A chance in hell." Cain hit Gabriel, enjoying the crunch of nose cartilage beneath his knuckles.

Cain saw Gabriel's gaze focus behind him. Cain swung him around, a split second before the blast of

Sheriff Lassiter's rifle. Gabriel stiffened, throwing both men off balance. Cain shifted, trying to break free but Gabriel hung on. Cain caught the surprise in Gabriel's eyes, even as the other man struggled to regain his balance. Unable to, the killer stumbled into the ledge. His calves smacked the brick, tripping him backward over the edge. Taking Cain with him.

"No!" Gabriel screamed as Cain made a frantic grab, his fingers catching only wisps of icy air. Doggedly, Cain struggled to keep his hold on the man as they both dropped.

Their bodies hit hard against iron. Cain felt the sickening thud, heard the crack of bone before he slammed against Gabriel, then dropped to the ground—alone.

Fire burned Cain's chest and he struggled to suck air into his lungs. His eyes locked on to Gabriel. The other man lay face up, impaled on the wrought-iron fence surrounding the Cambridge graves. Several spikes, now crimson with blood, pierced him mid-abdomen. His body hung across the top rail about four feet above the ground—like a broken puppet.

Cain scrambled to his feet, cursing his throbbing side, swiping at the blood running into his eyes.

"Don't you die yet, you bastard."

Gabriel gasped. Desperate, Cain grabbed the man's head and shoulders, and lifted them, knowing he was only adding a few precious seconds to the man's worthless life.

Gabriel's eyes fluttered open. "You think you've won, Prometheus?" A death rattle vibrated in his throat with each grinding syllable. "She'll die before you can reach her." His body spasmed. Blood and spittle frothed from his mouth and nose, forming crimson streaks down his chin and across his cheeks. He struggled for oxygen.

"Tell me, damn you!" Cain shouted into his face, his chest heaving, the rage and helplessness consuming him.

A sadistic smile played at the edges of Gabriel's mouth. "Tick. Tock," he whispered with his last breath.

In seconds, Cain was surrounded. He immediately placed his hands on his head and dropped to his knees. Two agents shoved him to the ground, face-first in the snow-patched dirt.

Something stung his eyes, dirt, blood—tears. He blinked them away. Other agents and troopers staggered around, still under the influence of the pellets' sedative— while many more still were out cold on the ground.

A foot pressed into the base of his neck, jarring his injury. Cain gritted his teeth. "Damn it, save the president," he yelled.

Ian and Lara hit the ground beside him, each eating dirt. In three quick snaps, Lara, Ian and Cain were handcuffed.

"Bring Cambridge over here." Cain tried to rise and took an elbow in the kidney for the effort.

"That'd be funny if he wasn't dead, you son of a bitch," Lassiter retorted, blood dripping from his forehead. The sheriff gripped his hair, yanking his head back, then cold steel dug into Cain's cheek. "Give me one goddamn reason you shouldn't join him," Lassiter asked, pressing the gun barrel hard enough for Cain to taste blood.

Ian swore. "Was she worth it, Cain? Enough to kill the president?" The betrayal was there, cemented in his brother's face. "Protect Cambridge and not harm anyone. That was the plan. That's why we used the smoking walls, the knock-out pellets." Ian jerked his head toward the dead man hanging on the fence. "Even Gabriel wasn't to die. Was this your backup plan?" Leveraging his chest off the ground, he twisted around to face Cain fully. "If Lara is brought down in this—"

"Shut up," the first Secret Service agent yelled and slammed the butt of a rifle across the back of Ian's head, knocking him back to the ground. "Or so help me, I'll—"

Lara hissed. Cain caught the flicker of concern in her green eyes before they flared. She struck out with her heel and nailed the agent in the kneecap. The man collapsed, howling.

The other raised his weapon, his intent clear. Ian rolled, caught the agent's leg with his ankles and yanked. The man hit the ground, his gun discharging into the air.

"Release them. Now!"

Chapter Seventeen

"I said release them!" President Cambridge stepped from the crowd of drugged troopers and agents. He grabbed Lassiter's arm, forcing the sheriff to let go of Cain. "Let them up! We don't have time for this!"

Blood dripped from the president's lip. His normally well-groomed hair stood in unnatural disarray. Instantly surrounded by protective bodies, the president shoved. "Get out of my way, you bloody idiots." Robert Cambridge grabbed his forehead and pulled. Prosthetic skin broke away from his face, revealing the stern expression of a younger man beneath.

The baritone voice was replaced by a clipped British accent. "You're one lucky bugger, Cain. If it had been Her Majesty's guards, your head would be lying next to your bloody ass by now."

"Damn it, Jordan, you took long enough." Cain raised his wrists behind his back. "Get these off," he ordered, urgency stressed every syllable.

"You heard the man. Unlock him," Jordan Beck demanded, wiping his bloody lip with the back of his

hand. His eyes narrowed, looking for the calm, calculating Prometheus who once had existed in his friend.
"Your president is at the White House." He tossed a
phone to one of the agents but didn't wait for the real
president to verify. "Now! Take off all their handcuffs,"
Jordan snapped, while Cain, finally free, grabbed his
confiscated gun from one of the troopers.

"I couldn't get out of the hole," Jordan complained.
"You nearly broke my bloody back, Yank, when you
tackled me." He undid his damaged shirt and threw the
concealed pad, filled with a thick red dye, to the ground.
"We got Bowden though. Nailed the bastard. When he
saw me move, he decided to try to stab me himself
while everyone was distracted. The ass didn't realize it
was a trick knife until it was too late. He won't be contracting any more hits."

Ian stepped toward one of the Secret Service men—
the one who had pistol-whipped him. He helped the
agent up before glancing at Lara. "Didn't think you
cared, Red."

"I don't," Lara snapped, shrugging off Ian's helping
hand. "I'm getting tired of being left in the dark, MacAlister," she continued, rounding on Cain, then shot a look
at Jordan. "Who the hell are you?"

"Jordan Beck," the Brit replied easily, picking off bits
of plastic and adhesive from his face.

"You're Jordan Beck?" Lara crossed her arms, taking
in the lanky body, the sharp British features.

"You've heard of me." Jordan grinned, then dropped
his voice. "Who else would MacAlister contact for this?
Roman convinced the president that he needed a decoy.

That's why the burial happened fast, and was kept so secretive. Even your father didn't know Cain had authorized the switch."

"Well, I'll be a—" Ian bit off his expletive.

Lassiter stepped forward and grabbed Cain's shirt. "You bastard!"

"You can have a piece of me later, Lassiter" Cain growled and yanked free. "Gabriel hid Celeste. She'll die if we don't find her soon." He'd been running Gabriel's last words through his mind. "Tick, tock. Tick, tock." His little voice kept nudging him. "Time's running out."

In the distance, shots ricocheted. Those who could, screamed warnings. Cain took off at a run, followed by the others.

It took only moments to reach the grave, but by then it was too late. Bowden had escaped. "Damn it," Cain roared. His eyes met Jordan's. "Go!"

Lassiter started running, directing those who were left to follow. Several agents and troopers had taken off through the woods, but none were capable of an aggressive pursuit.

Jordan shook his head, his features determined. "The way I figure, I owe Diana one, Yank. I'll get her."

"Her name's Celeste, damn it." Cain paused for only a moment, then looked at Ian. "Ian! You and Lara, go after Bowden."

Ian paused, "You need our help to find Celeste. Alone, you—"

"No. Do what I say!" Cain snapped, his fear palpable. "Nail the bastard, then come back and help me."

"Got it, boss."

"Tick tock." Jordan frowned as he watched Lara and Ian take off running. "A bomb?"

"Maybe," Cain bit out, not letting the fear take control. "He used one on her store."

"Too conventional," Jordan considered, his eyes narrowing on Cain's reactions. "Not clever enough."

"Clever?" Cain commented, then rushed back to Gabriel's body. Quickly, he searched his pockets, finding the coins in the coat. "Maine.

"The lighthouse," Cain yelled, shoving the quarters in his pocket, already running. "It operates with a clock mechanism."

THE GLOOM, chillingly eerie, darkened the interior of the tower, leaving only the lever in its limited light.

A queer calmness filled her. The weight, now little more than a foot above the nitroglycerin, told Celeste she had no choice. Her ankle no longer throbbed, nor did the raw wounds of her wrists burn.

Sweat drenched the T-shirt stuck to her back.

In the distance, beyond the walls of the tower, she heard the muffled burst of orders. Cain!

A sickness, dark and terror-filled, roiled within her belly, when she caught the fear that underlined his commands.

The noose tightened, biting into her neck, and she tried to still the trembling in her legs. Moments. They were only moments away.

She heard him brush against the door, heard his words through the pine. "Celeste, we're here, honey. Hold on!"

"No!" Celeste screamed, realizing even as she did that duct tape would stifle her warning.

And warning Cain would be useless.

Tears ran unchecked as she tightened her muscles. Her thoughts focused on the lever, and she shifted her hips, putting her feet in a front-kick position. She would only have one shot.

No regrets, she thought, her heart pounding. With her last thought of Cain, she launched forward.

Time slowed. In the back of her mind, she heard the crates crash, felt the rope tighten. Her foot hit the lever and the splintering snap of the wood ricocheted through her leg.

She swung back, self-preservation driving her to search for stability though she knew she wouldn't find it. The rope squeezed her throat, blocking what little air she had in her lungs.

Gabriel had sabotaged the lever.

She understood that in the split second that followed her kick.

Her lungs burned, her mouth parted, straining against the tape, unable to gasp. Through it all, she heard the clicking of the gears.

They both would die.

CAIN BRACED his foot against the door, levering to kick the pine in—when his little voice stopped him.

"Damn it!

"What?" Jordan came up from behind, and put his shoulder to the door, already primed to help.

"If I'm right, he'll use a bomb to kill her. Celeste said

he'll follow the same MO if he can." Cain ran his hand down the crevice of the door, searching for wires. "If that's the case this door will be rigged."

Cain glanced at Jordan. "Do you have your penlight?"

Jordan nodded, already reaching for his pocket. "You want to cut through?"

Cain snagged his own, then turned the thin dial at the base. "Set the length just past two inches. Any deeper we might cut through something other than the door."

Jordan copied his movements, then punched the black button.

The twin lasers sliced through the pine like butter. Within moments, Cain yanked the four-by-four square free and threw it to the ground then scrambled through the opening.

His heart lurched: Celeste was swinging in midair, her neck trapped in a noose.

Jordan raced to the mechanism brake, and spotted the broken lever. "Serious trouble," he gritted viciously.

"See how much time we've got," Cain yelled as he tossed his gun down—the laser already out and slicing the rope above Celeste's head.

"Celeste!" he shouted in her ear over the rush of his own pounding blood.

The rope parted and he slid the noose from her neck. When he pulled the tape from her mouth, she whimpered in pain as the adhesive tore skin from her lips.

"The bomb?" Her question came out raspy, sandpaper on sandpaper.

"We've got to get you out of here. Hold still," Cain said as he lasered through her cuffs.

"Coins." Celeste's throat was on fire, her jaw stiff.

"We don't have time—"

"No." She shook her head, wincing as a thousand hot irons stabbed her neck. "Use…coins…in…gears."

Cain jerked his head, his eyes narrowing on the gearbox. "Jordan!" Hastily he set Celeste onto the ground and dug into his jeans pocket for the quarters from the cemetery.

Jordan was already there with his penlight laser, cutting the cover off. "Got it!"

Cain threw the quarters into the mechanism and slammed the lid shut. Time suspended for a moment as the coins rattled through. Suddenly a loud screech hit the air—the grinding of metal against metal—a high-pitched whine that threatened their eardrums.

Then silence. Sudden, deafening silence. The weight stopped, poised mere inches from the explosive.

Bracing himself, Cain lifted Celeste into his lap using the warmth of his body to give her strength. He smoothed away the sweaty tendrils of hair that clung to her forehead. He murmured unintelligible words against her cheek—rocked her back and forth.

"Now isn't this sweet?" Dan Bowden stood in the doorway, his eyes glinting with madness, his hand holding a 9mm Glock. "Can anyone join this party?"

Chapter Eighteen

The vice president nodded toward the bomb. The cruel twist of his mouth left his lips bloodless. "Looks like Gabriel's handiwork."

Cain froze, aware that his gun lay at least a foot away. And with Celeste in his lap, he wouldn't be able to move fast enough to reach it.

"I heard them, you know. Mercer and Olivia. She was concerned about her." He pointed his gun at Celeste but was talking to Cain, his breath coming in ragged bursts of air. "The old bat made the mistake of discussing it at a banquet when she thought no one was listening."

His teeth bared, Bowden yelled at Celeste. "You were supposed to be dead. You just couldn't leave it alone. You couldn't let Bobby Cambridge rest in peace!"

"She's dead now," Cain spat, but his eyes never wavered from Bowden. "She can't hear you." To prove his point he dropped her to the floor, praying she'd stay there. Then he stood, carefully placing himself between Bowden and Celeste.

"Don't move!" Bowden screamed, the shrill cry

came from somewhere amidst his madness. He waved his gun between Jordan and Cain while his other hand, out of habit, straightened the strand of hair from his forehead. Pushing it back. Pushing it back. In a steady continuous rhythm.

"Both of you will just have to listen for her," he insisted, spittle flying from his mouth, his pistol settling on Cain. "I've made deals, guarantees that would have put the United States back on the map. I would've gone down in history as the man who changed the world. But I couldn't do it walking in Cambridge's shadow." His laughed bitterly, but his eyes darted wildly, no longer settling. Watching for inner demons.

"You murdered a ten-year-old boy," Cain explained as fear clawed up his back with sharp talons. He beat it back down. "How does that make you a leader?"

Bowden sneered, his hand only stopping momentarily. "A necessary casualty. We are at war."

Cain heard Jordan inhale, knew the Brit was going to make a move. Cain's muscles tightened. "But the war isn't here." He gauged his chances and shifted a few inches toward his Glock.

"Of course it is. People must see it here to be impressed when I save them."

Celeste moaned and a cold sweat slicked Cain's skin.

"Look, Yank." Jordan's voice rose over another moan. "There's no need—" Jordan took a step forward, one hand raised, the other reaching for his gun.

"Don't!" Bowden fired his pistol. Jordan fell back, hit the wall and slid to the ground, leaving a stark trail of blood on the concrete behind.

"Damn it!" The Brit hissed with pain as his hand stifled the flow of blood at his shoulder. "What the hell happened to that ninety percent effective rate of this bloody material?"

"Don't worry," Bowden pointed his gun toward the nitroglycerin. "We're all going to die anyway—"

"No!" Cain barked, trying to draw Bowden's fire. He dove for Jordan's weapon, rolled and came to his knees, his finger compressing the trigger.

But he was too late.

The shot seemed to come from nowhere, but it caught Bowden right in the heart. He jerked once, dropping his gun, the dark eyes no longer glazed with insanity, only murky with confusion. Slowly, he crumpled onto the granite. Dead.

"No," Celeste whispered, Cain's pistol slipping from her fingers. "Not us, just you." Then her eyelids fluttered shut.

"THEY'RE going to be fine."

By the time the paramedics arrived, the firefighters had contained the nitro and Cain had gotten Celeste and Jordan out safely.

Celeste's wrists were bloody, the skin that wasn't torn already bruising. She'd fought hard to break free, fought hard to save Cain.

The handcuffs dangled from Cain's hand, while he watched the paramedics strap her to the stretcher. They'd made one attempt to treat Cain's injury, but the steel in his eyes drove them away.

Ian stood next to his brother, studying the play of emotion on Cain's features. "I like the change." He slapped Cain on the shoulder, but the tone of his voice softened. "It's nice to see you've got your soul back, big brother."

Celeste lay still, pale as death. Cain brushed her cheek, the only skin exposed. It had been so close. Too close.

Outside, while they waited for the helicopter to arrive, the paramedic had commented on the two things that had saved her life—the thick rope Gabriel had used and her petite frame. If not for those, she'd have broken her neck. As it was, she'd been only moments from unconsciousness and then strangulation.

It was too soon to tell if there'd be permanent damage to her vocal chords or scarring to her neck.

Yep, the paramedic had said, Miss Pavenic sure was lucky.

Cain disagreed. It was Celeste's strength that had saved her, not luck.

"Jordan?" Celeste rasped the question.

Cain pointed to the other stretcher where Jordan lay. "The bullet glanced off the collar bone. The hospital's going to keep him a few days, I'm sure, but it looks like he'll make it."

Celeste's eyes flickered. With relief, Cain eased over, placing his ear next to her lips. Her breath brushed against his cheek, tightening his gut, reminding him how close she'd come to dying.

"Cain."

He tucked a stray end of the blanket around her shoulder. "Don't talk, Gypsy, you could be damaging your voice."

She ignored the order. "Lighthouse…how?"

"Gabriel had the last set of quarters in his pocket. Maine. Once the president was dead, he would've left them for me, I'm sure."

Celeste's eyes fluttered closed on the tears starting to gather. "Why didn't you…tell me…about Mercer?"

"At the time, I wasn't sure he'd survive. It wasn't important to the mission."

"Like…Quamar…at warehouse?" Her voice, now grits of sandpaper, bit into him. "Like…Lassiter's…interrogation?"

Her tone was filled with more than pain from the injury, more than fatigue or sorrow. Underlying both, Cain heard accusation, defeat.

"I had my reasons, Celeste. Good reasons."

"No."

He should've welcomed the finality in her answer. He'd gotten his answers, his pound of flesh. That's what he'd wanted only the day before. Instead, bitterness rose up in him, savage and mean. In spite of it, he kept his voice gentle. "I did it to protect you, Gypsy. The more you became involved, the more chance—"

"I…protect…me," Celeste protested weakly. "You… me…" she rasped. "Never…us." She turned her head away, tears flowing unchecked. "Never…trust."

Vulnerability welled in him, unexpected, riding shotgun to his anger. "Damn it, this isn't the place—"

"No…done," she argued. "You…agreed…stay… away."

The loud whop of the helicopter could be heard in the distance. "Sir," one of the paramedics, a gray-haired man, his face lined with experience, insisted. His eyes were sympathetic but determined. "We need to take her up to the road."

"All right," Cain agreed, knowing it wasn't the time to settle things between them.

"Sir, you really need to get yourself treated." The paramedic pointed to Cain's side where dried blood kept the shirt sealed to the wound. "I can have someone take you to the nearest hospital."

Cain nodded to the man, not recognizing him from the fire the night before.

God, had it been that recent? It seemed as though a lifetime had passed, but it had taken them a little less than twenty-four hours to stop Gabriel.

Still, he couldn't stop the whispers of his little voice.

They'd won against Gabriel, but what had he lost in the process?

Chapter Nineteen

Everything was white outside. Not a stark, hurt-your-eyes kind of white, Celeste mused absently, but the soft-focus white that soothed and tempted most to be lazy. Just the kind of weather that made kids wish for a day off from school.

For the hundredth time that week, she forced the heartache away. After all, she thought stubbornly, how many people get to spend an evening visiting—

"Miss Pavenic?"

Startled, Celeste swung around from the window overlooking the snowy White House lawn.

"Miss Pavenic?" A female voice questioned again.

"Yes." Celeste cleared her throat, embarrassed still over its unnatural huskiness. A permanent reminder of her heroism, the specialist had said. "I'm sorry, I'm a little jet-lagged."

"I understand." The woman appeared to be in her mid-forties, a short, stylish brunette in an efficient dark burgundy business suit. In one hand she carried a day planner, with the other she gestured toward a long hall.

"I'm Martha Fisher. President Cambridge's personal assistant. The president is ready to see you now."

Celeste followed the older woman through a door into a narrow hall.

"I apologize for the delay. Our schedule is a little bit off this evening."

"I understand." Celeste smoothed a hand over the V-neck of her simple navy-blue suit, trying not to let her fingers touch her bandaged neck self-consciously.

Turned out Gabriel had been nothing more than an ex-mercenary named André Bovic. A man who'd advanced his career by refining his talents and education.

It had been two weeks since he had died. Two weeks of interviews, flash bulbs, crowds and the paparazzi's attention that had turned her into an overnight celebrity—something she didn't want, but suspected Jon Mercer had triggered.

Once Mercer's resurrection became public, the frenzy was unimaginable. After all, it wasn't every day the vice president was involved in a scandal. The media sensed blood, and, like piranhas after prey, they demanded details.

And they'd gotten them. The vice president had left detailed notes of his plot, maybe hoping one day to publish it. Bowden had revealed his desire for an almost Hitleresque world. In order to have it, he needed to guarantee his place as president. He'd contracted the hits and planted Bremer's phone number on Celeste's cell.

Saddened, Celeste thought of all those people dead because of his madness. Bobby, Grams, Olivia Cambridge, the prostitute Joyce Raines. Bowden had manipulated the phone records, forged documents, provided

Gabriel with Cain's file and details of Mercer's injuries that the president had entrusted him with.

The felony counts were endless.

As was the media's interest.

Celeste's legs wobbled only a bit as she followed Ms. Fisher down the last of the wide halls.

Martha Fisher held open a door and Celeste stepped into the Oval Office.

Robert Cambridge turned from the large windows overlooking the famous Rose Garden and crossed the deep, navy-blue rug emblazoned with the Presidential Seal. A flutter swept through Celeste's stomach. She couldn't believe she was actually standing here, alone, with the President of the United States.

And he wasn't having her arrested.

"Miss Pavenic." He grasped her hand, his smile warm and reassuring. She noticed he'd taken off his suit jacket, loosened his tastefully patriotic red-and-blue pinstriped tie and rolled up the cuffs of his white Armani shirt. The casualness could've come from a long presidential day, but she figured that more than likely he'd dressed down to put her at ease.

"I want to thank you for coming today." His eyes, a soft leather-brown, shadowed with remorse when they touched first on her neck then on the bandages around her wrists. "Frankly, I wasn't sure if you would."

"I have to admit, I was surprised." Celeste smiled and discreetly—because of a sharp twinge of pain—tugged her hand free. The lacerations, although deep, were healing quickly, along with her neck bruises, which had faded to a dull yellow.

"Please, so we can talk." He indicated a plush cream couch to her right. Instead of taking the opposite couch though, he sat next to her, surprising her. "First of all, I want to apologize for my actions and conduct after Bobby's death. You did your best, just as I did, in trying to protect him. But I couldn't see that at the time."

"Understandably. You were set up just as much as I was." Slowly, Celeste sorted through her words. "More so because of your emotional state at the time. I believe the worst thing that can happen to parents is the loss of a child." It emptied the soul of the family, leaving their spirits whisper-thin. Bobby's murder would be an experience that would haunt her for the rest of her life. "And to be honest, Mr. President, you couldn't have blamed me any more than I blamed myself."

"I'm sorry for that, too," he said gently and cleared his throat. Instantly changing the mood, he smiled. Not the politician's smile she'd seen plastered across the papers but a genuinely kind smile. "I haven't thanked you properly for saving my life."

"It really isn't necessary—"

"But it is. If I had my way, you'd receive a medal. And you still may." He patted her shoulder. "But for now, I want to thank you personally." He leaned over until his lips lightly brushed her cheek. "Thank you."

Startled, Celeste stared at him until he winked. A smile tugged at her lips. "You're welcome."

"Now…" He settled back into the cushion and studied her for a moment, his solemn expression reminding her more of a father's than of a world leader's. "…I have an official favor to ask."

Celeste waited, felt the hum of nervousness between her shoulder blades.

"I want you to work for us again. Work for Labyrinth."

A month ago, Celeste would never have considered it. But a month ago, she'd believed herself a failure.

"You are under no obligation, of course." The president cleared his throat. "But I'd like to point out that with no store and a only a hotel for your current home, your future—"

"I accept."

It was President Cambridge's turn to be startled. "You do?"

"Oh, yes." She laughed slightly, understanding his surprise. It was no greater than her own. "But I do have one concern." All humor disappeared. "I've achieved some notoriety because of the events in Shadow Point."

"Your notoriety, in this case, will help us. For now, your speaking schedule can be adapted to wherever we need you. You've proven quite effective in the field. Later, we're hoping to utilize your talents in our recruiting process." He patted her hand. "Hold on one moment." In two quick strides, he reached his desk and hit the intercom. "Ms. Fisher?"

"Yes, Mr. President."

"Could you please catch my prior appointment? I need him to join Ms. Pavenic and myself for a moment."

"Yes, Mr. President. He's still here."

Celeste quirked a brow in question just as the door opened behind her. Apprehension skittered up her spine. She twisted around.

Cain.

He crossed the room with his usual predatory grace, dressed in his customary black snug-fitting slacks, tie and shirt. Leaner, with sharper edges, Cain studied her. His jaw, she noted, was shadowed with dark whiskers. If she'd thought he looked lethal before, it didn't compare to now.

"Mr. President." He shook hands with Cambridge. The greeting was casual, almost too casual, Celeste realized and squared her shoulders.

"Cain." The president nodded toward Celeste. "Miss Pavenic has agreed to rejoin Labyrinth."

"Good." Cain replied evenly, his features impassive.

Celeste's mouth tightened, understanding. "You've taken over as director."

"Jon decided to retire earlier than expected." Cambridge's answer did nothing to disperse the growing tension in the air. "And although it hasn't been made public yet, he has graciously accepted my appointment as vice president. Of course, both Houses need to agree. But considering his record, there shouldn't be any problem."

"You'll be working for me, Celeste," Cain emphasized.

Under duress, she was sure.

"Your field duties will be limited, of course."

"Is that right?" Irritated that Cain was still protecting her, Celeste turned to Cambridge. "I've reconsidered, Mr. President. And although I'm flattered, I'm declining your offer."

"Why?" Cain's question was bland, almost bored. She understood the thinly veiled warning for what it was. He wasn't going to back down.

"Because I have that right." She scowled, her fist

tightening on the strap of her leather purse. She tried to calm herself with a deep breath.

"Of course you do." The president hesitated, obviously puzzled. "But I was hoping—"

Cain grasped her arm and started toward the door. "I know you're a busy man, Mr. President. So we'll take our…negotiations…elsewhere."

"No, we won't." Her mouth firmed, her heels dug in. "Since the president offered me the job, I expect to deal with him and only him."

"Yes, well…" Robert Cambridge moved to the door, his brows furrowed with curiosity. "Actually, Cain requested your reinstatement. I merely lent my support. So you do need to discuss your concerns with him, Miss Pavenic." His gaze moved warmly over Celeste. "Thank you again for all you've done for my family."

"Thank you, sir." Realizing she'd lost her only ally, Celeste turned on Cain. "Unfortunately, I'm running late for another meeting. I'll contact your office so we can set up an appointment."

"No," Cain drawled.

Before Celeste could react, he picked her up and swung her over his shoulder like a sack of potatoes. Careful to avoid her injuries, he walked through the door.

Cambridge's stifled laughter followed them.

Chapter Twenty

Celeste arched her back, hoping to elicit some help, but no one from the offices along the corridor moved, although several men and women stared. Her cheeks flushed with embarrassment, feeding her fury. Apparently, not even the Secret Service challenged Cain MacAlister. "Are you crazy? What are you doing?" she hissed.

"If I've learned nothing else in the past few weeks, I've learned you don't understand the word *stay*." He readjusted his arm, pinning her skirt to the back of her knees. "And frankly, you could drive any man insane."

Cain reached the elevator and jabbed the button. "I'm taking you somewhere private, so we can talk about the future."

"Put me down!" Longing pulled at her, hard and deep, igniting a flare of irritation. She punched his backside, almost hurting her knuckles on the tight, firm muscles.

"No." The elevator doors slid closed, and Celeste buried her face against his back. He smelled of leather and soap. Her fists curled against the temptation to inhale more deeply.

"Why, Cain?" She gritted her teeth in frustration. Frustration not from being carried through the White House in such a humiliating manner, but from fear of letting her feelings for him show. "Why did you come here? Ms. Fisher didn't just *catch* you. You were waiting." They hadn't fooled her, and she wanted him to know it.

"The pretense was the president's idea." His voice, husky with patience, vibrated across her thighs. Desire shot through her, causing a sharp intake of air.

Outside, a limo was waiting. Celeste only caught a glimpse of it before he slid her down the front of him, causing a jolt when thigh touched hip. "He wanted the chance to thank you personally for what you did," Cain continued casually, as if his carrying a woman through the White House was an everyday occurrence. "And to find out if you'd forgiven him."

Before she could reply, the limousine driver swung open the door, and caught Celeste's eye. "Jordan!"

"At your service, Poppet." Relieved to find another ally, Celeste couldn't help but smile over the nickname he'd given her. For the last two weeks, Jordan Beck had made it his business to become her friend. He'd confessed to being the reason Cain hadn't been with her during Bobby's kidnapping and the aftermath. When Celeste admitted that she'd already come to terms with Cain's decision, knowing it couldn't have happened any other way, Jordan seemed relieved.

"I'm so glad to see you," she told Jordan, returning his quick hug, careful not to jar the sling that held his arm.

Dressed in a leather jacket and jeans, Jordan Beck looked nothing like a chauffeur. "Actually, I insisted on driving. I thought you needed someone to cover that lovely tush for a bit, and I wanted to make sure this bloke here didn't intimidate you."

For the sake of time, Cain let the comment pass. "All right, Beck. You've said your hellos." Capturing Celeste's elbow, Cain urged her inside the car, not surprised when she refused to move.

He sighed, letting his impatience show. He wanted her in the car and in his arms. So much so, he didn't care if Jordan heard. "I've waited long enough to talk to you, Celeste. You wouldn't see me at the hospital, wouldn't return my calls at the hotel. If I have to pick you up and toss you in, I will."

Uncertainty had her biting her lip, and Cain pushed his advantage. When she slid a glance at Jordan, Cain's glare followed.

Jordan shrugged, but a grin tugged at his mouth. "It's the least you could do, Poppet. The man has been chomping at the bit all week."

"Jordan—" Cain warned, biting off the rest of his remark and instead turned back to Celeste. "Get in."

Lifting her chin, she stepped into the limo. "Raise the privacy window, Beck. You know where we're headed." Cain eased onto the leather upholstery after a quick salute from his friend. Celeste sat as far away from him as possible. Which, considering it was a stretch limo, was quite a few feet. His mouth twisted wryly over the distance. "Just in case we decide to neck."

The slight widening of Celeste's eyes, and the subtle flush to her cheeks pleased him and he poured himself two fingers of whiskey. MacAlister whiskey. A present from his father. Cain lifted the glass, asking, and she shook her head.

"Just where are we headed?"

Deliberately misunderstanding, Cain said. "That's what I want to find out." He drank the whiskey, then set the glass aside.

"You never used to play games, Cain," she whispered.

Wanting to skip the words, but knowing the explanations needed to come first, he leaned forward and placed his forearms on his knees. "Remember when you said we all have our pasts to deal with? Well, you were right, we all do. Mercer, Quamar. You. Myself."

Her jaw flexed but she didn't look Cain's way. Instead she continued to gaze through the window as Washington, D.C., passed by. "How is Quamar?"

"He came out of the coma a few days ago." Cain's hesitation brought her around.

"But," she prompted.

"He's blind, Celeste." Cain had visited Quamar the day before. The giant seemed in good spirits, but Cain had recognized his friend's underlying fear. "He's undergoing a battery of tests and his doctors are considering surgery. The prognosis is good."

"Is he allowed visitors?"

"Yes." He reached over to touch her arm, but she shifted away. "Damn it." He yanked a hand through his hair. It was either that or yank her into his lap.

"Remember when you accused me of being the self-appointed protector of mankind? You were right." He braced his elbows on his knees, and locked his hands together. "Prometheus was the god who provided man with fire against Zeus's wishes. So, in retaliation, Zeus had him chained to a rock where a giant eagle tore at his liver all day, only to have it grow back every night for the eagle to devour again."

"I know the story."

"Part of me *is* Prometheus. And I wouldn't change that. Because that's what kept me alive."

"If we agree—"

Cain wasn't finished. "But you're Lachesis, too, Celeste. And Diana. No matter how much you run away, they remain a part of you. That's why the Labyrinth job is yours. Not to prove anything to you, but because I know you'll do a damned good job."

"It's mine with restrictions," she corrected, not bothering to hide her bitterness.

"That's right. Not to protect you, but to train you. I wouldn't send any operative out in the field without proper training. Especially not one I'm in love with."

A small flame of hope flared, but she brushed it away. "Loving me is not enough. Not anymore. I'm not sure it ever was." Celeste swung away, unable to deal with the hurt that squeezed her chest. "I thought that the more I cared for you, the more I'd understand you. But the reality is that the more you care for me, the more barriers you put up preventing me from seeing into you. Even when we're…" She stopped unable to continue.

"Making love?" he murmured rhetorically. "Not any more. No more secrets—unless I'm held to the restrictions by my job."

"Why should I believe you?"

"You think I'm lying? This thing between us—you

think that's a lie, too?" Through his fury, he recognized the truth. Why should she believe him? Up to this moment, the only time he'd shared any part of himself with her was when he'd whispered it as she lay half-unconscious in the lighthouse.

Celeste stared at him, confusion rimming the deep blue of her eyes, furrowing her brow. A strange tenderness swept through Cain, dissipating the anger, the frustration.

He almost gave in to the urge to touch her, the ache to hold her. But unless she came willingly, the gesture was hollow. "Fate bonded us. Maybe I'd been so lost in a dark, emotionless hole that I needed someone like you, something like this to bring me out of it."

He joined her on her seat, craving her nearness, wanting to comfort her. "Gabriel's dead. He wouldn't be if you hadn't done your job. I…" He gave in then and tipped her chin up. "…would be dead, if you hadn't."

He brought his face close, until they were nose to nose. "You made the call, Celeste." Anger flashed across his feature, startling her.

For the first time she noticed. All his emotions—love, hurt, rage—were there on his face, something the old Cain would never have allowed, would never have shared.

Anger, frustration, desperation gushed through her. She fought them off. And the tears. The tears were the hardest. "I don't know what you want from me, but whatever it is, I can't give it to you."

"I just want your love. And your trust—when I've earned it again. Nothing else. I had to fight through hell and back to get to the feelings I have. And like Prometheus, I've had my insides eaten out again and again."

His forehead tipped against hers. His breath came in shaky heaves. He was frightened. Just as she was. Through her mind flashed an image of a two-story house, kids running through a sprinkler screaming, a puppy nipping at their ankles.

"You once told me you loved me, Celeste. I won't let you take it back, because only you can save me."

"No," she whispered, but she felt the wall around her heart splinter, each shard driving deep. Her jaw trembled, and she clenched it. "It's not that easy. Finally, in the past few weeks, I'm beginning to realize who I am. What I am. I'm strong. Not invincible, but strong. All my life I leaned on Grams, Jon, even you— using what others thought of me to fill the empty void inside me. I don't need that anymore. I don't need you or anyone anymore, for that matter. I can rely on myself, take care of myself, Cain. I might love you, but I don't need your love back. I'll survive better without it."

"Do you hear yourself?" he growled, his gaze pinning her to her seat. "You can survive by yourself and take care of yourself. You don't need love or emotion or anyone in order to live the life you've chosen?" Desperation laced each syllable he uttered. He shifted away, almost as if he couldn't bear the closeness any longer.

The car slowed to a stop and the privacy window lowered, the hum of it doing nothing to dissipate the tension. "Cain."

Cain scowled, the bite in his words showing his displeasure over the interruption. "What is it, Jordan?"

"Our guest is getting restless up here. He's starting

to take his irritation out on the passenger seat. I thought I might toss him back with you for a while."

A sharp yowl hit the walls of the limo. Celeste glanced over as Jordan, one-handed, dropped Pan through the window onto the bench seat below. An emerald-green bow puffed up behind the back of his head, but it wasn't until Pan sauntered forward that she saw the sapphire ring hanging from his collar. Her eyes widened, but she didn't acknowledge it, didn't want to think about its meaning. "Where did you come from?"

"Your hotel." Cain uncoiled from beside Celeste, then leaned over and picked Pan up. "I snagged him from your room along with your luggage."

"Why?"

"Because I thought you and your family would like to spend some time with my family before you started work." Cain's scowl darkened; his response was surly and impatient.

"I think I'll pass, Cain. There's no need to prolong—"

"What about Pan?" He handed the cat to Celeste. "Do you still need him?"

"Of course." She stroked the minklike coat, hearing the purr of pleasure, ignoring the ring clinking against his collar. "He's my responsibility." Her hand froze, realizing.

"Your responsibility?" Startled, she caught the stab of anger in his question, the accusation. "Only two weeks ago, you would have said he was your family."

"He is." She gathered Pan close to her chest, burying her trembling fingers in his fur. "I love Pan. You know that."

Cain wouldn't let her off that easily. Couldn't. There was too much at stake for both of them. He rubbed his eyes. "Don't become what you hated, Celeste. Don't become me—or at least what I used to be."

"You did what you had to do. Duty means you make sacrifices." Celeste put Pan onto the floor.

"That's the excuse I used." He took her hand, humbled when she unconsciously gripped it back. "Three years ago, I deliberately seduced you. I didn't care about you or what you wanted. I'd wanted the serenity you brought to my life and made sure I left you with no other choice."

"I wanted to be seduced," she admitted quietly, but it was the underlying shame that caught like a hook in his heart. "You didn't do anything I hadn't wished for."

"But you also wanted more. At the time, I knew I couldn't give it to you. But I can now," Cain rasped, his voice raw with what he'd lost. He brushed away a tendril of hair from her cheek. "I've never begged anyone. But I'm begging you now."

His words pierced Celeste like tiny, sharp arrows, bringing down the last of the barriers that constricted her heart. She searched deep into the pewter of Cain's eyes, now tinted with regret.

"I'm sorry, Celeste. Forgive me." His hand slipped over her heart, his forehead tipped against hers. "I love you. I loved you the first moment we met, I've loved you with every breath I've taken since."

He used his thumb to brush away a tear on her cheek. "I can't promise a life of bliss," he whispered. His hand curved around the back of her neck, tilting her head back. "But I do know that without you, I'm only half alive."

Her hand caressed his jaw, her fingers traced the hard lines of his features—knowing that the power that lay just beneath the surface would not make their life easy.

Celeste realized that she wanted the flesh-and-blood man before her—and the exciting roller coaster of emotions that came with him. A small smile tilted her lips. "Partners?"

He groaned, trembling as his hand gripped hers. "Partners." He lifted her onto his lap. Automatically, her legs locked around him as his mouth found hers, this time with a need she felt confident she could fill. And she gave herself freely. Because Cain had saved her too.

"I'm going to work for Labyrinth," she said against his lips, and happiness flowed through her, sweet and warm.

"I'm going to be your boss," he reminded her, determined.

"That's okay." She nipped his jaw, finally feeling complete, whole. "Because someday I plan to be *your* boss."

"What makes you think so?" he teased, while his hands danced up her spine, making her squirm, making the heat between them flare.

"If I'm tough enough to love you…" She tugged his hair to make him stop, but instead her fingers caressed its silky texture. "…then I certainly have the guts to boss you around."

He nuzzled her neck, laughing, and the rumbling sent shivers quaking through her limbs. She'd done that, she thought. She'd made him happy.

"I do love you, Cain."

With a groan, his hand caught hers, warm and welcoming. Slowly, he slid her body back onto the seat then

knelt before her. Ignoring a high-pitched yowl from
Pan, he tugged the green ribbon and the solitaire ring
free from the cat's neck.

"Cain?"

"Celeste?" Cain mimicked her softly, then held out
the ring. Blue fire flashed beneath the limo's interior
lights. "I know this might be too soon, but I can't wait."
Cain's mouth tilted, sexy, teasing—taking her breath
away. "I guess impatience has become one of my newly
discovered traits."

"Could work for me." Her lips curved in a secret
feminine smile as he slipped the sapphire band on her
finger.

"I didn't think I had anything—not even you," she
said, not bothering to hide the tears that welled in her
eyes. "Now I don't want anything but you." Cain gathered her close, and she felt the tension drain from his
body. She shivered as his breath fanned her skin. Tipping
her head to one side, she allowed him more access.

Cain leaned back, taking her with him until she
sprawled over him, limbs entwined. His hand slid up her
thigh, groaning when he touched a spot of bare skin
above the silken hose. "White cotton?" he asked rhetorically, passion turning his eyes sleek silver.

"Always."

Gently, almost reverently, he kissed the side of her
mouth. "I love you," he murmured, linking her hands
behind her back, drawing her tight. Desire tripped
through her and she melted into him.

"You pick the damnedest times to go soft on me,
Gypsy."

"And no bed in sight." She laughed wickedly, letting her love filter through.

His fist hit a button on the nearby bar. Suddenly the lounging seat on the other side of the limo flipped, and the backrest slid down, revealing a full-size bed.

He caught her earlobe tenderly between his teeth. Goose bumps chased down her neck. "You were saying?"

Pan jumped onto the bed and looked at Celeste, his eyes hooded and lazy. With a languid yawn, he circled twice and settled down with a flick of his tail. Celeste glanced from the cat to the bed to her man. With tender fingers, she cupped his cheek and lowered her lips to his.

"Stay."

The Private Bodyguard

DEBRA
COWAN

Many thanks to John Hager, for answering my questions about the courthouse. You were a tremendous help!

And to Linda Goodnight, nurse, writer and friend, for all things medical.

Chapter 1

At two o'clock on a cold February morning, Dr. Meredith Boren came face-to-face with a dead man.

Asleep in her family's Oklahoma lake house, she'd been awakened by a noise in the kitchen and gotten out of bed to investigate. She'd crept down the long hallway that led from the master bedroom, edged around the foot of the stairs and frozen between the living room and kitchen.

In the melding shadows of night, a man stood over the sink. Meredith's breath lodged sharply in her throat. Moonlight glanced off lean muscle, flashing a series of impressions. His right shirtsleeve was ripped and hanging down his arm. His left hand pressed against his bare shoulder. Something dark stained his flesh and the edge of the sink. The first aid kit lay open on the counter beside him.

Hazy moonlight filtered through the window, mixed with too many shadows to discern the color of his hair. She had a gun in her bedside table. She couldn't see if he had one or not.

He didn't appear interested in anything except patching himself up. Still, Meredith was calling the police.

She retreated a step, intent on slipping back to her room and dialing 9-1-1. At that moment, the man sagged against the counter as if it was the only thing holding him up. The movement brought his face into profile. Pale silver light skimmed his temple, the long planed line of his jaw, part of a strong neck.

Meredith's heart stopped. He looked like…

No, it couldn't be. This had to be a dream, which made sense considering the reason she'd come to the summerhouse at Broken Bow Lake. The cool tile beneath her feet, the whiff of cinnamon from the living area, the underlying metallic scent of blood drifting from the kitchen all felt real, *smelled* real, but they couldn't be.

Gage Parrish was dead, had been dead for a year. It was a dream. Yes, it had to be. If this was real, the man would've seen her from the corner of his eye and reacted.

Operating on less than four hours' sleep out of the last forty-eight, Meredith rubbed her forehead. "No," she murmured.

In the deep stillness, the quiet word shattered the silence.

The man jerked toward her, his hard gaze zeroing in like a laser. Before she could blink, he roared, "What the hell are you doing here?"

She snapped to full attention just as she did when

jarred out of sleep at the hospital to tend a new arrival in the emergency room. This was real. *He* was real. How?

Something fell from his shoulder to the floor—a stained cloth. He didn't grab for it. "You're not supposed to be here."

"Neither are you!" Numb, she stared at the filmy silhouette of her ex-fiancé. She could barely think. Was she breathing?

With his left hand, the man—Gage—gripped the counter's edge. Even in the dim light, Meredith could see his unsteadiness, the waxy sheen of his face.

It was the blood tracking down his shoulder and arm that got her moving. "You're hurt."

She reached him about the time he crumpled into the cabinet, banging it hard. She grabbed his left arm to steady him.

This wasn't possible. He was dead. Dead!

Her mind was unable to process anything except that he was wounded, bleeding. She draped his uninjured arm around her shoulder and started slowly toward the nearest bed. Her bed.

"Are you hurt anywhere else?"

"No," he said hoarsely. "Gunshot."

Surprise jolted her. He'd been shot. Why? How far from here? And completely apart from the gunshot wound, how was it even possible that he was alive? Meredith's head began to pound. Sweat broke out over her body. What was happening was too unreal, too much. Too raw. She couldn't function if she dealt with that right now. Judging from how heavily Gage leaned on her for support, he wasn't up to it, either.

He faltered, his weight pulling her into the wall with him as he propped himself up there.

His warm breath feathered against her face and an unexpected knot of longing shoved painfully under her ribs. She dismissed the emotion.

He struggled away from the wall. "Okay."

She wondered if he'd be able to make it the rest of the way. They reached her room, painstakingly crossed the silver carpet to her queen-size bed and she eased him down on the edge of the mattress. Reaching over, she flipped on the bedside lamp and stood, paralyzed.

Her mind fought to sort this out, to make sense of it. *Believe it.*

Blood smeared his shoulder, her sheet. He groaned, jerking her out of her stupor. He was hurt. She knew how to deal with that. Unbuttoning his black button-down shirt, she eased it away from his injured shoulder, then stripped it off.

"Meredith."

The deep, grainy voice had her looking straight into his pure blue eyes. Eyes she'd thought to never see again. Meredith started at the realization that there was more than pain there. He looked exhausted and… haunted. Tenderness tugged at her. She tore her gaze from his.

Putting herself on autopilot, she palmed off his shoes then eased his legs onto the mattress and laid him back on the pillow. Leaving his jeans on, she knelt beside the bed and got her first good look at the wound. The bullet had gone through his shoulder, entering close to his clavicle. Where the subclavian vein and artery ran. Concern streaked through her.

"You're...not s'pposed to be here."

His words were slurred. Depending on how much blood he'd lost, he'd be getting dizzy. And thirsty.

"It's winter."

She understood his surprise. The lake house was used only in the spring and summer, for fishing, boating and water-skiing. And with her Thunderbird in the garage, it looked as though no one was here.

"Never would've come." He reached up, his fingers brushing her mouth.

Hit with panic and a sudden streak of fear, she jerked away.

"Baby, I'm sorry."

"Be quiet!" She didn't know if he was aware of what he said. She didn't want to hear the endearment he'd always called her. All she cared about was stopping the bleeding.

"Don't move," she ordered. Pushing to her feet, she hurried to the kitchen and grabbed the first aid kit, snatched some hand towels from the nearest drawer then returned to him.

He was still, unnaturally so, and dread stabbed at her. She felt for his carotid pulse. Weak, but there.

"Thirsty," he croaked, his eyes slitted against the pain.

She hurried into the adjoining bath and filled a small glass with water, then returned to hold up his head and help him drink.

After placing the glass on the bedside table, she examined his wound. He was bleeding out externally, not into the chest. Of the two, that was preferable. No broken collarbone, no collapsed lung. The man was beyond lucky. "How long ago did this happen?"

"An hour." He struggled to get out the words. "Or two."

Using one of the towels, she pressed firmly on the wound, noting the deep penetration, the torn flesh, his shallow breathing. "You need to go to a hospital. McCurtain County's hospital is about thirty or forty minutes away."

"No. No hospitals."

"Gage."

"They'll report it." His raspy voice was firm. "No cops."

"But—"

"A cop shot me." His agitation started his blood flowing heavily again. "No hospital."

"You need to calm down." A *cop* had shot him? What was going on? Blood seeped out from under the towel and Meredith pressed harder against the wound.

"Promise me." His face was colorless, and desperate. He groped for her right forearm with his left hand and squeezed hard. "Promise," he rasped, struggling to sit up.

"Be still." Her voice was sharper than she'd intended. She pushed against his opposite shoulder until he eased back into the mattress. "I promise. Now be quiet and let me do what needs to be done."

He must've been using every bit of his strength because when she finally agreed not to contact anyone, he passed out.

Questions hammered at her. Emotions, too. Anger,

confusion, pain. But there was no time to deal with that right now. She could only deal with Gage and his GSW.

Working quickly, she slowed the bleeding, cleaned the wound with alcohol as best she could then stitched the ragged hole near his collarbone. There was no anesthetic. She prayed he'd be out for a long time.

She was cool, precise, steady. She trimmed the stitches. Applied a pressure bandage. Then sat back on her heels and stared at him, her heart thundering in her chest as if she'd run the two hundred and fifty miles from here to Presley.

She began to shake all over.

His dark blond hair reached the base of his neck, longer than she'd ever seen it. His skin was weathered by the sun, putting lines around his eyes that hadn't been there eighteen months ago when she'd broken things off between them. Six months after that, she'd gotten word he was dead. She'd believed it. They all had. So how could he really be here? Really be alive?

Swept up in a sudden swirl of anger and confusion, she wiped streaks of blood from his neck and lower jaw, the back of her hand lingering on the sandpapery roughness of his skin.

His familiar woodsy scent was faint beneath the antiseptic, but she could smell it. Smell him. The lanky, wounded man in her bed was really Gage and he was alive.

She thought she'd shed her last tear over him, but one fell anyway.

Gage opened his eyes, increasingly aware of the searing pain in his right shoulder and torso, a comfortable bed and a soft feminine fragrance. A familiar apricot scent on the sheets, his pillow. Then he remembered. "Meredith," he murmured.

The bathroom door across the room opened and there she was. She paused, soap-scented steam floating around her. Her hair was freshly dried, wild blond curls loose around her shoulders. Her cream-and-rose skin was free of makeup, her blue eyes crystal-bright and wary. She was so beautiful, it hurt to look at her. His memories didn't do her justice.

He'd missed the hell out of her, but despite the telltale spike in his pulse, seeing her was the worst thing for both of them.

Last night hadn't been a hallucination due to pain and blood loss. She was really here. And looking damn good.

"You're awake." She stepped into the bedroom. Her tall lithe figure gloved in a long-sleeved red T-shirt and faded jeans brought to aching life the memory of every bare inch of her.

A slight flush pinkened her skin from her bath. She preferred those to a shower, he knew. And bubbles to bath beads. Apricot or vanilla to any floral scent. Hell. Gage wished he'd forgotten things like that in the past eighteen months, but he hadn't.

Forcing his gaze away, he glanced at the bandage curving over his shoulder and clavicle. "You patched me up."

She nodded.

He made a lame attempt at humor. "Will I live?"

Her eyes went cool. She looked at him as if she

didn't know him. "Won't that interfere with your being dead?"

Ouch. There were a thousand things he should say, all starting with "I'm sorry." He soaked her in, storing away another image for when he had to leave. "You're really here."

"I think that's my line." Her words were as sharp as her laugh.

She was angry. What did he expect? "No one's ever at this house in the winter. I never would've come if I'd known you would be here."

Hurt flared in her eyes. "You're lucky I was or you would've bled out over my sink."

She thought he meant because he didn't want to see her. There wasn't anything he wanted more, but it was dangerous. He couldn't involve her any more than he already had.

Quietly, he said, "Thanks for saving my life."

She gave a curt nod, eyeing him warily. Gage hated it. And there was nothing he could do about trying to correct it before he left. "What time is it?"

"Almost noon. Are you hungry?"

"I could eat." Once he did, he would have to say goodbye. Again.

"All right, I'll get you something." She folded her arms under her breasts and nailed him with a look. "Then I want to know what's going on."

He could tell her some, not all. Nodding, he pushed himself up on his left elbow.

"You lost a lot of blood," she snapped. "You shouldn't try that yet."

"I'm almost there." It was an effort to rise into a half-sitting position against the headboard. He bit back a moan as agony ripped through his shoulder.

She stood close enough for him to see the light brush of freckles across her nose, but the distance between them yawned like a canyon. Her eyes were remote, blank. He wanted to see her smile, just once.

But the steady gaze she trained on him said that wasn't going to happen. He knew what she wanted. Letting out a shaky breath, he asked, "Where do you want me to start?"

"How about with when you died? I'll get your lunch. We can talk while you eat."

She left and he sagged into the headboard. He had no energy, felt as if he could barely lift his hand. Through a fog, he looked around the room where he and Meredith had stayed during their frequent visits.

His gaze moved left to the closet and the piles of clothes stacked neatly beside its open door. In the back of the closet, he could see what he knew was the tip of his slalom water ski. The pale gray walls were missing a couple of pictures, but he couldn't call them to mind at the moment. He felt outside of himself, as if he were barely holding on to consciousness.

Meredith returned with soup, a ham sandwich and a large glass of water on a tray that she set across his lap. "I imagine you're thirsty, but even if you aren't, you need to drink that."

He nodded. "You're not eating?"

"Not hungry."

She'd cut the sandwich in half and still the effort

required to pick it up surprised him. He hadn't realized how weak he was. It took him a while, but he was able to eat without help. By the time he finished the soup, he felt stronger and sleepy.

Meredith walked to the window beside the bed and glanced over. He thought he saw a glint of tears before she looked away and stared out at the gray day, the private dock and lake less than a hundred yards away.

"Your grandparents and I— We thought…"

"I know," he said softly.

She turned, anger crossing her face before she closed it against him. "Why did you let us think you were dead?"

He couldn't tell her everything. The less she knew, the safer she'd be. Breathing past the pain, he stared.

Despite the shadows in her eyes, she was gorgeous. He'd been a self-absorbed fool to let her go. Her creamy skin was velvet-soft. Her blond curls were pulled back in a neat ponytail that made him want to mess it up.

After what he'd done to her, he'd be lucky if she ever let him get close enough to touch her hair, let alone put his hands on her.

Whatever she saw on his face made her frown. "Gage."

"Sorry. I just can't believe I'm seeing you."

"Ditto," she said drily. "Now talk."

"Yeah." He drew in a deep breath, struggling to focus. "Okay, here it is. After you—after we—our—"

After she'd broken their engagement.

"I know what you're talking about," she said stiffly. "Go on."

She'd thought she hadn't regretted returning his ring.

Until six months later when she'd gotten word he was dead and she kept hearing her last words to him over and over. *You don't need to push me out of your life any longer. I want you out of mine.*

They'd been engaged for nearly two years and she'd never been able to get a wedding date out of him. That, along with being repeatedly put second to his job as a fire investigator, had made his obsession with Operation Smoke Screen the last straw. She understood priorities and no one knew better than a doctor that sometimes work must take precedence. But not every time.

So Meredith had finally called it quits. Her last words to him had filled her with guilt. She thought she had gotten past it and now he was here, stirring it up all over again.

His woodsy, body-warmed scent settled in her lungs and notched up a sense of dread. A steadily growing anger. She didn't see how anything he said could be good.

"There was a series of fires. None of us Oklahoma City fire investigators could get anywhere on the case and neither could an investigator hired by an insurance company." He paused, pulling in a shallow breath, looking pale and wasted.

"The residents of one burned-out section went to the State Attorney General with evidence against the torches. He ordered an investigation, asked me to be part of a task force. We discovered an arson ring, a conspiracy made up of gang leaders, city officials and city employees. It was the easiest money they'd ever made, and the more they got, the more they wanted.

"Our evidence was strong. They were all arrested for

murder, conspiracy to commit arson and fraud, and indicted. The trial is scheduled to start in ten days."

"Okay," she said slowly. After sitting with him through the night, never looking away in case he disappeared, some of the shock had worn off, but now it surged inside her again. She shook her head. "I can't believe this is happening."

"It's pretty wild," he admitted.

"Does the trial have anything to do with you being shot?"

He hesitated. "I was in the wrong place at the wrong time."

"That doesn't explain why you let us believe you were dead."

He wanted to touch her, pull her close, but he'd given up that right when he'd let her walk away. And again when he'd made the choice to let her believe a lie. A lie necessary to save his life, but still a lie. "There were two attempts on my life."

Her only sign of distress was the sudden way she paled. Her gaze skipped over him, thoroughly, dispassionately. Looking for proof of his claims. His wounds weren't visible and he wasn't talking about them.

"After those attempts, the Attorney General involved the marshals. They put all of us in WitSec."

She frowned at the term.

"Witness Security," he explained. "Their witness protection program."

"All the investigators?"

"Yes. We argued against it, but by then the decision was out of our hands." Gage had agreed to it in the end because it was his only option, which made him hate it even more. "The police and the AG's office announced that they believed the gang leaders had succeeded in the attempts on our lives. We were all 'pronounced dead,' different ways. One a hunting accident, one a car wreck, one simply disappeared."

"And you," she said hoarsely, "in a fire."

"Yeah." He hated seeing the ravage of grief in her eyes, the pain, the betrayal, but he'd had no choice then. Just as he had no choice now.

"So shouldn't you still be whoever you are now?" She frowned. "And back wherever it is you live now?"

"Getting shot changed my plans. I knew there were medical supplies here and I thought the house would be empty this time of year. It always has been before."

She studied him for a long moment. "There's more."

There was, but he didn't want to give her one iota of information more than necessary. He was determined to keep her safe.

Under the guise of making sure Gage was ready for trial, the marshal assigned to his case had arrived at the house where he'd been living for the past year. It was there that Gage had overheard the man being threatened into killing Gage. If he had to literally give up his life for Meredith, he would. He never should've pushed her out of it.

He'd been half-dead since leaving her, anyway. *Dumbass.* He clamped down on the thoughts. She was a regret he lived with every day and looking back on it didn't change one thing. He had to look forward, *move* forward.

He knew he'd lost a lot of blood. He knew how

crappy he felt, but he also knew the risk of staying. "I need to go."

She eyed him critically. "Think you can?"

"I have to."

"How'd you get here?"

"Drove an SUV I've been fixing up. It's at the side of the house."

"You should stay in bed for another twenty-four hours."

The longer he stayed, the higher the chances of Meredith getting involved and he *wasn't* involving her. "It's best."

"Suit yourself."

He wished he could. Tearing his gaze from hers, he asked, "Where's my shirt?"

"I threw it away. It was ruined."

"My leather jacket?"

"It's on a bar stool in the kitchen, along with your laptop. I'll find you something to wear."

She left and came back with a man's long-sleeved denim shirt. "This is Wyatt's. You can borrow it."

"Thanks." Gage was about the same size as Meredith's younger brother, which was good because the only clothes Gage had left here were shorts, T-shirts and underwear.

"Need help getting it on?"

Yes, he did, but if she touched him, Gage didn't think he would be able to make himself leave. "I can do it."

"All right. Let me know if you change your mind. I really don't think you're strong enough to go anywhere."

He sure as hell didn't want to. "I'll be okay."

After studying him for a moment, she shook her head. "I'll get your jacket and laptop."

Her tennis shoes scuffed softly on the hallway's wooden floor as she walked away. Regret welled up inside him. He wanted to stay here, look at her, *be* with her, but he knew he couldn't. He hated this. It was just as painful as it had been a year ago, letting her believe, along with his grandparents, that he was dead.

He sat up and eased his feet to the floor, gripping the edge of the mattress as the room spun. Long seconds later, the dizziness receded. Biting back a moan, he pulled the right sleeve up his arm.

The next thing he knew, he was on the carpet, his shoulders propped against the side of the bed and Meredith was kneeling in front of him.

"What happened?" he asked groggily.

"You passed out."

"Passed out?" Pain pounded through his shoulder, his skull. He felt himself fading. "You have to help me so I can leave."

"And then what? Drive you wherever you need to go? Babysit you? You can't even get dressed on your own." She leaned over, her sweet-smelling hair tickling his jaw as she fitted her shoulder under his, supporting him to his feet.

Light-headed and wobbly, Gage was aware of the blackness at the edge of his vision. He couldn't feel his legs, had no control over them.

Meredith got him prone on the mattress and pulled the blanket over his bare chest. "Don't try that again until I tell you it's all right."

He was fading, his vision blurring, but as she straightened, he said, "Are you okay with this?"

"Does it matter? You can't even walk the three feet to the bathroom let alone out of this house."

"I just...don't want you to get hurt, Meredith."

The look she turned on him was glacial. "It's a little late for that, don't you think?"

Yes, he did. As he watched her walk away, regret rolled over him. The hurt he'd caused her—*them*—was only one more reason he needed to leave ASAP. He'd avoided going to Presley and had come here solely for the purpose of keeping her out of this hell. Instead, he'd made her a target.

Chapter 2

Hours later, Gage jerked awake to the sound of harsh, labored breathing. The wind lashed brutally against the house, crackled in the trees. He thought he'd been done with the nightmare. Staring into the heavy morning shadows, he could still feel the pain and the flames as if they were real. Burning him, burning Meredith. A swirling fiery mix of present and past.

He scanned the room slowly as he tried to level out his pulse. The sheet and blanket were shoved to the foot of the bed. His jeans hung neatly over the back of a chair in the corner, socks tucked into his black running shoes. Meredith.

Gage had tried to call the state attorney general to update him but couldn't reach the man. Not trusting anyone else in Ken Ivory's office, Gage planned to call again later.

Agony bored deep into his injured shoulder and sweat slicked his face, his chest. Fine tremors worked through his body. As pale gray daylight seeped past the blue bedroom curtain, his pulse hammered sharply in his temple. He lay unmoving, trying to deal with the images the nightmare had driven into his fatigued brain. Regret pumped through him like adrenaline. Always the regret. Over his grandparents, over Meredith. Especially over her.

Exhaling a slow breath, he drew a shaking hand down his damp, whisker-stubbled face. He'd gone almost two months this time without having the dream, but sometime during the night, it had grabbed him by the throat. Had him reliving over and over what he couldn't control or change. The lie all his loved ones believed. That he was dead.

The task force Gage had been assigned to had arrested and indicted six coconspirators in an arson-for-hire ring. Those men had ties to a gang, so death for the investigators working Operation Smoke Screen was only a matter of time.

Months ago, Gage had been shot at and escaped unharmed, but he hadn't been so lucky with the second attempt. Yes, he'd survived a vicious pounding by a baseball bat and a lead pipe, but there were aftereffects. Parts of him still didn't operate fully and probably never would.

In addition to a broken nose, jawbone and two ribs, he'd lost his peripheral vision on the right side. A fracture to his orbital rim had damaged the optic nerve.

After two surgeries, he was amazed he didn't look like a completely different person.

Local law enforcement already had plans in the works to provide protection for all the investigators and witnesses, but after Gage had been beaten and left for dead, and a day later, the ATF agent assigned to the task force had also been attacked, the State Attorney General had requested assistance from the Marshals Service.

Gage's time had come a year ago. He'd been unable to tell the grandparents who'd raised him. And Meredith wouldn't welcome any contact, a fact she'd made emphatically clear six months before when she'd returned his ring. Per instruction from the marshals, he had ignored the phone calls from his best friend and firefighter, Aaron Chapman.

As clearly as if it were happening right then, the images scrawled across his brain in painful technicolor. The bitter February cold sliced at him like a knife, so sharp it stung his lungs. The tang of gasoline and winter-fallow earth mixed with the faint aroma coming from the coffee plant a mile away.

As his life had gone up in flames, Gage thought about his grandparents and how unfair this was to them. Thought about Meredith and wondered if she would even care when she heard the news.

He felt sick to his stomach and slowly became aware once again of where he was. In the present, with his ex. Frustration and helplessness over the situation still ate at him like acid.

He now lived as a mechanic in the northeastern Texas town of Texarkana. He was sick to death of reminding himself that this lying was necessary. That he was doing it for his job, doing it to protect those he loved, to protect future victims.

The past months had been spent with him alternating between self-loathing and flat-out ambivalence. He'd grown impatient and more uncertain that the deliberate erasure of his life made a damned bit of difference.

He had found himself sinking into an apathy he'd never experienced. His job had always motivated him, challenged him, but now it was a ball and chain. He wanted his life back and he was starting to wonder if it would ever happen.

Noises penetrated his thoughts. Down the hall, he heard a drawer opening, water running. He pinpointed the sound as coming from the kitchen. He hadn't had the nightmare in a while and he knew why he'd had it now. Meredith.

Seeing her had sprung the lock on Gage's tightly guarded memories. He'd thought there was no regret left in him, but the disbelief, the dazed shock and apprehension on her face last night had proved him wrong.

His chest still ached from the emotion that exploded inside him upon seeing her. He felt raw, exposed. Unprepared. Why was she at her family's summer lake house in the dead of winter?

A chill settled over him and he shifted uncomfortably against the burning pain in his shoulder. He'd spent the past year consoling himself with the thought that at least his grandparents and his ex-fiancé weren't involved in this mess, that he didn't have to worry about their safety. Finding Meredith here had shot that all to hell. She'd probably saved his life and the longer he stayed, the more he endangered hers.

She'd come here to bury the past; instead it had blown up in her face. Throughout yesterday and last night, Meredith made hourly visits to check Gage for fever, shock or signs of more bleeding. She made him drink plenty of water and gave him antibiotics as well as ibuprofen, which was all she had for pain. In between, she had cried, paced and fought the urge to yell at him.

Gage wasn't dead. He hadn't ever been dead. She'd taken his pulse, touched his flesh and yet she could barely absorb it.

At first, she was numb, then she felt...everything. By late last night, incredulity had given way to nerves. And fear for him. She didn't buy his explanation of being shot because he was in the wrong place at the wrong time, but she hesitated to press for an answer. She wanted to know and yet she didn't.

For the past year, he'd lied to her, to everyone. She understood why, but that didn't stop the feeling of betrayal or resentment. It wasn't surprising that he'd given up his whole life for his job. Everything came second to the fire department and always had. Including her.

After moving his silver SUV into the garage next to her car, she'd dozed off and on in the twin bed across the hall with the door open so she could hear and see him.

Except for her interruptions, he'd slept deeply the past

eighteen hours. He appeared to be still asleep when she rose at dawn and went to the kitchen to start coffee. On the way back to her room, she stopped to check him again.

There was enough watery light to make out his motionless, half-naked body. He'd kicked the quilt and sheet to the foot of the bed. Last night, she hadn't had the time or the presence of mind to notice any physical changes, but she did now. He'd always been rangy, and now he'd become sleeker, more defined. His arms and shoulders were solid slabs of muscle.

The dark lashes laying against his winter-reddened skin were the only soft thing on his sharply planed face. She'd removed his jeans, making him as comfortable as possible and now her gaze skimmed his hard chest, lingered on the lean hips in gray boxers. When she caught herself staring at his plank board–hard abdomen, she mentally shook herself.

Pressing the back of her hand against his cheek, she registered light perspiration, but no clamminess, no fever. She didn't realize she was caressing him until her gaze returned to his face. And found him watching her.

His blue eyes heated in the way that had always sent a shiver through her. And still did, she realized with a jolt as she withdrew her hand.

He gave her a weak grin. "Couldn't wait to get me out of my clothes, huh?"

"How can you joke about this?" she snapped.

He shrugged and she saw it then—the bleak shadow of pain in his eyes. He was only trying to cope with his injury, she chided herself. And maybe some of the same awkwardness she felt.

Off balance and unsure about exactly how to act with him, Meredith decided the best thing for her to do was deal with him as she would any other patient. Professional, efficient, distant enough to remain clinical about his injury.

She eyed his pressure bandage. Without access to a hospital or clinic, she couldn't be sure he *wasn't* bleeding inside so she had left on the thick ABD pad a little longer than twenty-four hours. There was nothing more she could do except keep a close eye on his pulse and blood pressure.

The supplies she'd had on hand were better than she would've gotten from a drugstore first aid kit. Since both she and her brother Wyatt were doctors, they kept the lake house stocked with bandages, sutures, antibiotics and syringes. Through the years, they'd needed those things plenty of times due to fishing or waterskiing accidents.

"What do you think?"

"You can wear a regular bandage now. What you need is food and lots of rest. And you can't exert yourself."

He levered himself up on his good hand.

Startled at his movement, Meredith reached for him. "What are you doing? Did you hear what I just said?"

"I'm sitting up." He winced. Though he didn't push her away, he didn't accept her support, either. He got his feet on the floor and remained on the edge of the bed.

She pressed two fingers to his carotid artery, feeling

for a rapid or thready pulse. It was fast, but not dangerously so. Not yet, anyway. "You used to be a paramedic. You should know better."

"I'm a little rusty," he said drily. "But I remember."

"So go easy, all right?"

He nodded.

"Are you dizzy at all?" she asked quietly.

"I'm fine."

She studied him. He was pale, but his eyes were lucid. "I'll change your dressing. Be right back."

A few moments later, she returned with fresh supplies. His head was bowed, but he straightened when she halted in front of him and placed the items on the nightstand.

"Doing okay?"

"Yeah," he rasped.

She carefully removed the ABD bandage then began to clean the sutured wound with antiseptic.

Hissing in a breath, his body went rigid. Meredith's attention locked on his broad chest, the hair there that grew a little darker than the sandy-blond on his head. As awareness tugged low in her belly, she forced her attention back to his shoulder.

He watched as she checked for inflammation, heat, additional swelling.

"Nice stitch job," he said in a slightly rough voice.

"Thanks."

"You still at Presley Medical Center?"

"Yes."

"And still working with the senior citizens program?"

Her gaze met his, seeing the same memory there that flashed in her own mind. It was how they'd met. His grandmother was part of the city's planning committee for seniors' activities and so were Meredith and her mother. Millie Parrish had known Meredith all of two weeks when she and Meredith's mother, Christine, set up Gage and Meredith on a date.

From their first meeting, there had been something special between them. They'd shaken hands and it was as if a current of energy traveled from her to him. Nothing like that had ever happened to her with any other man.

"Yes, still working with the older people." Shoving away the memory, she reached for a fresh gauze pad.

He grazed a hand against her thigh. "I want to clean up."

Aggravated at the way his touch burned through her jeans, she ignored the sensation and considered his freshly swabbed wound. "Your dressing can't get wet. I'll tape some plastic over it and you can take a bath."

"Great." He dragged a hand down his face.

As she took in the whisker stubble, the exhaustion on his face, she felt battered by the past and by the staggering reality of the present. "I'll see what there is to cover your bandage, then I'll run your water."

He nodded as she left the room. Under the kitchen sink, she found her mom's neat stash of plastic bags from a discount store. Meredith took one and retraced her steps to the bedroom, then walked past Gage into the restroom.

She turned on the tub's faucet and adjusted the water temperature. When she turned, she found him in the doorway. Features strained, he braced himself against the jamb. His boxers dipped low on his hips.

This awareness she had of him irritated her. "When I said don't exert yourself, I meant doing things like walking without support."

"I've got all the speed of a snail. I'm okay." He moved to her left, his good hand gripping the edge of the counter.

Meredith eased past him to get a clean towel, then hung it within easy reach of the tub. Turning back, she caught his dark woodsy scent and a faint hint of clean sweat. He smelled more than good. He smelled familiar, reassuring.

She wanted to bury her face in his neck and breathe him in, pretend the past eighteen months had never happened. But they had and both of them were changed because of it.

When the bath was more than half-full, she turned off the water and stepped aside. His good hand clamped on the edge of the counter and the flex of muscle up his forearm told her he was using a fair amount of strength to hold on.

Her gaze slid down his chest and to the waist of his boxers. Under her regard, the thin bands of muscle across his stomach clenched and his reaction had her looking away.

Okay. She was letting him affect her way too much. After a moment, her brain kicked in. Reaching around him, she scooped up the plastic bag. She double-folded it, then taped it snugly over the bandage so it was covered. "There you go."

She gently smoothed the edges, her hand moving over the hard curve of his shoulder.

Abruptly, he drew back. "I'm good. I'll yell if I need anything."

That heat flashed in his eyes again, making her aware that she'd been practically petting him. She needed to get out of here, although she wouldn't walk away from any other patient at this point. "You're probably going to need help getting in."

"I'll be fine, Meredith."

The steady, unreadable look on his face had her edging past him, careful not to touch as she stepped into the hall. "I won't close the door completely. I'll be right here. Call me if you need help getting in or out or…with anything else."

"Yeah."

She pulled the door toward her, leaving it ajar. "Toss out your underwear and I'll wash them."

"What am I supposed to wear?"

"There should be something around here that will fit." Either of his own or her brother's.

After a moment, he said, "Here."

Looking down, she saw his boxers in the V of the open doorway. Long seconds later, the slosh of water and a groan told her he'd settled into the tub. She picked up his underwear, examining the blood-stiffened waistband.

She leaned back against the wall, listening. Waiting. Reviewing her treatment of his injury. He'd be gone soon and she'd probably never see him again. The thought hurt her heart.

A splash sounded then a heavy thud against the tub.

Before she could ask, he offered, "Dropped the soap."

"Oh." Hit with a sudden image of the two of them in that tub, naked, she exhaled a shaky breath. The memories slipped in. The veins cording his neck, the tapering of his wide shoulders to lean hips, the way his hair clung to the wet sinew and muscle of his chest. She could almost feel his slick warm flesh beneath her hands.

She swallowed hard, grateful when he rasped, "What about Aaron?"

Glad to have her thoughts occupied by Gage's best friend rather than his naked body, Meredith turned her head toward the open doorway. "He's been working some of his off days with the Oklahoma City fire investigator's office. He wanted to work at Presley, but Terra and Collier can't hire anyone else so he decided to go to Oklahoma City."

Terra Spencer, one of Meredith's best friends, and Collier McClain were the two fire investigators allowed by Presley's budget.

"Aaron wants to be a fire cop? He never had any interest in that before."

"That was before you—what happened to you."

"What do you mean?"

She heard the frown in his voice. He and Aaron had grown up together, attended the fire academy and fought blazes in the same station house for years. "He's never quite believed the story we were told."

"Do you think he suspects?" he asked quietly.

"I don't see how." She eased back against the wall.

"Maybe I'm naive, but I sure never would have guessed the truth. In my job, when people die, they really die."

There was a long moment of silence. "Have you talked to my grandparents?"

"I saw them last week. At the cemetery."

He cursed. It was weak, but she heard it and she knew why. It had been the anniversary of his death.

"I helped your grandmother make the funeral arrangements." She paused, working to still the quiver in her voice. "Your grandfather and I scattered your ashes—well, *someone's* ashes—off the dock out back."

Talking about it brought back the heartbreaking pain on Owen's and Millie's faces, the devastation and denial Meredith had felt upon hearing the news of his death.

"Meredith, I had no choice. The situation was out of my control."

She believed him, but she couldn't keep the anger from her voice. "It's a little hard to take in, Gage."

"I know."

The ache beneath his words reminded her that things hadn't gone the way he wanted, either. "I don't want you passing out."

"I'm okay." He sounded drowsy.

She had to keep him talking. "So whose ashes were those?"

"The Marshals Service said it was a body donated to one of the state's medical schools. They had my DNA, dental records, everything they needed to make my death believable."

She was glad Gage was alive. Relieved and grateful, but she wanted to know if it had been as difficult for him to pretend to be dead as it had been for his grandparents to deal with the loss of their only grandchild. For Meredith to deal with the fact that the only man she'd ever loved was gone.

She tried to tamp down her resentment, thought about the man and woman who'd raised Gage after his teenage junkie mother died in a meth house. "Do you want me to tell Owen and Millie anything?"

"You can't," he said quickly. "I won't put them at risk. I never meant to put *you* at risk. Hell, you were the last thing I needed."

Which was why she'd finally walked away. The old wound cracked open and bitterness welled up. "That sounds familiar."

"No, Meredith. That isn't what I meant."

"It's okay." There was hurt on both sides. Hadn't she told him she wanted him out of her life? She'd gotten that, all right. Completely. "How're you doing?"

"Fine."

Was his voice uneven, his strength fading? "You should get out of the tub."

"Yeah."

"Do you need help?"

He gave a hoarse laugh. "That wouldn't be a good idea for either of us."

He was right. Even so, she stood poised to go in at the first hint he needed help. The slosh of water told her he'd managed to stand on his own. "Gage?"

"I'm all right."

He didn't sound all right, but Meredith stayed where she was.

On a groan, he asked, "That swing still on the back porch?"

Her gaze cut to the door. Making conversation was probably his way of dealing with the pain or struggling to stay alert, but why did he have to ask about the swing? They'd all but had sex in it. Talked, laughed. Gotten engaged. It was an effort to keep her voice steady. "Yes, it's still there."

No answer.

"Gage?"

"Just need…a sec." He sounded winded.

"Are you dizzy?"

No answer.

Meredith straightened, concerned. "Gage!"

"M'okay."

The slurred words had her dropping his boxers and pushing open the bathroom door. The toilet lid was closed and he sat there with his good shoulder braced against the wall to his left. His lower half was barely covered by the white towel she'd left.

He'd done too much, too soon. Glad to see the plastic had protected the bandage, she moved in front of him. "I let you stay in there too long."

"Just…wait."

His waxy skin had her pressing a hand to his forehead to find it slightly clammy. She checked his pulse and though rapid, it was strong. "Do you feel faint?"

"No, but not steady, either." He straightened and immediately clutched her hip with his good hand.

Meredith's heart skipped a beat.

"Sorry."

"No problem."

His hold gentled, but he didn't let go. It didn't matter that he touched her strictly for support or that he wasn't even looking at her. Despite her determination not to let him affect her, sensation shot straight to all her nerve endings.

She breathed in his fresh-soap scent, uneasily aware of the weight of his hand on her, the heat of his palm. An ache lodged in her throat and she couldn't stop her gaze from dragging over him. His stomach was taut with muscle and sinew. Powerful thighs, one almost completely exposed by the parted towel, were dusted with hair a shade lighter than his golden skin.

He wasn't pretty-boy handsome, but there was an unadorned maleness about him that drew the eye. The combination of his solid, planed features and his meltingly blue eyes, kind eyes, made for a compelling face. Before she even knew what she was doing, she grazed the tips of her fingers against his temple.

Gage's hand curled into Meredith's flesh. For a long moment, he sat there and let her warmth seep into him, her light apricot scent. He barely had the energy to stand, but he felt a stirring in his body. Pain throbbed in his shoulder and after a few seconds, he was able to focus his mind there, and only there.

"Gage?"

He stared up into her gorgeous blue eyes. "I'm ready."

She looked doubtful, but stepped back so he could stand. Flattening his palm on the wall, he levered himself up. Weakness washed through him and he stilled. He wanted to get back in bed and he wanted Meredith with him. He wanted to stay here with her, but he'd put her in enough danger.

Dipping her knees, she braced her shoulder under his good one and slid a slender arm around his waist.

He draped his arm around her and they started slowly toward the door. "Thanks," he said.

They had taken only two steps when the towel slipped. Despite making a grab for it with the hand on his injured side—which hurt like hell—Gage was too late. The towel fell.

"No way," he gritted out.

Meredith's breath left her in a rush. "Oh."

Damn. She'd seen him bare-assed naked plenty of times and she probably only had her eyes on him this time for less than a second, but Gage felt his body tighten.

Flushing a deep rose, she quickly scooped up the towel, then pulled it around his waist, holding the edges together.

Her reaction was calm, but the feel of her cool fingers against his flesh had Gage anything but. He went hot, muscles clenching. Hell!

She was acting as if nothing had happened and despite his body's reaction, he didn't have the energy to act any differently.

As they shuffled out of the restroom and back to his bed, her hand stayed at his hip, keeping the towel secure. She eased him down onto the edge of the mattress then straightened, still pink-cheeked.

Turning away, she went to the closet and knelt in

front of a neat mound of clothes on the floor then returned with a pair of blue-and-white-striped boxers and black sweats. *His* boxers and her brother's sweats.

Her gaze didn't quite meet his as she handed him the garments. "Do you need help with these?"

"No, I can do it." Maybe. Maybe not. But it was better for both of them if she didn't touch him.

Glancing again at the items in front of the closet, he realized with a sinking feeling what he was seeing. She was getting rid of his stuff. *This* was why Meredith had come to the lake house in the dead of winter.

She was putting him in the past, moving on. He told himself not to ask, but he did. "Are you seeing someone?"

Startled, her gaze swerved to his and for an instant, he saw loss and regret on her face. He thought she wouldn't answer. It was none of his business, but he had to know.

She glanced away. "Not exclusively."

The idea of some other man putting his hands on her had a red mist hazing Gage's vision.

He had no right to want anything from her, not after what he'd done. Over and over, he'd put his job ahead of her, of *them*. She'd tried talking to him about it, pleading with him to step back just a little from work, especially from Operation Smoke Screen, but he couldn't—*wouldn't*.

When she'd broken their engagement, she had said his job had taken over his life. Neither of them could have guessed that it literally would.

Now, he didn't even have the job he'd chosen over her. He had a life that wasn't his own, no family, no nothing.

The past year had brought home to him in brutal terms what a mistake he'd made with Meredith. For six months after she'd walked away, he'd let himself be swallowed up by this case, had refused to admit he was to blame for their split, but since then, he'd had plenty of time to think about it. To admit it.

Her gaze held his, her blue eyes now remote. He wanted to pull her into his lap and kiss her until she went soft for him, but she'd lay him out flat if he tried it.

He might never touch her again, see her again and the thought snarled in his gut like a hook. He couldn't change the hurt he'd caused, but he could do one thing.

She began to untape the plastic over his bandage. Half expecting her to pull away, he took her closest hand.

She stiffened as she stared down at him, but didn't move.

One of the hardest things he'd ever done was look straight at her. "I hate that I hurt you."

Her eyes widened, turned wary. "Gage—"

"Let me." He squeezed her hand. When she remained silent, he continued, "I know it's a cliché, but if I could go back, I'd do things differently. For the rest of my life, I will regret pushing you away."

Her eyes darkened and for a heartbeat, he hoped she might say she forgave him.

Then her face went carefully blank and she slid her hand from his, crumpling the plastic bag she'd removed and turning to go. "Put it in the past. I have."

Chapter 3

Gage followed Meredith's orders to stay in bed. Throughout the day, she moved in and out of his room, keeping a close eye on him. At first, his body reacted every time she walked in. Part of that was due to having her hands on him earlier when she'd held that towel in place, teasing him with the possibility that her touch might slide lower.

Yes, he was a dog, but he couldn't stop thinking about it.

He slept quite a bit, which satisfied Meredith enough to bring him what she probably thought was his laptop. It was Ed Nowlin's laptop. Just the thought of what had happened with the marshal had a firestorm of anger flashing through Gage.

He reined in his fury, hoping like hell the computer

would give him some sort of clue about who had coerced the man into trying to kill him.

After sunset a couple of hours ago, he and Meredith had eaten dinner. He'd returned to bed as he'd promised, rebooted the marshal's laptop that he had snatched earlier from the man's car and continued opening files. Looking for something about the murder attempt on him or any of the other witnesses. About why he'd heard Nowlin mention the name Larry James, the disgraced ex-fire investigator Gage suspected of being the mastermind behind the arson plot. He needed something. Anything.

While he worked, Gage could hear Meredith puttering around the house. Which distracted him, slipping images into his mind that he didn't want there. Like the two of them on the back porch in that swing. Kissing, touching, undressing. And the time they'd tried to have sex there. It hadn't worked, but they'd had fun trying.

That memory kicked off others. Her amazingly soft skin against his, the delicate line of her spine beneath his hands, the sweet taste of that place on her nape. Kissing her there always pulled this breathy, pleading sound from her that charged him up like a straight jolt of adrenaline.

Drawn out of his thoughts as she passed by his room, he wondered if any other man knew those things about her. The possibility had anger roaring through him and he tried to stop thinking about her. About *them*. But the memories crept in like smoke, circling him until he was lost in them before he even realized what had happened. Which was why it took him staring at the computer screen twice before he realized what he was seeing.

He'd opened a desktop icon innocuously labeled "shortcuts," which brought up a drawing. The schematic of a building.

There was no address, no specific room delineation or boundaries, but there was a detailed rendering of the ventilation system for the eight-story building. Enough detail to have him cursing under his breath and zooming in on the diagram. A hard knot in his chest told him the drawing was likely that of the Oklahoma County courthouse, where all the witnesses would congregate. Nowlin could've easily obtained the schematic by using the ruse that he was doing prep work for security at the upcoming trial.

All the serial arsons Gage had worked in Operation Smoke Screen had started in the ventilation system. No remains of the accelerant had ever been found at the scenes. Even collecting samples immediately after the fires hadn't yielded anything to test. But Gage knew by the total involvement of the buildings, by the speed of the burns, by the multiple points of origin that there had been an accelerant.

Even ATF Agent Wright hadn't been able to figure out the mystery accelerant. That only strengthened Gage's suspicion that the arsonist was someone with extensive fire knowledge, enough to invent a burn agent that evaporated. Someone like Larry James, who had vowed revenge against the city employees he thought had wrongfully fired him. The city employees who were now awaiting trial for arson, fraud and murder.

Gage had notes back in Texarkana full of chemical

combinations, results of tests he'd performed to no avail. The schematic on the computer screen wasn't much, but it was a starting place. It was too much of a coincidence that the man who'd been coerced into trying to kill Gage would have this kind of detail. Which likely meant that whoever had threatened Nowlin wanted the diagram and was planning something explosive at the courthouse when the trial began.

Gage had already planned to leave Meredith's tomorrow morning. Not because being this close to her was torture, although it was, but because his staying put her in danger. The thought of walking away from her again ripped at his insides.

"Gage?"

The impatience in her voice meant she'd tried to get his attention more than once. He stared up into her blue eyes. "Yeah?"

"Do you want to keep any of these clothes?" She gestured to the stack in front of the closet. "I can bag them up for you."

The fact that she had come here to get rid of his things still annoyed the hell out of him.

"There are a couple more pairs of boxers, several T-shirts and several pairs of shorts."

"All of them, I guess." It was difficult to keep the frustration out of his voice. He had no right to be resentful, but he was. How could she discard his things as if they were nothing more than clutter? As if *he* were?

That wasn't fair to her and he knew it. He was the one who'd done the discarding first. As she turned toward the hall, he said, "I'll be leaving in the morning."

She looked over her shoulder, mouth flattening with disapproval. "Not before I say you're up to it."

He stored away the memory of her sky-blue eyes, her refined features, that tempting mouth. He wanted to stay, but if Nowlin found this place or Meredith, Gage would never forgive himself. "It's for the best. This way, you won't be involved any further."

"You were shot. You lost a lot of blood. If you leave too soon, you'll end up flat on your face."

It didn't matter. If he suffered a setback, it had to be somewhere away from her.

She must've seen the decision on his face. Irritation flashing across her features, she threw up a dismissive hand and started out of the room.

"Meredith." He swallowed around the tightness in his throat. "I don't know how to say goodbye to you."

She froze. After a long pulsing moment, she whispered, "You just did."

She walked out, just as she had eighteen months ago.

"I don't know how to say goodbye to you."

Gage's words had hit her with the same bone-aching loneliness she'd felt when they'd split up.

And it annoyed her, as did his announcement that he was leaving. Being annoyed made no sense because saying goodbye to him was exactly why she'd taken two weeks off work and come down here. It was his physical well-being that concerned her, Meredith told herself. And his stubbornness. It still made her want to wring his neck. He wasn't recovered enough yet to go, but she knew that look in his eye, that forged-steel cast to his jaw. He wasn't changing his mind. The man drove her crazy.

Proven by the fact that she couldn't dismiss the image of him naked this morning. His taut sculpted chest, those powerful legs and the prime everything-in-between she'd seen when the towel fell had made her melt from the inside out.

Good grief, you'd think she had never seen a naked man, she thought as she got ready for bed. Working the emergency room as she did, she'd seen dozens. So what? The sight of Mr. Gage Naked Parrish shouldn't have affected her as much as it had, but when he lost that flimsy covering, she'd nearly been affected right off her feet. She wanted to touch him, rub up against him.

She stifled a groan and squeezed her eyes shut tight, wishing the image away. Trying to focus on something else, she thought back over what she knew of his sudden reappearance in her life. Not enough, that was for sure. She'd had to bite her tongue more than once to keep from asking further questions about the GSW, his insistence on not calling the police.

Meredith resented that she was so curious, that she still cared so much. She was thrilled he was alive, overjoyed for his grandparents, but that didn't mean she wanted to be with him again. She should be glad he was leaving. She *was* glad.

Repeating that over and over in her mind, she climbed into bed. Only to be jerked awake sometime later by a harsh shout. A door slammed against the wall.

In the shifting pattern of shadows and dim light, she

saw two people—men—on their knees in her doorway. They jumped to their feet.

Heart hammering, she yanked open the drawer of her nightstand, reaching for her dad's loaded .22 caliber handgun. Her clammy hand closed over the grip. In a blur of movement, the person closest to her shoved the other into the hallway. A heavy thud told her the man had hit the wall. There was a masculine grunt, the sound of fist hitting flesh.

Thumbing off the safety, she rushed to the door in time to see Gage stumble into the wall. The intruder raised his arm.

Meredith caught a glint of light off the barrel of a gun aimed straight at Gage. "No!" she screamed.

Everything happened in staccato flashes. The unidentified man hesitated. Gage drove a fist into his jaw. The stranger leveled his weapon and fired. So did Meredith.

Her bullet hit him in the back. He jerked, his gun discharging into the bedroom beyond as he fell face-first to the floor. The man didn't move. Gage kicked the gun away then braced his good elbow against the wall, steadying himself. In the grim light, his eyes glittered like polished steel.

"Gage?" On shaking legs, Meredith stepped into the hall. "Are you okay?"

"Yeah. You?"

She nodded. Sweat slicked her palms. The smell of gunpowder burned the air as she stared at the darkly clothed motionless body. Nausea churned in her gut. "He's dead."

"Yeah." He was breathing hard, just as she was.

Jittery and trembling, she caught a movement from the corner of her eye and swung toward it. The living-room lamp provided a soft glow into the kitchen and Meredith saw a short Hispanic man at the corner, looking down the hall. Aiming a gun at them.

She froze in shock as he fired. Gage threw himself at her, knocking her back into her room. They both grunted when they hit the floor.

"Stay here." He pried the .22 from her hand, belly-crawling to the doorway.

Gage fired at the man. Two more shots sounded. Bullets struck the door frame, spraying slivers of wood. Fear had her muscles drawn taut. Dazed, Meredith curled into herself, struggling to breathe, to make sense of what was going on.

More gunfire. Another round zipped past and hit somewhere she couldn't see.

Gage got off three shots, then Meredith heard... quiet. An engine revved, then the sound grew faint. Silence closed in on them, abrupt and almost disorient-ing after the rapid-fire bursts of noise. For a long moment, all she heard was her and Gage's labored breathing.

Heart racing uncontrollably, she lay on her side, her chest aching. She wondered if her ribs were bruised. What had just happened? That man had tried to kill her. He might have succeeded if Gage's shots hadn't sent him running.

On a groan, Gage risked a look around the door frame, then straightened. "I'm going to make sure he's gone, see if anyone else is here. Got another clip?"

"In—in the drawer," she stammered.

He took the ammunition and disappeared. She told herself to move, to go to the bedroom's doorway to see if someone else *was* there. Mind numb, she managed to stand, but couldn't feel her legs. Still, she made it to the door. Long drawn out seconds raked at her nerves. Where was he? Was he okay?

She flinched when she heard the faint sound of the front door closing, then saw him move back into the kitchen and start down the hall toward her.

"He's gone. There's no one else here."

She tried to answer, but she couldn't get a breath.

"Meredith?"

Tears filled her eyes. Reaction, she knew. She sagged into the doorjamb.

"Baby?" He halted in front of her, flicking on her gun's safety and reaching around behind her to lay it on the dresser. Looking panicked, he cupped her face. "Talk to me! Are you hit?"

"No." She shook her head, managing to speak around a painful knot in her throat. Her lungs burned. She kept seeing herself shoot that man.

Gage's thumbs stroked her cheeks as he tilted her face to his. Even in the darkness, she could see the concern in his eyes. And anger. "Tell me you're all right."

"I am. I'm fine." Her body began to quiver.

Relief softening his features, he rested his forehead against hers. There was a faint trembling in his hands as he smoothed them over her hair, then her shoulders, down her sides, caressing the length of her body as if he didn't believe she was in one piece.

"I'm okay, Gage." She caught his hands at her waist. Her nerves were humming and his touch only magnified the sharp stinging sensation beneath her skin. "Just…had the wind knocked out of me."

He squeezed her fingers. "I'm sorry."

"For what? Saving my life?" She laughed weakly, struggling to regain her composure.

His face hardened. After another long look at her, he pulled away and reached over her shoulder to flip on the bedroom light. He cupped her elbow, his eyes cold and savage in a way she'd never seen. He looked…intimidating.

His gaze swept her from head to toe, taking in her pink cotton pajama top and leopard-print pants. "You sure you're okay?"

"Yes." Dazed, she stared down at the dead man lying a few feet away. She had killed him. Her, Meredith Boren.

Gage cursed. "He found me quicker than I thought he could."

"What! You know him?" Her stunned mind struggled to sort things out. Then she understood. "He's the man who shot you."

"Yes."

"Oh, my gosh!" She thought her knees might buckle. Backing into the edge of the dresser, she stared at Gage. "I killed him."

"It's a good thing you did or I'd be dead. For real." As if he couldn't help touching her, he stroked her arm, then her hair.

Her heart still pounded frantically. "I didn't hear anything until you knocked him down."

"I couldn't sleep. Heard a noise and saw him move into your room. I'd forgotten about your gun. Good thing your dad left it that summer there was a rash of burglaries down here."

Meredith nodded, only then noticing his shoulder. "You're bleeding!"

He glanced down. "I'm okay."

"Let me see." Taking an unsteady step toward him, she peeled the tape from the square gauze pads and removed them. Considering Gage had fought the jerk who'd broken in then tackled both the intruder and Meredith, it was no surprise his sutures had torn.

Only the top three, thank goodness, but blood welled up and tracked down his chest thicker and faster than she wanted to see. Still shaking, she took his hand and pressed it firmly against the wound. "Keep pressure on this while I get some bandages."

Shuddering, her legs wobbly, she inched past the dead man's feet and moved toward the kitchen in a fog of fear and relief. The events of the past few minutes played through her mind like a grainy film. With unsteady hands, she picked up the plastic box filled with medical supplies and returned to Gage.

He now sat on the end of the bed, his face ashen. As she went to him, she clumsily scooped her cell phone off the dresser. She dialed 9-1-1 then placed the phone between her shoulder and neck, snapping open the box of supplies.

Gage worked the phone away from her and disconnected. "You can't call 9-1-1."

"That man is dead!"

"You can't call anyone."

Meredith had never heard his voice flat and hard like that. The reality of everything began to sink in—his showing up here, the dead man just outside her room, bullet holes in the walls. She'd killed a man.

Suddenly light-headed, she thought she might have to sit beside Gage on the bed. "What am I supposed to do about him?"

"It'll be all right. It was self-defense."

"Who will know that?" Her voice rose. "Who will believe us?"

"Listen." Gage held her at the waist. "The AG knows what's going on. I used your cell phone this morning and let him know about the marshal trying to kill me a couple of days ago as well as you treating my gunshot wound. When we get away from here, I'll call him and tell him about the shooting. He'll take care of the body, everything."

"But—"

"It'll be okay. I promise."

She wanted to believe him. If the government could fake Gage's death, they could hide a real one, couldn't they?

Still she couldn't stop a shudder. The shooting looped over and over in her mind. She knew she'd had no choice. She hadn't shot to kill; she'd shot to protect. And if she hadn't, Gage would be dead.

"Meredith." The urgency in his voice snapped her focus back to him, what needed to be done.

Still woozy, she pushed his hand away from the wound and covered it herself. She pressed hard in an effort to staunch the bleeding and also to stop her hands from trembling. After a long moment of firm pressure, the blood flow slowed.

Hands still unsteady, she began to carefully clean the injury. He hissed out a curse, but didn't move. Adrenaline drained out of her, making her feel weak and slightly nauseous. A cold sweat covered her whole body. Once she was satisfied the bleeding had stopped, she placed a clean gauze pad over the reopened part of the wound. "Keep pressure on this and tell me what's going on. Who's that man?"

"Marshal Ed Nowlin." Gage's lips twisted. "He was assigned to me. Until two days ago, I trusted him."

Her eyes met his, silently urging him on.

"I heard him on the phone. The person on the other end found his elderly mother and was threatening to kill her unless he agreed to kill me."

She drew in a sharp breath, barely aware she was stroking his shoulder. "Who was on the phone? How did they know Nowlin was the marshal assigned to you?"

"Nowlin accused the caller of bribing someone to hack into the marshals' database. He was probably right. All the hacker had to do was find the files listing the marshals on this case and the witnesses assigned to them."

Gage's mind was stuck on the second man who'd shown up in Meredith's house and shot at them. From the statements of the men in prison, Gage was almost sure the man was Julio, the go-between who worked for the mastermind behind the arson plot. "I grabbed Nowlin's car keys, then tried to slip out the back bedroom window."

"That's when he shot you."

"Yeah. I managed to get away in his car and went to the garage where I work. I took his laptop and switched vehicles to the SUV I drove here."

Meredith's lips were tight and Gage wondered if it was because of what had just happened or because they were talking about the case that had been the last straw for them. She'd made no secret of her resentment about that.

"My plan was to go to the State Attorney General in Oklahoma City, but I knew I couldn't drive for five-plus hours. I was losing too much blood."

"So you came here for medical supplies."

He nodded, regretting that decision more every second.

"How did he find you?"

"My guess is he went to Oklahoma City first. When he couldn't find me with my grandparents or at a hospital, he probably checked your house. Once he figured out you weren't home, he would've called your hospital and learned you were out on vacation."

"But no one at the hospital would've told him where I went."

Gage could blame himself for the man finding them. "I talked about you and this place to Nowlin, told him we used to spend time here. This was probably his only lead so he drove down here. He must've run a property search to find this house."

Her face was carefully blank. He couldn't tell what she was thinking.

"Who was the other man?" She shuddered. "The Hispanic man?"

"I think his name is Julio and he works for whoever's

behind the arson ring. Each of the coconspirators stated they only ever met with a man matching his description to contract for the arsons and receive their cut of the money once the job was done. My surviving Nowlin's murder attempt must've prompted Julio's boss to send him with the marshal and make sure he killed me."

She was silent for a moment. "Who is Julio's boss?"

"I can't prove it, but I think it's a man named Larry James. He was a fire investigator, terminated for—"

"I remember. He was suspected of selling drugs, but it couldn't be proven. He was fired for bad job performance or something like that. It was all over the news because he took it to arbitration and lost."

"Yeah. Since I could never isolate the flammable material common to all the fires, the task force couldn't identify the torch or the person pulling the strings on the fire-for-hire plot. All of us working Operation Smoke Screen thought the suspects would give up a name once they were indicted, but we finally had to accept that none of them knew the identity of the mastermind. None of them ever met with anyone except the Hispanic man."

"So if Larry James is the one behind the arson ring, he did it for revenge?"

Gage nodded. "And he got it. He pushed money at the very men who cost him his job then turned them in."

"They must've gotten involved with him because they didn't know he was the same guy they'd gotten fired."

"Right. I've always thought the anonymous tip we received right before we made our arrests was from him, but like everything else about him, I can't prove it."

"Did those indicted men get involved in the arson ring because of greed?"

"Maybe one, but the others really needed the money. One to pay off a large debt, one to provide twenty-four-hour care for his elderly mother, one to pay for intensive care for his premature baby. Stuff like that."

"James involved those men, then exposed them? That's cold."

"Yeah," he said grimly. "He's ruthless and if my suspicions about Julio are right, Larry James is going to know you're with me. We have to get out of here."

"Look at you! You can't go anywhere yet."

"The SOB who ran out of here saw you. We can't stay."

She opened her mouth. To argue, he knew. He jumped in first. "Describe him to me."

She blinked. "What?"

"The bastard who shot at you. Tell me what he looks like."

She barely hesitated, though her voice shook. "Shorter than me, about five foot six. Hispanic features, baggy sweatshirt and jeans. The sweatshirt was red, I think. The lamp in the living room was on, but I couldn't see a lot of detail. There was something shiny around his neck, some kind of chain."

The more she related, the more ill Gage felt. "You saw him well enough to probably ID him. And *he* saw *you*."

Alarm widened her blue eyes. Gage wanted to hit something. Someone. He'd put her right in the line of fire, could've gotten her killed. "We have to go."

"But—"

"We can't stay, baby. He could come back and he

might not be alone next time." Gage saw anxiety cross her face, then heat spark in her eyes. She was angry at him. He didn't blame her.

She reached into the box for the sutures. "I want to know everything."

"I said I'd tell you, and I will, but not now." He noted she hadn't regained her color; her pulse still fluttered rapidly in her throat. "Get your things together and let's go."

"Let me patch you up first. That wound needs to be closed."

"There's no time for that." Her reluctance, the uncertainty in her face tugged at him and he softened his voice. "I know you want to think this through. You always do. But you'll have to trust me."

The look she gave him could've withered steel. She was already picking up another bandage. "It won't take long."

"The bleeding's nearly stopped, anyway," he said impatiently.

Her jaw firmed. "I'll butterfly it."

Knowing it would take less time to let her do it than to argue with her about it, he agreed. Maybe the task would help calm them both. Urgency pounded through him as she carefully applied the winged bandage. Gage's gut knotted when he noticed that her hands still trembled and she hadn't regained her color. They needed to get out of here.

Meredith glanced toward the marshal's body and Gage turned his head to look, too. His warm breath tickled the inside of her arm. She barely registered the shiver that rippled through her and the sudden tightness of her nipples.

Was this really happening? She'd been asking herself that about one thing or another since seeing Gage again.

"We have to go, Meredith. Right now, the only thing that matters is getting you out of here, so move it."

She bristled, but the increasing strain in his voice and the grim look in his eyes kept her quiet. She finished with his shoulder and snapped the plastic box shut, feeling as if she'd stepped outside of herself. After tossing all her clothes, her makeup case and her hair dryer into a soft-sided leather bag, she shoved his T-shirts and boxers into a tote.

His injured arm was useless so she had to help him put on his jeans and shoes. Which almost used up the last of her calm and took twice as long as it should have because she couldn't stop quivering. She felt as if she were breaking apart, piece by piece. Though she hated to admit it, she wanted to curl up next to him and pretend this wasn't happening. "Where are we going?"

"Somewhere not connected to you or your family. Maybe to the other side of the lake."

"I know a couple with a place across the highway. They winter in Florida."

"Across the highway? Back in all those trees where people rent out trailers and cabins for vacationers?"

She nodded, her chest tight because she still couldn't get a full breath. "The place I'm thinking of is a cabin, owned by the Greens. They keep the utilities on in the winter so the pipes won't freeze. I'm sure they wouldn't mind us staying there for a bit."

He'd met the retired schoolteachers at one of the Borens' summer cookouts. He rose and picked up both bags in his good hand. "All right."

"I'm bringing the medical kit, too."

He nodded and led the way out of the room. She could tell by the intent look on his face that his mind had shifted completely away from her. Well, some things never changed.

Flipping off the light, Meredith glanced one last time at the bloody, motionless man on the floor. She stared at him in disbelief as fear skittered up her spine. Dead people were no rarity in her line of work, but she'd never been the one who'd gotten them that way. She followed Gage to the unlit kitchen, waiting as he stared out the window over the sink, scrutinizing the dark. After a moment, they continued to the garage.

His shoulder had to hurt and she was concerned about renewed bleeding.

Focus on his care, she told herself. Not the dead man in your hallway.

"I'll drive." After turning on the garage light, she opened the back passenger-side door of the silver SUV with a crumpled front fender and motioned him inside. "You need to lie down. I'll get our coats, the food I brought and a couple of blankets for you."

He frowned, angling his body so that she was caught against the door, surrounded by his heat. Blue eyes glittered down at her, fully aware of her now. "I don't want you to drive. If that guy is tailing us, he'll see you. He might shoot."

"Well, I don't want to do any of this, but if he is following us, he'll shoot regardless of who's driving. I've spent every summer of my life down here and I know this area well enough that I can drive the back roads without my lights if I have to. A stranger to the area won't be able to keep up."

The tic of his jaw told her he didn't like the idea, but it made sense. Even though she knew he wouldn't let her drive solely because it was best for his injury, she added anyway, "You need to be as still as possible. The best thing for you is to take the backseat."

When he nodded curtly in agreement, she gave an inward sigh of relief.

"I'll keep an eye out for a tail." He ducked his head, slowly lowering himself onto the edge of the leather seat. His knees still outside, he curved a hand around her hip, startling her. She had no time to brace herself for the current of energy that zinged to her toes. She told herself it was the stress of the situation that had her pulse going haywire, not the man she'd nearly married.

His fingers flexed on her flesh. "I'm sorry about this. The last thing I wanted was for you to be involved." His eyes were dark, tortured. "But you're in this as deep as I am now."

She said nothing. What was there to say? That *he* made her as nervous as what had just happened?

He was her patient and as a doctor, she should've had no problem being with him, but as a woman who'd been in love with him, she had a big problem.

Right now, all she could do was put one foot in front of the other. She returned with the blankets and coats as well as the food she'd brought here. Who knew how long they'd have to stay at the Greens'?

Meredith was relieved to see Gage was inside the car and lying on his good side, facing front. His knees were bent because he was too tall to stretch out. Once she was behind the steering wheel, she adjusted the seat to give him more room. And to give herself another moment to deal with the emotion churning inside her.

She shook so hard, it took two tries to get the key in the ignition. Then her hands wrapped tightly around the steering wheel.

She'd come here to say goodbye to a man she thought was dead. Instead, she'd learned he was very much alive and there was no goodbye in sight.

Chapter 4

He was in bed with Meredith and it wasn't a dream.

In the first wash of daylight, Gage looked across the king-size mattress. There she was, closer than he'd had her in eighteen months. She slept on her back, one arm resting on her forehead, blond curls spread across the pillow. The hem of the dark green long-sleeved shirt she'd thrown on when they'd left her family's lake house rode up enough to bare a thin strip of creamy flesh.

He remembered fighting to stay alert as they'd driven across Highway 259 and weaved along the twisting roads in the heavily forested area. They hadn't been followed. Meredith had parked behind the Greens' secluded cabin, then searched for a key. She'd found it inside the porch light fixture.

The last thing he remembered was her taking off his

shirt and restitching him. He still wore his jeans. There was no memory of her getting into bed with him.

He was going to enjoy it as long as possible, since it might not happen again. Inhaling her subtle apricot scent, he rolled over on his good side to study her.

He watched the rise and fall of her breasts beneath her shirt. An extra blanket she'd found was a soft mound of yellow bunched at her waist. Very carefully, he inched over until he could skim his fingers over her sunshine hair. His injured shoulder throbbed, but it didn't matter. He itched to touch her cream-and-rose skin, stroke the fine bones of her cheeks and jaw. The elegant line of her nose. Her lips.

Thick dark lashes lay against her cheeks. He wanted to see her eyes. He wanted to see all of her. Peel away the covers and find out if she had on her jeans or only panties. Just look.

His gaze rose again to her face as he propped himself up on one elbow.

She stirred, shifting on her side to face him. Her eyes were still closed. The unguarded vulnerability on her face had a sudden fierce protectiveness welling inside him. As well as the regret he'd lived with for the past year.

He rolled to his back, then carefully sat up and got his feet on the floor. His hands clamped on to the mattress as weakness swept through him and he bowed his head. Silently, he cursed himself up one side and down the other for involving her.

He hadn't done it on purpose, but that didn't mean she was in any less danger. He couldn't let anything happen to her. He wouldn't.

"Gage?" she said in her smoke-and-velvet voice.

He looked over his shoulder, his entire body going tight at the sight of her tousled hair and sleepy blue eyes.

"Are you okay? Do you need some ibuprofen?"

"I'm fine." The pain helped dull the want burning in his belly. A little.

In the growing light, he searched her face. The warm flush on her cheeks and the fall of unruly curls brought to mind all the mornings he'd woken to see her looking just like this. The way she used to look at him before they had split up.

Her eyes were that clear endless blue he wanted to drown in, and a wave of longing hit him. Just the sight of her put a hard throb in his blood. And the dreamy way she stared at him, as if she hadn't yet remembered why they were together, what he'd done, unraveled every reason he had to keep his hands off her.

He wanted to pull her across the bed and bury his face in her hair. Kiss her sweet, warm neck. Taste her delicate skin. Her lips. He wanted to get his mouth on her. He didn't care where.

There was about as much chance of that happening as there was of no wind in Oklahoma. Furious that things had come to this, he was unable to stop the roughness in his voice. "Why don't you shower and I'll see if I can find something for breakfast?"

At his tone, the drowsiness faded from her eyes. She stiffened. "I should look at your shoulder first."

"It's fine. You can check me before I clean up, when you put something over my bandage to keep it dry."

She sat up and shoved her silky hair back out of her face with both hands. "All right. I won't be long."

He faced front, staring down at the floor, staying put until he felt her get out of bed and heard her close the door to the small bathroom behind him.

He might've lost a lot of blood, but his body still responded to her and he couldn't have hidden it. Once she was out of the room, he carefully pulled on the denim shirt he'd borrowed from her brother and moved over to the window adjacent to the bathroom door.

His SUV sat undisturbed where Meredith had left it under a winter-stripped oak. The pines and cedars were a vivid burst of green in the midst of the gray-and-white landscape. Frost glittered on the windshield and windows, covered the branch-strewn ground. There was no sign anyone had been out there.

After snagging Meredith's cell phone, Gage made his way to the front of the cabin. This place was smaller than the Borens' lake house, but comfortable. Besides the one bedroom, there was a black-and-white kitchen with sparkling appliances, glowing wood floors and a red front door with tall narrow windows on either side. The living area was small, with a red leather sofa and overstuffed chair grouped around a rock fireplace. So much for Meredith sharing a bed with him because she wanted to. Apparently, there was nowhere else for her to sleep.

Gage kept to the side of the window until he'd checked the front porch and copse of trees on both sides of the house. He saw no one.

The place was secluded and Meredith had said the neighbors to the right used their cabin only in the summer. She wasn't sure about the neighbors on their other side. Both houses were about two hundred yards away from the Greens' cabin. The gravel road leading to the porch gave a clear view of anyone approaching from the front.

Satisfied for the moment that the Hispanic man hadn't found them, Gage called Ken Ivory again. Last night, Gage had told the State Attorney General the bare bones of what had happened at Meredith's lake house. Ivory had offered to send protection, but Gage objected, saying it could draw attention to where he and Meredith were. Not to mention that he feared someone like Julio could be working in Ivory's office or watching every move the man made. Gage had been relieved when the AG said he would handle the incident discreetly.

Nowlin's body had been moved and no local law enforcement involved. After answering a spate of questions and asking some of his own, Gage hung up and opened the plastic bag of food Meredith had brought. There were two giant cinnamon bagels—her favorite—a half loaf of bread, coffee, chili, soup and crackers. He started the coffee and turned on the oven to toast the bagels about the same time he heard the creak of pipes in the bathroom, the faint rush of water.

It took zero imagination for him to picture her in the shower. His mind jumped straight to memories of water sluicing over her full pink-tipped breasts, down her sleek belly and legs. His hands would follow, then his mouth.

He narrowly missed slicing the tip of his finger with the knife he used to halve the bagels. Remembering was the worst thing he could do and not only because it might cost him more blood.

Several minutes later, she walked into the kitchen, shaking her hair free from a loose knot she'd piled on her head. She eased to the side of the front windows, checking outside the way Gage had. Good.

Turning, she padded toward him wearing socks, slim jeans and a thick blue sweater that made her eyes glitter like sapphires. "How's it going?"

"Found bagels and coffee." There were dark circles under her eyes. "How are you doing? About the shooting?"

"I don't know. I'm not sure how I'm supposed to be." Looking subdued, she peeked into the bag. "If we need anything, we can go into Broken Bow. We should probably get you at least a sweatshirt and another long-sleeved shirt. All you have are short-sleeved T-shirts and underwear."

"You can't go to town." The faint scents of soap and her apricot body wash teased him. Her skin glowed with a sheen of dampness. "You could easily be spotted."

Irritation crossed her face. "Right."

They sat down at the round stone-topped table to eat and silence hung heavy between them. Vibrating with regret and apology and shades of the past.

Gage had plenty of that stuff in the present, too. "I called the Attorney General and told him what happened last night. Once we get to Oklahoma City, we can give our statements, answer any questions we need to."

She swallowed visibly. "What about…the body?"

"Ken will handle it and inform all the appropriate authorities."

"I guess that includes the Marshals Service."

"Yeah. They already know their computer system was breached and Ken will let them know that the witnesses should be switched again to new handlers."

"Does that mean you'll get one, too?"

"I refused," he said tightly. He didn't trust anyone with Meredith's life. "There's no way I'm taking a chance that another marshal could be coerced into killing me. Or you."

The apprehension on her face had every muscle in his body clenching against the urge to hold her. He couldn't stop looking at her. As he studied the magnolia smoothness of her face, the gentle sweep of her jaw, he recalled the sweet taste of her skin, her mouth.

Meredith fixed him with a look over her coffee cup, making him realize he had been staring.

He wasn't apologizing, especially when he saw a delicate blush on her face and knew it was hueing her breasts, too.

Her eyes went frosty. "You said you'd fill me in on what was going on."

As much as he hated it, she deserved to know what they were up against.

Shoulders tense, he explained in detail how he'd come to be shot and had escaped by taking the marshal's car. How he had then exchanged the sedan for his SUV at the automobile garage where he worked. "The laptop I have is Nowlin's. When I switched cars, I took it, hoping to find something on there about who wants me killed. I haven't found anything like that yet, but when I was looking around on it yesterday, I came across a schematic of a ventilation system."

She frowned. "All the fires associated with that arson ring started in ventilation systems."

"Yeah." She'd kept up with the case. Interesting.

She squirmed, giving him a look that told him he was watching her too intently. Tough.

"That's too much of a coincidence. Less than two weeks before the trial starts, the marshal assigned to me is threatened and I'm nearly killed. A diagram for a ventilation system—part of the signature of the arsonist behind the fire-for-hire ring—just happens to show up on his computer? No."

"Does the diagram identify the building?"

"No, but I think it's the Oklahoma County courthouse. It's the one place where all the investigators in WitSec will meet."

"Could the drawing be of a system in another building? Could he have it for another reason?"

"What would it be?" He tore his gaze from her luscious mouth. Damn, he was pathetic. "If Nowlin got the schematic for a legitimate reason, like to plan security, why didn't he have blueprints of the whole building? There's no way this is a fluke. No, whoever threatened Nowlin is planning to do something using a ventilation system and the Oklahoma County courthouse is the logical place."

"And they're going to try and kill as many task-force members as possible," she said hoarsely. "Including you."

He wanted to deny it, wanted to reassure her. He couldn't.

If possible, her face paled even more. "Can't you tell the cops you suspect Larry James of being the person behind the arson ring and have them pick him up?"

"I've got nothing solid on him, even though I've been working on that the whole time I've been in witness protection."

"By doing what?"

"Trying to figure out the composition for an accelerant that leaves no trace after it burns." Gage attempted to focus solely on the discussion, not about putting his hands on her body. "Not in wood, fabric, cement, nothing."

"Then how do you know an accelerant's being used?"

"By the speed of the burn, the distortion of certain objects, points of origin. Someone has invented an agent that disappears. That requires extensive fire knowledge. I've tested dozens of different chemical combinations, trying to figure it out and so far, I haven't been able to."

"Would learning that help lead you to who's behind the arson ring?"

"It might point me in the right direction. As of now, it's the only possible lead I have, so I can't ignore it."

"Do you need a lab to do that?"

"No. I've been doing tests on my own and keeping notes."

"So you could work on it here."

"Yeah, but I need my notes and some photos I have that show the same burn pattern was found at all the fire scenes in question. Proof that the same accelerant was used."

One look at his face and she blew out an exasperated breath. "Let me guess. They're at your house in Texarkana and you want to go there."

He nodded. "As soon as possible."

"Of course you do," she said drily. "You've gone a whole six hours without bleeding or reopening your wound."

"Meredith, I need to do this."

"I know," she muttered. After a moment, she sighed. "Will you at least rest a little longer? You lost more blood when you fought with Nowlin last night."

"How about midafternoon?"

"All right." She leaned toward him, reaching out as if to touch his jaw, then pulling back. "You have a bruise there. Your knuckles are probably banged up, too."

He glanced down so she wouldn't see how badly he wanted her to touch him. He wanted to take her hand and kiss her palm, run his tongue across the delicate blue veins on the inside of her wrist.

She must've seen the intent on his face because her eyes narrowed and she pushed her chair away from the table. "I'll keep watch while you take a bath."

"All right." He needed to follow her lead and stick to the present. There was plenty to handle without dwelling on the gut-twisting ache he had for her. "It's less than a two-hour drive to Texarkana. I don't want you to go—"

"So, you don't need me anymore," she broke in hopefully. "I could—"

"I wasn't finished," he gritted out, irritated at how anxious she seemed to get away from him. Of course, why wouldn't she be? "I don't want you to go to Texarkana with me, but you have to. You sure as hell can't go back to your lake house or to Presley. And there's no way I'm leaving you alone. As much as you hate the idea, you're stuck with me until this is over."

He didn't like the idea much himself. Not only because he'd never forgive himself if something happened to her, but also because the longer they were together, the harder it became to keep his hands off her.

Meredith exhaled a shaky breath as she finished covering Gage's bandage and left him to take a bath. His blue eyes had been hot and intense on her. She needed some space and she wasn't going to get it anytime soon.

Stuck with him, he'd said.

Seven more days. She would be with him that long or until they got to Oklahoma City. What had started out as annoyance at his announcement had turned to panic. Because she'd spent the past thirty minutes trying to ignore his frank male appraisal. Because she'd dreamed about him. *Them.*

One night on the same mattress and boom. She couldn't remember the last time she'd dreamed about him before this. Her jaw clamped so tight she felt a twinge in her cheek. She was restless and hot and mad. She'd been that way since waking up next to him, feeling his warmth like a touch. Glimpsing the dark hunger in his eyes.

When she had climbed into bed with him last night, she knew she could be tempting herself, tempting him, but she'd done it anyway. Because there was no way she was sleeping alone after killing that man.

She was an idiot. She'd thought getting away from

her lake house and going somewhere else would be better because there would be no memories in the new place. They wouldn't be in every shadow or corner or possession she touched. But this was just as bad.

While Gage was in the bath, she cleaned bagel crumbs from the table and swept the floor. Called her parents and told them it was taking longer down here than she'd expected.

Wandering to the small living area, the quiet pulsed around her. Everything kept at bay by thoughts of Gage caught up to her—shooting the marshal, nearly being shot herself, the fear, the fight, the blood.

Just like that, tears started. She sank down onto the red leather sofa, dabbing at her eyes. A physical release of stress, she knew. But she couldn't stop. The more she swiped at her tears, the faster they flowed.

Suddenly a big warm hand covered her left one. "Meredith?"

Gage's hushed voice was soothing and she tried to check her sobs. Through blurry eyes, she saw the concern on his face.

"Nowlin?"

She nodded, tears burning her cheeks.

Warm and steady, he sat in the chair next to the sofa, loosely clasping her fingers. His knee brushed hers. After a few minutes, she had herself under control.

Still she couldn't suppress a shudder. "I shot him. I killed him." She gave a watery laugh. "Like you don't know that. I just…can't believe it happened."

Gage brushed his thumb lightly back and forth across her knuckles.

"It's only now sinking in, I guess. It's a delayed reaction. I know that, but I can't seem to help it."

"You don't have to. You've been through a lot, Meredith. Just let it out."

He didn't try to hold her or fix her, just waited patiently as more tears fell. They finally stopped. Slowly she became aware of the hum of the refrigerator, the coarse caw of a bird outside. The familiar scent of soap and man settled her.

She squeezed his hand. "Sorry."

He thumbed away a streak of wetness on her cheek. "You okay?"

"Yes," she said hoarsely. The tenderness in his eyes had her chest going tight. "It's overwhelming. I know I saved your life and I'm not sorry for that."

"Good to know," he said drily.

She smiled. "It's just…he's dead. In med school, we were taught how to deal with death, but it's different with patients. The marshal wasn't a patient."

Gage listened as she worked her way through it, keeping hold of her hand. As she calmed, she took in his damp hair, the steadiness in his hands, the hard hair-dusted chest visible between the edges of his open shirt. And the heat in his blue eyes.

His thumb softly stroked her ring finger. Had he been doing that all along? Awareness fluttered down low and she slowly slid her hand from his. "I feel better now."

About the marshal. Not about Gage.

He laughed. "You don't have to sound so surprised."

"I'm not." Her mouth curved. She had always admired his patience. Except when it came to them and the wedding he had seemed content to wait on forever.

She might not like what he'd done to them, she might not trust him with her heart, but she did trust him with her life. "I'm not sure I would be able to handle this with anyone except you. Thanks."

His gaze sharpened. Maybe she shouldn't have said that out loud, but she meant it.

Shifting closer, he rested his elbows on his thighs. "I'm glad to return the favor."

"What do you mean?" She dried the last of her tears. "Oh, saving my life after I saved yours."

"No." He shook his head, seeming to consider his words carefully. "I'm talking about the past year. Thinking about you was what got me through."

She stiffened. "Gage."

"Remembering us."

She didn't want to hear this. She couldn't. She wasn't going back. "Stop. Please."

After a long, heavy minute that had her quivering deep inside, he looked straight into her eyes. Her pulse skipped. She couldn't ignore the fierce need on his face.

"I can't stop thinking about being in bed with you this morning. And how we used to wake up. Remember?"

Oh, she remembered, all right. This was why he'd been watching her with such blatant interest all morning. "Well, we didn't wake up that way today!"

"Trust me, I know. Every part of me knows," he added wryly.

Before she could stop herself, she glanced at his

groin and her eyes widened at his unmistakable arousal. "You can't— You're hurt!"

"I'm not dead."

Panic had her surging to her feet. She wanted to run, but where? "Okay, listen. There's one bed in this place. It's plenty big enough for both of us, so you better not try anything. You've been looking at me like you want to take a big bite."

His gaze did a slow slide down her body. "I'd be lying if I said I didn't."

Meredith wanted to smack him. "I'm not sleeping with you. We're not sleeping together. There will be no sex. None."

"What about—"

"No kissing. No touching."

He arched a brow and amusement glinted in his eyes. "I was going to say what about afterward? What about after this is over?"

She blinked. Was he serious? Regardless of how the trial turned out, their basic problem would still be the same. He would always put her second to his job. "There is no 'after this.'"

"No?"

"No."

His eyes darkened as he rose, his body almost touching hers. A frantic electric sensation screamed through her body, zinging clear down to her toes.

She wasn't sure what she expected, but it wasn't for him to lean close and whisper, "Whatever you say."

The soft arrogance in his voice didn't sound like agreement to her. It sounded like a challenge.

Her pulse spiked and her nipples tightened. She shouldn't want him ever again, but she did. Meredith folded her arms, trying to look as if she were unaffected, but she could tell by the infuriating satisfaction in his eyes he'd already seen. Her entire body flushed.

Before she could step away, he did. It scared her how quickly some of her old emotions had surfaced. The anger, the regret. And the want. Especially that one.

Seven days to go before the trial. Seven days of *this*.

She mentally braced herself. Things were what they were and she had to deal with it. She could suck it up for seven days. She could do this without getting involved again.

"We can come back here after we finish in Texarkana." He skirted the leather chair and walked down the hall toward the bedroom, hopefully to rest.

As Meredith watched his slow progress, her gaze took in the stubborn set to his shoulders, the jeans she only now noticed were loose on him. She went hot, then cold. Her legs felt like rubber. Those seven days loomed before her like a long stretch of desert. She was afraid she couldn't tough it out at all.

Because she had never gotten over him.

Chapter 5

She'd said no sex, but she still wanted him. Gage had seen proof in her body. Her eyes. And he planned to get her to admit it. He was driven by ego, but he didn't care.

She hadn't wanted to hear that sometimes thoughts of her had been the only thing to keep him going. Maybe he shouldn't have confessed, but he wanted her to know how much she still meant to him.

His day had been spent sleeping off and on, and searching through more files on Nowlin's computer. Even though Gage chafed at the inactivity, he knew he had to regain his strength. And leaving Texarkana after dark was a precaution they should take.

Meredith had dodged him most of the day. She was skittish though he didn't know if it was because of what he'd admitted in the living room or because there was still a spark between them.

This morning had started a slow throb of anticipation in his blood. Knowing this might be the last chance he had to ever spend any time with her made the hunger sharper, deeper, and being with her until the trial was going to test his restraint.

His awareness of her sawed away at his control as they drove to Texarkana later that day to pick up his notes and fire-scene photos. The sun was setting in a ball of pure orange. Gage didn't mind Meredith being behind the wheel; he just wished he had something to do with his hands, his mind. Something to override the sweet scent of her wrapping around him, the memory of how she'd responded to him earlier.

Tension arced between them. Because of him, he knew. He was making her uncomfortable, but he couldn't quite bring himself to be sorry. Waking up with her this morning had done more than fire his blood. It had unlocked memories of all the mornings he'd woken with her before. And all the ones he hadn't.

He tried to think about other things, other people. Maybe the silence was getting to her as well because she slid a look at him. "How long have you worked at the car garage?"

"Since I got there last year."

"You always could fix anything," she said, her lips curving.

Not us, he thought. Her smile still pushed his buttons, made him itch to get his hands on her. Hoping to hide his reaction, he glanced out the window. He didn't want to talk about him. He wanted to know what had been going on in her life. "How are Terra and Jack?"

Presley's first female fire investigator was one of Meredith's best friends. She and her husband, Jack Spencer, had become good friends to Gage, too.

Meredith accelerated past a semitruck. "They're doing great. They have a baby now, Elise."

Gage had never thought about having babies with Meredith, but he thought about it now.

"She's a little over a year old."

"That's nice. Before I went into Witness Security, I ran into Terra at a fire investigator seminar, so I knew she was pregnant. How's Robin?"

Meredith's other close friend was a highly regarded cop on the Presley P.D.

"She's well. She's a detective now. Last year, she was hurt in a fire."

"How badly?"

"Luckily she wasn't burned. Her leg was gashed by some falling debris, badly enough to need quite a few stitches."

Gage shifted in the corner of the seat, trying to keep pressure off his injured shoulder. His gaze fixed on Meredith's face, the creamy skin he knew was velvety soft. All over. The need to touch her was even worse than it had been this morning. "She ever get married?"

"No." Meredith shook her head emphatically. "I don't think she ever will after what happened."

"Can't say I blame her. Her fiancé jilting her right before the ceremony probably doesn't make her inclined to get serious about anyone."

Meredith nodded. "It's been almost five years and she still doesn't know which of Kyle's groomsmen convinced him that she was the worst person he could marry."

"Brutal."

"It's horrid. At least that didn't happen with—"

Us. He knew what she'd been about to say. Remembering the stark pain in Meredith's eyes when they had split up, Gage figured what he had done had hurt her just as badly.

She filled the awkward pause. "Your grandparents got a new dog."

He grinned. "How does Rex like that?"

Regret flashed across her face. "Rex died about three months ago."

"Oh." The news about his bird dog jarred him. "That had to be really hard on Gramps."

She nodded. "Fifteen years is a long time to have a dog. He was a member of your family."

Gage stared out the window. Rex, gone. One more thing that had happened without Gage knowing. He and Gramps had trained the black Labrador together. The animal had been a big part of Gage's growing up. His chest felt hollow. Not only because of losing the dog, but also because of everything he'd missed.

There were chunks of his life he would never get back. People he might never see again. People he'd let down. He should've been there for his grandparents, for Meredith. Failing his grandparents could be blamed on his having to go into hiding, but not his problems with Meredith. No, he'd screwed up their relationship before his supposed death.

Talking with her, being with her, put a sharp bite in his blood. Over the past year, he'd been able to numb himself to some extent, he realized. Since seeing Meredith again, his body had been slowly unthawing. Spending time with her brought back every emotion he'd locked away—want, need, regret, loneliness. Love. He hadn't been aware of how completely he'd shut himself off. How empty he'd felt.

As they headed east, then south through Arkansas on U.S. 71, he asked questions about some of the arson cases he'd seen reported over the past few months in Presley's online newspaper. She told him Terra Spencer now had another full-time fire investigator, Collier McClain, whose first case had been a serial arsonist-killer.

They talked about changes in Presley and other friends they shared. As best she could, Meredith answered his questions about his grandparents, about Aaron and Gage's fellow fire investigators. All things he should've gotten to experience. Life—*his life*—had gone on without him. As had the woman sitting beside him.

Looking at her, aching at the memory that he hadn't been able to touch her the way he wanted this morning, he'd never felt more alone.

They reached Texarkana just after dark. Along with the notes and photos, Gage intended to pick up some clothes at his house and if they were careful, purchase anything else they needed from a store here.

So far, there had been nothing on the news about him or Meredith so Gage felt Ken Ivory was handling everything the way he'd promised.

Gage directed her to an older neighborhood of small

frame houses and had her park around the block. They walked through the field that ran behind a row of fenced backyards. This way, there was less chance of being noticed, especially by his widowed neighbor, Ralph, a former Army Ranger.

When they reached Gage's yard, he helped Meredith over the four-foot chain-link fence, catching sight of Ralph's tabby cat prowling the length of the back porch. Light from the fat white moon showed the back bedroom window through which Gage had escaped was still open. Fishing his keys out of his pocket, he opened the patio door and stepped inside.

He froze, his grip tightening on the semiautomatic he and Meredith had brought with them from her lake house. "Sonova—"

He scanned the living area. The dark tweed couch cushions were slashed, the drawers of both end tables had been yanked out and dumped, lamps broken. Shock shifted to apprehension.

"Stay here," he whispered over his shoulder. He checked the other rooms. Once convinced they were alone, he returned to Meredith. "The whole house is torn up like this."

She followed him across the living room and down a hallway littered with linens and books and papers. They passed one ransacked bedroom before reaching his. Clothes were thrown from his closet and drawers. His mattress was shoved half off the bed.

"What were they looking for?"

Unaware that she had eased up on his right side, Gage jerked toward her.

"Sorry," she breathed at his abrupt movement.

"Maybe whoever broke in was looking for my notes or photos. Maybe info on me. Hell if I know."

"Do you think it was Julio?"

"Could've been. Or Nowlin could've trashed everything before leaving here and finding us at your lake house."

Gage moved to the solid oak headboard and tried to pull it away from the wall with his left hand.

Meredith made an exasperated sound and hurried to the other side of the bed to help him.

"Thanks." Shoulder aching, he felt his way down the frame toward the lower half then pushed in on a section. A square piece popped out and Gage removed it. Anyone who didn't know about the hiding place he'd cut into the wood wouldn't notice anything unusual.

Relief pumped through him when his hand closed over the small notebook and fire-scene photos. He passed them to Meredith. "Would you hold these while I grab some clothes?"

Taking a duffel bag from his closet floor, he stuffed in sweatshirts, jeans and socks. He stepped into a small bathroom and grabbed his shaving kit. "Let's get out of here."

They left the same way they'd come, hurrying silently across the crackling winter grass and back to the SUV. The silence, the heavy chill coiled Gage's muscles tight. And it wasn't lost on him that his wrecked house mirrored the shambles his life had become.

At the edge of town, they stopped at a discount store for some clothes, then a convenience store for gas. Impatient and edgy, Gage knew he wouldn't relax until they reached the cabin. He and Meredith took turns in the restroom then she filled the gas tank. When he protested, she said, "You're moving as if you're hurt. Someone might notice that, but they won't notice me."

In an effort to hide her face in case there were working security cameras around, she wore one of Gage's baseball caps he'd found under the seat. He stayed in the SUV, scrutinizing the driver's side where she stood and the passing vehicles on the street beyond.

As they continued on their way, Gage kept watch on the highway behind them.

Features pinched with concern, Meredith glanced over. "Do you see anything suspicious?"

"Not yet."

"We weren't followed down here, so maybe we're in the clear."

"Maybe." He wasn't assuming anything.

The image of his ransacked house looped through his brain, a grim reminder of the danger they could still face.

The traffic wasn't heavy, but it was steady. When they crossed the border into Arkansas, they began to see more semitrucks than automobiles. Some truck trailers were loaded with lumber or machinery, some were empty.

Gage and Meredith made it through DeQueen, Arkansas, without spotting a tail. There was about twenty-four miles to go until Broken Bow, then another thirteen or so miles to the Greens cabin. The tight pressure across his chest eased. They would be all right.

But when they stopped at the light on Park Drive to

turn toward the lake, his attention was caught by a distinctive pair of round headlights. Exactly like some he'd seen on an older car at the convenience store in Texarkana.

As he and Meredith started out of town, Gage swore.

Her gaze jerked to him. "What? What is it?"

The vehicle held its position a few car lengths back. He touched Meredith's leg. "We're being followed."

She drew in a sharp breath, looking in the rearview mirror. "Do you think it's Julio?"

"That's a good possibility. Don't change your speed."

"Okay." Her voice was thin. "What do we do?"

Gage's hands curled into fists. He'd been vigilant about watching for anyone following them. How had the tail suddenly appeared? It didn't matter. They had to get rid of him. "We can't go back to the Greens' and I don't know if we could lose the tail in Broken Bow. The town's too small."

For a long minute, neither spoke. The silence turned heavy with apprehension.

"We need a plan B," Meredith said.

"I'm fresh out of those."

"I might have an idea." She glanced in the rearview mirror.

Gage was glad to see the tail hadn't gotten closer. "What?"

"We'll go past the lake, past Smithville and take one of the logging roads into the mountains. If the person following us manages to make it as far as the logging road, they won't make it much farther."

It was a good idea. Gage had hunted in the heavily forested area with her brothers and knew how easy it was to get lost on roads that were often no more than lumber-truck ruts. "It's really difficult to find your way out, even in the daylight."

"Not if you know where you're going."

True. Her brothers, as familiar with the area as Meredith, had managed to get in and out of their hunting camp just fine.

"All right. Let's lose him."

She nodded, her face ghost-pale in the darkness. Gage bit back a curse. He wanted to tell her everything would be okay, but as long as she was with him, it wasn't.

As they passed the lake and traffic thinned, the speed limit increased. And the car trailing them closed in. Meredith hoped she could lose him. She thought she could.

Fear was a cold lump in her throat. She focused on keeping at least one vehicle between them and their pursuer as they passed the entrance to Beavers Bend State Park, then a lake area called Stevens Gap. Meredith drew on her years of E.R. experience to stay calm when what she wanted to do was scream, pretend none of this was happening.

She thought she could hear Gage's heart pounding as loudly as hers. He kept watch out the back window while Meredith monitored the rearview mirror. In the flash of a passing semi's lights, she saw the grimness, the guilt on his face, and knew he blamed himself.

Meredith was starting to see the price he'd paid the past year, was still paying.

A road sign listed the upcoming towns of Smithville, Bethel and Battiest, then a billboard-sized sign welcomed them to the Ouachita National Forest. The highway curved and they were heading east. The moon was bright and in the distance, Meredith could see the night-draped forested mountains.

The tail still followed. Meredith accelerated, driving over the Eagle Fork Creek bridge. Hands clammy, chest tight, she drove through the small town of Watson, then turned right toward the cemetery, slowing when the road became dirt and gravel and holes. Coming to a fork in the road, she again went right.

There were huge gouges in the red dirt road, deep enough to crack teeth if they hit one going too fast. The SUV's lights were a beacon to the person behind them, but she couldn't turn them off, not yet.

The forest of trees along both sides of the road blocked most of the moonlight. Gage's vehicle bumped and rattled as the road twisted and climbed.

He spoke loud enough to be heard over the noise. "We could get lost, just like him."

"Maybe."

"I never could get my bearings when we came here to hunt."

That was because the only landmarks this far into the mountains were trees and more trees. One might be marked with a band of white or red spray paint, but the next one would be, too. "Let's hope whoever's behind us can't find their way, either."

Meredith put the SUV in four-wheel drive and started up a steep incline. She could see the car keeping pace behind her and she was nearly frantic to put more distance between them. At least that person couldn't travel any faster than her and Gage.

Deep, rock-pitted ditches ran along the road. Suddenly, she steered into one. Their vehicle bounced hard enough to slam her and Gage's heads into the ceiling. Hissing out a harsh breath, he grabbed the dash to steady himself.

"Sorry." Meredith searched for a narrow opening and took it, driving up a small rise and over felled tree limbs, decades-old cushions of pine needles and twigs, mounded mud. When the ground leveled out, she stopped, killing the lights and the engine.

Their labored breathing was loud in the abrupt silence.

The quiet was palpable. The grind of a car engine sounded over the chirps and rustles of night animals. Bright lights speared through the trees, but didn't reach them. Chest tight, Meredith fought the urge to grab hold of Gage's hand, hoping they couldn't be seen in the dense growth. The car passed, the engine's rumble faded.

Meredith and Gage stayed frozen, waiting. Soon, she heard a car coming back toward them. Was it the one that had been following them? Had they been found?

Seconds pricked her nerves like needles. When the vehicle drove past their hiding place and she saw it *was* the car that had been tailing them, she felt Gage's relief as strongly as her own.

Neither of them spoke until they could no longer

hear the automobile. He reached over and squeezed her waist. "You did it."

Tension drained out of her and she slouched down in the seat, boneless. "For a minute, I was afraid he might find us."

"Me, too." Gage looked at the surrounding woods. "Do you think we could get out of here using the other route you know?"

"Not in the dark, and we can't go back the way we came. If that guy manages to make it to the highway, he could be waiting down there."

"So…"

"So?" Meredith glanced over, realization dawning at the same moment he spoke. She opened her mouth to tell him not to say it, but he beat her to it.

"Looks like we'll be sleeping together again."

She rolled her eyes at his choice of words, while trying desperately to keep the panic off her face.

Her with Gage. In much closer quarters than a king-size bed. This morning, he'd seen how much he still affected her. She had to be careful.

It didn't take long for a chill to settle in the car and the windows to frost from their breath. They moved to the backseat and laid it flat to give them room to sleep. They traded places so Gage could rest on his good side if he wanted.

From behind the driver's seat, he broke the silence. "If we're going to be here all night, we should use the sweatshirts we bought earlier."

"Those blankets we took from the lake house are still in here, too." As he pulled the new garments out of the bag, Meredith stretched to the back corner and retrieved the blankets, passing one to him. She slipped off her coat to pull on the sweatshirt.

He tossed something soft and white at her. "I figure you're going to want a pair of these socks, too."

Despite his teasing tone, they stared at each other in tense silence. Her feet were always cold in the winter. When she and Gage had been together, she would filch a pair of his socks to wear over her own.

Judging from the knowing glitter in his eyes, he was remembering, as she was, how she would beg him to rub her feet and warm them up. She didn't want to think about their past. Spending the night with him was going to be hard enough.

Pulse hitching, she drew her blanket around her shoulders, searching for something to say, anything to prevent other reminders of their past. "You know, there are several Vietnam veterans who live up here."

After giving her a long, measuring look, Gage leaned against the back of the driver's seat. "Your brothers mentioned that the last time we were here."

"No one ever sees them. I don't know if they ever leave the mountain. It's sad and intriguing at the same time."

Sitting cross-legged at his hip, she looked past him to the window and froze. Her heart skipped as two big dark eyes stared back at her. A brown face with white circling the eyes and inside the ears identified the animal as a whitetail deer. No antlers, which meant it was a female. Her jet-black nose with two white bands behind it pressed against the glass as the doe watched them, unblinking.

Gage turned his head, following Meredith's gaze. He went still. "Wow."

"Yeah. Think she'll do anything aggressive?"

"Not if we don't."

Amazing. They sat there in breathless silence as the animal snuffled, frosting the glass, then sniffed its way down the side of the SUV. After a moment, it disappeared into the darkness.

Relaxing, Meredith blew out a breath. "That was a surprise."

"Too bad I never saw a deer that close when I was hunting with your brothers."

Meredith smiled at him, but something about his words nagged at her. Something about seeing. Then things started falling into place. The night she'd found him in her kitchen, the night Julio had shot at them before Gage saw him. Previously tonight when she had come up beside him in his bedroom, startling him. And just now.

Given where the deer had stood, Gage should've seen the animal from the corner of his eye. And he hadn't. He should've seen all those earlier things when she had, if not before.

"You have no peripheral vision on your right side," she said slowly, certainly. "Why?"

She thought he might have winced. He opened another plastic sack and dug out a box of granola bars. "Hungry?"

"There are only a couple of ways that can happen. One is disease and the other is blunt-force trauma." She was afraid she knew which it was. Her heart started pounding hard. "Tell me."

"I'm fine."

She felt his reluctance like a wall. "You told me there were two attempts on your life. That was why you had to go into Witness Security, why you had to fake your death."

He stared straight ahead, his face stone-hard in the shadowy light.

"Gage." She heard the plea in her voice; she had to know. "They nearly killed you."

"Yes," he confirmed grudgingly. "Once with a gun, once with a baseball bat and a pipe. The bullets missed, but—"

"You were beaten horribly. That's what happened."

He dragged a hand down his face. "I'm fine now."

"Tell me what they did to you."

"Baby, we don't have to talk about this."

She scooted closer until her knees touched his thighs. She wanted him to look at her. Her voice shook. "I need to know."

After a long minute, he answered. "Broke two ribs, my jaw, my nose."

"And damaged your orbital rim."

He nodded.

She swallowed hard. Something inside her went dark and flat. For the first time, she *felt* how close he'd come to being killed. The realization was a razor-sharp slice through her heart.

Finally, his gaze met hers. "I'm okay."

She rose to her knees, the blanket sliding off her shoulders. With a trembling hand, she reached out and feathered her fingertip against the corner of his eye.

He froze. She shouldn't be touching him. Since waking up with her this morning, his body had been humming with tension. He closed his eyes, just for a moment, savoring her silky soft touch against his temple.

All the need he'd tried to smother the past year crashed over him. Gage couldn't help pressing into her touch.

Her hand on his face, the naked emotion in her eyes, her faint apricot scent. She was *right there,* her breath caressing his skin. All he had to do was shift, so he did.

His lips brushed hers, lingered. She stiffened. He waited for her to push him away. Instead, her mouth settled against his and a breathless broken sound came from her throat.

Driven purely by the hot slide of her mouth, Gage teased her lips open, trying to rein in the urge to drag her into his lap, bury himself in her.

He was shaking, unable to believe she wasn't fighting him. She tasted like every good thing he'd lost.

His heart nearly stopped when her arms crept around his neck. She was trembling, just as he was. He was starving for her. He told himself to go slow, savor the honeyed heat of her mouth, but he'd wanted her too long, missed her too much.

Still, he managed some control until she pressed hard against him and he felt the fullness of her breasts through her sweater and sweatshirt. He nearly lost it.

His hands cupped her skull and he ate at her mouth. Selfishly, greedily taking what he could get, knowing that any second she would pull away.

And she did.

Breathing hard, she placed her hands on his shoulders and held him back. "No," she panted. "Stop."

Yes, she was calling a halt, but for the first time since Gage had found her at the lake house, hope flared that she might give them another chance.

She must've seen it on his face. Shaking her head, she moved away. The dreamy desire in her eyes shifted to regret, then a cool remoteness. "No. We're over. I can't be with you."

"Even after the trial?" His body ached for her. He literally hurt deep down in his gut.

"The trial has nothing to do with us. We didn't end our relationship because of Operation Smoke Screen. It wasn't the reason things went wrong between us. It was just the last straw. I couldn't be second to your job anymore."

We hadn't ended their relationship. *She* had.

"You still want me."

"It doesn't matter."

"Baby—"

"I won't let you hurt me again," she whispered.

The way she was hurting him now. And it did hurt. He knew she had no reason to trust he wouldn't screw things up again, but that didn't stop the flash of anger he felt at himself, at her, the whole situation.

"Don't…kiss me again."

He wanted to point out that while he may have started it, she'd done as much as he had, but he bit back the words. Curling his hands into fists, he managed to keep from reaching for her.

As she edged away, he had the insane impulse to

keep kissing her until she changed her mind. There was no way in hell that would turn out well.

He'd hurt her too much and evidently he'd be paying for that jackass mistake the rest of his life. No matter how badly he wanted her, pressuring her about it was selfish. He couldn't do it, even though he knew she still felt something for him.

This time, maybe their last time together, had to be all about what she needed. He didn't want to hurt her anymore.

Chapter 6

Gage stayed where he was, leaning back against the driver's side seat, knees bent. He was rock-hard and it took a couple of minutes for his blood to cool. Frost filmed the windows of the SUV. Wrapped in the blanket Meredith had given him, his warm breath puffing out into the frigid air, he could still feel the hot slide of her mouth against his. The freezing temperature didn't do a thing to douse the burn she'd started in his body.

She lay a foot away, huddled in a ball under her blanket. In the darkness, he caught the occasional glimpse of her pale hair above the blanket, the white of her socks and part of her shoes sticking out the bottom. If there had been enough light, Gage knew he would've been able to see that her lips were blue. She shifted, turned, wrapped her feet in the blanket for the third time.

Neither of them would get any sleep like this.

He'd already dug a hole with her so he went ahead and dug it deeper. "We need to huddle together, Meredith."

He waited. One, two—

She rolled toward him, peeking over the edge of her blanket. *"What?"*

"It's really cold in here." The chill bored into his shoulder like a drill. "I think we can handle combining our body heat for one night. At least, *I* can."

He'd known that would get her. The sharp look she gave him pierced through the thick darkness like a blade. She sat up slowly, the shadows of the night shifting around her.

"If you're worried about me getting off on it, don't be." *He* would have to worry about it, but she wouldn't.

"I'm not worried about…that."

Even though he couldn't see her very well, he felt her gaze drop to his lap. All his nerve endings popped and his body clenched. Damn. "I got the message a while ago, Meredith. You're not interested in picking up where we left off."

"That's right."

Did she have to sound so certain about it? "We proved this morning we can sleep in the same bed without me jumping you. I want you, Meredith, but I do understand the word *no*."

"I know that." She sounded defensive.

"Okay, then."

She hesitated, which pissed him off. What did she think he was going to do? Tear off her clothes and start in on her?

"Yes or no?" he snapped.

"Yes, but I'll sleep behind you."

"Whatever," he muttered.

She crawled around him as he scooted to the middle of the vehicle. After he arranged his blanket beneath them, Meredith helped smooth it out then handed over their only pillow as she lay down.

Once she was on her side facing him, he settled the other covering over them, tucking it around her feet before he turned his back to her and stretched out as best he could on his left side.

They both ducked their heads beneath the blanket to trap as much heat inside their makeshift cocoon as possible. Behind him, she was as stiff as a rail.

The cold sank down around them one numbing layer at a time. Meredith had been taking care of him since he'd arrived. He would like to do the same for her once.

He caught the scent of her fragrant skin, her shampoo. "Better?" he asked quietly.

"Yes, thanks." Her voice was muffled, her breath a hot puff through his shirt.

She still hadn't relaxed. The only way she would was if he showed her she didn't need to worry about something happening between them.

"I'm going to sleep now, so don't try anything."

He felt more than heard her soft laugh at his teasing. After a few long moments, their breathing leveled out. Gage's muscles began to warm. Meredith burrowed into him. She had to be asleep or she wouldn't have done it.

Her cheek lay flat between his shoulder blades, her

breasts burned into his back. The cradle of her thighs held him tight.

Like a short-circuited screen, images flashed through his brain of them naked. His hands on her, in her. His mouth, too. Over and over and over.

Excellent idea, Parrish. You idiot. Finally, he could feel his toes again, his fingers. And every inch of Meredith.

Since forsaking his old life, he'd dealt with only memories, but this was her in the flesh. *Her* flesh against *his*.

Warm breath whispered past his ear. Her hair tickled the back of his neck. The sweet woman scent of her settled in his lungs. She shifted, her arm sliding over his hip and he ground his teeth. He wanted to reach for her, curve his hand around the back of her thigh and lock her to him, but he didn't.

He wanted her body, but he wanted her trust more.

He was going to keep his word, even though she had just kissed him as if she wanted to crawl inside him. He could handle this. He *would* handle it.

He'd have a lot more confidence in that if he hadn't been dreaming for the past year about having her right up against him.

When early morning light filtered into the SUV, Meredith came awake, toasty-warm, her cheek pressed against Gage's shoulder blade. Except for the occasional rustle of an animal outside, all was quiet. Meredith registered that her right hand lay flat against Gage's hard belly. As if she were holding him to her. Even beneath two shirts, she could feel the muscles of his abdomen. His heat pulsed against her like a furnace.

Cold air stung her ear and the side of her face. A thick frost covered all the windows.

Still half-asleep, she wanted to slide her hands under his clothes and rub against his hot bare flesh, stroke her hands across his chest, his stomach. Lower.

The fierce want startled her out of her drowsiness. After she'd told him there would be no touching, she was stuck to him like varnish on a dresser.

She could tell by Gage's utter stillness that he was awake, too. Great.

Before she could move, his body coiled tighter against hers. He shifted, his backside brushing against her and causing a tickle of warmth low in her belly.

"Morning." The word came out grainy, velvet-rough.

His deep slumberous voice stroked over her like a touch and triggered memories she didn't want. Meredith squeezed her eyes shut. "Good morning."

She sounded breathless and a strange urgency hammered through her. For cryin' out loud!

She'd told him no touching, no kissing and last night, they'd done both. She might have been unaware of putting her arm around him while asleep, but she had gone into that kiss knowing full well what she was doing. Despite telling herself to pull away the instant she'd seen the intent in his face, she hadn't been able to make herself move. She'd looked in his eyes and her stomach had tumbled, just like the first time he'd kissed her.

So far, she'd done everything she'd told him *not* to

do. Irritated, she dragged her hand off him and scooted back, huddling inside her coat, which she'd slept in.

He sat up, scrubbing a hand down his face. "Did you get any sleep?"

"Yes." The frigid air had goose bumps breaking out all over her body as she came up on her elbow.

Half expecting him to gloat over the fact that he'd kept his hands to himself and she hadn't, she couldn't look at him. Meredith pulled her coat tighter around her.

They climbed out and quietly checked the area then scraped the frost from the windows as best they could. She knew Gage was as relieved as she was when they discovered they were alone. The quiet around them made Meredith fairly certain there were no other vehicles nearby.

Feeling it was safe enough, Meredith started the car and turned on the heater. They waited only a couple of minutes before slowly forging their way out the other side of the thick woods. Getting through and around the crowded trees, and over mounds of packed dirt and twigs required all of her concentration.

At some point, she stopped expecting Gage to taunt her about draping herself all over him. She certainly wasn't going to mention it.

Descending the twisting, steep roads down the back side of the mountain took over an hour. Then another hour to circle around and reach the highway a few miles south of where they had turned off it last night. There was no sign of anyone following or posted near the highway, watching for them. If the person who had tailed them was waiting, he was probably north of them, close to where they'd left the highway to take the road leading to Watson.

Once Gage and Meredith were back at the cabin, they carried in the things they'd picked up in Texarkana.

He'd been quiet during their drive, but when he walked past her into the cabin, admiration glinted in his eyes. "That was some slick driving, Doc. Good hiding place."

"Thanks." She didn't want to admit how his praise warmed her. "Growing up, I never thought I'd have to go up there to lose a tail."

They left the blankets and pillow in the SUV. While Gage put away his small suitcase and shaving kit, Meredith heated up chili for lunch. After eating, she checked Gage's wound and put on a fresh bandage. She showered, then he did.

They were both quiet throughout the day. Restless and frustrated about waking up all over him, Meredith wanted more than the space of one room between them, but she wasn't going to get it anytime soon. She started a load of laundry and tried to take a nap.

Gage sat at the round kitchen table with his notebook and the dead marshal's laptop. Meredith finished folding and putting away the laundry, wondering how long they would be here.

Gage was completely, totally focused on his notes, seemingly unaware of anything else. Of her. How irritating. And familiar.

Turning off all but the kitchen light, Meredith made her way into the living area. She discovered the fireplace in the corner burned on fake logs, not real wood.

They could have a fire without having to worry about smoke from the chimney.

She settled on the red leather sofa and turned on the television to watch the news, relieved when there was no mention of a dead marshal, protected witnesses, Gage or her. An image of Nowlin lying dead in her hall blazed across her mind.

Since shooting him, she thought about it frequently and would for a long time to come. But she didn't want to think about it now. She didn't want to think about anything although she couldn't stop her thoughts from going to the big man at the table behind her. Or that panty-melting kiss they'd shared. Or waking up this morning draped over him like a blanket.

Across the few feet separating them, Meredith caught his woodsy masculine scent. Shoulders angled into the corner of the sofa, she propped her head on her fist and tried to watch a late-night talk show, but her gaze kept sliding to Gage.

To look at him, one would think the only thing on his mind was his notebook. Meredith wished her thoughts would go to something else, but watching him made her think about that kiss, want more. And regret it at the same time.

She itched to offer any help she could, but she stubbornly, selfishly wanted to keep her distance from him. Especially since he acted as if last night had never happened.

That stung, she admitted grudgingly. How could their kiss be so easy for him to dismiss?

Finally, she gave up trying not to look at him. He wasn't aware of her, so she could look all she wanted.

In the white light of the fixture hanging over the kitchen table, his hair was the color of dark sand. The gray, long-sleeved T-shirt he'd bought in Texarkana stretched taut across his wide shoulders and deep chest. Her gaze roamed up his strong corded neck, the blunt planes of his face, the smooth firm lips she could still feel against hers. That she wanted to feel in other places.

Her attention rested on his whiskered face. The four days' growth was more than she'd ever seen. The only times she'd seen him unshaven were when he'd gone on weeklong deer hunts with her brothers. The scruffy beard did nothing to soften his blunt features.

It did give him an unfamiliarity she found intriguing. As if he were a stranger inside a body she knew well. The contrast struck a chord deep inside her, kindling a dark, new temptation.

It made her wonder what things she didn't know about him.

Remembering the soft scrape of his beard against her chin when he'd kissed her, heat flushed her body. "What is your life like now?"

He looked up, his face guarded.

"Can you tell me anything? Should I not ask?"

"I can tell you some." He sat back, laying down his pen and easing his chair a few inches away from the table. "What do you want to know?"

"Do you have a different name?"

"The first name is Greg. I shouldn't tell you the last name."

She tilted her head. "I can't see you as a Greg."

"You're not the only one," he said drily. "Sometimes,

I still don't realize people are talking to me when they call me that. It's weird. I want to tell them my real name."

"That has to be hard." And it sounded agonizingly lonely. "You said you work as a car mechanic. Are you a volunteer fireman?"

"No. If you're in the Witness Security Program, it's best to keep away from any aspect of your former life. Or that's what they say," he added bitterly.

"You can have friends, though, right? You don't have to stay away from society, do you?"

"No, not at all. I have friends. My neighbor Ralph and I play poker one night a week. He's not as good as Aaron, but he's beat me plenty."

She caught the wistfulness in his words. "Do you socialize with anyone from work?"

"Not really. I get along with all of them, but don't feel comfortable just hanging out."

"Ever spend time with women?" The question was out before she could stop it.

His gaze measured her. "No."

She couldn't imagine that he'd been celibate since their breakup and she wanted to ask if he'd been with anyone. On second thought, she didn't want to know.

"Most nights, I work on trying to figure out the mystery ingredient in the disappearing accelerant." A grin hitched up one corner of his mouth. "Have you learned how to cook? Or do you eat out all the time?"

"Hey, I cook a little!"

"Pouring cereal in a bowl isn't cooking, Meredith."

She laughed at his dry remark. "Okay, I usually pick

up something and eat at home, unless Terra or Robin take pity on me and invite me over for a meal."

She remembered all the times he'd cooked for her. Especially his wonderful breakfasts in bed after she'd worked a wretchedly long shift. It would be better not to bring that up.

She gestured toward his face. "Are you planning to grow a beard?"

"No. I just can't shave—I mean, I haven't shaved yet."

Maybe he wasn't strong enough yet to shave on his own? Or his shoulder hurt too badly? "Do you need help? I could help you."

"No." The word was flat, hard and his face closed against her.

"I don't mind."

"No touching, remember?" He didn't snarl the words, but close.

Meredith's spine went to steel and she sat up straighter. So, last night *had* affected him.

His gaze fixed on her mouth, so long that she felt her body start to soften.

Flustered by his focus, frustrated by how badly she wanted him, she spoke without thinking, "We've done fine when I check your wound. That involves touching."

A muscle in his jaw flexed. "Not the same thing, not by a long shot."

"It wouldn't take very long. Think how good it would feel to shave it off."

"No."

"Oh, good grief, Gage! I didn't say we would do it naked."

His eyes went dark, savagely hot as he said in a harsh voice, "You touch me, I'm touching you."

She blinked.

"How much of that do you think I can stand?" He stood, his chair scraping across the tile floor. "Hell, I couldn't even close my eyes last night. All I could do was feel you."

"You're the one who wanted to share body heat," she muttered.

He gave her a scathing look. Her heart hammered hard.

He jerked his thumb toward the bedroom which they had to pass through to get to its adjoining bath. "If you're up for it, baby, let's go. Give me a green light. I've waited a long time to get my hands on you again."

Oh, wow. She couldn't breathe. The heavy-lidded look he gave her burned right through her clothes. Had he always been this intense?

He was aroused. So was she. But she also sensed pain beneath his words.

She rose, palms slick with sweat. "I'm sorry. You're right. I should've realized, but... I'm sorry."

She couldn't tell if it was disappointment or anger that had his jaw firming. She wanted to touch him. Wanted him to touch her. Talk about walking right into stupid.

"I think I'll get ready for bed." Her voice shook.

"I'll sleep out here on the couch."

"We should take shifts, keep watch."

He grunted.

Feeling hollow, she walked around the sofa, heading down the hall. "Let me know when it's my turn. You need to rest, too."

He didn't say anything. A glance over her shoulder showed him sitting back down. Instead of immediately opening his notebook, Gage closed his eyes and pinched the bridge of his nose. Tension vibrated in his body.

Last night had affected him as much as it had her. It didn't give her any satisfaction to learn he'd been as wound up over it as she had. Instead, she felt sad.

She shut the bedroom door, her heart aching.

All day, she'd wanted to touch him. She still did. She told herself to dismiss it, to stop thinking about that kiss, but she couldn't stop thinking about it.

Because she wanted him, too. And that was the worst thing for both of them.

She was killing him. Being this close to her was going to snarl his guts into a permanent kink, especially now that he'd finally had another taste of her. Gage wanted to hit something. Even now, hours later, he could *still* taste her. And one kiss wasn't going to be enough.

Thanks to Meredith being plastered to him like cling wrap last night, Gage had been hard and hurting for hours. It wasn't until they got to the cabin that he had finally managed to get a little relief. Then she'd asked questions about his other life and started in on the shaving thing. That had fired him up again and brought back the feel of her lush curves against his back, the dark sweetness of her mouth.

Arousal had mixed with anger, started a slow boil inside him. Which was why he had told her point-blank what she could expect if she touched him. She couldn't just change the rules whenever she felt like it. If she couldn't make up her mind about what she wanted, he'd do it for her. Because he knew exactly what he wanted. Her.

She may have finally gone to bed, but her scent still lingered. Even so, that was easier to deal with than her sitting in the living area looking at him with those liquid blue eyes.

He bit back a groan. He'd nearly tumbled her onto that couch and kissed her until she agreed to do anything he wanted.

His resistance to her was *thisclose* to finished. Despite the smallness of the cabin, he planned to keep as much physical distance between them as possible.

He hadn't been able to gather his thoughts while she moved around. Went back and forth. *Breathed.*

With his concentration split like that, it would've been easy to miss something helpful in his notes so he started at the beginning. It took him fifteen minutes to settle down and focus his attention.

After a few hours, a headache throbbed behind his eyes. He rose from his chair at the table and walked to the narrow window left of the front door. Bracing his good shoulder against the wall, he stared out into the night, over the shallow porch, the red packed-earth road, the trees beyond. The moon was a cold sliver of ice in an inky sky.

"Is everything okay?" Meredith asked.

He started, his head whipping toward her.

"Sorry. I tried not to come up on your right, but your other side was against the wall."

He wished he hadn't told her about his loss of peripheral vision, but with her training there was no way to get around it. She was barefoot, which explained why he hadn't heard her. Her hair was down and she wore her pink leopard-print pajama bottoms and the pink long-sleeved cotton top that snugged her breasts just right. In two seconds, he could slip right under her shirt and have his hands on her.

He directed his gaze back out the window. "Everything's fine. Why?"

"I saw the light on. Is it my turn to take a shift?"

"No, go on back to bed. I'll do it tonight."

"But you said you didn't get any sleep last night."

He sure as hell didn't need her to remind him. "I took a nap this afternoon. Plus I want to go over my notes again."

"Any luck figuring out your mystery accelerant?"

"Not yet." Even the smell of recently brewed coffee didn't mask her light frothy scent. He straightened, cursing softly. "The answer's probably right under my nose, an ingredient or a combination I haven't considered."

She came closer, close enough that if he reached out, he could stroke her silky skin. Jamming his hands in his jeans pockets, Gage clenched his jaw tight.

"Would it help to talk it out? I know a little chemistry."

Talking wasn't what he needed help with. He needed to get her out of pouncing distance. "I don't know."

"I might see something you didn't."

Her chemistry background would be helpful, but he'd only just gotten his body past their earlier conversation. As he dragged his gaze over her, he wanted to move in closer, kiss her, peel off her clothes. Especially when he saw her nipples tighten under his perusal.

She realized where he was looking and backed up a step, a delicate blush playing over her cheeks. Seeing her brother's denim shirt on the back of the chair where Gage had hung it, she grabbed it and slipped it on. Folding her arms, she met his gaze defiantly.

It didn't matter that she was warning him off. If possible, his body wound even tighter. Accepting her help would force him to share more space with her than he wanted, but he needed a fresh pair of eyes. And if he tried anything, she would knock him into next week. "All right, yeah."

Her blue eyes widened. "Oh. Okay, good."

He moved around her, trying to ignore her provocative body-warmed scent. She followed him, taking the chair next to his and scooting closer.

Hell. She'd told him she wasn't interested. That should've been enough to cool him off, but it wasn't. He pushed his notebook to her and while she began reading, he recounted his progress.

"So far, I've determined the accelerant is an egg-based gelled flame fuel."

She looked up, frowning. "Gelled, like jelly?"

"Right."

"Not a liquid."

He shook his head. "If it were, there would be a trail of accelerant. Even concrete can soak up liquids and none of the surfaces in these blazes—concrete, wood or fabric—have retained anything. The fire-starting material has to be something that doesn't penetrate."

"And a jellylike substance wouldn't?"

"It normally would, but it could be coated to prevent that from happening."

"Coated? With wax?"

"Probably."

"So, the flammable gel is made of eggs—"

"Egg whites."

"Okay. Egg whites and gasoline then thickened with—" She glanced down. "Salt and tea leaves?"

"Those are only two possibilities. Further in the notes, you can see I also tested cocoa, sugar, baking soda, Epsom salts." He leaned over her to flip the page and point to the details he'd noted.

His muscles clenched against the teasing drift of her breath against his cheek. When she bent her head to read, her hair brushed the back of his hand.

He pulled away.

"A lot of things can work as a thickener, but I'm trying to determine if more thickener is the secret to making the accelerant disappear or if it's a specific ingredient."

"That's why it's taking so long to find an answer."

"Yeah."

As she went back to reading, he eased away, his attention fully engaged by her even though he wasn't looking at her. He was riding the edge of want. Was she?

After a few minutes, she looked up, her eyes crystal-blue in the light. She indicated a place in his notes. "I think you're right about the coating on the flammable jelly being wax. It would prevent a rapid breakdown, but wouldn't the wax also leave a trace?"

"Generally, but I think the reason it doesn't is because of what is mixed with it."

"And that's what we need to figure out."

He murmured agreement, forcing his gaze away from the pulse tapping in the hollow of her throat.

"So, egg whites, gasoline, thickener and wax. What kind of wax? Candle-making wax?"

"I tested that and also the wax used for preserving food, for canning. So far, that one seems to work the best."

"Isn't wax flammable?"

"Yeah."

"Which means if it's too hot when the gas-jelly is dipped in it, a fire could start if the temperature is misjudged by even a small bit."

He nodded. "That's why I think whoever is behind this is someone with extensive fire training."

"Or they're a chemist."

"That's possible, I guess." Gage had considered that in the beginning, but his gut said no.

She thumbed through a couple of pages. "You've tried granulated cane sugar. How about powdered sugar? Brown sugar? Or syrup?"

He grinned. "I like the way your mind works."

The slow smile she gave him had his heart knocking hard against his chest.

"Let's make a list of what I've tested and similar products I haven't," he suggested.

Meredith read aloud while he jotted down the possibilities. She was methodical and thorough, one of the few people who had ever matched him in that regard. They had always been able to help each other with problems in their jobs, but they hadn't ever done it while trying to ignore this fierce awareness between them.

He didn't know how long he could hold out.

Chapter 7

The next day, just before noon, Meredith stood at the front window of the cabin, her nerves jangling. Where was Gage? What was taking so long?

He had left a note saying he'd discovered a flat on the SUV this morning and had gone to get a new tire. The drive from here to the nearest gas station took about twenty minutes. So, there and back equaled less than an hour. Maybe another half-hour to pay for the tire and mount it himself. But he'd been gone nearly four hours.

What if that Julio guy had found Gage? Or what if Gage had seen the Hispanic man and tried to lose him by going back up into the mountains, then was unable to find his way down? He had a cell phone, she consoled herself. So, if something had happened, he would've called.

Unless he was hurt and couldn't.

What if Julio *had* hurt him and Gage disappeared? Just like a year ago.

The thought put a hard knot in Meredith's belly. What would she do if he didn't return? What *could* she do? Call his friend, the State Attorney General, and tell him.

Meredith wasn't typically a worrier, but from the moment Gage had shown up in her lake house, bleeding profusely, things had been unpredictable and weird to say the least.

The crunch of gravel and the soft rumble of a motor had her easing to the side of the window, out of view. A silver SUV passed by—Gage's vehicle—and she leaned into the wall, eyes stinging at her overwhelming relief. He was all right.

After a few seconds, the automobile's door slammed and she walked to the back of the cabin, making sure it was Gage who got out of the SUV. Quickly wiping her eyes, she opened the door as he walked across the frozen, pine-needled ground and took the two steps up to the deck carrying a small plastic bag. Clean sharp air swirled inside as he walked through the door.

Not wanting him to know how worried she'd been, she managed to keep her voice light. "Everything go all right?"

"Yeah." He frowned as he shut the back door with his foot, glancing at his watch. "I guess I was gone longer than I expected, but we can't risk not having a good tire when we need to leave."

She preceded him to the kitchen, where he placed the

bag on the counter next to the sink. "I bought a couple of cell phones—untrackable."

Not wanting to reveal how worked up she'd made herself, she kept her face averted.

"There was no trouble," he said. "I just wanted to make sure I wasn't followed. And I wasn't."

"That's good." She stared blankly at the plastic sack.

Behind her, he opened the refrigerator door and studied the contents inside.

"The tire shop at the gas station where I stopped wasn't open yet so I had to wait."

"I see."

He hesitated then peered around her shoulder to look at her. His breath grazed her temple. "You weren't worried, were you?"

"No."

After watching her for a few seconds, he reached for her hand, then pulled back. "You *were* worried. I'm sorry. I should've called."

She wanted to brush off his apology, say she was fine, but instead she said, "If you'd gotten into some kind of trouble, I wouldn't have known what to do. Or how to find you. Or who to ask for help."

He stilled, as if the possibility had only then occurred to him, too. "If something happens and I can't contact you, call Ken Ivory. I'll write down the number for you."

"Okay."

He jammed his hands into the front pockets of his jeans. "Were you afraid I'd disappear? Again?"

That was exactly what she'd feared. She looked at

him then, her pulse skipping when she saw the concern in his blue eyes. After a moment, she nodded.

"I really am sorry." His gaze stroked over her, making her skin heat.

At that moment, Meredith really wanted to touch him. She caught herself and stepped away, giving a brittle laugh. "I'm fine. You know how I think everything to death. I just got carried away."

"Meredith—"

"You're here now and no one followed you," she said brightly. "That's what matters."

He studied her for a minute. "Wanna eat before we set up our lab?"

She nodded, taking his now-empty bag and folding it to place under the sink with the others. "I thought I'd call Terra."

His gaze sliced to her. "What? Why?"

"To ask for some chemistry help. I won't mention anything about you or the task force or any kind of trouble. If she asks, I'll tell her I can't explain why I need to know."

He was silent for a moment. "Use one of the new phones and keep it short. I don't think anyone's on to us, but the fewer chances we take, the better."

She agreed, calling her fire-investigator friend while Gage made grilled cheese sandwiches.

When she hung up and turned off the phone, he glanced at her. "Was she any help?"

"Maybe. I'll know when we start experimenting."

After a quick lunch and cleanup, they began. Meredith wished she hadn't been so transparent about her worry, but she couldn't just push aside her concern. Just as she hadn't been able to block the want that had started a slow throb in her blood last night when he'd warned her what would happen if she touched him.

That macho stuff usually aggravated her, but last night, for some perverse reason, she'd liked it. Enough that she'd dreamed about him. *Them.* Sweaty, hard-pulsing sex dreams that left her aching even now.

In an effort to cool her blood, she reminded herself how things ended between them eighteen months ago. Though she wanted him, she didn't want everything that came with wanting him.

But had she been the one to draw the line? Oh, no. It had been Gage.

After being stifled for so many months, her hormones were tap-dancing. She could tell herself it was because she hadn't been with anyone since him, but she knew her body wouldn't respond this way to just any man. It was Gage. He'd always affected her this way.

But Meredith wouldn't let herself get distracted by that. Or by brushing elbows with him. The glancing touches, the occasional graze of his hip against hers made her edgy, restless. Hungry. She didn't want to get involved with him again. Their problem was too fundamental—she'd always been second to his job—and he hadn't ever seemed willing to change. Meredith didn't know if a person *could* change that much. Or even if they should. Such single-minded focus was what made him excel at his job.

They stood shoulder to shoulder over the kitchen

counter. He smelled of the sharp outdoor air and woods and an earthy musk. She didn't know if their working so closely was such a good idea, but she wanted to help, so here they were.

They'd decided to test three thickeners at a time. That would enable them to keep track of their results without getting too much information at once.

To begin, they made the egg-based gasoline gel by separating the egg whites from the yolks, then pouring the whites into a jar and adding the fuel.

They chose powdered sugar, baking soda and Epsom salts as their first thickening agents. After adding those ingredients to the jars, Gage handed Meredith a cooking thermometer. "While I'm stirring the mixture, you heat up some water. Let me know when it's at sixty-five degrees."

"What are we doing?" She searched under the cabinet next to the store and pulled out a two-quart-sized saucepan.

"Making the gel thicker. After it cools to room temperature, we'll dip it in the paraffin."

They worked in silence for a bit and Meredith found her attention wandering to Gage. He worked with confident, yet careful movements. The smothering odor of gasoline grew stronger and she wrinkled her nose.

"Where are we going to set fire to this stuff?" she asked.

"Out back in the galvanized tub I found against the side of the cabin. We can fill some small buckets with water to have close by in case we accidentally torch something."

She nodded, watching as he delicately handled an

egg. She remembered his strong broad hands on her, touching her face, stroking the small of her back, trailing low across her stomach.

A sharp tug of desire jerked her to attention and she shifted away. Tension coiled in her shoulders. The cabin was starting to feel about as big as a cracker box.

She focused on the water heating on the stove. As she checked its temperature, she felt Gage's gaze do a slow glide down her body and back up. Even pretending to ignore him didn't stop the sparks of heat shooting through her whole body.

She wanted him just as much as he wanted her, maybe more considering she hadn't had sex since they'd split up. Had he? She wasn't asking.

He had loved her. Meredith had never doubted that, which made it more difficult to understand his unwillingness to get married. It had taken her months to realize and accept that he really didn't want to have a wedding, but once she had, she'd returned his ring.

She'd been willing to commit. He hadn't. Why?

She'd never known for sure. At the time, she'd been too hurt and angry to ask him. Did it matter why? Did it matter *now?*

Yes, she decided. She turned, resting her hip against the corner of the stove so she could see him. Water bubbled in the heating pot. A foot away, Gage stirred the contents of a jar, his spoon clinking against the glass.

In the quiet of the small kitchen, her words were stark, bald. "Why didn't you ever want to get married?"

He froze, spoon in midair over another jar, his back

to her. After a long moment, he laid the silverware on a paper towel and turned to face her. Both hands curled over the counter's edge, as if he were bracing himself.

"I did want to get married." His blue eyes burned into hers. "That's why I proposed."

If you'd wanted to get married, we would have! Meredith bit back the scathing words. "You wouldn't ever agree on a date or suggest one that worked for you."

He looked down at the floor, his jaw working. Then he seemed to come to a decision and lifted his gaze to hers. "I had this stupid idea that I'd be giving up more than I wanted to."

"More what?" She stiffened. "Freedom?"

"That, and control."

Stung, she couldn't breathe for a moment. "You make it sound like I was forcing you to get married. As if I could. You *were* the one who asked. When you propose to someone, it's supposed to be because you want to be with them, not because you feel like you can't get away from them."

"Don't put words in my mouth."

"Did I make you feel trapped?" Her voice thickened. "Chained to me?"

"No."

"Then what?"

"I never wanted to get away from you. I just wasn't ready for marriage, but I didn't know that until I went into WitSec. That's when I figured out my priorities weren't in good order. My priorities about a lot of things, not just us. But being away from..." He hesitated, making her wonder if he had started to say something else. "Being alone sorted them out pretty quickly. That's when I realized the things I'd been forced to give up, the things I'd been worried about giving up were the things I wanted the most."

"Gave up?" Blinking away tears, she couldn't keep the bitterness out of her voice. "Some of it you pushed away."

"I know, and I take responsibility for that. Losing you made me open my eyes."

"Oh, please."

"It's true, Meredith," he said fiercely.

Fiercely enough that she shivered. She softened. "It's better that you knew before we got married. I wish *I'd* known sooner."

"Why? So you could've broken up with me earlier?"

"No." His scornful tone tripped her anger, her hurt. "So I wouldn't have been disappointed over and over."

"Do you want me to apologize again?" His voice was rough with emotion. "Say what an idiot I was? Open up a vein?"

"No, I don't want anything like that."

"What, then?"

She thought he winced before he glanced away. The regret in his face was every bit as sharp as what she felt over them. Over what she'd just said. She mentally chided herself. She didn't want to hurt him, didn't want to hurt herself anymore. "It didn't work out and now I know why. I've always wondered. Thanks for telling me."

Right now she wanted to touch him more than anything. Those gas fumes must be going to her head. "I just wanted some answers."

"For closure?" he asked tiredly.

Meredith was afraid there would never be closure. She shook her head. "No, just answers."

He searched her eyes and it took supreme self-control to hide what was happening inside her. Finally, he nodded and turned back to stir the gas-gel mixture.

She felt as if she were going to shatter into tiny pieces. How could she stand so close to him and pretend she was over him? She didn't know, but somehow she would. He might've been the one to draw the line in their relationship, but she'd be the one to make sure they didn't cross it.

Damn it, she drove him crazy. Gage didn't see how he could be more conscious of her than he had been before the "marriage" talk, but he was.

As they worked together in the following hours, they kept their conversation strictly to the experiments or the news. But it was as if every second brought a heightened awareness of her, even outdoors.

The next afternoon, they stood on the small deck of the cabin, setting fire to another block of gasoline gel. The sun was bright, the air crisp. Images of Meredith, sharp and clear, and without the dark winter coat that hit her midthigh, looped through his brain.

He pictured the soft curve of her neck, the elegant line of her back, those long sleek legs and perfect backside. And even though the bite of gasoline drowned her subtle scent, Gage knew he could find it in the warm crook of her neck or at her wrist.

It was killing him.

Her question from yesterday still circled through his head. He hadn't wanted to tell her why he'd dragged his feet about getting married. Women never understood stuff like that exactly as men meant it, but he'd spent the past year letting her believe a lie. He wasn't lying to her about anything else.

He'd been crazy in love with her, so it had taken him a while to figure out why he hadn't wanted to set a date for their wedding. Now that he knew the reason, he didn't mind if Meredith knew, too. If he ever got a second chance with her—and he wasn't holding his breath—he wanted her to know he realized how wrong he'd been.

But explaining his reasons had put more distance between them. Gage told himself that was good because it was what she wanted. But it bugged the hell out of him.

Since yesterday, they'd tested and made detailed notes on nineteen combinations of accelerants. Each of the burned blocks of gel fuel had left residue from at least one of its ingredients, except for the last two. Only a trace remained of those so Gage wanted to test the same combinations using different amounts of certain elements and see what happened.

They were discussing which to try first when they were interrupted by a ring tone from inside the enclosed back porch. "Don't Stop Believin'" by Journey pegged the ringing phone as Meredith's. Setting Gage's notebook on the window ledge, she moved to answer it, the screened door clattering shut behind her.

With a cheerful greeting, she went inside the cabin. He wondered who was on the other end of the phone.

Four days. That was all he had left with her, depending on the outcome of the trial. And he had to keep his hands off her.

When she didn't return after a few minutes, Gage decided now was a good time for a break. They had yet to mix up the next gel sample so he gathered the tub and three small empty containers they'd used, then placed them just inside the screen door.

As he stepped into the welcome warmth of the cabin, he slipped off the down-lined coat Meredith had pestered him to buy in Texarkana. When he walked past the bedroom, he heard the low cadence of her voice. He hoped she didn't talk much longer. Just because they hadn't run up against any problems since their last cell phone call didn't mean their communications were safe.

He filled a tea kettle with water and set it on the stove to heat. After a couple of minutes, he heard her say goodbye to the caller and come down the short hallway toward the kitchen.

She stopped at the breakfast bar, looking across the counter where he stood next to the stove, dumping packets of cocoa mix into two mugs.

Before he could ask, she said, "That was Robin."

A call from Meredith's cop friend didn't automatically mean something was wrong, but the worry in her voice said there was. Gage's shoulders tightened. "Is your family all right?"

"Yes."

Relief rolled through him. When she didn't say anything more, he cocked his head. Her brow was furrowed and he could practically hear the wheels turning in her head. What was going on?

Sober-faced, she walked to the sofa and sat. Gage switched off the stove, moved the kettle of water to the hot pad on the counter and went to the matching red leather chair.

His knee brushed hers as he sank down into the seat. "What is it?"

The slow way she answered told him she was trying to remain calm. Concern shadowed her blue eyes. "Robin said someone broke into my house."

"What?" He stiffened in alarm.

"She's been going by my place to pick up my mail and check the house. When she went today, she discovered someone had been there. Nothing was taken that she could tell. They must have been interrupted."

Maybe, Gage thought, apprehension drumming through him.

"That isn't all. Early this morning, she had to stop by Presley Medical Center to take a statement. A nurse there told her a man with an Hispanic accent has called the hospital twice, wanting to speak to me, but when the nurse asked some questions, he hung up. Robin thinks that might've been the prowler's way of seeing if I was home."

After a minute, she said what Gage was thinking. "If the caller was Julio, he could've easily found out where I live *and* work from the dead marshal."

Julio also might've broken in to leave something, rather than take. The thought had Gage's nerves stretching taut.

"Robin's waiting to hear if any of the fingerprints found at the house are in the system."

Identifying prints would be a huge help. Gage hoped some were found. He had never gotten any prints from the Smoke Screen arsons because the torch had been careful not to leave any. Possibly because the arsonist knew that, despite popular belief, fingerprints didn't disappear in a fire. Which was another indicator that whoever was behind the arson ring had extensive fire knowledge. If the go-between who had set the Smoke Screen fires was the person who'd broken into Meredith's house, Detective Daly likely wouldn't get any prints, either.

"Terra told Robin about my call for some chemistry help."

The mention of Meredith's friend drew Gage's attention back to her.

"That plus the break-in and the fact that I've stayed down here longer than expected made her hinky. I told her everything was fine."

Her voice shook slightly and Gage checked the urge to take her hand. "That's good."

"That's why we haven't seen Julio." Meredith stood, her voice rising. "He's in Presley. There are pictures of Robin, Terra and me all over my house. What if he hurts them because he can't find me?"

"Let's not jump the gun." Gage got to his feet. "He probably can't identify them."

"If he's been watching my house, he'll recognize Robin from going there." Meredith sounded close to frantic as she paced to the opposite end of the couch. "And if she starts digging around, she could put herself in danger."

"She's a cop. She's good at protecting herself."

Meredith didn't look reassured. "I didn't breathe a word to either of them about you being alive or what we were doing, but Julio doesn't know that. He could think I told them."

It was true, which meant her friends might be in danger. Meredith definitely was, since the SOB was still looking for her.

Tension pulsed from her. Clasping her hands together tight enough to show white at the knuckles, she moved to the fireplace. "I need to warn them and my family."

"You can't." He reached for her, then pulled back. He hated this. He felt as if he'd be violating some sacred oath if he touched her in any way.

The flush of anger on her features didn't hide the fear also lurking there. "It's one thing for me to be involved in this, but them? What if my mom or dad go by the house? What if he hurts them?"

Gage understood her rising panic. It was bad enough when she worried about herself, but the idea that people she loved might be hurt stripped away her cool doctor persona. The same fierce loyalty and protectiveness had made her help Gage long after she should have stopped. "I'll call Ken Ivory and tell him what's happened."

"What can he do?"

"If it will make you feel better, I'll ask about having someone watch Terra and Robin. He won't be able to tell them about it, though."

"This is all because of you," she cried out, her eyes welling with tears.

It was, and the ripping, gouging hurt joined the guilt and regret he carried all the time. If he'd had any stones at all, he would've climbed right back into his SUV after she'd patched him up the first time, dragged himself out of her lake house on his belly if necessary. But he hadn't, and now here they were.

"I'm sorry, Meredith."

"I've got to call my family."

"We don't know what we're dealing with. Whoever broke in may have done nothing. Or he could've put a camera or microphones in your house."

Horror widened her eyes and she moved to the other side of the coffee table. "Robin won't know to look for anything. I need to tell her."

"You can't. Since nothing is missing, she'll try to figure out why someone broke in. She'll look at every inch of your house."

Gage cursed himself all over again for putting her in danger, but he couldn't let her warn her family. The risks to them *and* to Meredith would be even greater. If Julio thought her family might know about her killing the marshal or Gage coming back from the dead or the real mastermind behind those arsons, all hell would break loose.

Visibly trying to remain in control, she took a deep breath. "Can you call Ken now? Will you tell him about Robin and Terra, too?"

"Yes." The fear in her eyes hollowed out his gut. He wanted to go to her, put his arms around her, but he didn't. "If something were to happen, if Julio tries to threaten them, they can both take care of themselves.

Terra's husband is a cop. Robin is a cop. When I call Ken, I'll give him the addresses of your brothers and parents, too. He'll do something to help."

"Robin did say she planned to call Jack and tell him about the break-in and the phone calls to the hospital."

"That's good." Although Robin talking to Terra's husband didn't seem to reassure Meredith much. The rare vulnerability in her eyes had Gage's hands drawing up into fists so he wouldn't touch her. "Spencer will know what precautions to take and how to protect Terra."

"What if it's not enough?"

He had no answer. When he shook his head, a tear spilled down her cheek.

Gage couldn't help it. He went to her.

She edged away, around the corner of the sofa and he felt her withdrawal like a slap. "I need to be alone."

"Okay, yeah." Frustration and resentment rose at her obvious attempt to stay away from him.

She started down the hall.

"I'll bring you some hot chocolate—"

"No, thanks."

He ground his teeth. "If you need anything, I'll be on the deck."

She didn't respond, just went into the bedroom and shut the door.

He dragged a hand down his face. He wanted to go after her and just hold her, but it would be a mistake. Because if he got his hands on her again, he wasn't letting go.

Chapter 8

A few hours later, Meredith froze at the corner of the breakfast bar, her apology stuck in her throat. The round table was set with red earthenware plates, napkins, silverware and wineglasses. A toasty-lemony scent drifted to her. In the background, the Righteous Brothers crooned "You've Lost That Loving Feeling."

Gage looked up from the salad he was making. "Ready for supper?"

"What is this?" Her gaze skipped around the kitchen, over the two saucepans on the stove putting off a savory aroma, then back to the place settings. "What have you done?"

"Cooked?" With a crooked grin, he stepped over to the table and set down the bowl of mixed greens.

After what she'd said earlier, Meredith couldn't

believe he was even talking to her, let alone cooking. "I was awful to you earlier. Why would you do this?"

His gaze softened on her face before he turned away. "We have to eat, right?"

Her heart swelled painfully. He moved again to the table, carrying a bottle of chilled white wine and filling the two glasses.

"Have a seat." Returning with their plates, he placed them on the counter then opened the oven. The citrusy aroma of lemon-baked fish filled the small space.

She'd been planning to apologize even before this thoughtful gesture. "I'm sorry for what I said before, about this all being because of you."

"It *is,* Meredith."

"You have no more control over this than I do." Her nerves were raw from their close proximity, the waiting, being chased, hiding out, all of it. And the new fear that Julio could harm one of her best friends or family members had everything crashing in on her. "I was afraid and frustrated. You tried to reassure me and I jumped down your throat. I shouldn't have spoken to you that way."

"It's okay. You're entitled." Using a spatula, he slid one piece of fish from the baking pan onto a plate. "You were upset when you heard about the break-in at your house. I didn't like it, either. The situation is scary. You shouldn't even be involved in this."

"You wouldn't have put me in this position if you'd had a choice." She exchanged the filled plate for the empty one. "Will you accept my apology?"

"It isn't necessary, but okay."

She smiled, then noticed his smooth jawline. "You shaved."

"Yes."

The tautness of his voice tweaked at the tension that had been between them before she'd disappeared into the bedroom.

Changing the subject, she moved toward the table. "It smells wonderful."

He grinned and motioned her into a chair. "Stop stalling and find out for yourself."

They sat and Meredith bit into a flaky, tender piece of cod. "Oh, this is good!"

He took a bite, then gave a satisfied nod.

"You can't tell me you were getting tired of my specialty, sandwiches and soup."

"Just thought it would be nice to have something different."

"And wine. Wine is an excellent idea." Meredith studied him for a moment. While she'd been stewing, he'd been doing things, nice things.

In the background, Elvis began to sing "It's Now or Never." The overhead light glinted off the red plates. For a bit, the only sound, apart from the music, was the scrape of their silverware as they ate.

Gage glanced over. "I spoke to Ivory. He's going to have some people watch Robin and Terra. Your family, too."

"Thank you." The strong relief she felt had her wanting to grip his hand. Instead, she sipped at her wine, enjoying its crisp flavor.

As they ate, Gage asked about the man who had

been chief of the Oklahoma City Fire Department at the time of Gage's "demise" and Meredith updated him on current department politics.

She was still concerned about what might happen to her friends and family, but was reassured to know the State Attorney General was helping. She might've attributed her increasing calm to that, but when Gage made her laugh about something, she realized it was more due to him.

The atmosphere between them was comfortable as he told her he hadn't made any further progress with his tests that afternoon. They discussed everything from movies to music, and she began to relax.

He didn't act as if he were angry about her accusation earlier and Meredith was glad. Still, she noticed he was careful not to touch her. Not when she handed him her wineglass for a refill or when he passed her more steamed vegetables or reached for the salt. It drove her nuts.

Especially since she'd been thinking about what might have happened if she'd gone with him to the bedroom as he'd challenged a couple of days ago.

When they finished eating, he refused to let her help with cleanup. He poured her another glass of wine and sent her into the living room where he'd already turned on the gas fire. As she settled on the floor and rested back against the brick hearth, she snagged a magazine from a rack beside the television. Considering the way she'd acted earlier, she had expected coolness from Gage, not thoughtfulness. Her heart turned over in her chest.

The magazine was open, but her attention was on the big man in the kitchen. A faint lemony scent still hung in the air. He moved efficiently from the table to the sink, his shoulder looking stiff even though he didn't appear to be bothered by any pain there. Or by any of his other injuries.

The startling realization of how close he'd come to dying put a hard knot in her chest, just as it had when he'd told her that night on the mountain. The danger, the uncertainty weighed on her. It had to weigh on him, too.

Not wanting to put a damper on their evening, she turned her thoughts to dinner. When they'd been a couple, he had cooked for her frequently. He'd always said being a fireman gave him an edge over her because of the years he was responsible for meals on a regular basis at the firehouse. He was good at cooking, as he was at most things.

As he had been with her in the beginning.

From their first date, they had enjoyed each other's company without a single awkward, getting-to-know-you moment. And despite what had happened to them, being with him now steadied her. Even in these circumstances.

It also unlocked memories. The past was a dangerous place to visit and she'd tried desperately not to do it in the past eighteen months. She doubted Gage had intended for their supper to remind her of the way things used to be between them, but it did.

Without his wineglass, he joined her at the fireplace, easing down beside her. Bending one knee, he draped an arm over it. His other hand rested on his thigh.

"How's your shoulder?"

He glanced at it. "Not too bad."

"The stitches should be checked again tomorrow."

He nodded, reaching toward the coffee table for the television remote.

There was a good foot of space between them. Meredith should be glad for the distance; instead she was irritated. At him and herself. The less contact they had, the more she wanted.

When she'd come into the kitchen for supper, she'd been determined not to cross the line he'd drawn between them, but his thoughtfulness chipped away at her resolve.

"Remember the first time you cooked for me?" she asked. "It was breakfast." *In bed.* "You picked me up after a long shift and took me to your place."

"I remember." The way his voice deepened gave her a shiver.

After eating, they'd showered. And stayed in bed all day. A quick glance at his hot blue eyes told her he remembered everything as well as she did.

When an image of his hard naked body flashed through her mind, heat burned her neck and she looked away. "Thanks again for supper."

"You're welcome."

"You made me feel better. You always could." She was surprised at the sudden tears that stung her eyes.

Gage tilted his head back, staring at the ceiling. Her gaze trailed down the strong corded line of his neck. She wanted to trace it with her tongue, follow it to the hollow of his throat.

She sipped at her wine. He'd told her what would happen if she touched him. "You cooked for me, too, after the presentation I gave to the American Medical Association on burn treatment. That was the night—"

She stopped herself from reminding them both of the night she had realized she was in love with him.

They'd been dating about three months and that evening had been easy and quiet, much like tonight. Well, minus the danger and all the lies about his being dead.

"That's one of my favorite memories," she said.

"Mine, too," he murmured.

Sensation rippled through her, her smile faltering as she became aware of the words the Righteous Brothers sang. "Unchained Melody." Beside her, Gage stilled and she wondered if he was having the same memory that suddenly rushed over her.

A month after realizing her feelings for him, they'd come to her family's lake house. This song had been playing in the background the night he proposed on the back porch swing.

Suddenly, all the old feelings surged back. The deep joy they'd found in being together, the certainty that there was no one else for them, the belief they'd be together forever.

As she set her wineglass on the hearth, she looked over, her gaze locking with his. Yes, he remembered. His dark, half-lidded gaze made her body vibrate clear down to her toes.

Maybe it was the song—*their* song—but as the Righteous Brothers' smoky voices wrapped around her,

Meredith was swept into the past. All the good memories. She had missed him. She was tired of being without him. Before she even realized she'd moved, she leaned in and brushed her lips against his.

Gage froze, squashing the urge to haul her to him and crush his mouth to hers. After learning about the break-in at her house, he had seen how rattled she'd been. He'd wanted to do something nice for her, so he'd cooked. He hadn't expected *this* in return.

When he didn't move away, she kissed him again, a real kiss this time. Her soft lips coaxed his, teased, her tongue tickling the corner of his mouth before he let her in.

She tasted cool, honey-sweet. He wanted to strip her bare and drink her up. He wanted her to touch him. All over. All night.

By some unbelievable force of will, he managed to keep his hands to himself. Fierce need swelled inside him as he pulled back slightly. "Do you remember what I told you?"

Her gaze never left his. "Yes."

"Say it," he demanded roughly. Muscles coiling, he waited.

Waited to see exactly what she wanted, how far she would go. He saw a flicker of indecision and for one second he thought she would back off.

Then she whispered, "If I touch you, you touch me."

Hell, yes. He barely registered pulling her across his lap then taking her to the floor. Wasn't aware that he'd unbuttoned her soft plaid shirt until he pulled his mouth from hers to rake his teeth down her throat and found his fingers already curved around her breast.

He flicked the front clasp on her black lace bra. She spilled into his hand, soft and warm and perfect. His thumb rasped across her tight nipple.

She shifted beneath him, squeezing his thigh tight between hers and pushing her hands under his sweat-shirt to stroke his bare back. The broken way his name spilled from her throat jacked his pulse into overdrive.

Drawing in a deep breath of her faint apricot scent, Gage sank into a haze of sensation. He pushed aside the open edges of her shirt and looked at his sun-darkened skin against her creamy, petal-smooth flesh, flushed from his touch. He stroked his hand between her breasts then cupped her fullness. When he closed his mouth over her, she inhaled sharply. Chest tightening, his blood hammered in his veins.

The whole time he'd been in WitSec, he remem-bered being with her—how she felt beneath him, the way her breath caught when he slid inside her, the way she always linked hands with him afterward, as if she thought he might leave.

Murmuring, she pulled his head back to hers and kissed him. The hand on her breast trembled slightly. Beneath his touch, he felt her pulse jump.

He'd missed her like hell. He had no idea what was going on. All he knew was that she lay beneath him and he'd been waiting a damn long time to get her there.

One of her soft, hot hands dipped below the waist of his jeans, scoring the small of his back with her nails. Burning need spiked inside him. She slid the other palm around his waist to his stomach. A second later, his jeans were open and her hand moved inside his boxers.

She curled her fingers around him. The sigh she made against his mouth nearly set him off.

Some part of his brain still worked. Searching for control, he lifted his head, his breathing labored. Firelight chased across her rose-and-cream features. Dreamy blue eyes stared up into his.

"You sure about this?"

"Yes." Slipping one hand out from under his sweatshirt, she skimmed her fingers down his clean-shaven jaw. "I want you."

Wild blond curls fell across one cheek and part of her eye. He nudged them away, grazing his thumb across her cheekbone. She was so beautiful, it hurt to look at her.

His gaze tracked down her body and Meredith's heart nearly pounded out of her chest.

He slid her shirt off. She pressed against him, her lace and satin bra open so nothing was between their hot skin.

He kissed her until she couldn't feel her legs, drawing the strength from her before trailing his lips down her neck. Sliding one arm beneath her, he supported her as he laved and nipped his way to the swell of her breasts. He tugged off her bra, curling his tongue around her rosy puckered flesh.

"Oh, wow." She twisted against him. "Gage."

He opened her jeans, slipped his hand into her panties and curled his fingers inside her. A ragged moan spilled out of her throat.

The feel of his slightly rough flesh against the smoothness of hers had heat flashing across Meredith's skin and she thrust her hands into his hair, trying to steady herself. His every touch was slow and thorough. She'd always loved that, but she couldn't handle it this time.

That intensity focused on her was thrilling. And terrifying. She didn't want to feel everything she'd always felt with him. The emotion was too raw, tapped too much of the pain from their past. She needed him to hurry.

Shoving up his sweatshirt, she flexed her hands in the wiry golden hair on his chest. He was hot and solid.

Reaching behind him, he pulled his shirt over his head and dropped it. She rolled him to his back, careful of his injured shoulder. He filled his hands with her breasts and lifted up to take one nipple in his mouth.

Her throat went tight. "Let me touch you, Gage."

He allowed her to slide down his body. His fingers skimmed over her back, her shoulders, as she kissed his neck, breathing in the scent of man and soap. She slid her lips to his chest, scraped her teeth over his nipples, kept moving.

A sound rumbled out of him. He was breathing hard, one hand cupping her head. "Slow down, baby."

"No." A low throb worked through her body and she was taken aback by a sudden sting of tears.

She wrestled his jeans and boxers past his muscled thighs. Following the garments down his body, she nipped his flat stomach just below his navel then moved lower to do it again.

"Son of a—" He pulled her up, fastening his mouth on hers.

Worked every time, Meredith thought as he rolled her to her back. He slid his big hands into her panties and pushed them off.

"Hurry," she breathed against his mouth. She wriggled, wanting—needing—him to move now.

Holding her head, he settled between her thighs. His hot straining flesh pushed against her. Meredith wanted to look away from the raw desire blazing in his eyes, but she couldn't move. She could barely breathe.

She tightened her legs around his hips and he pressed against her.

Then froze. "Damn it!"

"What?" she cried out, her short nails digging into biceps of pure steel.

He straightened his arms, bracing himself over her. Color burned across his cheekbones. He was breathing hard, his arousal throbbing against her inner thigh. "I don't have protection. I haven't been with anyone since you so I haven't needed anything—"

"You were my last, too." She urged him closer. "Don't stop!"

Eyes glittering with savage desire, his jaw worked as he stared down at their bodies.

The intensity on his face made her shiver. "I'm still on the pill. We're both cle— Oh!"

He thrust hard, his arms going under her and pulling her tight into his chest.

As she buried her face in his neck, emotions swamped her. Old, new, good and bad. As right as

Gage felt inside her, against her, her heart ached. She couldn't bear it.

He began to move and her vision hazed at the sharp tight contractions that started almost immediately.

"No, baby, hold on." Taken aback by her quick climax, he could barely get the words out. He fought to control his body. "This is too fast."

"It's good." Breathing in his heady male musk, she pulled his earlobe between her teeth.

He hissed in a breath, fisting a hand in her hair and bringing her head up so he could crush his mouth to hers.

She shifted, her body meeting his at a higher angle. He moved deep and sure, driving into her until she came apart beneath him, then he went, too.

As their pulses slowed, her hands stroked the supple length of his spine.

He nuzzled her neck. His voice was thick, gritty. "Damn."

"Yeah." Both her voice and body shook. She tried desperately to keep from letting him back into her head, her heart. She told herself to get up, say good-night, but she couldn't move. Didn't want to.

Nor did she want to allow the thought that had gnawed at her since she'd jumped him, but it pushed through, anyway. She had more than crossed the line he'd drawn. She'd plowed right over it.

And she hoped she wouldn't come to regret it.

A few hours later, Gage woke in the king-size bed where they'd moved after making love in front of the fireplace. The empty space next to him registered about the same time he saw Meredith at the window, wrapped in a blanket. Bright moonlight washed through the half-open blinds, tinting her profile with silver, gilding her hair.

Was she all right? She'd acted fine after they'd made love, had been the one to lead him to the bedroom. Now she stood perfectly still staring out the window.

Gage slid out of bed, ignoring the chill as he padded over to stand behind her. He cupped her shoulders, pulling her back against him and murmuring into her hair, "You okay?"

"Yes." She snuggled against him. "It's snowing. I was watching."

He slid his arms around her waist and pressed a kiss to her temple. "Pretty, and I'm not talking about the snow."

He felt her smile. "Aren't you cold?"

"You could warm me up."

She slipped off the blanket and he wrapped it around both of them. For a few minutes, they watched the snow swirl and dip in the frosty light.

Holding Meredith like this—naked and warm against him—wound him up tight. Of course, it didn't take much. He wanted her again. The first time had been great, but too fast. It had been about quenching a need, about taking. The whole time he'd half expected her to pull away, but he kept going. He'd wanted her for so long he wasn't going to let anything stop them.

They were surrounded by the quiet fall of snow, the stillness outside and in, the bare hum of the heater. He pressed tight against her bottom. When she pressed back, he nuzzled her neck. Lifting her left arm, he anchored it behind his head, opening her body to him, causing the blanket to sag off his shoulders.

She held his free arm to her stomach, catching their covering. Gage trailed his fingers down the underside of her arm, coasted them lightly against the curve of her breast to her waist.

A giggle escaped her as she jerked against him. "That tickles!"

He grinned and turned her to face him, her soft breasts teasing the hair on his chest. In the pearly light, her eyes glittered with dark desire. Keeping the blanket around them, he lightly grazed his mouth over her cheekbone, her lips, the line of her jaw.

Her eyes closed and the pleasure spreading across her face had him moving in for a kiss. Long and deep and slow. He knew she liked it that way. He tried to throttle back and give it to her as he feathered his thumb across her taut velvety nipple.

Both her hands flattened against his chest. He could stand here all night kissing her, but when he felt her shiver from the cold, he scooped her up and carried her to bed. As he followed her down, she tossed away the blanket and scooted close as he pulled the comforter and sheet over them.

Her kiss was fierce, demanding, but he wasn't going to be rushed this time. Rolling her to her back, he moved between her legs, linking his fingers with hers to bring their arms slightly above her head.

He dragged his mouth to her ear, down her neck. At the feel of his tongue there, she melted into him, shifting with him, using the length of her body to stroke him every time he touched her.

His lips glided down her throat and she bent her knees to give him more room. He took his time, teasing heated, openmouthed kisses all over her breasts, low across her belly, the inside of her thighs. By the time he put his mouth on her, she was trembling, his name a breathy plea that had him sliding inside her.

He struggled to still the urgency, pausing when her eyes fluttered shut. "Look at me, baby," he commanded raggedly.

She did and Gage thought he caught a flicker of wariness in the blue depths. He stroked her hair and moved slowly, even when she locked her legs around his hips and tried to speed him up. As she neared climax, he backed off.

A broken moan rose from her. He could feel the heat beneath her skin, the pumping of her heart against his. Kissing her deeply, he took her up again and again. Long minutes later, when the demanding pulses of her body sent him hurtling toward the edge, he nudged her over. She let go and so did he.

His spine felt like mush. He rested his head beside hers, soaking in her sweet fragrance, not wanting to move. Finally, he propped himself up on one elbow and brushed her hair off her face. "I've missed you."

She smiled, but it didn't reach her eyes.

He rolled to the side, taking her with him. His pulse slowed and she settled close. She was unlocking places inside him, stirring up something he hadn't felt in over a year—hope. Being with her felt familiar, but now he appreciated even more what he'd gone without for the past eighteen months. Maybe that was what made him finally realize she was holding back. She had the first time, too.

At first, anger swirled inside him. She was the one who'd initiated the sex, not him. But after their broken engagement, the way he'd hurt her, why wouldn't she be guarded?

Maybe she needed to know he wanted a lot more than this. He pulled her half on top of him, stroking his hand up and down the velvet of her back.

"Mmm," she breathed into his chest.

He brushed a kiss against her hair. "You can count on me, Meredith. I'm in this all the way."

She stilled, her fingers plucking at the hair on his chest. "In what?"

"This. Us. I want more of you than in bed."

She lifted her head, looking dazed. "What?"

"I want you back. I want things like they were before."

Unease suddenly pulsed from her. "What we're doing right now is nice."

Her wariness irritated him. "You saying you don't want more? Baby, you wouldn't have slept with me unless you were open to giving us another shot."

"I wanted you."

"You only wanted sex, nothing else?"

"Yes."

He snorted. "Bull."

She untangled herself from him and sat up, taking the sheet with her. Pushing her hair back out of her face, she turned toward him. "Gage—"

"So you won't even talk about giving us another chance?"

Her pale silky breasts swelled over the top of the sheet. Unable to resist the tempting fullness, he traced a finger into her cleavage.

She drew the sheet tighter around her. "After the trial, I may never see you again."

"Yes, you will," he growled, pulling his hand away from her soft flesh to push up on his elbows. "And that's not an answer. If everything at the trial worked out so that I didn't have to go back into witness protection, if I came back to my old life, my *real* life, would you give us another chance?"

"We don't know what will happen. Why are we even talking about this?"

"'Cause we just had sex. Twice. And it meant something to me."

When she looked away without responding, his gut hollowed out. What was going on with her? He sat up, turned her face to his. "I never forgot how things were with us."

"Not forgetting is very different from going back."

"It's a start." He trailed his thumb down her neck, grazing the delicate line of her collarbone. "Neither of us has moved on. That's significant."

"I don't know what you want me to say."

"I want you to tell me you want more than this."

"We have right now. That's enough."

Since when? Who was this woman? "You can't expect me to believe sex is all you want."

"It doesn't matter what either of us wants." Her voice

was steady, almost flat. "Not until the trial's over, anyway. After that, you're probably going back into WitSec."

Her pragmatic statement irritated him even though she was probably right. She still felt something for him—he knew she did—but what exactly? He searched her face, his heart squeezing tight at the careful blankness there.

Gage wanted to push her for an answer, but he was afraid it would be no. Plus, he couldn't ignore the bleak and very real possibility he might have to disappear again.

"I want to be with you. You want to be with me, so what's the problem?" She let the sheet fall, placing a hand on his thigh.

He wanted to hit something, but maybe in the time they had left before the trial, he could convince her he was serious about a future with her. A future he wasn't going to screw up. As soon as possible, he would figure out how to make that happen.

He cupped her nape and pulled her to him. Angry that she wouldn't talk about their life after this, his kiss was hard at first. Until she climbed into his lap and straddled him, her breasts teasing his chest, her soft silky heat scattering his thoughts.

Sex was all she wanted to give him, and it was damn good. But it wasn't enough. Even now with their bodies locked together, an emptiness hollowed out his chest. He needed to prove she could trust him, which meant he had his work cut out for him.

He wanted all of her. And he was going to have her. Somehow.

Chapter 9

Gage had thought nothing could add to his frustration about Meredith and her refusal to consider anything with them beyond right now, but he was wrong.

Late the next afternoon, he rapped on the bathroom door. In response to Meredith's "Come in," he walked into a warm fragrant haze of woman smells.

"I figured it out." Gage paused, taking her in. She lay stretched out in the tub, her head resting against the rim. His gaze slid from her upswept hair to the elegant line of her neck and the damp sheen of her shoulders. What the water didn't cover of her breasts, the bubbles from the apricot-scented bath wash did. He thought about getting in there with her, even though he hadn't been invited. "I know what it is."

Her drowsy blue gaze met his. "You figured out the mystery ingredient?"

"Yeah." Remembering how she hated cool air interfering with her bath, Gage closed the door before she asked. Bracing his backside against the sink, he crossed his feet at the ankles.

He and Meredith had worked on the experiments together until about twenty minutes earlier, when she had announced that she would fix supper after taking a bath. Thick perfumed steam swirled around him, settled in his lungs. Man, her scent drove him crazy.

He paced the two steps to the opposite wall then back to the door. "And my big discovery isn't going to do us any good."

"What do you mean?" She shifted so that water covered her shoulders, rosy skin peeking through the light froth of bubbles. A few damp blond strands escaped from the messy topknot and stuck to her nape.

His blood was on slow simmer for her anyway and the frustrating discovery about the accelerant edged him into a full-blown burn. He wanted to grab her and…do stuff.

He tried not to look at her. "The mystery ingredient that enables the gas-gel to disappear is—get ready—powdered sugar."

"Powdered sugar?" Her surprise was as palpable as his own. "You're sure?"

"Yes." He shoved a hand through his hair. "I tested it five times. Every time, the accelerant disappeared without a trace."

His gaze touched on her delicate earlobe, the droplet of water in the hollow where her neck met her shoulder. Stopping at the swell of her breasts, he re-membered the softness of her fine-grained skin. He wanted to feel it again.

Noticing where he looked, she sank down a little lower in the tub. "…Larry James?"

Realizing she was talking, Gage jerked his gaze to her face. "Sorry, what?"

"I asked if there was any way for you to tie the powdered sugar to Larry James?"

"No." Gage's body tightened in anticipation of her getting out. "I was really hoping the ingredient I isolated would be some sophisticated compound or specialty material like that used in fireproofing or by stunt people. If it had been one of those, I could've at least checked to see if James had a connection to any company or person with access to something like that, but it's just plain powdered sugar and paraffin wax."

"What is it about the powdered sugar that makes the accelerant disappear?"

"From what I can tell, it's the amount." He fought the urge to pound his fist through the wall. "Damn it, this is all I have."

"You'll find another way."

"I hope so," he muttered, realizing she was finished with her bath and had been for some time.

But she stayed in the water, her body hidden beneath the bubbles. Why didn't she get out? It wasn't as if he hadn't seen and touched every inch of her. "Want me to get you a towel?"

"Not yet."

She wouldn't look at him and Gage ground his teeth.

Did her guarded behavior mean she regretted last night? She hadn't pushed him away, but everything she did was marked by wariness.

What had he thought? he jeered. That one night with him would erase her doubts, make her as certain about him as he was about her?

He wanted to grab her and kiss her until she melted. And she would, he knew. But there was too much at stake. As frustrated as he was with her, Gage knew he had to let her work it out on her own. When they'd been engaged, he'd made it all about him. This time he couldn't do that. Not if he wanted to show her he'd really changed.

"Are you going to get that?" She arched a brow.

"What?"

"Your cell phone."

At her words, he realized it was ringing. Pulling the phone from his jeans pocket, he answered. "Yeah?"

"Parrish, it's Ivory."

Gage mouthed the Attorney General's name to Meredith.

As the other man spoke, tension coiled through Gage's body. He could feel Meredith's concerned gaze on him.

He disconnected and she sat up straighter in the tub. The water gave her skin the luster of a pearl. "What is it?"

"A body matching Julio's description was discovered, shot execution style." Gage knew Meredith had worked the E.R. long enough to know that meant a bullet or two to the head. "Ivory needs us to look at the body, see if it's the piece of scum who broke into your lake house and shot at us."

"And tailed us?"

He nodded, feeling as if his chest were being crushed.

"I'm sorry." She searched his eyes. "If it is Julio, you may have just lost your last chance to connect Larry James to the arson ring."

"Yeah. Ivory wants us to come to Presley to look at the body."

"Now?"

Gage nodded, biting back a curse.

Meredith looked into his face for a long moment and he wished he knew what she was thinking. He wasn't ready to end their time together. He was no closer to getting his life back than he had been before running into her at the lake house.

"Let me look at your stitches before we leave."

"Okay. I'll check around the cabin outside, make sure no one's waiting to ambush us." He didn't care how tentative she was. He was damn well touching her. Pushing away from the counter, he stepped over to the tub and ran the backs of his fingers down her cheek.

She didn't pull away, but didn't relax into his touch, either. "What happens when we get back? Are you going to check in with the Marshals Service?"

"No. Even if the dead man is Julio, we still don't know the identity or whereabouts of the mastermind behind the arson ring. I don't trust anyone but myself to keep you safe." He frowned, suddenly hit by a thought. "We need a place to stay. We can't go to your house and I don't even have one now."

"Do you need to be close to the courthouse in downtown Oklahoma City? Does it matter?"

"I'm more concerned about safety than proximity."

"We could probably stay at Robin's," Meredith ventured. "But we would have to tell her some of what's going on and you might not want to do that."

"Does she still live outside the city limits?"

"Yes, on the acreage she bought several years ago for her horses."

Gage thought for a moment. "That might be good. She's a cop. We know she can keep a secret. She can protect herself, if necessary. But as you said before, there's a chance Julio and the ringleader might have made a connection because she's been house-sitting for you. And no one would think to look for us there. Do you think she'd mind?"

"No, but I need to find out if it's even an option."

"Okay. Use the second throwaway phone I bought in Texarkana to call her, then turn it off. We've been testing our luck with the personal phones."

"All right."

He reached over to the bar on the wall and snagged a towel, holding it open for her.

After a hesitation that had his jaw clenching, she gave him a small smile. "I'm still not ready to get out."

Gage fought the urge to reach down and pull her wet, slippery body right out of there. She wasn't ready to get out. She wasn't ready to talk about giving them another chance. What the hell *was* she ready for? If it had to do with him, apparently not a damn thing.

The watchfulness in her blue eyes told him whatever she felt about last night hadn't settled a part of her the way it had him.

Did she regret sleeping with him? He sure as hell

wasn't asking, but why else would she act this way? He knew what they'd shared meant something to her. It wasn't like Meredith to sleep with him just to scratch an itch. Or at least it hadn't been her way before he'd hurt her, he reminded himself harshly.

She hadn't hinted that she was thinking about what he'd said last night, but he hoped she was. He had to figure out a way to convince her he was in it for the long haul this time.

If the body discovered by the Attorney General *was* Julio, Gage was glad the bastard had been eliminated as a threat, especially for Meredith's sake. But as she had pointed out, he could possibly have just lost his last connection to Larry James.

Gage had made no progress on the case or with Meredith. He hoped he hadn't lost his last chance with both of them.

He was getting to her. Meredith had known he would and she was prepared. Sort of. Though she was jittery, so far she had managed not to give in to the hope that things could be different for them.

The sex was as good as ever, although now there was an added poignancy. Every time he touched her, it was as if he thought it might be for the last time. And it might be. The closer the trial got, the stronger the possibility grew.

Because Gage's SUV could be recognized by the still-unidentified man who'd followed them in Broken Bow, they'd decided to leave it at the lake house, returning to Presley in Meredith's Thunderbird.

When Meredith had called to ask her friend for a place to stay, Robin had agreed immediately. She'd also said she knew something weird was going on and wanted Meredith to fill her in when she arrived. There was no way Robin would guess Gage was at the center of that something weird.

A sense of sadness had swept over Meredith when they left the Greens' cabin. She wasn't sure if it was because of the uncertainty about the upcoming trial or because she had realized how difficult it was going to be to walk away from Gage again.

While secluded with him, there had been no choice except to live in the moment. And Meredith thought she was handling it fine until late that night as they stood on the wide wraparound porch of Robin's century-old farmhouse. When her longtime friend answered Meredith's knock, doubt sizzled through her.

With her dark hair pulled up in a ponytail and wearing flannel pajamas, Robin Daly looked more like a teenager than a decorated detective. She opened the screen door and pulled Meredith into a hug. "I'm glad you made it without any problems. I was starting to wonder. Come on in."

"I didn't tell you everything."

The other woman laughed. "You can tell me inside. It's cold out here."

"I'm not alone."

Robin frowned, looked past Meredith's shoulder to the circular gravel drive beyond. "Okay."

Gage stepped silently out of the deep shadows to Robin's left and she spun toward the movement.

"Hey, Robin," he said quietly.

For two heartbeats, the petite brunette looked nonplussed, then her classic features slipped into a polite unreadable mask. Her cop face. "Gage Parrish? Wow."

Despite Robin's reputation for being practically unflappable, Meredith was surprised at how quickly her friend regained her composure upon seeing a supposedly dead man. She was probably already sizing up the situation.

"Witness protection?" she asked evenly as she ushered them inside and closed the door.

Meredith exchanged a look with Gage as he confirmed the other woman's guess. It was a good thing he'd already decided to tell Robin everything. His main concern was Meredith's safety and even if her friend was furious with him, he believed she would keep quiet for Meredith's protection.

Robin crossed the living room, the large area warmed by a fire burning in a gray stone fireplace. The space was updated with dark furniture, wood flooring and cheerful rugs in a deep red. Family portraits in antique frames, an old grandfather clock and a rocking chair in the corner integrated the old with the new. "Put your stuff down somewhere in here. Y'all want something to eat?"

"No, thanks." Meredith draped hers and Gage's coats over the back of a taupe ultrasuede sofa and followed their hostess into the kitchen.

"How about something to drink— Okay, I have to sit down. This is too wild." She plopped into a chair at the light oak dining table. "I *knew* something was hinky when I talked to you, but I never figured this."

Meredith had only seen her friend this rattled one other time and she wasn't sure what to make of it. "How did you put together so fast that he's been in the Witness Security Program?"

"His death was obviously faked and the trial for the arsonists he busted is coming up. Makes sense the prosecution would want to protect their witnesses. I guess none of the other task-force members are really dead, either."

"The last I heard, they weren't," he answered somberly as he pulled out a hard-backed dining chair for Meredith then eased down into the one next to her. "But that was a year ago. I don't know about now."

The same dark flooring carried over from the living area. The dining table was centered in the big room finished with dark blue counters and white cabinets. A large picture window gave the kitchen an airy, open feel. Meredith noticed her friend's holstered gun and badge on the nearest counter top.

She hadn't been sure how Robin would react to seeing Gage. The policewoman had always made clear that she thought he was a bonehead for letting Meredith get away.

Meredith glanced over at Gage. "This okay?"

"Sure, if it's okay with Robin."

A slight frown gathered on the other woman's brow as she looked at them both. "Of course, you can stay. Meredith, did you know about this? His being alive?"

"Not until several days ago."

"It was a big surprise to her, too." Gage linked his fingers with hers.

At his touch, Meredith stiffened, but didn't pull away. Nor did she respond when he gave her a sideways look. "That's an understatement. I nearly passed out when I saw him bleeding over the sink."

She related how Gage had believed the Borens lake house to be empty and had gone there for medical supplies.

"Gunshot wound," he offered. He described how he'd been shot by Marshal Nowlin, about how he and Meredith had been caught off guard when the marshal and an Hispanic man showed up at the lake house.

Robin's eyes widened as she looked at Meredith. "You shot the marshal?"

"Good thing she did or I'd be dead," Gage said. "She's saved my life twice."

Robin stared hard at Meredith. "Damn, girl."

"Tell me about it," she muttered.

Gage continued, "We plan to lay low until the trial."

"Which is supposed to start in two days," Robin said.

He nodded. "I called the Attorney General on our way up here. He wants us to identify the body of a man matching the description of the intruder who shot at us in Broken Bow. And we both have to be deposed about the marshal."

"You can stay here as long as you want."

The offer was sincere, but Meredith could see the frost slowly gathering in her friend's eyes and in her manner toward Gage. Robin hadn't completely forgiven him for the way he'd hurt Meredith.

"I've been working the break-in at your house," Robin said. "But haven't gotten anything new. Didn't find any prints, not even a smudge. Do you think it was this Julio guy?"

"Very probable," Gage said. "We never found any prints at the arson fires we think he started."

Meredith recognized the glint in her friend's blue eyes. Robin was about to burst with questions—for Meredith, not Gage.

He finally caught on, too, and stood. "I'm outta here so y'all can talk."

Their hostess indicated the hall on the other side of the living area. "There are two guest bedrooms. Take your pick."

"Thanks." Gage lightly squeezed Meredith's hand before starting into the living room.

"Be careful with your shoulder," she cautioned as he scooped up her bag along with his. She watched him go, feeling a mix of uncertainty and longing and regret.

Robin muttered something under her breath and pushed out of her chair. "Parrish?"

Meredith's gaze shifted from Gage to her friend on the other side of the table. Uh-oh. She had seen that give-me-a-reason-to-shoot-you look before.

Turning, Gage paused in the archway. "Yeah?"

"Because of what happened at my 'wedding that wasn't,' I've made it a point to stay out of other people's business."

His big frame tensed and he waited. At Robin's mention of being jilted at the altar, Meredith frowned. Her friend hardly ever talked about that horrible day anymore.

The brunette nailed Gage with a look. "But if you hurt Meredith again, that will become my business. Got it?"

"Robin!" Meredith exclaimed, but neither her friend nor Gage looked at her.

His eyes narrowed and Meredith could practically see sparks shooting off both of them. One second stretched into another. Even though Robin's gun was still on the counter, Meredith's heart began pounding hard. Robin started to stand.

"Got it," Gage said.

Startled by his response, Meredith drew in a breath. She felt surprise from Robin, too.

With a half grin, he raised one hand in the air as if surrendering and said in his best John Wayne imitation, "I don't want any trouble. I'm gonna walk out of here real slow, Detective."

It broke the tension and Meredith smiled. Robin's mouth curved slightly.

His gaze shifted to Meredith. "See you in a bit."

"Okay."

Robin remained standing until Gage disappeared from sight then she plunked down in her chair. "Good grief! Seeing him had to be a huge shock."

"It was."

"Are you okay?"

"I'm fine. The first couple of days weren't so good."

"I wish we could tell Terra about this," Robin said. "Just what all happened down there? Are y'all back together? What are you thinking?"

Meredith drew one foot under her. "Which question do you want me to answer first?"

The brunette made a face. "Well, I don't want to know *exactly* what all happened down there, but are y'all back together?"

"For now."

"For now," her friend repeated. "Not forever?"

Meredith shook her head. "Last time, I didn't know things between us would end. This time, I do."

This past week, she and Gage had come close to being killed. She *had* killed someone. If anything had been hammered home to her, it was that all you had was the moment.

"If the guy who shot at us and trailed us around the lake is dead, that means Gage has lost his last chance to find something incriminating to nail the mastermind behind the arson ring."

"So even if those on trial are convicted, his life will still be in danger and he'll have to disappear again."

"Yes."

"Meredith, this could really happen. Are you sure you want to let him that close?"

She started to say she'd gone into this with her eyes open, that she knew what she was doing, but she *didn't* know. The only thing she felt certain of was she couldn't handle more pain like that of last time. "I won't let him hurt me again."

"How can you help it? You're still in love with him," her friend asserted quietly.

The comment caused Meredith's stomach to fall to her feet, but she didn't deny it. "This isn't about love— it's about commitment. To each other first, then our jobs. He still has the drive, the single-minded focus he had before, but he seems to genuinely regret how things ended."

She explained how Gage had apologized, how he had taken responsibility for what had happened to break their engagement. "And he's been acting differently. More…thoughtful toward me."

"That could be because he hasn't seen you in a year and a half," Robin pointed out wryly.

Meredith nodded in painful agreement. "I've thought about that. Before, he didn't value our relationship enough to put me ahead of his job. What's to say he would give it any more priority than he ever did?"

Compassion and understanding darkened Robin's eyes. "I don't want him to break your heart a second time."

"It's not high on my list, either." The memory of last night swept over her. His tenderness, his refusal to make the sex as casual as she had wanted. His sincere desire to go back to the way things were. Her heart squeezed. "I've never felt this way about another man, but I don't trust him not to hurt me again."

"So, what about after the trial? What will you do if he doesn't have to go back into the program?"

"I don't know." She couldn't think in terms of the future. Gage might believe he could reclaim his life, but Meredith didn't. She couldn't afford to. "I just don't know."

Annoyed and impatient, Gage lay on the fluffy queen-size mattress in the bedroom closest to the kitchen.

He'd caught snatches of Meredith's conversation with her friend, enough to remind him how deeply he'd hurt her. As if he needed reminding.

He would never forget the raw pain in those blue eyes—pain he had caused—when she'd broken off their engagement and he wondered, not for the first time, if she could ever get past it.

The women's voices dropped to murmurs and he heard them say good-night. The kitchen went dark, leaving a lamp glowing from the living room to throw light into the hall.

He heard the soft scuff of shoes against the carpet, then Meredith paused in the doorway, blocking the light. For a long moment, she stood in silence outside the half-open door. Her hesitation to enter the room set off a burst of anger inside him. Damn it!

She still didn't trust him. He didn't blame her—she had plenty of reason not to. But, hell, what did he have to do?

She may have gotten naked with him last night, but she had been skittish ever since. When he'd taken her hand earlier, she'd gone as stiff as a tow bar.

Mounting frustration and deep regret snarled his gut into a knot. He knew he couldn't pressure her even though every cell in his body strained for her to come to him. So he waited. And hoped.

Chapter 10

Gage's irritation about the case and now Meredith edged into anger. If he clenched his jaw any tighter, he was bound to break some teeth. He was surprised enamel wasn't shooting out his ears. The next morning, he and Meredith drove south on Hefner Parkway from Robin's house.

He'd eagerly accepted her offer to let him drive the fiftieth-anniversary-edition car, but tension still vibrated between them as it had since they'd eaten, dressed and started this trip to the Oklahoma City morgue to identify the man suspected to be Julio.

Meredith's light, luscious scent taunted him as did the tousled blond curls she'd tamed into a neat twist. He wanted to sink his hands into her hair and mess it up, touch her petal-soft skin. But her blue eyes kept him from doing anything. They were distant, a reminder she wasn't his and might never be again. As if he needed a reminder after last night.

After long moments of standing outside the bedroom door last night, she'd finally come to bed. She had slept against him, but she hadn't really been there. Just like now.

She was with him, but not *with him.*

She wouldn't let him in past a certain point and he had no idea what to do about it. Force the issue? That would be suicide, but ignoring it bugged him, too.

She was the first to break the silence. "Maybe we'll learn something at the morgue."

"That would be nice," he said tightly.

"Do you have a plan for after this?"

He didn't know what the hell it would be. Do his part at the trial and hope someone else found something to incriminate Larry James so Gage could get his life back? "Not really."

"I'm sorry. I know how frustrating this is for you."

"That isn't the only thing frustrating me." He wasn't fazed by the sharp look she gave him. His discontent about their relationship—about *her*—was no secret.

She opened her mouth as if to say something, only to be interrupted by a burst of song from her cell phone. After a quick glance at the call screen, she looked at Gage in surprise. "It's my neighbor Sarah."

"It's okay to take it."

"All right." She answered, then grew eerily still. "Wait, slow down."

At the shock on her face, concern shot through him, then surprise as she reached for his hand.

Meredith held on tight, grateful Gage was with her. A buzzing had started in her ears at her neighbor's first words. She managed to reply to the other woman calmly, but her nerves wound tighter and tighter. After a few moments, she hung up, feeling ill and detached.

Gage squeezed her hand. "Baby?"

Reeling, she shook her head. "Sarah said there's been a fire at my house."

"What!"

"She saw the smoke and called 9-1-1. The fire department got there quickly and the fire's out now, but she doesn't know how much damage was done." Her voice thickened. "She said it's still standing. That's good. Maybe it isn't too bad."

He cursed under his breath as he changed lanes. Meredith was riding the edge of numbness and fear. She wanted to curse, too. Or scream at someone.

She still had a home, but how much of one? She felt completely lost, bereft. For an instant, on a lesser scale, she had an inkling of how alone and displaced Gage must've felt when he lost his home. His whole life.

She began to tremble. "I can't believe this."

"Are you okay?"

The worry that carved lines in his face had Meredith trying to shake off her dazed lethargy. "Yes."

She was amazed at how calm she sounded. She wasn't calm. She couldn't even make herself release her choke hold on his big hand.

It was a second before she realized he'd exited the parkway. "What are you doing?"

"You sure you're all right? You look pale."

"I'm okay." Her voice quavered.

Gage turned the car around and drove to the ramp going the opposite direction. Once again on the parkway, they traveled back the way they'd come.

Meredith frowned. "Where are you going?"

"To your house."

"But… What if someone sees us there?" Her grip tightened on his. She couldn't stop trembling.

"We'll stay a fair distance away."

"Are you sure this is a good idea?"

"We need to go there, baby."

"To check the damage? If it's risky for you, we shouldn't go."

"Partly to see the damage. We'll lay low, stay out of sight."

After struggling to steady her racing heartbeat, she nodded. Having Gage with her helped managed this adrenaline free-for-all.

With so many questions yet unanswered, she tried to figure out what might have happened. "It was probably an accident of some kind. Electrical. Sarah said she never saw anyone hanging around my place."

"Yeah, it could've been an accident." The cynical brusqueness of his tone told Meredith he didn't believe that. "That's one reason we need to check it out. We need to know exactly what we're dealing with."

Something in his voice had her considering another likelihood and her gaze locked in on him. "Do you think this is arson? Do you think it's related to your case?"

"I don't know, but I seriously doubt it's random.

Julio or whoever tried and *failed* to kill us is nowhere to be found, and now a fire is set at your house? You're still in danger. It can't be a coincidence."

The hair on her neck rose.

"I have to get inside and determine if the blaze was arson. I think it was, but I need to be sure."

Her hand felt cold in his. "How are you going to get in?"

"I don't know yet." He linked his strong, warm fingers with hers and Meredith held tight. "We'll figure it out."

Twenty minutes later, they pulled into her housing addition, able to get within only a block because of the police cruisers forming a border to keep people away from the fire scene. Red and blue lights strobed here and at the opposite end.

Parked on the next curb were two SUVs bearing the names and logos of Oklahoma City television stations. A helicopter belonging to another station circled overhead. Gage intended to stay under the radar.

He backed away from the cordoned-off area then parked on a side street half a block down. He and Meredith settled in to wait until the rescue personnel left her house. The acrid stench of smoke burned the cold air. The white-gray haze dissipating into the clouds told Gage the blaze hadn't been caused by petroleum products. Otherwise, the smoke would be dark.

Neither of them spoke. Waiting in the heavy silence, surrounded by Meredith's frothy scent, turned Gage's thoughts to them.

He was trying to give her the space and time she needed to make up her mind about them, to see he had changed, but it was gnawing a hole inside him. He told himself to be patient, just as he would be in an investigation. But he had trouble reining back when Meredith was concerned. Still, he had to try.

He couldn't do anything about his situation with her right now, but he could focus on this fire, determine if it was arson and find out if it was related to his case.

Finally, the police cruisers and fire trucks left the scene. As he and Meredith carefully made their way toward her house, midmorning sunlight speared ruthlessly into the shadowed corners of the established neighborhood. They stayed behind trees and kept an eye out for neighbors or anyone else they might see.

She had bought this house after she and Gage had gotten engaged, and though he had been inside plenty of times, they had split up before he could move in.

About a hundred yards from her cottage-style home, they stopped beside a gray brick house on the same side of the street as hers and Gage scanned her now-soggy front yard. Water from the fire hoses soaked the cold packed ground, streamed down the pavement and glistened on nearby trees. Yellow crime-scene tape stretched around the house and yard.

A policeman watched the scene from his patrol car at the curb.

After scanning the area again, Gage said in a half whisper, "I don't think Presley's fire investigators have shown yet or they'd still be working inside. Since they aren't here, it means they're probably at another scene. A big one, if it required both Terra and Collier McClain to work it. That's good for us."

"What are we going to do? That cop is looking this way." Meredith kept her voice quiet. "It's not as if we can just stroll inside."

"I'll figure out something."

A few minutes later, they had a plan. Gage waited as Meredith returned for her car, then drove into the neighborhood as if just arriving. When she walked toward the patrol car, Gage took advantage of the officer's distraction and slipped over a chain-link fence behind the gray house and then another, moving toward Meredith's backyard through those of her neighbors.

He encountered a basset hound inside one fence, then a mastiff inside another. Both dogs began to bark. They continued to make noise as Gage kept moving and finally climbed over Meredith's taller wooden fence into her backyard. Though he couldn't hear her, he knew she was doing as they'd agreed by telling the patrolman the damaged house was hers and asking to be let inside.

Knowing the cop would refuse to allow her into a scene that hadn't been processed, Gage used the key she'd given him to let himself in the sliding glass doors at the back of her house.

He quietly closed the door and took in his surroundings, noting there was no odor of kerosene or gasoline. That, along with the absence of black smoke, told him another type of accelerant had been used.

The center of the house was the open living room. An attached dining room looked out the front and the kitchen, which looked to have sustained the most damage, was to his left. He relaxed slightly, knowing the kitchen wasn't visible from the front windows.

The smell of wet ash hung in the air. Meredith's light gray carpet was soaked, covered with soot. Grime streaked the white walls and boot prints clearly showed the path the firefighters had taken to douse the blaze. Among the many questions Gage wanted to ask was if they'd used the typical wide or "fog pattern" spray to kill the fire. But of course he couldn't ask.

Nor could he dig for answers since he was without his shovel. Even though he hadn't performed fire investigations for a year, his hand still felt empty without his most essential tool.

The firefighters had entered through the front door, moved into the charcoal-filmed living room then the kitchen. The room's cabinets, counters and floors were blackened. At the kitchen's back wall, the doorway that led to the laundry room was charred. The kitchen was the point of origin and the alligator-patterned frame was the low point, the specific place the fire had started.

Using Meredith's cell phone camera, Gage snapped pictures of the sooty foyer and living room before turning to the kitchen to search out more detail.

He started at the kitchen's back wall, his attention immediately snagged by a cloudy yellow blob of gel attached to the other side of the door frame. This was no electrical fire.

His heart rate kicked into high as he moved closer.

Bingo! Gage knew this signature. The gel block in front of him appeared to be exactly like those he'd made for his experiments. All the torch had to do was adhere the accelerant to where he wanted and light it. Just like what had been done to start the arson ring fires.

He was barely able to stop himself from calling out to Meredith. Thank goodness for her neighbor who had gotten the fire department here in time to prevent major damage to the house, especially the kitchen. And to keep the evidence from burning and disappearing.

A nice-sized chunk of gel remained, enough to test and maybe lead to the mastermind behind the arson ring. And hopefully prove that person was Larry James as Gage had suspected all along.

Since there was no dead body at this scene, the fire department wouldn't need to work with the police department, but seeing as how both a cop and Presley's lead fire investigator were close friends of Meredith's, Gage was pretty sure he could get information about anything discovered here.

This fire was definitely arson, likely connected to Operation Smoke Screen. And this time, he had evidence to prove it.

Meredith could feel frustration rolling off Gage in waves. An hour after leaving her house, they were driving away from the Oklahoma City morgue and back to Robin's farmhouse. The man they'd been asked to identify had indeed been the man who'd tried to kill them, the one Gage said was the go-between who'd set the fires for the mastermind of the arson ring.

Julio Garza. They had his whole name now, and that

was all they had. No connection to Larry James, nothing on Garza's body or in his effects to point to anyone. Disappointment was a sharp keening pain in Meredith's chest. Judging by the way Gage's jaw muscles bunched, he felt the same way.

She drove while he used her cell phone to call Robin and take more notes. As he told the detective what he'd discovered about the fire at Meredith's house, she regained her mental balance enough to sort through what had happened. She realized with a flutter of panic that the first thing she'd done upon hearing the news about her house was turn to Gage. It had been natural, but she couldn't let herself depend on him. For anything. It would only lead to hurt.

Forcing away thoughts about the two of them, she listened to his conversation with Robin.

"We're leaving the morgue. The scum we identified was the guy who tried to kill us in Broken Bow. Since he was lying on a slab at the time, I know he didn't set the fire at Meredith's."

He paused, listened, then continued, "He never left prints at any of his scenes, but whoever torched Meredith's house might have. As thorough an investigator as Terra is, I'm sure she checks everything for prints at her fire scenes."

After answering a couple of questions and asking Robin to call with any news, he disconnected. Even though his voice had been steady while on the phone, Meredith heard the strain beneath his words. Recognized the stress that made his shoulders rigid and cut deep lines around his eyes.

As far as evidence went, Julio was the end of the road for Gage unless Terra discovered something at Meredith's house. Chances were high Gage would have to return to the Witness Security Program, and the possibility left Meredith feeling empty, sad.

He stared out the window of her car as she drove north in the noon traffic. Glancing at her, he pinched the bridge of his nose. "Did I sound as desperate as I feel?"

Meredith's heart ached. "There has to be something else we can do, somewhere we can look."

"I don't know what it would be."

His voice was gritty with exhaustion, his features haggard. The strain of the past couple of weeks rode him hard. She hated this. She might not know what she wanted for them, but she knew she wanted Gage to get his life back, wanted his grandparents to get their grandson back. Right now, it didn't seem likely.

"Maybe you could go through my house again," she said. "Or give your test notes to Terra and see if she can find something you may have missed."

He was quiet for a long moment, then reached over and took her hand. "What I care about more than anything is that you're safe. I want that for you, no matter what happens with me after the trial."

Tears stung her eyes. His going back into Witness Security would be the worst thing for him and his grandparents. It had cost him enough. Why did the person doing the right thing have to pay the price?

"Robin's going to keep me in the loop." He dragged his free hand down his face. "She'll let me know as soon as she hears anything from Terra."

Meredith squeezed his hand. "That's all we can do for now?"

"Yes." And it pissed him off.

His gut told him he'd uncovered something key at her house and it grated that he had to sit around on his hands and wait on someone else to find out what it was. Terra Spencer was one of the best fire investigators he knew, but Gage wanted to be the one working that scene. It was *his* life on the line.

Between that frustration and the feeling Meredith was getting farther from him, he was ready to chew nails. It didn't help that his damn shoulder was aching worse than it had in the past few days.

His patience, already flimsy, only wore thinner as the hours passed. Hours spent between reviewing everything he'd found at Meredith's house and thinking about his woman. Was it his imagination or was she spending most of her time in whatever room he wasn't in?

Irritation, resentment, bubbled up until his insides felt on fire. When his mood didn't improve the next day, Gage went in search of more things to do. He entered the last of the results of his and Meredith's experiments on the marshal's laptop, then e-mailed the schematic he'd found to Ken Ivory.

The ache in his shoulder had him looking on the Internet for some range-of-motion exercises. Sitting on the end of the queen-size bed he and Meredith had been sharing, he was about five minutes into the first set when her voice came from the doorway, startling him.

"What are you doing? You know I should check your stitches before you do something like that."

"My shoulder feels fine." He rolled it to demonstrate.

Looking pale and concerned, she walked toward him. "Let me see."

He unbuttoned and slid off his dark green long-sleeved shirt then sat quietly as she examined his injury. He drew in the deep scent of woman and apricot.

"It's healed well. Well enough to take out the stitches." She moved to the corner of the room where she had put the medical supplies she'd brought and returned with a small pair of curved scissors.

As she carefully removed the stitches, he watched her face, the tiny line between her brows as she concentrated. Watery winter light streamed through the window. His skin pulled with the removal of each suture. When she finished, she ran a gentle hand across his scar.

He looked at it. A healthy pink and healing scar. "Thanks."

"You're welcome."

He wanted to pull her into his lap, but didn't. Normally, he would've touched her before she did him, yet for the past couple of days he'd felt as if he needed to wait for her to make the first move on everything. It bugged the hell out of him.

Things between them were fine as long as he didn't talk about anything other than what was in the moment. When he did, Meredith closed up.

When she lightly ran her fingers through his hair, he settled a hand low on her hip, looking up at her.

"Are you about to go stir-crazy?" She moved away

to dispose of the sutures in a wastebasket the same navy as the other accents in the bedroom.

He stood, pulling on his shirt and buttoning it. "Yeah. I'm trying to keep my mind occupied."

Before she could reply, her cell phone rang. She answered then handed it to Gage. "It's Robin."

He took the phone, tamping down restlessness and a demand for the detective to tell him what she'd learned.

"Terra was able to get a couple of sets of prints, even one from the accelerant, but they were smeared," Robin said. "No match points at all."

Damn! Gage felt as if a massive weight crushed his chest, cutting off his air. What the hell was he supposed to do? How was he supposed to walk away from his life again? From Meredith? Would he ever nail the mastermind behind the arson ring?

His brain was churning so hard he almost missed Robin's next words.

"But we got something better."

He froze. "What?"

As he listened, adrenaline shot through him. His gaze went to Meredith, who watched him closely.

Whatever she saw on his face had her moving closer.

Excitement mounting, he struggled to wait for all of Robin's information. He wanted to be sure he had everything right. He could hardly wait to get off the phone. When he did, he grinned and scooped Meredith into his arms.

Hooking an arm around his neck for balance, she ordered breathlessly, "Tell me!"

"Terra found DNA."

"DNA! From what?" The elation in her voice matched his. "Blood? Hair?"

"She managed to extract it from oil left behind by the fingerprints."

"I've read about that process. I didn't know our lab could do that now."

Gage nodded. "The best part is that the DNA matches Larry James."

"Oh, how wonderful!" She hugged him tight.

Saying the words out loud made it seem real. Gage could have the bastard locked up for years. He wouldn't have to stay in witness protection. None of the task-force members would.

He actually felt weak with disbelief. Sorting through a flood of emotion, he buried his face in Meredith's thick fragrant hair. Finally, *finally,* he could nail that son of a bitch. He was going to close this case.

His mind was so full it took him a second to register Meredith's question.

"How was Terra able to get his DNA to test against what she found at my house? Is he in custody?"

"No. Robin said she's trying to serve a warrant on him, but so far he can't be found. Terra was able to match his DNA because it was in the system."

"Why would it be in the system? Oh, wait, I remember. Like a lot of cities after 9/11, Oklahoma City and Presley began storing samples of blood from rescue workers, like firefighters. That way, if something happens and they can't be identified by sight, they can be identified by DNA."

"Right."

"James's DNA would still be in the system even though he was fired?"

Gage nodded. "The city can barely afford to pay people to enter all that data. They sure aren't going to pay them to take it out."

Satisfaction filled him. He finally had the bastard. It didn't feel real yet, but it was. "Robin also said they'd gotten a warrant to search his house and turned up a gun along with some records. She thinks the ballistics will match the bullet that killed Julio."

"Did she say anything about the records?"

"Only that her first glance revealed details about fires. She thinks I'll be able to tell if the information concerns the arson ring blazes."

"Oh, Gage, I'm so glad for you." Her eyes filled with tears as she hugged him tight. "Your grandparents will be overwhelmed."

"That isn't all." Keeping her close, he drew back to look at her. "I'll have my life back, baby. *We'll* have our lives back."

Her bright smile faded.

"This isn't over yet, but I can see the end of it." He stroked a hand over her hair. "I may have to go back into Witness Security for a while, until Larry James is apprehended, but once he is, I'm coming back for you. We can be together."

"Gage."

The low warning in her voice had dread piercing through his euphoria, but he wanted her to know he was serious about a future with her. He'd kept quiet since the night they'd first slept together, but he wasn't keeping quiet now. "I know you think you can't trust me, but you can."

"I can't…do it again." She stepped out of his arms. "I can't be with you."

Her words didn't surprise him. Tension over this had been bubbling from the moment he'd told her he wanted things to be the way they were before.

"I've tried to give you space, Meredith. To show you I mean it when I say I've changed."

"It's not your sincerity I doubt. It's your commitment to me—to *us*. That a relationship means more than your…dedication to your job."

She'd been about to call it his obsession, he realized. And she would've been right, back then. "After what happened, the way I was last year, it's understandable why you'd still think so, but—"

"Before I returned your ring, I spent so much time trying to figure out what was wrong with me." Her voice shook and he couldn't tell if it was from pain or anger. "But I wasn't the problem."

"No, you weren't. It was all me." His heart clenched that she'd ever thought the fault had lain with her. "My job meant too much to me."

"I didn't leave because you cared about your job. I left because that was *all* you cared about."

She walked to the other side of the bed and he felt every inch of distance like a blow.

"Watching our relationship die nearly wrecked me. For weeks after I broke our engagement, I was out of it. Once I had to leave a surgery because I didn't trust myself not to botch it. I'm not willing to go there again. I'm not strong enough to handle us falling apart a second time."

Hadn't she noticed any difference in him at all? He told himself to be patient. They could work this out. "I'm nuts about you, Meredith. And I know you still feel something for me."

"That wasn't enough before. Why would it be now?"

"Because now I know what I gave up. I'm willing to compromise, not expect you to do it all. I finally understand how badly I hurt you and I'm not going to break your heart again. Look at me. You can see I'm telling the truth."

Her eyes, full of anguish, searched his. "I believe you."

"Then why won't you say yes?"

"Right now, you don't have to give your attention to anyone or anything except me. But once you're settled back into your life, your *job,* that will change."

"Things aren't going to be the way they were before, baby. Whatever it takes, I'm not going to lose you again."

"Please don't say things like that. We're…over. We both need to move on."

Irritation streaked through him. "If that's what you want, then why did you sleep with me?"

"Because I wanted to be with you," she said quietly. "It doesn't mean I think we can work."

"Then what *does* it mean?"

"I… Goodbye, I guess."

The sorrow in her voice didn't stop anger from roaring through him. "Did you ever even consider giving me another shot?"

"I can't."

"You mean you won't."

She hesitated. "Yes, that's what I mean."

His gut twisted into knots. "Is that why you slept with me? Because you figured it would never go anywhere? Damn it, Meredith, I can't prove I've changed if you won't let me in!"

"This isn't easy for me, either, Gage. In some ways, we're very good together, but not when it comes to forever. Not when it comes to putting us as a priority."

"That's on me and I'm different now." He shoved a hand through his hair, fighting not to panic. It couldn't be over. "I don't know how many ways to say it."

"I can't let you hurt me like that again."

"How long do I have to pay for my mistakes?"

"This has nothing to do with punishing you." She wrapped her arms around her waist, her eyes troubled. "It has to do with protecting myself."

From him. "I get it, okay. I should probably do the same damn thing, but I want to work through this."

After a long moment thick with pain and regret, her gaze lasered into his. "How do I know things will be different?"

His heart thumped hard. Was she softening? Would she give him another chance? Hesitantly, he reached out. When she didn't shy away, he stroked her cheek. He fixed his gaze on hers.

"Because while I was gone, I woke up every day wanting you with me and I don't want to wake up that way for the rest of my life. I know what it's like to be without you," he murmured. "I don't want to ever feel like that again. I can't make you believe me. Or trust me. The only thing I know to do is stick around and show you."

He saw the uncertainty in her eyes, held his breath in hope she would agree, even reluctantly, to give him another chance.

Then he saw her decision and her words shot his wish all to hell. "Don't. This is hard enough for both of us already. It's not fair to you or me."

His chest felt like a wide gaping hole; his voice turned sharp. "Why are you completely closing the door? Because I can't make any guarantees about us? Neither can you."

"We just don't work. You know it, even if you won't admit it."

"In the past, maybe that was true. Not now."

She shook her head, her blue eyes dark and sad.

"You can really just walk away?"

"I have to."

"Well, I can't. I won't."

"Don't make this any more painful for either of us." Her voice quavered and tears filled her eyes. "If you really do still care for me, let it go."

"That's exactly why I can't."

She moved past him, not even pausing at his words. As he watched her leave the room, desperation and near-panic choked him. Was she truly finished with them?

He didn't want to believe it was over, but he didn't see how he could believe anything else.

Chapter 11

A little before eight the next morning, Meredith, Gage and Robin were shown into an empty courtroom the Attorney General had found to use as a waiting room. Meredith and Robin would wait here while Gage gave his deposition to Ken Ivory. Per Ivory's instruction, the three of them had arrived before court convened at nine o'clock.

As Meredith watched Gage and the AG walk through a corner door leading to the jury deliberation room, she was one big throbbing nerve.

Gage would be deposed first about her killing Marshal Nowlin and then how the marshal had tried to kill Gage. When it was time for her deposition, she would trade places with him.

Once he was out of earshot, Robin turned to Meredith,

concern in her blue eyes. "Sheesh, I nearly got frostbite in the car on the way down here. What's going on with you two?"

Tears tightened her throat. After her talk with Gage, she'd spent last night in Robin's other guest bedroom. Meredith had seen hurt in his eyes the first time she'd broken up with him, but if memory served, it hadn't been as raw or bleak as what she'd seen yesterday.

She and Gage had ridden to the courthouse with Robin at his insistence. He wanted more than himself watching out for Meredith. They had talked little during the drive and when they had, it was about things concerning the trial.

Her heart ached. "Once all this is over, he wants to try again, but I said no."

"So, that's why he looked like he wanted to shoot someone. Are you doubting your decision?"

"No. I don't know." She didn't think she should second-guess herself, but it was difficult not to. "I feel like I made the decision I should have, but it's not the one I wanted. I really do believe he's changed, that he wants to make our relationship a priority, but I can't trust he'll stay that way."

"After he settles back in and goes to work, you mean?"

"Yes. All I can think about is how he became obsessed with his job and put it ahead of everything else, including me. I can't let him hurt me like that again."

Robin gave her a quick hug. "I'm sorry."

"Thanks." Meredith wiped at her teary eyes. "I'm so ready for this to be over."

The pain was sharp and deep. One of the first things she'd learned in med school was to detach emotionally from certain situations. She had to distance herself now, from Gage, or she wouldn't be able to make it through the trial. And she needed to be here for him one last time.

Robin and Terra had offered to attend court with her for moral support, and Meredith was so grateful for her friends. They'd been through a lot together.

Terra's divorce, losing her friend and mentor to a serial arsonist, marrying the sexy cop she'd met on the case. Robin being jilted at the altar and nearly being killed in a fire. Meredith's breakup with Gage and her subsequent belief that he was dead. And now as she walked away from him for the second time.

Maybe Gage was right and being with him had been her way of saying goodbye. She'd foolishly believed they could spend these last several days together and she wouldn't hurt when it was over, but her heart felt just as shattered this time as it had the last.

She glanced at Robin, who wore a smart-looking navy pantsuit. "How long do you think his deposition will take?"

"Hard to say." Though Robin wasn't on duty today, she wore her badge, gun and holster clipped to the waistband of her slacks.

"I'm going to make a trip to the ladies' room."

"Why don't you go to the one used by the jury? Even though no one has spotted James, it's better if you don't go out to the public restrooms. While you're gone, I'll call Terra and check on her ETA."

Meredith nodded as she walked past the jury box and through a door made from the same dark wood as the rest of that in the high-ceilinged room. The facilities were across from the deliberation room where Gage was being deposed.

After a quick trip, she started back to the courtroom. Startled by a noise behind her, she glanced over her shoulder and saw a dark-haired man easily more than six feet tall. He was replacing a vent cover high on the wall.

At first, she tagged him as a maintenance worker. She smiled, then looked again. There was something familiar about his sharp-edged cheekbones, the slitted, cunning gaze—Larry James!

She'd seen his picture on the television enough the past couple of days to be sure. Managing not to betray the fact she'd recognized him, she played it cool and kept walking. She'd tell Robin, then Gage—

Something hard slammed into the side of her head and she crumpled to the floor in a burst of pain before everything went black.

Gage rubbed his nape as he walked out of the room where he'd been deposed by Ken Ivory and into the courtroom where he expected to find Meredith and Robin waiting. The room was empty.

Outside the main door, he could hear the increasing din of voices in the eight-story building. The tap and click of shoes echoed on the polished marble floor.

Where were Meredith and Robin? If Meredith had gone into the deliberation room, he would've passed her. He knew neither woman would leave this area. Most likely, one or both of them had gone to the restroom.

Stepping into the jury box, he eased down into the nearest chair and closed his eyes. Meredith had made it clear she was in no mood to talk, but they needed to. He intended to. He just wasn't sure if he should leave her alone a few hours or try to talk to her now.

"Son?"

At the familiar masculine voice, Gage jumped to his feet and pivoted. "Gramps? Gran?"

Owen and Millie Parrish rushed toward him. He met them halfway.

The tall, white-haired man and petite woman with frosted hair swept him up in a tight embrace.

"It *is* you! Thank goodness!" His grandmother's voice was tremulous.

He pulled back slightly to look at the older couple. "What are you doing here? Did you come for the trial?"

"Mr. Ivory wanted us to come. We didn't know why until just now." Owen Parrish's voice cracked.

Gage's grandmother touched his face, her soft hands shaking. "I can't believe it. You're alive."

She burst into tears and grabbed him to her. His own eyes stung as he met his grandfather's gaze. Looking as if he were having trouble holding back tears, too, the older man put a hand on Gage's shoulder.

After a long minute, Millie stepped away. She kept touching Gage, on the face, on the arm.

His grandfather hugged him hard. "Mr. Ivory filled us in on what's happened the last year. How are you doing?"

"Have you been eating?" Gran asked. "You look thin. And you need a haircut."

Chuckling, he urged them each into a chair in the jury box before taking the seat between them.

He quickly caught them up on his life for the past year, including how Meredith had found him wounded at her family's lake house and probably saved his life.

A fresh set of tears started in his grandmother's eyes.

He hugged her again. "I'm fine, Gran. And thanks to the investigation at Meredith's house fire, there's evidence to put away the scum who masterminded the arson ring. That means I don't have to stay in the Witness Security Program."

"That's the best news we've had in a year," his grandfather declared.

Millie's blue gaze pinned Gage. "And what about Meredith? How were things between y'all while you were together? I know you still have feelings for her. Is there any chance—"

"She's said no. Twice."

"She can't forgive you for putting her second to your job?"

"I think she has, but she's afraid I'll make the same mistake. She doesn't trust me."

"You did let work take precedence over everything, Gage," his grandmother reminded softly.

"I know. And I regret it. Living in WitSec has taught me a hard lesson. I won't make a mistake like that again."

"And you've told Meredith this?" Owen asked.

Just as Gage was about to answer, the door leading

from the jury deliberation room jerked open. Robin looked quickly around the courtroom, her face chalk-white.

Dread hammering through him, he slowly got to his feet. "What is it?"

"Meredith went to the jury's restroom. When she didn't return after a few minutes, I went to check on her. She wasn't there. I looked in the offices for the clerk and bailiff, and the court reporter. Finally, I found one of her shoes down the hall, near the door leading to the stairs. There's no sign of her."

"It's James, that SOB." Gage knew it without a doubt. He started toward the petite detective.

His grandfather rose, too, his deep voice concerned. "What can we do? Where should we start looking?"

"The best thing would be for y'all to stay here." Robin glanced at Gage. "I need to tell Ivory."

"We'll cover more ground if we help," Owen pointed out.

Robin glanced at Gage, her expression saying she was leaving the decision in his hands.

He shook his head. "This guy's out to get me, Gramps. He won't care who he hurts. It will be better if we don't have to worry about y'all, too."

The older man started to protest, but Gran put a hand on his arm. "We don't want to make things more difficult. If there's something we can do from here, tell us."

"Okay, thanks."

"Parrish!" Ken Ivory appeared in the doorway behind Robin.

The Attorney General's face was tight with worry. "I've contacted security and the police department. A

SWAT team is being deployed right now. They'll be here shortly."

"We can't wait on them!" Why were they standing around here talking? Irritated, Gage shoved a hand through his hair. "We need to find her now. Whatever Larry James is planning, he'll do it and get out. He won't stay to play hide-and-seek."

"Security has covered all the exits," Ivory informed him. "And when the SWAT team arrives—"

"I'm not waiting on them. I can't." Gage started around the man and Robin, who both stood in front of the door leading to the deliberation room.

Robin snagged his elbow. "Hold on—"

"The longer we wait," he gritted out, "the better the chance he'll get her out of here. Or do something worse. He wants me and the other witnesses dead. He won't care if he kills anyone else in the process. It's my fault Meredith's involved in this. I won't stand here and do nothing."

"I'll go with you." The brunette turned to follow him, pulling her weapon and checking it.

As they started down the hall, Ivory called out, "Parrish, tell me where you're going so I'll know how to direct SWAT."

"James will be looking for a way to get out without being noticed by too many people."

"He'll take the stairs," Robin predicted as they started down the hall. "He could go to the third or fifth floors and take a walkway over to the county office building."

"Or he could go down to the concourse," Gage said.

The detective nodded. "That connects to a parking garage north of the courthouse."

"Got it!" Ivory was already dialing his cell phone.

When Gage and Robin reached the door to the stairwell, she volunteered to take the flight leading up. Gage headed down, panic squeezing his chest. He had to find Meredith. If anything happened to her—

He cut off the thought, putting himself on autopilot, pushing his feelings away so he could do what needed to be done.

Down one flight of stairs, he passed a door marked Storage. He paused, turning to look back. This room would make a perfect place to hide while people checked exits first. The heavy door groaned as he opened it.

Well-used chairs, discarded tables made two neat rows. Past the furniture, battered and sagging file cabinets formed a line of corners and shadows that would make it difficult to be found.

Gage reined in the urge to sprint to the other end of the room. The fluorescent bulbs didn't provide the best lighting, but that wasn't the reason he had to jog rather than run.

Due to his loss of peripheral vision, he was forced to move slower and look at everything head-on or risk missing something that might help find Meredith.

A couple of minutes later, he was giving thanks for that same handicap. If he hadn't needed to make allowance for it, he would've missed the tip of a black shoe peeking out from behind a shadow-draped file cabinet.

Not just any black shoe. A woman's shoe. Meredith's shoe.

Gage knew because he remembered everything about what she'd worn to court. She looked sleek and professional in a black herringbone suit, her blond curls drawn into a neat twist at her nape. Those high heels made her legs look even better than they normally did.

Keeping his gaze on the shoe, he stopped several feet away. "Meredith?"

"Gage!" She stumbled into view, pushed from behind by Larry James.

The bastard held her in front of him with one arm locked around her torso. He towered behind her, holding a cell phone.

Meredith was calm, pale, but Gage saw the fear in her eyes. And a streak of blood at her left temple. Rage tore through him. "Are you okay?"

She nodded.

His voice was hard, vibrating with anger. "What did you do to her, you son of a bitch?"

"Nothing nearly as bad as what I'm going to." The ex-fire investigator held up the cell phone and Gage knew what the man had planned.

He'd planted his gel blocks and intended to detonate them all at once. The courthouse had been crawling with security since last night, so it was possible James had chosen a location other than the ventilation system for his accelerant. There was no way of telling how many gel blocks the scumbag had placed.

Gage's mouth went dry. "Let her go, Larry. There's no reason to keep her."

"After I kill you, I'm going to need her to get out of here."

Alarm flared in Meredith's eyes, then anger. Gage forced himself to keep his gaze on the other man, trying to think of a way to get his hands on that cell phone without hurting Meredith.

"The police department and a SWAT team are on their way. You're not going to get very far."

"With her, I can get as far as I need to."

The man was so bitter over being terminated from his job, he was willing to take revenge against someone who had no part in it at all. "She's not involved in this. You've gotten your revenge against all the men who had anything to do with you losing your job. You set them up, used a middleman to offer them bribes, which they took. All of them are locked up."

"And I'm not joining them."

"I wouldn't count on that. You threatened the marshal to get him to kill me, but he died instead so you had to send your go-between, Julio Garza, after me."

"You can't prove any of that." The other man tightened his arm around Meredith until she winced.

Gage barely managed to keep from going for the bastard. "Is that why you killed Garza? Because he didn't kill me, either?"

"Who says I killed *anybody?*" James sneered.

"It may never be proven and you may not pay for that murder, but you're going down one way or another." He kept his voice level. "You left your DNA at the fire at Meredith's house."

The man laughed. "Bull!"

"Our lab extracted oil from a fingerprint off the gel

block and from the oil, they managed to collect enough DNA to test. The sample matched yours."

For the first time, Gage saw a flicker of uncertainty in the bastard's eyes.

He quickly sized up the situation. Meredith still clutched her purse tightly to her chest, her other arm locked against her side by the man holding her. How could Gage get her out of the way before Larry James ignited the whole place? Neither he nor Meredith had a weapon.

"Parrish, back off or I'm going to start pushing buttons."

No way in hell was he backing off. Mind racing, his gaze locked on Meredith. She stared intently at him, almost desperately, and he realized she was going to make a move.

Before he could warn her to wait, James said, "This is what's going to happen. Parrish, you're going to leave—"

Moving suddenly, Meredith dropped her purse and reached back, grabbing James's throat.

The man choked and twisted away from her. She jerked around, chopping at his windpipe with the knife-edge of her hand. Gage lunged for the bastard and the cell phone.

Air gurgled in the back of James's throat and his face went fire-red. Dropping the phone to make a grab for Meredith, he fell to his knees.

Gage snatched the phone and punched the off button.

Before he could breathe a sigh of relief, a loud thud had him wheeling around. Larry James lay unmoving at Meredith's feet. Her gaze met Gage's and all the color drained from her face.

She wobbled and he reached out, putting a steadying hand on her elbow. His jaw clenched as his gaze went to her blood-streaked temple. "What did he do to you?"

"Hit me with something."

"You okay?"

"Yes." The cut looked stark and darkly raw against her pale skin. "Are you?"

"I'm fine, except for my heart nearly stopping when I found out he had you." Gage moved to plant his knee between James's shoulder blades and reached for the scumbag's arms. "You're sure you're all right?"

She nodded, gingerly fingering the side of her head.

"That was too damn close." He frowned down at a still-motionless Larry James. "That was some move. Learn it in med school?"

"Self-defense class," she half whispered.

Her trembling voice made him want to hold her, but he knew better than to try right now. There was still clear distance between them. Rage pumping through him, he shook James, who still hadn't moved. "Get up, you bastard."

Gage thought it odd that the SOB hadn't stirred. He found out why when Meredith knelt next to him and pressed her fingers to James's neck.

"No pulse," she said quietly. "He's dead."

Chapter 12

Minutes later, they were surrounded by SWAT, several OCPD officers, Attorney General Ivory, Robin and Gage's grandparents.

Meredith wasn't sure how many times she repeated her story. Because she'd seen James actually planting the accelerant, he couldn't leave her unconscious or dead. The risk was too great that someone might find her body before the explosion and alert people, so he had taken her as a hostage. Thank goodness Gage had shown up when he had.

Sitting in a chair several yards from James's body, Meredith answered questions from the Attorney General as she watched the steady activity around the scene.

Ken Ivory closed the notebook he'd been using to

record her answers. "I still need to depose you about the marshal, but I can do it another time."

"Could we go ahead? I'd prefer to finish everything now."

The man's gray gaze measured her. "If the paramedic says you're okay, we'll go back to the room we used before. Until things wrap up here, no one will be using that courtroom."

"Thank you."

She watched Gage talking to his retired boss as well as the new fire chief, Bill Haynes. Several firefighters passed by, all pausing to slap Gage's back or shake his hand, disbelieving smiles on their faces.

Presenting the evidence found at Meredith's house and the past pattern of James's behavior at the arson-ring fires, Gage had managed to secure a couple of fire stations on standby. If James had managed to detonate those gel blocks, the fire department would've had a good chance of dousing the blazes before anyone was hurt.

She told herself to stop watching him.

A lanky, dark-haired paramedic approached and knelt next to her chair. "I need to check you out, Dr. Boren."

She nodded, recognizing him as a firefighter-paramedic who often brought patients into the Presley E.R. "Are you working for Oklahoma City now?"

"No, just doing some training with their SWAT medic program."

"I'd forgotten Presley started a program like that. It's a good idea to take paramedics on police calls. You look familiar, but I'm afraid I can't remember your name."

"Walker McClain." He gently examined the cut at her temple. "A while back, you saved my sister-in-law, Kiley, after she was shot."

"Oh, yes, you're Collier's brother." Something else about him nagged at her, but Meredith couldn't call it to mind. "Terra Spencer, the fire investigator who works with him, is one of my closest friends."

He nodded, moving in front of her to check her pupils. The hollowness in his eyes tugged at a memory. She felt as if she had treated him or someone with him at one time.

She knew she was focusing her attention on him rather than Gage because watching her ex was too difficult.

Then she remembered. Two years ago, she'd treated Walker McClain's pregnant wife after she'd been beaten. Sadly, neither the woman nor the baby had lived. Her heart clenched.

He cleaned the wound on Meredith's temple. "You don't need stitches. I can just put a butterfly bandage on this."

"Okay, thanks." She gave up trying not to look at Gage.

This might be one of the last times she saw him. She swallowed past a lump in her throat, admiring his big frame, the hard muscular line of his body. Seeing him with his former co-workers filled her with a bittersweet certainty. He was back where he belonged.

Walker's green gaze followed hers to where Gage stood with his former boss and his grandparents. "My brother's mentioned Parrish a few times. He's a good fire investigator."

"Yes, he is," she murmured. "He's outstanding."

And she couldn't take that away from him. She wouldn't. She'd been right before. Their lives just didn't mesh. Neither of them should have to change the core of who they were in order to make their relationship work.

Walker grinned. "Just before I got to you, I heard the new chief offer him his job back."

"That was fast." A razor-sharp pain lodged in her chest. She looked away, fixing her attention on the floor. "They'd be lucky to have him."

Walker finished bandaging her cut. "Okay, you're all set."

"Thanks." She rose, her attention again shifting to Gage.

The current fire chief approached Gage and after a minute, drew him aside. The two men talked intensely, then shook hands. Gage was taking the position. And why shouldn't he? Meredith asked herself. He no longer had to feel torn between his job and her. Before long, he would be immersed in another case.

Tearing her gaze from him, she found Robin and Terra waiting several feet away and joined them. As she walked away to give her deposition, she fought the urge to turn around and look at Gage one last time.

Ending things for good between them had been the right thing to do. And she didn't know if she'd ever get over it.

* * *

A few hours later, Meredith angrily dashed away a tear as she walked into the guest bedroom at Robin's. Her mind was filled with images of Gage, memories. Regrets. Why couldn't she just move on? She was only making herself miserable.

She'd made the right decision. Things had turned out well for Gage and she was glad for him. Part of her wished she'd waited at the courthouse after her deposition to say goodbye to him, but hadn't she done that already? Seeing him again would only make her pain worse. It was better for both of them that she'd left when she had. There was no need to drag things out.

She slipped off her black velvet-trimmed jacket and heels. She planned to change into jeans then go home and determine what needed to be done before she could move back in. Until her house was ready, Robin had offered her a place to stay.

"Meredith?" her friend called out. "I'm going out for a few minutes."

"All right." Tugging her black silk blouse out of her skirt, her mind whirled with thoughts of Gage. She wondered if he'd spoken yet to Aaron Chapman. His friend would be ecstatic to learn Gage was alive and returning to the fire department.

"Meredith?"

At the sound of Gage's deep voice, she whipped around, her heart beating painfully in her throat. His blue eyes flared hotly as he looked her up and down.

Swallowing hard, she committed to memory how good he looked in his dark suit with a blindingly white shirt and muted paisley tie. "How did you know where to find me?"

"Robin told me."

She frowned.

"I know. Surprised me, too." He rubbed his nape and she noticed he was sweating.

Concerned now, she took a step toward him. "Has something happened?"

"Nothing bad. The trial has been delayed until tomorrow, because of James."

The uncertainty on his face had tension winding Meredith's nerves.

He cleared his throat. "I wanted to leave the courthouse with you."

"I thought it was better to go on." This was too much. She couldn't bring herself to look at him. "You saved a lot of people today."

"*We* did. We saved them. If it weren't for you, I wouldn't have been able to stop that detonation."

Meredith couldn't work up any regret over the death of Larry James, not when he'd intended to kill anyone and everyone he could.

Gage continued, "I had to take care of some things, finish giving my statement, then walk with the fire department through the courthouse until we found all the accelerant James had planted."

"What about security? Why didn't anyone notice him?"

"We think he came in yesterday before the building closed and hid in the ventilation system last night and again this morning before people arrived for work."

Gage shifted from one foot to the other. "It was hard getting away from Haynes, but I finally did."

At the mention of the fire chief, Meredith knew what was coming. Her heart fell and she had to force her gaze to meet Gage's. "I heard you were offered your old job. That's great. I really mean it. No one is better at fire investigation than you are."

"I wanted to talk to you about that."

How could this still hurt so much? She turned away. "I should finish changing clothes and get home to see what needs to be done."

She felt him walk up behind her, stiffened when he curved his hands over her shoulders. "Gage."

He hoped with everything in him Meredith would listen to what he had to say and change her mind about them. She *had* to change her mind, although he was prepared to dig in for however long it took to convince her he was totally committed this time.

"I'm crazy in love with you," he said huskily.

She stepped away and turned, the anguish in her blue eyes tearing at him. "There has to be more."

"Compromise on both sides." He wanted to go after her, pull her to him, but he didn't. "I know."

"We've tried it. It didn't work."

"You tried. I didn't. But I will this time."

Her voice quavered. "The only way we can be together is if one of us is miserable."

"No, it's not." He knew she truly believed that and he was determined to convince her differently. Only sheer will kept him from gathering her close.

"After the last year, I know what I can't live without, and that's you." Chest tight, he refused to give in to the dread pounding through him. "I have an idea."

She shook her head, looking confused.

"I'm going to open a private fire-investigation company. That means I can choose my clients and more important, my hours. We can accommodate your work schedule when we need to."

"But you were offered your old job. Did you turn it down?"

She was still listening. That was good. Despite the vicious knot in his gut, he gave her a half grin. "If you'd waited at the courthouse, I would've told you I'd made this decision before Haynes even talked to me about my old position."

"You can't leave your job."

Instead of the pleasure he'd hoped to see in her eyes, she looked horrified. "Meredith, this is a chance to start over. It's something I want to do."

"You couldn't live with that! You shouldn't have to. Quitting my job is something you would never ask me to do."

"You didn't ask, baby. I thought of the idea as I was talking to Gramps earlier."

"You should be with someone who doesn't need you to change."

"I want us to work, no matter what it takes."

"Not this. Your job is who you are. You're incredible at it."

"And I like it, but I *love* you." He took her hand, encouraged when she didn't pull away.

She shook her head. "You'd be unhappy. Our lives just don't mesh, Gage."

"They could, if you'd let them." He tamped down his exasperation. "I know what it's like to be without you. That's a price I'm never paying again."

Tears filled her eyes and he felt a burst of panic when she said, "I don't want you to do this."

"Well, I am. Can't you meet me halfway?"

"You'll resent it one day."

"Damn, you're stubborn. What I'll resent is not getting another chance. My time away has been one regret after another. If I let you walk away, that will be the biggest one of all."

She stared at him. He'd refused his old job. For them.

"You still love me. You know you do."

There was no denying it.

He dragged a hand down his face. "Is it that you really haven't forgiven me?"

"No, it's not that."

"I'm on my knees here, Meredith. Giving you whatever you want."

She *wanted* to believe things would be different this time, but she was afraid to. "Do you mean it?"

"Yes," he said firmly, his gaze intent on hers. "Just a chance. That's all I'm asking."

The wall she'd built against him weakened. "It isn't fair for me not to trust you the same way you trust me."

"We'll get there. I'll earn it."

"No!"

"Baby—"

She put her hand on his arm, the first contact she'd

initiated. Hope flared. "No. You don't have to *earn* my trust. If I decide to try again, I *will* trust you."

His heart kicked hard. "If? Are you saying… Will you give it a shot?"

"Yes."

Her voice was so soft he had to lean forward. Even then, he was afraid he'd heard only what he wanted. "Meredith?"

"Yes." She moved into him, flattened her hands on his chest. "I want to try again."

Emotion tightened his chest as he covered her mouth with his. After a long moment, he lifted his head. "I love you."

"I love you, too. I never stopped."

How damn lucky was he? "You're never going to doubt me again. I'll make it work this time."

"*We'll* make it work."

"You're really saying yes?"

She nodded, her arms going around his neck as she pulled him down for another kiss.

He turned her, walking her backward toward the bed before he realized he didn't have everything he wanted. Lifting his head, he said hoarsely, "Wait."

"Why?" She nuzzled his neck.

Holding her to him with one arm, he pulled a slim leather notebook from his suit jacket with his other.

"What is that?"

"My calendar."

She laughed, her eyes full of the light he'd almost given up ever seeing again. "What are you doing? Writing this stuff down?"

He was going for it. All of it. His lips feathered across her forehead. "I'm talking marriage, too."

She started.

He pressed her. "Meredith, tell me you mean marriage, too."

"We don't have to hurry—"

"Tell me."

His voice was husky with emotion and his face held a raw vulnerability she'd never seen before. Was his hand shaking? He was putting himself on the line, hoping she'd say yes, but probably expecting her to say "maybe" or "no."

Here it was—the total commitment she'd once wanted from him. How could she give him any less?

"I want forever." His eyes blazed down at her. "I want you to want that, too."

"I do." When she'd been so angry last year, she'd tried and failed to imagine herself growing old with someone else. She didn't want anyone else. "Yes, I'll marry you."

"What about April 21?"

"What about it?" She pushed his dark jacket off his shoulders, loosened his tie and began unbuttoning his shirt.

He laughed. "For our wedding."

She snapped to attention, her blue eyes searching his. "You want to set a date?"

"Yes."

"That's less than two months away."

He kissed her. "Yes."

"We don't have to hurry."

He tossed the calendar to the floor and wrapped both arms around her. "Did you agree to marry me or not?"

She nodded.

"I don't want to give you a chance to change your mind, but if you're not sure—"

"I just thought it might be a good idea to take some time."

"And make sure I mean to do what I say?"

She studied him and whatever she saw in his face had a soft smile curving her lips. "Okay, April 21."

"You believe me, right? Us first."

"Hmm." Giving him a look from under her lashes, she slid her arms around his neck and breathed in his ear, "Why don't you convince me? Right now."

And he did.

* * * * *

So you think you can write?

Mills & Boon® and Harlequin® have joined forces in a global search for new authors.

It's our biggest contest yet—with the prize of being published by the world's leader in romance fiction.

Look for more information on our website:
www.soyouthinkyoucanwrite.com

So you think you can write?
Show us!

Special Offers

Every month we put together collections and longer reads written by your favourite authors.

Here are some of next month's highlights— and don't miss our fabulous discount online!

On sale 17th August

On sale 7th September

On sale 7th September

Save 20% on all Special Releases

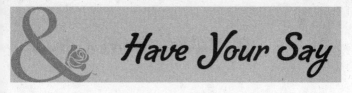

The World of Mills & Boon®

There's a Mills & Boon® series that's perfect for you. We publish ten series and, with new titles every month, you never have to wait long for your favourite to come along.

Blaze®
Scorching hot, sexy reads
4 new stories every month

By Request
Relive the romance with the best of the best
9 new stories every month

Cherish™
Romance to melt the heart every time
12 new stories every month

Desire™
Passionate and dramatic love stories
8 new stories every month